Michelle Smart's love affair with books started when she was a baby and would cuddle them in her cot. A voracious reader of all genres, she found her love of romance established when she stumbled across her first Mills & Boon book at the age of twelve. She's been reading them—and writing them—ever since. Michelle lives in Northamptonshire, England, with her husband and two young Smarties.

USA TODAY bestselling, RITA®-nominated and critically acclaimed author **Caitlin Crews** has written more than one hundred books and counting. She has a Master's and a PhD in English Literature, thinks everyone should read more category romance, and is always available to discuss her beloved alpha heroes. Just ask! She lives in the Pacific Northwest with her comic book artist husband, she is always planning her next trip, and she will never, ever, read all the books in her 'to-be-read' pile. Thank goodness.

THE FORBIDDEN GREEK

MICHELLE SMART

HER VENETIAN SECRET

CAITLIN CREWS

MILLS & BOON

First published in Great Britain 2024
by Mills & Boon, an imprint of HarperCollins*Publishers* Ltd,
1 London Bridge Street, London, SE1 9GF

www.harpercollins.co.uk

HarperCollins*Publishers*, Macken House, 39/40 Mayor Street Upper,
Dublin 1, D01 C9W8, Ireland

The Forbidden Greek © 2024 Michelle Smart

Her Venetian Secret © 2024 Caitlin Crews

ISBN: 978-0-263-32008-4

05/24

This book contains FSC™ certified paper
and other controlled sources to ensure responsible forest management.

For more information visit www.harpercollins.co.uk/green.

Printed and Bound in the UK using 100% Renewable Electricity
at CPI Group (UK) Ltd, Croydon, CR0 4YY

THE FORBIDDEN GREEK

MICHELLE SMART

MILLS & BOON

For Pippa, who made our second collaboration
as much fun as the first. xx

CHAPTER ONE

TRAVELLING BY PRIVATE jet was every bit as amazing as Kate Hawkins had imagined. The cabin crew catered to her every need and whim, serving her an array of food that passengers on commercial airlines could only dream of along with every possible drink her tastebuds could fancy, alcoholic and non-alcoholic alike. She had her own lounge, a dining room, a bathroom and even a bedroom with a mattress so comfortable you'd have to be a world-class insomniac not to fall into a dreamless sleep on it. Or too frazzled with the task you'd volunteered yourself for to switch your brain off enough to sleep.

In the space of thirty-eight hours Kate had travelled to seven different countries over two continents, zipped through so many different time zones she'd no idea if it was currently Sunday or Monday wherever in the sky she was, and if Leander Liassidis wasn't to be found at the next stop, there was a high probability she would do more than stamp her feet and scream in frustration like she'd done in Manhattan.

She pulled out the list Helena had written, the paper now a crumpled, grubby mess, and stared moodily at the places still to be crossed off. How could one man own so *much*? Kate's property empire consisted of her childhood bedroom, which she'd moved back into full time after completing her veterinary degree two years ago. Leander, wildly successful technology tycoon worth billions, owned fourteen properties, and if it turned out he'd bought another one that Helena knew nothing of then there was an excellent chance Kate would throw herself out of the plane. Cabin fever had well and truly hit.

By the time it was politely requested that she buckle up for the landing, she couldn't be bothered to ask where the private airport they were flying into was located. All of Leander's properties were located within a thirty-minute drive of an airfield. She couldn't even be bothered to summon a glimmer of interest at the view as they descended of the Pacific Ocean lapping onto California's sandy shores. At least when descending over New York she'd grunted appreciation at the iconic skyline. Now her body clock was too shot to give a hoot.

'Grand Cayman next,' she said to her favourite of the crew with a weary smile as she left the plane. Kate was convinced she'd have to travel to every ruddy country listed before she found the runaway groom and dragged him back to Greece. The way she was feeling, she'd have to resist killing him. Maybe just settle for maiming him.

'We will await your call.'

As at all her previous stops, the efficient crew, who'd thus far organised everything, had arranged for a car to meet her at the foot of the plane. She had time to be grateful that she hadn't stepped into a furnace as she'd done in Manhattan before slumping into the back of it.

They hadn't left the airfield before her heavy eyes started fighting with her wired brain to stay open. Or was that to close? Images flickered in her retinas of the wedding, voices from it echoing in her head. The shock of seeing the wrong Liassidis twin waiting at the altar, the surrealness of hearing Leo recite his vows in Leander's name, time skipping to Helena, the beautiful bride, ashen faced with shock at what Leander had done, Kate's vow to find him and bring him back, of Leo giving her access to a company jet and...

Her eyes suddenly sprang open. She'd drifted into one of those vivid waking dreams and now found herself being driven through high trees on a road with No Trespassing signs displayed at intermittent intervals. High up in front of them loomed a huge glass-fronted property. As they drew closer, she saw that although framed by trees, the mansion faced the ocean. The driver glided to the smoothest of stops at the foot of a wide, curving path that led up to what she assumed was the main entrance.

Climbing out, Kate craned her neck upwards, trying to take it all in, trying to spot signs of life, waiting for the security guard that would appear at any moment and politely inform her that Mr Liassidis was not in residence and that he was unable to make contact with him because Mr Liassidis was on his honeymoon.

Mr Liassidis certainly was on his honeymoon. The only problem was, it was the wrong Mr Liassidis.

She supposed any of the security guards in Athens, Rome, Milan, Vienna, Frankfurt, London, New York and Toronto could have been lying to her but she hadn't sensed life behind those closed doors. Here though...

Exhausted legs dragging halfway up the path, she was just thinking that this was the most perfect of secluded hideaways when the requisite security guard appeared in front of her.

* * *

Leander Liassidis spotted the black four-wheel drive appear through the foliage and grimaced.

He supposed this meant his brother's minion had finally found him.

Hauling himself out of the pool, he rubbed a towel over his soaking body. He didn't need to tell Mason to send the visitor away. He'd already made his instructions explicit on this. Leander wasn't there. Leander was on his honeymoon. His visitor would leave Marina Sands empty-handed.

He briefly wondered how many of his properties the minion had visited to get this far. He could find out if he wanted but he was on a self-imposed communications blackout. Since satisfying himself that Leo had stepped up and taken his place, Leander hadn't wanted to know anything about the outside world.

For the first time in his life, Leander needed solitude. Outside his Californian household staff, whose loyalty and discretion was assured, only his PA knew his location. Sheree had been with him for ten years. Practiced at lying for him, her loyalty and discretion were also assured.

Slinging the towel around his shoulders, he popped the lid off a cold beer and drank a good slug of it. The bitter taste matched the way he felt towards himself for not going through with the wedding.

Leander loved Helena. An incredibly ugly baby who'd turned into an incredibly cute toddler and then a delightful child who'd followed him about like a puppy whenever their families had got together—which had been a lot, their families in business together and as close as if they were bound by blood—she was the one non-blood female constant in his life. She'd turned into a beautiful and smart woman, and he always looked forward to meeting up with her, adored being in her company. One thing he didn't have was any romantic inclinations towards her. Maybe it was over-familiarity, maybe it was because she was like a sister to him, whatever the reason, he'd never looked at Helena with the same eyes he looked at other women, and even if he had and even if it had been reciprocated—which it wasn't, being platonic ran both ways—he would never have acted on it for the simple reason that he loved her too much to hurt her.

And now he had hurt her. He'd broken his promise, and it tore his heart to think of the hurt and bewilderment that absconding the way he'd done must have caused her.

At some point in the near future he would return to his Greek homeland and face her, face his brother too, and step into the role of husband that he'd promised to play for her, but that point wasn't yet, and he downed the rest of his beer to drown the burn of bile in his throat at the thought of putting on a loving display to the world until Helena got her inheritance sorted and they could dissolve their sham marriage.

He *had* to get his head together.

Popping the lid off another beer, Leander settled his mind with the promise of spending the rest of the day getting rip-roaring drunk. About to head inside to shower, a lull in the ocean breeze carried the whisper of a voice up to him.

The hairs on the nape of his neck rose.

In four quick strides he was at the glass balustrade that overhung the path to his home.

* * *

Kate took one look at the security guard's face and pulled her own. 'Let me guess, Mr Liassidis isn't here?'

'Mr Liassidis is on...'

'His honeymoon,' she finished for him. 'And you are unable to contact him.'

'I'm sorry for your wasted journey.'

It was exactly what she'd expected, exactly what she'd experienced during her pitstops at Leander's other homes. And yet...

There was nothing in the security guard's demeanour or expression to make her think he was lying but something felt different, different enough for Kate to fold her arms over her stomach and flatly say, 'I don't believe you.'

'I can't help what you believe, ma'am, but Mr Liassidis isn't here and now I'm going to have to ask you to leave.'

She looked around him and up, trying to see through the glass that so effectively blocked the viewer from seeing anything of the beautiful home's interior.

'You need to leave now.'

Ignoring him, she continued scrutinising the exterior of what had to be the most spectacular home she'd ever seen.

'I must insist.'

'Must you?' she murmured absently. Kate's instincts were telling her loud and clear that the security guard was lying. Someone was resident in this house, she could feel it in her bones.

'Ma'am, I don't want to have to use force.'

That snapped her back to attention. 'Lay one finger on me and I'll sue you to kingdom come, got it?' Cupping her mouth, she shouted, 'I know you're in there, Leander Liassidis. Get your backside out here and stop hiding!'

'This is your last chance. You are trespassing. Either leave voluntarily or I carry you to your car. I can give you directions to the nearest law enforcement offices if you want.'

Her hands flew to her hips. 'What I *want*,' she stressed, her patience stretched way past boiling point, 'is for your boss to stop hiding away like a big baby.'

'Mason, let her up.'

Kate's gaze shot back up to where the heavily accented gravelly voice had rumbled from.

There, hands gripping the darkened glass balustrade, stood Leander.

Energised vindication overrode her shock at his appearance, and she couldn't resist poking her tongue out at the security guard as she skipped past him. Moving as fast as her short legs would carry her, afraid the man she'd been sent on a wild goose chase to find would disappear as suddenly as he'd appeared, Kate wasn't sure if relief or fury was the strongest emotion raging through her. At least her instincts were working, so that was one plus. She'd *known* Leander was here the second she'd stepped out of the car. Known it, known it.

The top of the path led onto wide marble steps that fanned out, one side leading to the balcony, the other to the house itself. Leander had opened a section of the balustrade for her, and she steamed through it, more than ready to let rip at him. Except all the abuse she wanted to hurl suddenly tied itself on her tongue when she rounded to face him and was confronted with Leander wearing nothing but a pair of tight black swim shorts. The towel around his neck hardly covered any of him.

'Whoa!' Immediately she turned her back, scrunched her eyes closed and covered them with her hand for good measure. 'Put some clothes on, will you?'

'If my state of undress disturbs you, you know the way back to your car,' he said sardonically from behind her.

'I've just spent the best part of two whole days trying to hunt you down. I'm not going anywhere without you and you know it, so put some clothes on before I'm sick everywhere.'

She heard a put-upon sigh and then, 'You can look now. I am decent.'

'You're sure?'

'The floor tiling out here cost a fortune. I don't want it ruined with your vomit.'

Gingerly lowering her hand, Kate unscrewed her eyes and turned her head, only to immediately squeeze her eyes back shut. All he'd done was wrap the towel around his waist. 'That is *not* decent.'

'I didn't realise you were such a delicate flower.'

'Only when my eyes are bleeding.'

'Have you travelled all this way to insult me?'

Still keeping her back to him, she tightened her hold on her small handbag and imagined it was his neck. 'Leander, I'm moving to Borneo in a week and as you very well know, I've a million and one things I need to do before I go, so stop mucking about and put some ruddy clothes on. You'll need to be dressed for the flight back to Greece so do it now, otherwise you'll find I haven't even got started on the insults.'

There was a short but heavily loaded silence.

'How can I put this…? No.'

'What are you saying no to?' she asked indignantly.

She felt rather than heard him walk away.

'All of it,' he replied. 'I'm not going anywhere so why don't you save your breath and my ears and get back in your car, drive back to the airport, fly home, and start packing for your new life.'

Furious, she spun back around.

Leander had sat himself on one of the light grey L-shaped outdoor sofas that surrounded the swimming pool, both arms resting lazily along the back of it, a bottle of beer in hand, long tanned legs stretched out. He'd put a pair of shades on, his gaze fixed musingly at the sky as if judging what the weather planned to do. If Kate could command the weather she'd make it chuck it down with freezing rain on him.

'Well, I'm not going anywhere without you,' she snapped. 'I promised Helena and that brother of yours that I'd drag you back to Greece and that's what I'm going to do.'

'Tell that brother of mine that I'll return to Greece as promised before the honeymoon is over but it will be at a time of my own choosing, so fly away, little flower, and ruin someone else's day.'

'Nope.' Spotting an unopened bottle of beer in a bucket of ice on the table, Kate snatched it up and removed the lid with her teeth.

'Neat trick.'

'Isn't it?' She flopped onto the sofa closest to his and mimicked his pose, although keeping her gaze trained on his face. 'One of my brothers taught me that on my eighteenth birthday.'

'Sounds like my kind of guy. Go and ruin his day.'

'I've ruined many of my brothers' days over the years which means I've had *mucho* practice in annoying men, and now I'm going to stay here and annoy you until you give in and fly back to Greece with me.'

His jaw clenched but his gravelly voice retained the sardonic calm that had laced it since her arrival. 'Kate, go home. I'm not leaving.'

'I promised Helena I would drag you back,' she repeated stubbornly. 'And unlike *some* people, I don't break promises.'

'I told Leo I would be back before the honeymoon is over and I meant it.'

'Yes, I heard the message you left for him—aren't you lucky he heard it in time to take your place?' she retorted. 'You also told Helena you would be waiting at the altar for her. You *promised* her.'

The strong jaw clenched again. 'Leonidas stepped in for me.'

'Yes, and he is *not* happy about having to pretend to be you, and Helena is worried he'll pull the plug on the whole charade before the honeymoon's over, and you know what that means—if she's not married, she has to wait two more years for her inheritance, and she needs that money now.'

'Leo will not pull the plug.' He finally looked away from the sky and turned his shaded stare to her. 'Everyone should stop worrying. I will return before the honeymoon is over. No harm will have been done.'

'How can you say that with a straight face? Your

brother is furious, your parents are…' She shook her head. 'Actually, I don't know what your parents are thinking—they went along with the pretence but if you looked closely enough you could see their bewilderment, and as for Helena…'

'Helena got the marriage she wanted.'

'To the wrong brother! And the wrong brother is not a happy bunny. I get the feeling he likes Helena as much as you like me.'

'What do you mean by that?'

She laughed. 'Oh, come on, Leander. Don't pretend. I know you don't like me and you know I know because Helena asked what I'd done to offend you.'

In the almost fifteen years that Kate and Helena had been friends, Kate had heard a lot about Leander Liassidis but circumstances meant that until Kate had flown to the Liassidises' Greek island the week before the wedding, she'd never actually met him. She'd been looking forward to finally meeting the man Helena had always spoken so highly of, had been certain they would hit it off, and for the first days of their acquaintance her hopes had been realised. Leander was as fun, gregarious and charming as Helena had promised. On Kate's fifth night there, he'd flown the two English women to Athens for a night of food and dancing at an exclusive nightclub near his Athenian apartment. Kate had had the *best* time, and when they'd ended the night at his apartment, she'd been more than happy for the party to continue, the three of them and a handful of Leander's friends drinking cocktails, downing shots and dancing until the sun woke up.

It had been early afternoon when she'd finally dragged

her hungover body out of the gorgeous spare room she'd crashed—literally—in, and though it had to count as the worst hangover of her life, she'd still been buzzing from the fun they'd all shared. In many ways, it had been the celebration she hadn't even known she wanted, her chance to whoop it up and celebrate being just weeks away from starting her new life and the fulfilment of all the dreams she'd held since she was a little girl of seven.

She'd practically boogied into Leander's kitchen and had found him slumped over the kitchen island that was bigger than her bed. She couldn't remember exactly what she'd said but she'd cracked a joke about hangovers and when he'd lifted his head something had flickered on his face before he'd closed his eyes and in the gravelly voice that had up to that point been warm, icily said, 'I have a headache. I would appreciate some silence.'

Although stung at his unexpected coldness, she'd assumed it was his hangover talking and tried not to take it personally, expecting gregarious Leander to re-emerge soon enough. And he did. Gregarious Leander was fully back before they returned to the island...but not for Kate.

He didn't exactly blank her but there was something cool, almost dismissive about his new attitude to her. It had bugged her but it was only when she'd been sunbathing around the Liassidis pool the next afternoon, Helena having popped back to her room to get her portable phone charger, and Leander had appeared on the terrace, taken one look at her and, without a word, turned around and walked away, that she'd known he really had taken a dislike to her.

She'd mentioned it to Helena because it had bothered her and she'd worried she'd inadvertently done something to offend him. If she had, she would have apologised.

'You told Helena that you didn't have a problem with me but I'm not stupid, Leander, and quite frankly, I don't even care about your reasons any more. You need to—'

'I didn't want to hurt Helena with the truth but I'm more than happy to tell you my reasons for disliking you,' he cut in, removing his shades and fixing his dark brown eyes on her. 'You are like a buzzy bee in my ear.' He made a snappy gesture with his fingers and thumb for emphasis and leaned forwards. 'You don't know when to shut up and the stuff that comes out of your mouth is hardly worth the air you use to expel it. I can only assume you got someone to take your veterinary exams for you because you are a walking, talking template of the dumb blonde that people of our parents' generation used to make jokes about.'

He rose to his feet and, top lip curved in a sneer, added, 'Tell Helena and my brother I will be back before the honeymoon is over, as already promised. You can see yourself off my property.'

CHAPTER TWO

LEANDER'S BLOOD WAS still pumping hard as he washed his hair under the shower.

Of all the people his brother and Helena could have sent to track him down, why *her*?

Wiping the suds off his face with his hands, he wished he could wipe the look of shocked hurt on Kate's face from his eyes. Banish it.

It was for the best, he told himself as he lathered shower gel over his body. It had needed to be done. Kate couldn't be here.

He'd known Leo would send someone to find him because it was inconceivable he would take Leander at his word to come back. Leander had broken his word to his twin fourteen years ago and Leonidas had never forgiven him for it. Even though it had been five years since Leo had responded to any of his communications, Leander knew he could tell his brother it was raining and Leo would open a window to check for himself.

So yes, he'd expected Leo to send someone and demand he return to Greece immediately, and had prepared his staff accordingly. He would stay in seclusion until his head was together and his emotions under control, and only then would he return. A week was plenty of time to achieve all this.

But Leonidas and Helena had sent *her* to find him.

Why the hell had he revealed himself to her? It was a question still raging through his mind when he pulled a pair of heavy knee-length canvas shorts on. If he hadn't felt that strong compulsion to see if the voice was who every one of his senses had told him it was, Kate would have left Marina Sands in ignorance of how close she'd come to finding him.

He hoped like hell that she didn't take his cruel words to heart, but he'd needed to get rid of her and that had been the only way to achieve it.

Another sin he could add to his tally. The sin that cut the deepest. The most necessary of all his sins.

He needed to eat something. His usually healthy appetite had deserted him in recent days. It was almost lunch time and he hadn't eaten a thing, which for a man of six foot four was normally unthinkable.

He'd let his chef enjoy the balmy weather and make himself an omelette. Anything to do with eggs he could fix for himself. An omelette, a bucket of wine and a crap movie...

He stepped into his main living room and his plans dissolved in an instant.

Kate was on one of his sofas. Not just on it but stretched out, her head propped on a cushion, bare ankles hooked together below smooth, slender golden legs covered only to mid-thigh in khaki green shorts, busy doing something or nothing on her phone.

'There you are,' she said cheerfully, tucking a lock of blonde hair behind a little sticky-out ear, not looking away from the screen inches from her face. 'I was starting to wonder if you'd run away again.'

'I told you to leave,' he said roughly. Damn her. It had never occurred to him that she would stay after he'd spoken so cruelly to her. Anyone with an ounce of pride would have driven away cursing his name.

'For the sake of accuracy, you told me to see myself out. Now, I've messaged Helena with the good news that I've found you and updated her about your resistance to returning straight to Greece.' She turned her head and fixed the heart-shaped face that reminded him of the pixies of folklore and eyes the colour of jade on him with a steely smile. 'I've promised to do everything I can to get you back there sooner rather than later—reading between the lines, your brother's being an arse, which doesn't surprise me given everything Helen's told me about him—so consider me your houseguest until such time you agree to return.'

'Absolutely not.' He'd rather have radioactive cockroaches as houseguests.

'I'm afraid I only chucked a few bits of clothes in a bag when I set off to find you and I've left them in the plane, so I'll have to borrow some clothes off you, and also some toiletries and stuff—unless you don't mind having a stinky houseguest that is—and—'

Leander had never known a man's guts could clench so tightly. 'This is all out of the question. You need to leave.'

'Can't.' Her smile widened. 'I've sent the driver away.'

'I'll get my driver to take you.'

'I'm not going anywhere without you, Leander, so unless you plan to physically throw me out of your home, you're going to have to put up with me annoying you and buzzing like a bee in your ear until you're so sick of me that you give in and do the decent thing and go back to Greece, and put Helena and Leo out of the misery you've inflicted on them.'

'How many times do I have to tell you, I will return to Greece before the honeymoon is over?' he demanded.

She turned her stare back to her phone and swiped at the screen. 'You can repeat yourself until you're blue in the face; no one trusts you to keep your word, and even if they did, this is supposed to be *your* honeymoon, and it's selfish of you to expect your brother to step away from all his responsibilities just because you can't cope with the idea of being tied to one woman without any sex for a few months at the most. If you need to get your leg over that badly, use some discretion. Helena won't care.'

'You think this is all about *sex*?' Swearing loudly, Leander paced the room, torn between doing exactly as Kate had said and throwing her over his shoulder to march her out of his home, and not wanting to even share the same air as her. The thought of touching her was too intolerable to contemplate.

'Well, you did tell your brother in that message you so kindly left him that something had come up, and you are known as Leander the Lothario,' she reminded him sweetly, 'so it does stand to reason.'

The tabloid moniker for him. It had never bothered him before. He'd actually found it quite useful. Women knew not to expect anything permanent from him. He could work hard and play hard without ties or responsibilities and enjoy his life and indulge in short but sweet

successive flings without any expectations being lev-
elled on him.

Kate attempted to keep her stare on the screen and
not let it drift to Leander because she was still trying
to banish the sight of him semi-naked from her retinas,
which considering she'd sunbathed next to him numerous times—before he went all cold on her—and had
barely paid his semi-nakedness the slightest bit of attention other than in a general *he's got a great body* way,
was as disturbing as the pulses fluttering in her stomach.

'If it isn't about sex then what is it?' she asked when
his only response was to glare malevolently at her. She
couldn't see the glare but she could feel it. 'You told me
only a week ago that you thought a fake marriage to
Helena was *no big deal.*'

She'd asked him about it when they'd been sunbathing on her third day on his family island and Helena had
been on a phone call. It had been Kate's first opportunity to grill him.

'What's in all this for you?' she'd asked, turning onto
her side to face him.

He'd been lying on his back, fabulous body glistening
under the searing sun, dark shades covering his eyes.
He'd turned his face to her. 'You mean marrying Helena?'

'Yes. I know why she needs a quickie marriage and
why she asked you—'

'Why was that?' he'd asked lazily.

'Because you're her second-best friend—'

'Only second?'

'Of course,' she'd grinned. 'I'm number one.'

White teeth had flashed.

'And she asked you because you have no ties and apparently no intention of ever marrying.'

'Oh, I might marry for real one day.'

'When you meet the right woman?' she'd teased, very much aware that Leander's playboy reputation was well deserved.

'That sounds remarkably romantic for a woman who wants to marry an orangutan,' he'd teased back, making her splutter with laughter. 'Life is for living, not being tied down, but I can see myself wanting children one day. If that happens, I might consider marriage, but it wouldn't be for a long time. Helena needs her inheritance now and the only way she can get it is by marrying, and as she won't accept money from me...' He'd flashed his teeth again. 'I just thought, why not? It's no big deal for me. It'll be for a couple of months at the most. As soon as the inheritance is signed over to her, we will tragically go our separate ways.'

Kate's recollection of this conversation only made Leander's cold feet on the morning of the wedding even harder to understand. How could he be so blasé about it one day and then only days later flee thousands of miles? It just didn't make sense.

Leander could see from the way Kate had stilled that her clever brain was ticking and the clenching in his guts tightened to a point.

Folding his arms across his chest, it occurred to him that he could use that tabloid moniker and the reputation it had established to his advantage.

'You know what, Kate? You're right. This is all about my insatiable need for sex, and when I return to Greece, I'll be sure to tell Helena that I'll be taking lovers—discreet lovers, naturally—until she gets her inheritance and we can dissolve the marriage.'

She turned her face back to him brightly. 'Oh, good. Does that mean we can leave now?'

'You can leave whenever you want but I'm staying here. But seeing as you've put me in the mind for sex...' He gave her a meaningful stare.

Her nose wrinkled, just as he'd anticipated. Kate was the only woman he'd met in adulthood who gave no signs at all of desiring him. From Kate there had not been the slightest sign of awareness that she saw him as a man.

'God, you're disgusting.'

'Most women find me irresistible.'

'Then most women are stupid.'

He shrugged. 'If you won't oblige, my phone is packed with the names and numbers of women who would be happy to come over and satisfy my needs.'

Distaste written all over her face, she shrugged in return. 'Knock yourself out.'

'Some of my lovers have a tendency to be...how can I put this delicately?...vocal.'

She shrugged again. 'If they're too noisy I'll stick some cheese in my ears.'

How could she be so damned blasé? So unaffected?

Pulling his phone out of his back pocket, he waved it at her. 'Hundreds of obliging women.'

'Your mother must be very proud.'

'My mother understands me very well.' It was his identical twin who didn't. Or wouldn't.

Perching his backside on the side of the sofa next to Kate's head, glancing at the screen of her phone and seeing she was playing a word game which, for some reason added to his internal fury, Leander scrolled through his contacts. 'Who should I call? Grace? Hettie? Ah, Elle's in Santa Monica. That's not far. What do you think, Kate? Shall I call Elle? She's a real beauty.'

She tilted her head back to look up at him. The movement sent strands of her blonde hair brushing against his thigh. 'If you think Elle would be happy to be summoned to act as a vessel for your selfish pleasure, then by all means call her.'

'Stick around long enough and you'll find the pleasure is entirely mutual.'

'I'm sticking around until I get you back to Greece, even if it means using a whole block of cheese as ear plugs.'

He smiled cruelly down at her. 'I would suggest two blocks of cheese, and speaking of cheese, I'm hungry. If you're still planning to hang around where you're not wanted, you can make yourself useful and make me an omelette.'

'I'm happy exactly where I am, thanks.' And to prove it, she looked back at her phone and made another attempt to guess the day's word.

He laughed mockingly. 'You'll have to vacate your spot when Elle gets here—unless you want to watch as well as hear?'

Her mouth opened in a wide yawn she didn't bother to cover. 'I'm sure watching you have sex will be riveting.'

'I can go for hours.'

'Congratulations. You should add that to your email signature.'

'It's gauche to brag.' He got back to his feet. 'I'll call Elle now. I imagine she'll be here within the hour so if you see sense and decide not to ruin your dream job, dial one on the intercom and my driver will take you to the airfield. I'm going to make myself some food.'

'No onion in my omelette thanks.'

'If you want to eat, you'll have to go somewhere else. I will provide you with nothing.'

Unperturbed, she wiggled her toes. 'That's fine. I was a hungry student for five years, and besides, I'm sure the sight and sound of you having sex will kill my appetite for ever.'

Teeth clenched so tightly his jaw locked, Leander strode to his kitchen, more determined than ever to drive Kate Hawkins out of his sanctuary.

Kate waited until she was quite certain Leander wasn't planning to come straight back into the living room with another psychological attempt to make her leave before placing her phone on her chest, closing her eyes, and expelling a long breath.

She would not let his disdain for her affect her like he so obviously wanted it to. If he didn't like her and didn't want her in his home then tough luck. Kate had never broken a promise in her life and wasn't about to start now, especially not when that promise had been made to Helena. If not for Helena, she would never have survived boarding school and if she hadn't survived boarding school she'd have had to attend the local secondary school which was infamous for its lousy teaching and so would never have achieved the grades she needed to study to be a vet. She wouldn't be seven days from flying off to start her dream job, working at what was essentially a charity-run orangutan orphanage.

Kate had been one of only three full scholarship girls

at her boarding school, one of the only girls who didn't spend the holidays in St Tropez or Klosters or wherever else Mummy and Daddy had a second or third or fourth home. The Hawkins annual family holiday was normally a fortnight in Spain or Portugal at an all-inclusive three-star resort which the other girls had all thought hilarious, and not in a good way.

Helena had been different. She hadn't cared that Kate's parents drove second-hand cars, lived in a semi-detached house and didn't have food delivered from Fortnum & Mason. Their friendship had been instant and had endured for almost fifteen years. As close as sisters, there was nothing they wouldn't do for the other, and if Helena needed Kate to cling like a limpet to Leander Liassidis until she could drag him back to Greece then she would forego any personal discomfort and do it. She knew exactly what was at stake for Helena if she failed and Leander's twin refused to carry out the pretence of being him any longer.

She didn't believe for a second that Leander would call Elle or any woman over. She had no idea where this certainty came from, but just as she'd instinctively known that he was in residence here, she also knew he was playing dirty psychological tricks to try and get rid of her, and she would swallow away her pride and the pangs that kept smashing into her chest that he made no bones about disliking her.

At least he was making it easier for her to despise him in return, and she would not allow herself any sadness that a man she'd struck such a great rapport with, someone she'd felt a real kernel of friendship unfold for, had turned out to be such a hateful bastard.

* * *

Leander's omelette looked pretty damn good, even if he did say so himself. Loaded with cheese and Serrano ham, he'd deliberately not put any onion in it, just to tantalise Kate's tastebuds. He would starve her out, and as he carried his plate out of the kitchen, he locked the door behind him. He'd never understood why the previous owner, an architect who'd designed the futuristic-looking mansion, had put locks on all the doors including the kitchen and now he could only assume they'd had a Kate invade their home.

Stopping at his floor-to-ceiling wine fridge, he selected a bottle of Chablis, plucked a glass from the cabinet beside it, and carried his haul into the living room.

The comment he'd planned to needle Kate with went unsaid when he crossed the threshold and found she'd fallen asleep.

He could do nothing to stop the swelling in his chest that rose all the way up his throat.

Still stretched out on her back, an arm had flopped down the side of the sofa, the tips of her fingers brushing against the rug on the floor. Her breathing was deep and rhythmic, the motions making the abandoned phone resting on her chest move and slide with each exhale.

Jaw clenched, he forced the swelling to subside and sat himself on a reclining armchair close to her. The aroma of cheese and ham would wake her up, he told himself, and if that didn't work, turning the television on and upping the volume would do the trick. Pressing the remote, the television sprang to life, a daytime home improvement show. About to increase the volume to eardrum bursting levels, he made the error of letting his eyes fall on Kate's sleeping face. The swelling set off again.

He'd been so intent on getting rid of her that he'd ignored the exhaustion lining her delicate pixie features.

He turned the television off and left the Chablis unopened.

Three bites of his omelette and he could stand it no longer. Putting his plate on the floor, he padded quietly over and gently removed the phone from her chest, being careful not to allow his fingers to make contact with the round-necked blue and white striped top she was wearing, and set it on the floor beside her sparkly flat sandals, close to the hand trailing on the rug.

The delicate fingers twitched.

His heart stopped.

Swallowing hard, he backed away and finished his solo meal.

The figure moved from the shadows of the door and stalked towards her, only a small towel hiding his nakedness. The closer he got, the more magnified his demonic beauty and the higher the thuds of anticipation in her chest. She couldn't open her mouth to speak but when his face hovered over hers, her lips parted. Threading her fingers into the black silk of his hair, she tightened her grip and moaned into the hungry possessiveness of his kiss...

Kate pulled herself out of the dream with a start. Eyes springing open, the deep blue of the crushed velvet sofa she'd fallen asleep on dominated her vision. Her heart was thumping so hard and so fast it was a burr against her ribs. If her hand wasn't already gripping her top she'd have to pat herself for assurance that she remained clothed.

It took an age before she found the courage to turn her head.

Leander was in an armchair reading, the strong jaw covered in thick black stubble set, the slightly too wide mouth compressed into a thin line.

'What time is it?' she mumbled, striving desperately to shake the dream and sleepiness off, and was more grateful than she could ever express that he didn't look up from his book when he answered.

'Seven.'

She'd slept for hours.

It took much more effort than it should to swing her feet to the floor. 'I need to use the bathroom.'

'I'm afraid the facilities here are unavailable for you.' His voice was as tight as his features.

That was better. Right then she needed him to be as mean as possible, to grow horns and develop cloven hooves.

'Fine. How about I pee on your rug?'

That made him look at her, and God did she wish he wouldn't, not until she'd scratched that dream from her memory for good.

The lips that had just kissed her in her dream pursing in a put-upon motion, he nodded at the arch he'd gone through earlier, before she'd zonked out. 'First left.'

She crossed the vast living space, past the enormous central feature fireplace, and almost hoped he was sending her to a broom cupboard or something, just so she had something else to hate him for. But no, it was a bathroom, an ordinary downstairs bathroom with a toilet and a sink and which just happened to be one of the plushest downstairs loos she'd ever stepped in.

Only once she'd locked the door was she able to snatch a lungful of air.

Her heart was still racing when she washed her shaking hands with the deliciously scented hand wash and splashed cold water on her flushed face. It wasn't just her face that was flushed. Her insides felt liquidised.

God help her, that *dream*... It had felt so real.

She pulled more air into her lungs then ran her fingers through her mussed hair and rubbed away the last of the mascara applied over two days ago from under her eyes, forcefully reminding herself that it *hadn't* been real.

Even so, there was something frightening about her reflection, a feverishness she didn't recognise and which made her splash her face with more cold water.

One more deep breath and she left the bathroom.

Each step back to the living room made her heart race a little bit faster.

It was decidedly colder when Kate crossed the threshold. Most of the glass wall facing the ocean had been opened, cool evening air pouring in.

Leander's set profile was still focused on his book. He made no acknowledgement of her return.

The racing of her heart turned into a painful thunder. If she'd thought she could scorch the image of Leander's practically naked body from her retinas, her dream had put paid to that.

CHAPTER THREE

FILLING HER LUNGS deeply one more time for luck, Kate brought Helena's face to her mind. Helena was the reason why she was here, in the home of a man who couldn't stand her. Helena.

It had been a dream, that's all. A vivid dream but still just a dream. It didn't mean anything. She would shake it off and forget about it before the evening was done.

'I take it I missed Elle,' she said with determined breeziness as she reclaimed her spot on the sofa she knew perfectly well would be her bed for however long she ended up staying there. At least it was as comfortable as a real bed.

Leander didn't look up from his book. 'You missed all the fun.'

'She can't be that vocal if I slept through it all.'

'I doubt you'd have heard anything over the noise of your snores.'

'I don't snore.'

'How would you know? You were asleep. You sounded like a warthog.'

'You say the nicest things.'

A buzzer sounded from the ceiling.

He closed his book with a snap. 'That means my dinner is ready.'

'Don't let me hold you up.'

'Moussaka.'

She refused to let her expression change in the slightest. Kate had never tried the dish before her trip to the Liassidises' island and had fallen into raptures on her first taste. Leander had found this love for something that was so ordinary to him amusing, and they'd fallen into a long, detailed conversation about all their favourite foods.

'Try not to choke on it.'

'If I do, I'm sure you'll perform the Heimlich manoeuvre on me—after all, a dead Leander is no good for Helena, is he?'

'I'd be tempted to let you suffer a while first before saving you.'

'Then I'll make sure to chew thoroughly like a good boy.' With a tight, sarcastic smile, he disappeared from the vast room.

There was hardly the time for Kate to compose herself into a picture of serenity for he quickly returned carrying a tray with a plate heaped with an enormous mound of food and a gigantic glass of red wine.

'Not going to eat in your dining room?' she asked, affecting boredom.

'What kind of host would I be leaving my *guest* to her own devices while I eat?' He sat back on his armchair, took a drink of his wine and then took his first mouthful.

'Mmm…mmm,' he said appreciatively after he'd tried a sample of everything. 'You know, I think this might be even better than the moussaka we ate last week. And

the lemon roasted potatoes...' He smacked his lips together and forked another mouthful in.

There was nothing Kate could do to stop her stomach
from rumbling. It had to be a good sixteen hours since
she'd last eaten. She was thirsty too, having not drunk
anything since the beer she'd pilfered on the pool terrace.

The smile Leander gave proved without him having to say a word that he'd heard the rumble. He put his
knife and fork on the plate, held a finger up to indicate
he had something to tell her, then expertly held the tray
with one hand as he stood and pulled a bottle of water
from his shorts pocket.

'For you,' he said once he'd sat back down, and lobbed
the bottle to her. 'Can't have my *guest* getting dehy-
drated.'

She caught it and smiled. 'Oh, you're just too kind.'
Then she noted it was sparkling water. 'Just too kind,'
she repeated, unscrewing the lid and putting it to her
dry lips. Deliberately keeping her stare on his, she drank
half the contents and tried not to let her aversion to the
carbonated taste show on her face. Leander knew perfectly well that she hated sparkling water.

She watched him eat every last scrap, and when he'd
finished and the empty plate was replaced with a pasta
bowl of hot chocolate fudge pudding with whipped
cream, she gave not the slightest reaction, not even when
her stomach betrayed her hunger for the fourth time.

'There's a great restaurant two miles from here,'
he confided as he steadily demolished a portion large
enough to feed four people. 'It's in a cove and serves
fresh seasonal seafood but it's the desserts it's famous

around here for. They make a key lime pie that is out of this world.'

'Sounds great.'

'It is.' He pulled a face as if something had just occurred to him. 'You like key lime pie, don't you? I seem to remember you couldn't make up your mind what your favourite dessert is. Hot chocolate fudge cake with whipped cream or key lime pie.' He drank some more of his wine before holding up his glass. 'They also serve great wine. I'm told even the house red is palatable.'

'I'll be sure to pay it a visit if I ever return to this part of the world.'

'It closes at eleven if you want to try it now.'

'I'm good,' she said, even as her stomach betrayed her yet again.

His smile was knowing. 'Most Marina Sands' restaurants stop serving food by ten but there's a couple of twenty-four-hour drive-throughs on the outskirts. I've heard one of them serves food that doesn't taste like cardboard. I'm quite sure they all sell still water too.'

She pulled a shocked face. 'Still water? Wow. That's certainly something for me to think on.'

'My driver is at your disposal. Dial one on the intercom and you will be taken anywhere you wish to go.' His dessert finished with, he disappeared again, this time returning with a coffee that smelt so good Kate had to clench her buttocks to stop herself from jumping off the sofa to snatch it out of his hand.

Revenge was soon hers when Leander reclined his chair and turned the television on and found a film clearly designed to bore as it was a spy thriller without any thrills, and she proceeded to annoy him by chatter-

ing away about everything from the protagonist's im-
practical shoes to the implausibility of the plot line, not
giving her mouth a rest long enough for him to take
any of it in.

He thought she was annoying? Well she was delighted
to prove just how annoying she could be.

It took less than thirty minutes for him to jump up
from his recliner and announce he was going to take a
walk on the beach.

'Sounds like fun,' she immediately enthused. 'I'll join
you...' And then she caught the glint in his eyes and in-
stinct told her that the moment she left the glass walls
of his home, all the doors would be locked to her. 'Actually, I think I'll stay here.'

His smile as tight as his clenched jaw, he walked out
without another word and disappeared into the darkness.

Leander filled his lungs with the salty ocean air and
cursed himself for not thinking to put shoes on. Or a
sweater. The breeze from the ocean kept the daytime
temperatures in Marina Sands temperate all year round
but the evenings were often much cooler. When he
stepped onto the sand at the foot of his private path to
the beach, his toes curled in protest.

He supposed it was a good thing Kate had resisted
walking the beach with him. The temptation to throw
her into the ocean might have proved too much. To throw
her into the ocean would have meant having to touch her,
and a memory flashed of her dancing in his Athenian
apartment, one hand clutching a cocktail, the other waving above her head as she sang along loudly to the track
playing, and Dimitri sidling up to slip a hand around her

waist and palm her flat stomach over her pretty summery dress, Kate's scream of laughter and—

Leander upped his pace.

She'd be gone soon, he told himself grimly. He'd locked all the rooms so she was confined to the main living room which turned chilly overnight and all she had to wear were those shorts and that top that only reached her elbows. Opening the external doors had already driven out the residual heat. She was already hungry. Come the morning—if she lasted that long—she'd be freezing and starving. Even Kate, with all her tenacity and stubbornness, would have to admit defeat and leave.

By the time Kate figured out how to close the external doors of the living room that was twice the size of her parents' entire home, all the warmth had escaped. A search of the house for something warm to drape over herself ended in failure. Of the internal doors, only the downstairs bathroom was unlocked. The only fabric she'd found to warm herself with was the hand towel in the bathroom.

Back in the living room, she had another look at the central fireplace. Stumped at how to turn it on, she called out for Leander's staff—she knew there had to be staff around seeing as his dinner hadn't cooked itself. Her shouts went unanswered so she dialled one on the intercom. It was answered before the first ring had finished.

'Where would you like me to take you?' a feminine voice on the other end of the line asked.

'Actually, I was hoping you or another member of staff could turn the fire on for me,' Kate said. 'It's freezing in here.'

'I'm sorry, ma'am, but I'm not authorised to do that. I am only authorised to drive you to any destination of your choice.'

'Would you drive me to England?'

'If that's what you asked of me. It might take some ingenuity to manage it but I would do my best.'

'So you can drive me to England but can't turn the fire on?'

'I'm sorry, ma'am, but we have our instructions.'

Kate sighed. 'Thanks anyway.'

Ramming her hands into her shorts pockets, she took stock. She was cold and hungry but not defeated. For all Leander's bull-headed determination, her very presence was an aggravation to him. And the good thing about being cold meant the heat of her dream had finally disappeared.

She just wished the dream itself would vanish. Forget the current circumstances and the not insignificant fact that he couldn't stand her, she had no right allowing Leander into her dreams. He was as off-limits as off-limits could be and it didn't matter that Helena had no romantic feelings towards him or that their marriage was a sham and probably not even legal considering the wrong twin had made the vows and signed the certificate; in Kate's mind he belonged to Helena.

In her almost twenty-six years on this earth, Kate had never dreamt about a man, not even Euan, her two-week university fling that hadn't even been a real fling but which she'd ended abruptly when—

Outside lights came on.

Heart suddenly thumping, she hurried back to her

original sofa and curled up on it, warming her feet as best she could under her bottom, and turned her phone on.

The glass door slid open.

Her heart thumped harder.

Leander's gaze zoomed straight to her. The instant his dark brown eyes locked onto hers, Kate's thumping heart stopped and her breath caught in her throat.

Barely moments passed before her heart kick-started itself with a roar, sending hot blood pounding in every direction.

A slow blink and then Leander's huge shoulders rose and a tight smile pulled against his set features. 'Still here I see.'

She had no idea how she was able to summon a quip through the loud pulsing in her ears. 'Your powers of observation are astounding.'

'Nearly as astounding as your capacity for self-torture.' He slid the door shut. 'I'll keep this unlocked so you can see yourself out. I'm going to bed.'

'Not going to call one of your pleasure vessels to keep you company?' She had no idea where that remark came from either, knew only that it was a remark that should have gone unsaid because the last thing she wanted to think or talk about in that moment was Leander having sex, not when she was already feeling so...*aware* of him. Her only comfort was that her tone had been pithy rather than bitchy.

The tight smile pulled a tiny bit wider. 'The call's already been made. I'll keep my bedroom door open so you can watch.' The sensual lips pulled wider still. 'If you get too cold my bed's big enough for three.'

Even though she knew this was just another mind

game that she'd been stupid enough to leave an open goal for him to score in, a hot flush crawled through her, enflaming her bones, her skin…enflaming *everything*.

Somehow she managed to retain the pithiness to say, 'I'm sure I'd much rather freeze.'

'A night in here without the heating on and no blankets and you will do just that.' The smile dropped. 'Remember, dial one on the intercom and my driver will take you anywhere you want to go.'

It had been many years since Leander had gone to bed so early and the first time he'd slid under the blankets with fury snaking through his veins. Anger was only ever a fleeting emotion in him. His twin held onto it enough for them both. Leander had been the one to cut the invisible umbilical cord conjoining them as identical twins but Leo had been the one to sever it in its entirety. For five years Leo had acted as if he had no brother, every message Leander had sent him remaining unanswered, although not unread. He hadn't even RSVP'd the wedding invitation.

Leander had known though, that Leo would never refuse a direct request for help just as he would be unable to refuse Leo if the roles were reversed.

Theós, it had been surreal hearing his own voice down the end of the line after so long, even if it was only a short invitation for the caller to leave a message.

At the time he'd made the call, Leander's only thought had been getting as far from Greece as quickly as possible, but since then he'd thought of his brother more than he'd done in years. He'd kept tabs on him through family and news reports just as he knew Leo kept tabs on him, but he hadn't consciously thought about him. If he was being truthful, he'd actively avoided thinking about Leo. To think of his twin was to acknowledge the wound in his heart.

When he'd told Leo his decision all those years ago he'd known it would hurt him. He would have hurt too if the roles had been reversed. What he'd had no way of knowing was that things would deteriorate so badly and culminate with Leo cutting him from his life.

All of Leander's thoughts during that first contact in five years had been clouded by the woman currently sleeping on the ground floor below his bedroom. She couldn't know it but the sofa she'd made herself at home on lay directly beneath his bed.

Damn her. Damn her for treating her invasion of his home as one big game. Damn her for being so... *Kate*.

His wired brain refused to shut down. His heart refused to settle into a natural rhythm. His unwanted houseguest refused to remove herself from his mind's eye.

Midnight chimed and she was still there.

How could she be so stubborn? If she didn't leave soon she was going to give herself hypothermia.

He turned over and angrily punched his pillow. So what if she gave herself hypothermia? It would be her own damn fault. He'd given her every means to leave. One call and she could be driven in a heated car to a drive-through and then on to the airfield. There was no need for her to put herself through this unnecessary suffering.

Kate had huddled as deep into the sofa as she could go, knees hugged into her chest. The hand towel was draped over her feet but still goosebumps scored her flesh. She couldn't stop shivering. So cold was she that even the hunger pangs had gone into hibernation.

At least she wasn't thirsty. After leaving the living room, Leander had returned with two bottles of water for her, which he'd placed silently onto a sideboard before disappearing again without looking at her. Naturally, they were sparkling water.

As much as it pained her to admit it, she didn't think she could endure this for much longer. It was two a.m. and despite her long sleep that afternoon, she was still exhausted but sleep refused to come. She was just too cold. There were hours more to suffer before the sun rose and warmed the vast room.

But it wasn't just the coldness driving sleep away and making the thought of pressing one on the intercom ever more tempting.

Her brain was torturing her too.

Every time Kate closed her eyes the terrible dream was right there, dancing before her eyes, making her pulses accelerate and a terrible fever break out on her freezing skin. The deeper her exhaustion, the worse it all got, and her only successful attempts at driving the dream away were a failure of a kind because to replace them her mind filled with memories of all the fun and laughter they'd shared before he'd turned against her.

What had she done to provoke the change? In the stillness of the cold night, it was the one question that loomed larger than anything.

She must have done *something* because, for all his talk of her being an annoyance, his coldness had been too sudden for that excuse to be credible. Her last concrete memory of Leander and that night in Athens was shimmying over to where he was making cocktails. Leander had shimmied with her, shaking the cocktail maker in time to the beats pumping loudly through the whole apartment, the joy of good music and the excellent atmosphere flowing between them, and then he'd filled a glass with his creation and passed it to her with a mock bow. She'd shimmied away, blowing him a kiss that he'd caught with a huge grin and slapped to his stubbly cheek. Barely ten hours later she'd found him slumped over his kitchen island and he'd been cold with her ever since.

Leander punched his pillow for what had to be the fifteenth time and then something in him snapped.

Throwing the duvet off, he stormed down the winding stairs and into the living room.

Kate must have heard the heavy tread of his angry feet because he could see through the silvery light dancing through the windows that she'd lifted her head.

'Do you have some kind of damned death wish?' he demanded as he slammed his hand against the switch that turned on the soft up-lights rather than the main lights that would have blinded them both.

Immediately she turned her face into the sofa with the rest of her curled-up body. She was pressed so tightly into it she was close to being a part of it, but it was the small hand-towel wrapped around her feet that ripped through him the hardest.

'Why won't you leave?' he shouted into the unnerving silence. 'Why put yourself through this? What are you trying to prove? Do you think giving yourself hypothermia is going to make me soften and let you stay?

Do you think Helena would want you to make yourself ill for her sake?'

But still she didn't answer. Still she kept her stubborn little back turned to him.

Cursing in Greek at her sheer bloody-mindedness, Leander stormed back up the stairs.

Kate heard a distant door slam and stuffed her fist into her mouth to stifle the sob that wanted to break free.

She'd wanted to shout back at him, remind him of the promise she'd made to Helena but her heart had been pounding so hard the beats had rippled in her throat.

It was seeing him emerge from the darkness that had set the reactions off. The silvery light had magnified his demonic beauty. Just like in her dream. He'd been wearing only a pair of boxer shorts, as little as he'd been wearing in her dream.

But in her dream he hadn't used his mouth to be cruel to her.

She took a long shuddery breath and turned over. Annoying Leander into submission was one thing but the way he'd just shouted at her...

She'd been right that his attitude towards her ran deeper than mere annoyance, but she'd underestimated the depths to which his dislike had reached.

Leander didn't just dislike her. He *hated* her.

What had felt, in part, like a game, a battle of wills between them, now tasted very different under the weight of his visceral loathing.

Heavy footsteps crashed back down the stairs.

If his demonic beauty had struck her dumb before, now it was the bundle he held in his arms.

He dumped it on the end of her sofa, snatched the

top item and threw it onto her lap. 'Put this on,' he said roughly.

It was a black long-sleeved brushed cotton top.

He pressed his huge hand onto the rest of the bundle. 'Duvet and pillow. I'll leave you to make yourself comfortable.'

He stalked across the living room and disappeared.

Stunned at the unexpected gesture, Kate spent an age gazing at the duvet and pillow until her shivering flesh forced her into action.

Shaking the duvet out…oh, it was so wonderful and heavy…she hauled it over herself then stuck the pillow where her head rested and slipped the lounging top over her head. It smelt of fabric softener. It smelt clean.

Lying down, she huddled under the heavenly duvet and, while she waited for her body to accept the warmth and defrost, became aware for the first time that her bra was digging into her shoulders and ribs, and the button of her shorts was pressing into her belly.

Sitting back up, she took the lounging top and her own top off, then, while keeping the duvet around her shoulders for warmth by trapping it beneath her chin, unclasped her bra. The relief was so immediate that she wondered how she hadn't noticed the pain it had been causing her before. With the duvet still trapped between her chin and neck, she slid the straps off and scrambled again for the clean lounging top. There was a shock of cold against her breasts when she released the duvet to pull the top over her head and it flumped down to her waist, but then, once her arms were in, tugged it down, untucked her trapped hair and…

And noticed Leander as still as a statue by the fireplace, holding a crystal tumbler filled with a dark liquid.

Suddenly Kate found she didn't need the top or duvet for warmth. The flush that crawled through every inch of her was hot enough to generate heat for the whole of Marina Sands.

Time stood suspended. She couldn't drag her stare from Leander, could do nothing to stop the flush deepening and pulsing as the perfectly sculpted tanned torso fully etched itself into her paralysed brain, all the tiny details she'd never allowed herself to acknowledge before, from the dark hair covering the defined pecs and washboard abdomen to the indentation of his navel. All the tiny details that saturated her heated brain even while her eyes remained trapped in his stare.

His throat moved—how had she never noticed how strong it was before?—and his shoulders—broader than she'd ever recognised—lifted before his strong Roman nose flared and his lips compressed into a line so tight they disappeared.

A moment later he crossed the room to the archway that led to the stairs and the whole of him disappeared.

CHAPTER FOUR

LEANDER DRANK HIS Scotch in one huge gulp.

His skin had never felt so tight. The beats of his heart had never drummed so loudly in his ears.

God help him, Kate's breasts...

He gritted his teeth.

It had no effect.

God, they were every bit as beautiful as he'd refused to allow his mind to imagine. More so. Fuller than her petite frame suggested. Nipples the colour of dusky rose...

A groan rose up his throat.

He'd never experienced such painful arousal before.

He needed a shower.

Setting the temperature as low as he could withstand, Leander stood beneath the cold spray and willed the unwanted arousal to abate. If it was only in his loins he could have handled it, relieved himself and be done with it, but this was everywhere. Every cell in his body. Every cell begging for one little taste but one little taste would never be...

God damn it, why had he allowed himself to soften enough to strip a spare bed for her? Telling himself that it wasn't the same as inviting her to sleep in the spare bed cut no ice. The only reason he hadn't invited her to use it was because he couldn't endure Kate sleeping on the same floor as him. Bad enough knowing she was curled on the sofa he doubted he would ever use again. He would throw it out. Replace it.

And what had possessed him to give her an item of his own clothing? If he'd resisted, she would never have thought to take her clothes off and he would never have seen...

He squeezed his eyes as tightly shut as he could manage to eradicate the image of her breasts from his mind, but all he succeeded in doing was replacing them with the look that had slowly crept over her face in those moments when he'd been unable to tear his gaze away from her.

It was a variant of a look he'd seen so many times that he hardly noticed it any more. But he'd never seen it on Kate's face before and it made everything a thousand times worse.

Leander beat the sun up. He'd had little sleep, his brain too wired at the presence of the woman haunting his home to fully shut down. Before his eyes opened, the memory of Kate's naked breasts and the feel of that look that had passed between them hit him with vivid colour and he was wide awake in an instant, painfully aware only the floor beneath his bed separated them.

He needed to hit the surf. Once he'd driven out the angst that had his guts clenching so tightly and his pulses beating so strongly he'd be in a better frame of mind to up his game and force her from his home. If that look should pass between them again...

He descended the stairs quietly, intending to leave through the utility room, but before he could stop himself, he stepped into what had quickly turned into Kate's domain.

She was turned away from him, curled into the sofa fast asleep.

The churning in his stomach was violent enough to induce nausea.

Turning on his heel, he slipped back out of the room.

Kate's eyes pinged open. Although crushed blue velvet lay in her immediate vision, it was Leander she saw, his expression in that terrible, terrible moment that had passed between them, the complete stillness that had quickly morphed into disgust.

It was an expression that had made anything more than snatches of sleep impossible. She had the awful sense she would remember it for the rest of her life.

Being an annoyance she could handle, but being hated? That cut deeper than she could have believed. She'd never been hated before, not even by the snobby boarding school girls who'd taken cruel delight in patronising and mocking her, and to experience that hatred from the charming, fun, attentive man who'd made her laugh so hard and whose company she'd revelled in...

It didn't help that she'd developed this awful awareness of him that didn't seem in any hurry to shake itself off. During their week on his family's island, when the two of them and Helena had spent almost all their time together, Kate had acknowledged Leander was a hunk, mainly because she wasn't blind, but his hunkiness had had no effect on her.

Whatever protective layer had been on her eyes and mind in Greece, being alone with him here had stripped it away. The dream had ignited it and switched her awareness on. One little dream. One little dream that had roused something in her, awakened her to the fact that Leander wasn't just a hunk of a man but the most rampantly sexy man alive.

Rolling over, she squeezed her eyes shut in an attempt to eradicate the disgust on his face from her retinas, then swung her feet to the floor and rubbed her temples.

She needed to pull her big-girl knickers up and think practically. Her mission was to drag Leander back to Greece before his brother pulled the plug on the whole thing, and in good time for Kate to return to England and make the final preparations needed before she flew off to start the new life she'd worked so hard for. Leander's wild success in life and the way he'd treated her since her arrival here suggested he had an ever-flowing tap of ruthlessness, but she was stubborn, and her love and loyalty for Helena meant she'd wear him down before he broke her spirit. Admittedly, she needed to find a new approach to wear him down with, but so long as she kept her focus on the mission in hand and ignored all the terrible things happening inside her, she would complete it successfully.

Feeling clearer in mind if not in body, Kate headed to the downstairs bathroom. Her heart jumped to find a toothbrush and toothpaste on the ledge above the sink.

She stared at the two items, absently rubbing her bottom lip as her brain raced at all the possible meanings behind it. Was Leander softening? Feeling guilt? Had he caught a whiff of her breath and decided this was the one amenity he would provide? Had it even come from him? Had a member of his invisible staff put it there out of concern for Kate's oral hygiene?

No point wondering about it, she decided, and spread the minty paste over the brush.

Once she'd scrubbed her teeth and cleaned the rest of herself as best she could with only hand wash and a hand towel to use, she returned to the living room, lighter in heart than she'd been since waking from the dream.

Padding to the glass wall, she pressed her forehead to it and gazed out. The rustling of the trees and the movement of the ocean suggested a strong breeze and she felt a sudden yearning to stand out in it.

There was the same stillness to the house she'd felt when Leander had taken his walk on the beach, and on impulse she slid the glass wall open and stepped onto the terrace.

For long seconds she stood just past the threshold, alert to any sound, half expecting a member of his staff to come pouncing out to slam the door behind her, but the stillness behind her remained.

The ocean was the opposite to still, and when she moved tentatively to the balustrade to look out over it, Kate spotted a surfer riding what seemed to her untrained eyes as humungous waves.

It was the sigh of her heart that told her who the surfer was, a sigh that came after she'd spent Lord knew how long watching him, transfixed. It was a sigh that leapt up and stuck in her throat when he seemed to both ride and race a wave that continued to grow and had to be tens of metres high until the wave peaked and the surf swallowed him whole.

A puppy-like whimper sounded from her throat. The only movement her frozen body was capable of making was the tightening of her knuckles.

The thumping in her chest when he finally reappeared, feet secure on the board, knees bent, arms stretched out, still surfing that wave as it pounded onto the beach, was powerful enough to weaken Kate's legs.

Almost dizzy with relief, it took a long moment to register that he'd jumped off the board and was carrying it onto the beach…and that his gaze was fixed in her direction.

Kate didn't get the chance to act on her new, admittedly undecided, approach to her mission because for the whole of the day she was left entirely alone.

Leander had returned from his morning surf through an entrance that kept him out of her sight. He'd been out of her sight ever since.

But not out of her mind. She didn't know when but at some point Leander or one of his staff had removed the remote controls for the television, and now her phone's battery was close to death and she'd left the charger on the plane. With nothing to occupy her mind, it filled itself with Leander.

Hours she spent at the glass wall gazing out over the ocean, watching too the surrounding foliage sway in the strengthening wind. He wasn't out there in it. He was here, under the same roof as her, avoiding her as if she were a carrier of the plague.

As a tactic to wear her spirits down, it was an effective one. Kate wasn't used to having only her thoughts for company. She was used to her brain being continuously occupied and used to background noise, whether the noise of her family, her university housemates, or Helena and the general noise of an all-girls school. She'd long ago learnt the art of blocking out sounds so she could concentrate on her studies, but today there was no noise to block and nothing to fill her mind but the man actively shunning her, making her question again and again what she could have done to turn him against her so completely.

Memories of their days together on his island played continually in her mind, the two of them and Helena, carefree days Kate had known even as she'd been living them that she would one day look back on as some of the best days of her life. Leander had made those days special. Leander just being Leander.

Where was that man now? Not the physical body he was wrapped in but the fun, gregarious, surprisingly thoughtful man beneath the skin? Just what had she *done* to drive him away?

It was only the silence of her own company that meant she recognised his nearing footsteps long after the sun went down and enabled her to force her features into a version of nonchalance. If he could see beneath her skin he'd see the nonchalance was nothing but a front. At the first sight of him, crystal glass filled with what looked like Scotch or whisky in hand, her pulses surged.

The casual attire she'd always seen him in had been replaced with a suave dark grey suit that her inexpert eye knew had been tailored especially for his huge frame. The large collar of the crisp white shirt was opened at the throat, the contrast in colour highlighting the deep bronze of his skin. The black stubble on his face had been trimmed, his hair styled.

The scent of freshly showered Leander topped with carefully applied cologne filled the space surrounding them. It was a scent that threw her back what felt a lifetime ago but was in reality not even a week, to when she'd climbed into the helicopter transporting them to Athens and she'd inhaled this exact same scent, and chirpily said, 'Ooh, you smell nice.'

He'd grinned. 'Better than the orangutan you're going to marry.'

Kate's heart throbbed to remember that little exchange and remember the light, teasing nature of the friendship that had sprung up between them.

The easy smile that had never been far from the surface…no hint of it now. No hint of it for her since Athens. What had she *done*?

Lips compressed into a thin line, hard dark eyes fixed on her, he raised his hand and took a drink of his liquor. The movement exposed the fine black hairs on his wrist. For some inexplicable reason, seeing those hairs only tightened the throbs of her heart.

For all the hardness of his features, his gravelly voice was as smooth as silk when he said, 'I'm going out.'

Although she'd registered that Leander was dressed for a night out, it hadn't been a conscious thought, and she had no idea why it felt like a fist had wrapped itself around her throbbing heart. She cleared her throat and uttered her first word that whole day. 'Where?'

'That is none of your business.'

'But you can't.' She tried to think coherently through her wildly scattering thoughts. Was he leaving his bolt hole because of her? Did he hate her *that* much? 'You'll be seen.'

Leander shrugged and drank some more of what was his third glass of Scotch that early evening. 'No one knows me here. In Marina Sands, I'm just another rich guy who likes to surf.'

And even if people did know him here in this little pocket of California, it was a risk he would be willing to take because he could not stand another damned minute trying to kid himself that slender, pixie-faced Kate Hawkins with the dancing jade eyes wasn't ensconced in his living room, pacing the walls he'd confined her to, hungry...

Her hunger was her own fault. She wasn't a guest. She was lucky he was providing her with water. She could leave at any time of her choosing.

And so could he.

There was no risk in what he was doing. He'd chosen Marina Sands for its surfing and the ocean view. If anyone from his world should happen to be in a bar in a town so insignificant its name was barely known to anyone outside the immediate vicinity, they would assume he was Leo. That would be the natural assumption because anyone who'd even touched his social circle knew Leander Liassidis was on his honeymoon. The foulness of his mood meant he could pass himself off as Leo without any effort at all.

Driven out of his own home by a woman half his size.

Or should that be driven out of his own home because the woman half his size was driving him out of his mind? He must have been out of his mind to instruct his staff to arrange toothpaste for her. He shouldn't care if she got cavities. Any good done by his morning surf, cut short by the gusty winds, had gone to hell when he'd looked up and found her staring at him from the balcony.

With the weather as foul as his mood, he'd resorted to spending the day in his gym, working on every piece of equipment to distract himself from the infuriating woman who just didn't know when to quit. He couldn't even throw himself into work as a distraction because he was supposed to be on his damned honeymoon.

Damn Kate Hawkins and her dancing jade eyes for not having the grace to get the hell out of the sanctuary he'd escaped to.

Those jade eyes weren't dancing now. She was ten feet away from him but even that distance wasn't far enough to hide the emotion flashing from them.

The only person who'd ever looked at him with anything even close to that kind of emotion was his twin.

He turned his gaze from her.

'But…what if you *are* recognised?'

'This isn't a debate,' he said icily, finishing his Scotch. Forget going to a bar. He would call his flight crew and disappear again. He should have done that the moment he realised Kate was prepared to hunker down for as long as it took to drag him back to Helena. 'I am informing you of my plans as a matter of courtesy and so I can remind you that, should your few brain cells finally recognise you're in a no-win situation here, all you have to do is—'

A tiny body flew at him, a small hand gripping his wrist before he could finish repeating his mantra about the intercom.

She'd moved so quickly he'd barely had time to register her legs moving.

'Why are you being so cruel to me? What did I do to make you hate me so much?' she demanded angrily.

Caught off guard by the speed with which she'd flown at him, completely unprepared for her beautiful pixie face to be so close that he could see the swirling hues of her eyes currently firing hurt and anger at him, it was as much as Leander could manage to grit out, 'Let go.'

Her features were taut, her breathing ragged. 'Not until you tell me what I did.'

Fixing his sight on an abstract painting, he said through a jaw clenched so tight it felt in danger of snapping, 'Let go of my wrist, Kate. I will not tell you again.'

Her grip only tightened. 'You could easily move my hand if you wanted to but you won't touch me, will you? You won't even look at me. I've got a ton of photos on my phone of you smiling and laughing with me, and now you can't even bring yourself to look at me. For the love of God, tell me, *what did I do*?'

'You did nothing,' he dragged out. The blood pumping through him felt like fire. The torturous heat of her grip was spreading like wildfire through his blazer and shirt, burrowing beneath his skin and into his veins.

'If you're going to tell a barefaced lie at least have the courtesy to look me in the eye while you tell it,' she cried, and it was the underlying pain in her voice that snapped his stare back on her. 'We were *friends*, Leander. Those days we spent together were some of the best of my life. You went out of your way to make me feel welcome and accepted in your family's home, and you included me in *everything*. You looked out for me too—you insisted on escorting me to the ladies' room in that nightclub in Athens so I didn't get harassed by drunken men for heaven's sake, so don't tell me I didn't do anything when...'

Kate's emotional onslaught came to an abrupt end when Leander twisted his wrist from her grasp and captured her face in his hands.

Suddenly pressed against the sideboard, her demonic tormentor's face loomed over her, all coldness gone, his dark eyes staring intently into hers as if he were preparing to bite her head off in one snap.

'You did *nothing*,' he repeated harshly...but the harshness was counteracted by the molten intensity of his stare as his face drew nearer and his voice lowered to a husky, 'except be you.'

Kate's chest filled. Trapped in his molten stare, her pulses thrashed wildly, her senses springing to life as Leander's heat and scent engulfed her.

He pressed closer to her. Her breasts brushed against his chest. The floor beneath her feet shifted into sand.

She was sinking...

Their faces were so close she could feel his breath on her mouth...

Something guttural came from his throat and he abruptly dropped his hold on her cheeks.

In the blink of an eye the heat of his body vanished and in the blink of an eye that it took for her confused body to feel the loss of it, he strode to the sliding wall.

It took a few moments for the hot blood whooshing in Kate's head to clear enough for her brain to reengage with her body.

Running after him, she darted out onto the balcony.

Leander's silhouette had already reached the section of the balustrade that opened onto the pathway.

'What do you mean, *except be you*?' she shouted over the now howling wind.

The silhouette went through the gate. It slammed shut behind him.

'Leander!' She was all fingers and thumbs with the latch of the glass gate, and in frustration she kicked it with her bare foot.

He was halfway down the path by the time she opened it, yelling out his name but finding it lost in the noise of the strengthening storm. But he heard her, she knew it with the same certainty that she'd known he was in residence when she'd first walked this path.

Whether it was the smarting pain in her toe from kicking the gate or the awful, awful emotions raging through her or her inability to wrench her stare from Leander's rapidly retreating figure that stopped her watching where she was walking…running…but as she chased after him, shouting out his name, she missed a shallow step. Losing her footing, she went sprawling.

CHAPTER FIVE

LEANDER IGNORED ALL Kate's shouts. His mind was made up. He was leaving. He would make some calls from his car and get the hell out of California. Drive somewhere where a storm wasn't raging.

There was a storm enough raging in his guts, self-recriminations flying through his head.

Theós, he'd been on the verge of losing his head completely and kissing her. The ache of desire had infected the whole of him, an internal battle waging to turn around and go straight back to her, sweep her in his arms, carry her to his bed and devour her whole.

His driver opened the door for him and kept a secure hold of it to stop the wind from ripping it off its hinges.

About to climb in, Leander made the fatal error of turning his head.

Kate was quick on her feet. She should already have reached the natural curve the path made and be in sight.

When Kate ran out of English curses, she muttered all the Greek ones Leander had taught her when she hadn't been the anti-Christ to him, and fought the very real need to burst into tears.

This had to count as the worst day of her life, on a par

with the day she'd learned that she'd failed the final unit of assessment of her first module at university, bringing her overall mark down and so failing the entire module. Her second-worst fear had come true. Failing the module had terrified her, proved she couldn't take her foot off the gas even for a second. She'd ended her fledging relationship with Euan on the spot and thrown herself even harder into her studies. After resitting the assessment, she'd spent weeks living with cold fear while awaiting the results. A second failure would mean her ultimate worst fear coming true—being kicked out of university and her dreams being destroyed. All the sacrifices she'd made and her family had made would have been for nothing.

This day was as different from failure day as the sun was to the moon but she felt every bit as wretched. She was starving hungry, and physically and emotionally exhausted. It was like Leander had taken possession of her, and not only of her mind. If he'd kissed her, she wouldn't have stopped him. The difference between them would have been that if he'd kissed her, it would have been because she was female and had a pulse. If he'd kissed her she'd have responded because she'd have been helpless to resist.

There was no denying it any more. The thrills that had ravaged her entire being to have his hands cradling her cheeks and his breath on her face... She'd fallen for Leander. She'd fallen for the man she'd travelled thousands of miles to deliver back to her best friend so he could play the role of her best friend's husband, a man who'd been the light of her existence for five glorious days but had turned on a dime against her, and now she was sat on this stupid pavement in the dark, trees creaking around her in the wind, and with a gashed knee. She didn't know what was the most urgent: stemming her tears or stemming the blood.

The outside sensor lights came back on at the same moment a tall figure emerged on the path and a splash of rain landed on her nose.

Her throat choking, stemming the tears won, and she frantically swallowed the rest back. She would not let him see her cry.

It was only when Leander crouched on his haunches beside her and the humiliation of sitting on a path with a bleeding knee like a small child hit her and smashed into all the other emotions lacing her blood.

'Go away,' she choked, slapping her palm over the wound.

'You're hurt. What's happened?'

'I tripped.' How dare he fake concern? How very *dare* he?

'Let me see.'

'Why? So you can stick your finger in it?' Scrambling to her feet, she hobbled towards the car, raindrops mingling with the blood trickling down her leg. She didn't know what hurt the most, her knee, her toe, her pride or her heart.

She'd fallen for Leander and he despised everything about her. That was what he'd meant. She hadn't done anything to make him hate her except exist.

'Where are you going?'

'Home. You win.' She couldn't do this any more. Not now. Leander would go back to Helena when he was good and ready and not a minute sooner. The only thing

Kate would achieve by staying was starvation and, she painfully suspected, hurt of a kind that would leave her with a much bigger wound than a gashed knee. 'You can tell your driver to take me to the airfield.'

She could hear the gritting of his teeth as he called after her through the now pouring rain, 'You need to dress the wound. Come back up and I'll—'

Her anger and pain finally boiled over. Spinning around, she yelled, 'You'll what? Clean it with salt? I'd much rather take my chances with an infection than let you and your hatred anywhere near me, so why don't you just—'

He moved so quickly and stealthily that she didn't notice him close the gap between them until she'd been scooped into his arms.

'You are not flying anywhere in this weather or going anywhere with that wound,' he snarled, already striding back up the path before she found the voice to protest.

'I'm perfectly capable of walking,' she snarled back, kicking her heel hard into his rock-like abdomen.

He gave no reaction whatsoever, opening the gate without loosening his grip on her and then adjusting his arms to secure her more tightly to him as he marched her through the quickly accumulating rainwater deepening on the balcony. The rain now falling like a sheet, the collars of Leander's shirt and jacket were drenched against her sopping cheek.

She wriggled frantically, lashing out with her legs which, with Leander's arm now under her knees and his hand holding her thighs firmly to his chest, meant ineffectually kicking her ankles. 'Put me *down*.'

'You haven't got anything on your feet!' he told her

furiously. 'There is debris all over the place from the winds. Do you want to cause more damage to yourself?'

'Like you care!' she spat.

'Of course I bloody care!' he roared, coming to an abrupt stop and tilting his furious face down so his eyes bore into hers. 'You can have *no* idea...' He shook his head and sucked his words away, muttering something that sounded like one of his Greek curses.

He stared into her eyes another long moment and then something tortured contorted his features and, with another curse, his mouth came crashing down on hers in a kiss so hungry and possessive that she froze in shock. At least, her brain froze. The rest of her...

It was like a switch had been turned on. Before she could comprehend what she was doing, she was kissing him back with equal ferocity, melting into the dark heat of his mouth, her hand holding tightly to his neck as their tongues entwined and the fusion deepened. Dimly, she was aware of the rain still falling in a torrent over them, droplets pooling into the tiny pockets their mouths made as they moved together, her fingers now tugging at the sopping hair at the back of his neck, his fingers pressing tightly into her flesh, every passing second bringing them closer to being one entity until only the need for air forced their faces apart.

Blinking rainwater out of her eyes, she stared at him and shook her head in a futile attempt to clear the fog in her mind. It wasn't just the need to draw breath that made it hard to speak but the thrashing of her heart. 'Why did you do that?' she half accused. 'You hate me.'

Leander already knew he was defeated. He'd known it when the scratching of his heart at Kate's failure to round the curve of the path had led him to go and find her. He'd known it when he'd lifted her into his arms. And he'd known it when he'd looked down at her furious face and felt like he would die if he didn't feed the craving for her.

Pressing his forehead to hers, he expelled a long sigh. 'The only thing I hate about you, *agápi mou*, is the way you make me feel.'

Even with the storm raging around them, the silence that followed this admission was so total a feather swooshing to the ground would have been audible.

Jade eyes widened in dazed incomprehension.

A bolt of lightning crackled and lit the sky.

They both looked up and then back at each other. The dazed incomprehension was still vivid.

Wordlessly, he carried her inside and sat her on the sofa she'd made herself at home on. She didn't resist. She didn't say or do anything but keep her confused eyes fixed on his face.

'I'll get the first aid kit,' he told her as he straightened and ran his fingers through his hair to pull some of the water out.

She blinked as if not understanding. She looked like a drowned rat. A very beautiful drowned rat.

He dropped his gaze to her knee. The wound was still bleeding. All the rain had mingled with it and turned her calf and bare foot red.

Snatching a handful of tissues from the box on the coffee table, he pressed them to her knee. 'Hold that,' he ordered gently. 'I'll be back in a minute.'

She obeyed without uttering a word.

In the large utility off the back of the kitchen, Leander

pulled apart the medicine cabinet his staff kept topped up, grabbed the first aid kit, then snatched a couple of fresh towels from the laundry section and headed back to the woman he firmly believed had been put on this earth to make him lose his mind.

Theós, the taste of her mouth on his tongue and the heat and weight of her body in his arms and against his chest were still vivid.

Strangely, he felt calmer now. His heart still throbbed painfully and desire still racked his body but there was relief in not having to hide away from it any more. It was out in the open.

The last time he'd tried to bury his feelings and hide them from the person they most affected had ended in acrimony. When he'd finally admitted the truth fourteen years ago, Leonidas had taken it personally. He'd never forgiven him. But the truth had freed Leander even if the consequence had been to rip a piece of his soul off.

Nothing could come of the freedom that came with Kate knowing the truth. He'd known from the moment desire for her had almost doubled him over that it was a desire that was impossible. Days from marrying their mutual close friend, it had been easier to bear when he'd thought it a one-way desire.

His instincts that her feelings for him had shifted had been proved right. She did want him.

He should have left California when he first felt that shift.

Too late now.

What they felt for each other couldn't go anywhere.

His guts twisted to know he'd never cared if his desire could go anywhere before. Indiscriminate in his affairs, one night of pleasure, one week or one month, it had all been the same to him.

But those women had not been Kate.

Kate held the tissues now soaked in blood to her knee and swallowed hard when Leander reappeared. She was still reeling from the passionate kiss they'd shared and all the feelings that had erupted in her from it, still reeling from what he'd said to her, hardly daring to believe what he'd meant by it, terrified to even contemplate the implications.

He'd taken his jacket off. Her heart clenched to see smears of her blood on his soaked shirt. Something lower and deeper within her clenched to notice how his shirt had become translucent.

'I'm sorry, I've bled over your rug,' she whispered. She had a vague awareness the rug would have cost far more than she'd received for the battered car she'd sold the day before she'd flown out to Greece.

'It will clean,' he said, handing her a towel. 'For your hair,' he explained before pulling a footrest next to the side of her injured leg and sitting on it. 'Let me take care of your injury.' He gave a fleeting smile. 'No salt, I promise.'

Her heart expanded and caught in her throat. 'Leander...'

'Let me tend to your wound and then we can talk. Okay?'

Trying her hardest to keep herself together, Kate gazed into Leander's steady dark eyes and gave a short nod. Desperately needing to lighten the mood, she said. 'If it gets infected I'll have to sue you. I might sue anyway, seeing as it was your stupid step I lost my footing on.'

Deadpan, he answered, 'I'll give you my lawyer's details, now put your leg on my lap.'

Holding her breath, Kate lifted her leg and laid her calf on his thigh.

'Dry your hair,' he chided as he rummaged through the first aid kit.

She managed a half-smile and patted the towel to her hair. How, she wondered dazedly, was it possible for desire to spring from nothing to everything in the blink of an eye? When Leander shifted the footstool closer to her so more of her thigh lay on his lap, she concentrated harder on holding her breath and prayed he couldn't hear the thundering of her heart.

Oh, what did it matter? He already knew. Her ardent response to his kiss had given her feelings away.

What his own feelings were, she hardly dared to imagine.

Detaching from his mind that it was Kate's leg draped over his thighs and that the texture of her skin was even softer than he'd dreamed, Leander dropped the bloodied tissues stemming the wound on the rug and studied the gash on the base of her knee. It was already clotting, drying blood streaked all down the calf and ankle.

He dabbed at the wound with antiseptic and cleaned the skin around it, working as gently as he could. 'I think this needs butterfly stitches or you'll end up with a nasty scar.'

She gave a half-hearted shrug. 'It doesn't matter. I'm bound to end my career covered in them.'

Removing the backing off a large skin coloured plaster, he distracted himself further from the torture of touching Kate's skin by asking, 'Have you ever been bitten by a patient?'

'Not yet but it's bound to happen one day.'

'Let's hope it's not by one of those other wild creatures you mentioned.'

Although Kate was shortly to join a charity that cared for orphaned orangutans, the veterinary staff there also treated injured native wild animals as needed. She'd enthusiastically told him all about her upcoming move to South East Asia and what the job would entail at Helena's prompting on her second night, when they'd been eating at a taverna on a neighbouring island. He'd been struck not only by her single-minded focus—Kate had spent her whole life working to reach this point—but by the light in her eyes and the animation in her voice. *Theós*, she'd been fascinating. He could have listened to her talk all night. He could have *watched* her talk all night.

He should have known he was in trouble then.

He wouldn't have known how much damned trouble though.

The memory of Dimitri palming Kate's stomach and leaning his torso into her back to dance with her with that drunken leer on his face smashed back into him. One of his closest friends. A friendship Leander would have killed if he'd acted on the violence of his thoughts.

Coming hot on the heels of being doubled over with desire just from watching her dance, that was the moment he'd known just how much trouble he was in.

'I'm sure you'll be hoping one of them bites my entire head off,' she jested weakly.

It took everything he had to fight the swell of emotions rushing up his throat and spread the plaster over the wound.

She flinched when he pressed his palm down to secure it, only a reflex flinch, barely perceptible, but it broke something in him.

In an instant everything he'd been trying to tune out while tending to her injury, that this was *Kate's* leg draped over him, that this was *her* skin he was touching and it was the smoothest, warmest, silkiest flesh in existence, that the taste on his tongue was the taste of *her* tongue…it all slammed into his senses, and in that instant his senses refilled with her. With Kate.

Heart suddenly pounding furiously, breaths suddenly shallow, Leander lifted his gaze to the beautiful, delicate pixie face with its delicate features and delicate little sticky-out ears. Everything about Kate was delicate, a physicality that couldn't have contrasted more strongly with the vivacious substance contained within it.

Kate only had to walk into a room to light it up.

She only had to fix those incredible jade eyes on him to light *him* up.

Those eyes had lit him up from the very first moment they'd locked onto his, and they were locked on him now.

God help him but he'd hurt her. He'd knocked the light out of her eyes. He'd done that. Deliberately. And now he felt it, the full magnitude of it, as deeply as if he'd inflicted the wounds on himself, but even more than that, he felt the essence of Kate Hawkins feeding into the very fabric of his being.

Kate's heart was thumping so hard she could hardly draw breath. The pain in her knee was entirely forgotten.

The look in Leander's eyes…

It sucked all the air from her lungs.

She'd never seen anything like it before.

The emotion filling them was the antithesis of loathing.

Seeing that emotion…*feeling* it…

Everything fell into place, and suddenly she found herself clutching tightly to the towel and frantically shaking her head. 'We can't,' she choked. '*I* can't.'

'Why the hell do you think I've been trying so hard to make you leave?' he asked hoarsely.

Their gazes held for the longest time before a sharp pain sliced through her chest and she felt her entire being crumple.

This…

Oh, God, this was worse than believing he hated her. This…

With a heavy, sinking stomach, she realised that a part of her had sensed Leander's feelings. Sensed them and ignored them with the same zeal that she'd ignored her own feelings. Refused to even acknowledge their existence.

She'd thought the dreams had been about *her* feelings but they'd been much more than that.

This had been there between them from the start and she hadn't even known it, and now it was too late to wind the clock back to ignorance.

It hit her again. Leander didn't hate her. He had feelings for her.

Fresh hot tears welling, Kate blinked them away. 'Helena is like a sister to me.'

Hating to see the contortion of her face, Leander

rubbed the back of his neck. 'She's like a sister to me too. There is nothing else between us.'

'I know, but you're married to her.'

'I'm not.'

Her upset and frustration visibly grew. 'Your brother made his vows and signed the certificate as you.'

'I didn't make those vows and Leo will never allow the certificate to be registered.' This aspect, he was certain, was the most important point to get through to her. He'd seen the two women together, seen their closeness, knew that if Kate believed he was currently married to Helena even on a mere technical level then guilt at their fleeting kiss would eat her up.

'How can you *know* that?'

'Because I know him. He will leave it for me to register.'

She blinked rapidly and then breathed deeply through her nose and slid her leg off his thigh. Throat moving, she straightened, and when she next looked at him, it was beseechingly. 'Leander, you *have* to get the marriage registered, for Helena's sake. You know that.' Her throat moved again. 'And we need to pretend that nothing happened. Just forget about it.'

'That's impossible.' Leander could no more pretend that he'd not had a taste of Kate's sweet lips than he could pretend the earth didn't revolve around the sun.

Her eyes pleaded with him.

'Toothpaste cannot be squeezed back into its tube.'

She spluttered a tearful laugh. 'That is a *terrible* analogy.'

'But a truthful one.'

After the longest time she looked away from him and

rubbed her eye with the palm of her hand. Her melodious voice laced with misery, she said, 'I should go.'

'I know. But in this weather...?' Leander shook his head. It felt like a boulder had lodged itself in his chest. His efforts to force Kate from his home had finally worked but it was all too late. He'd treated her despicably for nothing, and he would have to live with it on his conscience for the rest of his life, just as he still lived with his betrayal of his brother. 'Are you hungry?'

Her blonde eyebrows rose in surprise at the question and then quirked as if she couldn't believe he'd been stupid enough to ask it.

'We can't put the toothpaste back in the tube but we can agree not to talk about it,' he said gently. 'I will get my chef to make us something to eat—'

Her eyebrows shot back up again. 'It's the middle of the night.'

'I have staff on call at all times. I think we could both benefit from a shower and dry clothes, and then we can eat and talk about everything except...*this*...until the weather clears enough for you to fly home. What do you say?'

The pulse at the base of his jaw throbbed strongly as he waited for Kate's answer.

The longing crushed Kate's heart against her ribs, and as she soaked in the face of the man who'd woken up a side of herself she'd barely been aware lived inside her, it hit her again that Leander had feelings for her. Strong feelings.

His toothpaste analogy had been terrible, but it had also been true. They couldn't pretend what had been revealed between them hadn't been revealed, but if they didn't speak about it then it could be squashed away and for a short while they could reset things and maybe even part ways with the spirit of friendship that had first bound them.

She took a deep breath. 'I must really stink if you're offering me the use of your shower.'

A glimmer of amusement passed between them and then Kate found herself laughing while simultaneously wiping a tear away.

CHAPTER SIX

KATE FOLLOWED LEANDER up the dark wood winding staircase and onto a magnificent mezzanine that overlooked a reception room with a marble fountain as its centrepiece.

He unlocked a door and opened it for her. 'My main guestroom. It has its own bathroom. You don't need instructions to work the shower—it is easy to use.'

'What, even for a dumb blonde like me?' she jested again, gripping the first aid kit he'd insisted she bring up with her in case the plaster came off in the shower. She needed to keep things light; anything to stop the tightness in her chest from loosening and for all the emotions she'd packed in it to come spilling out.

He stretched his neck and closed his eyes. 'I am sorry for saying that. I never meant it.'

'I know.'

His stare zoomed back on her. 'Do you?'

She nodded and sighed. 'I knew you were only saying it to get rid of me.'

He studied her a moment and nodded. 'Help yourself to whatever you need. I will find a shirt or something for you to wear.'

'Thank you.'

'I think it's the least I can do after the way I've treated you.'

Seeing him turn as if about to walk away, she impulsively said, 'Leander, when the weather clears and it's safe to fly...*please* go back to Greece. Leo was so angry and he seems to really hate Helena... I'm scared he's going to blow everything up.'

His huge shoulders rose slowly, dark eyes locking back to hers. 'He won't.'

'How can you be so certain?'

'Because he's my twin.'

'You seem so sure of what he'll do but you've barely spoken in years.'

'He's still my twin. I know him better than anyone. He will hate me and curse me but he will keep up the pretence until I return.'

'But what if he's discovered before then?' she challenged softly. 'The press will be itching to get that honeymoon shot of the bride and groom. One photo and everyone will know the wrong brother's on the honeymoon.'

'We are physically identical. No one will be able to tell the difference.'

'I knew it wasn't you the second we walked into the church.'

Her words punched into Leander's chest and sent blood pounding into his head.

Breathing deeply through his nose, he said, 'Our parents struggle to tell the difference between us.'

The first eighteen years of Leander's life had been spent correcting people that they'd addressed the wrong twin. Fourteen years later and any unexpected visit to his family always began with their eyes narrowing to scrutinise which twin was standing before them. His parents always got it right but with his grandparents it went either way. He'd had a girlfriend a few years back, before Leo had cut him off completely, who'd bumped into Leo at a party and spent five minutes talking to him before realising it was the wrong twin, and only then because Leo corrected her. This was a woman Leander had been intimate with. To think that Kate could tell from just one look that it was him...

'Leander, you're identical but you're not the same person,' she said, oblivious to the effect her observation was having on him. 'Your brother holds himself in an entirely different way to you—I knew it was the wrong twin without even seeing his face.'

For the second time in less than a minute it felt like Kate had winded him with her words, and he had to loosen his throat to say, 'Then you will just have to trust me that you are an anomaly on this.'

Leander folded the dark grey shirt and navy sweater over the mezzanine railing opposite the guestroom door, and went straight back into his bedroom to use his own shower.

It took all his mental strength not to let his mind wander to Kate and the fact that she was, at that moment, likely to be naked, and as he pushed the image of her breasts away, it was replaced with the bewitching smile that had lit her face when he'd caught her kiss in his apartment that night. If she hadn't then turned around and danced over to Helena, she would have seen him almost double over with the strength of the desire that had coursed through him.

That was the moment everything had changed for him.

Even if it hadn't been Kate, the strength of his feelings would have caused him to back away.

Leander was inherently selfish, something his twin had thrown at him too many times over the years to keep count of. Even now, whenever he pictured Leonidas, it was never as the man he was today but as he'd been at eighteen when Leander had told him he was leaving to pursue his life without him, and the hurt and disbelief that had rung from his eyes before cold anger set in. The ramifications from that day still echoed. A combination of living life on his own terms and never wanting to cause such hurt to someone again meant Leander had long ago decided that single life was the life for him. Short-lived flings without any strings or emotional attachments. No mess. No drama. No broken hearts. Perfect.

Pursuing your fake fiancée's maid of honour in the build-up to your sham wedding was low, even for him, and so when he'd met Kate there had been no thoughts of a potential fling. He'd been able to enjoy her company as one human to another, and her company had been fantastic. He'd never had long, intense conversations about absolute rubbish before and then in the next breath long, intense conversations about the world. Once desire had reared its ugly head...

Hours after his desire ignited he'd sat in his Athenian apartment's kitchen listening to the silence only people who'd spent the night over-indulging could make when they finally crashed out, and known he must never be alone with her again.

* * *

As Leander had predicted, Kate's plaster came off in the shower. After scrubbing every inch of her body in the most beautifully scented shower cream and washing her hair in equally beautiful shampoo, she wrapped herself in the huge, fluffy towel from the heated rail and put a fresh plaster on. Her skin still sang from when Leander had put the first one on.

She'd never known it was possible for skin to sing at another human's touch.

The song her skin was singing now though, was a lament.

Her throat closed at the impossibility of her longing.

In less than a week she would be flying to Borneo.

She felt like a runner who'd spent their whole life racing a marathon and could finally see the finish line. The marathon had been hard fought, not just by herself but her support crew, namely her parents who'd worked all hours to pay for the tuition needed to help her achieve the scholarship and all the other things they'd done to support her. Then there were her brothers, always so bemused at having a 'swot' for a sister, alternating between teasing and indulgence as the mood took them but always so proud with each marathon mile she passed. And then there was Helena. All the late nights in their dorm room helping Kate revise for school exams, a constant source of emotional support and understanding throughout her university years… All these wonderful people who loved her and were invested in helping Kate realise her dreams.

To do anything to derail that dream's realisation when she could almost touch the finish line was madness, and even if she did think the risk of letting something happen with Leander was worth the potential derailing, it didn't change the fact that very soon he would be flying back to Helena.

Leander was showered and dressed and staring out of the glass wall at the howling wind and lashing rain that kept activating the night sensors when he heard the rustle of movement behind him.

His heart tightened and then expanded like a balloon.

His shirt fitted Kate like an oversized dress. Landing just below her knees, it only enhanced her slenderness. Her dark blonde hair was damp and swung gently over her shoulders. Even with the distance between them he could smell the perfume of her shower and he knew that if he were to close his eyes and inhale deeply he'd be able to breathe in the clean heat of her skin.

He had to work hard to stop his mind fully registering that beneath it, she was likely naked.

For the longest time neither of them spoke.

'How's your knee?'

She held her hands out and pulled her shoulders in. 'I found some butterfly stitches in the kit to use on it. Shame you haven't got any superglue.'

He grinned. Kate's humour had made him laugh from the outset and to hear it now eased a little of the tension that had built back in him since they'd parted for their separate showers. 'Do you need painkillers?'

'It doesn't hurt that badly.' In comparison to the pain in Kate's heart, her knee didn't hurt at all. 'It's almost fully clotted. Can I smell pancakes?'

'Your sense of smell is incredible. Everything's set up in the dining room.'

'Ooh, am I allowed in there now?' she asked with a grin.

Appreciating the effort it must be costing her to make it appear that she didn't have a care in the world, he responded in kind, waving an arm expansively. 'I have unlocked all the doors. Consider yourself free to go where ever you please.'

Kate gave a mock curtsey. 'If I'd known all it would take for you to be nice to me was to cut my knee open, I'd have tripped on the pathway sooner.'

The dining room was as incredible as the main living area, with a glass wall that overlooked the rear—or was it the front?—of the mansion. It being pitch black outside meant any view was a secret waiting to be discovered. She would not allow herself to wish that the night and its accompanying storm lasted long enough for her to see it.

'What time is it?' she asked, taking the seat Leander pulled out for her.

'Just turned three.'

'Is that all?' she marvelled. She was determined to maintain a cheerful front. There had been enough bitterness between them these last two days to last her a lifetime and now she wanted it cleansed. 'I was sure it must be close to sunrise.' She wriggled her chair closer to the table. 'I've definitely lost all sense of time.' Which reminded her, 'I don't suppose you've got a phone charger I can borrow, have you? My battery's dead.'

'Of course. I'll get one brought in for you.'

No sooner had he answered than two members of

staff descended with a mound of American pancakes and bacon and a copper *briki* pot of coffee. If they were put out at having to work at this godforsaken time, they didn't show it. Still, Kate reminded herself, they did work for Leander, a man who played as hard as he worked. A man who had every intention of always playing hard.

Although Kate had gone nearly two days without food, her stomach felt so tight that she doubted she'd be able to manage more than one pancake, but a single bite was enough to get her tastebuds going.

'I'm sorry for trying to starve you,' Leander said, watching with a fist around his heart as she poured maple syrup over a third pancake.

She smiled. 'You would never have beaten me that way.'

He raised an eyebrow. 'And you know that how?'

'I spent five years as a hungry student, remember?'

'Even so, it was cruel of me.' The more he reflected on his behaviour these past two days, the more self-loathing curdled in his guts. Leander knew he was selfish and arrogant but he'd never known he was capable of cruelty. It was a side to himself that sickened him.

'I invaded your home uninvited. You were under no obligation to provide me with anything.' The tiniest sparkle glittered in her eyes. 'The moussaka was a masterstroke.'

He couldn't keep the carefree act up any more. 'No. It was cruel. I wish I could take it back.'

'You were doing what you thought you had to do and…' She shook her head. 'At least now when we say goodbye it will be as the friends we were before.' Her forehead creased and with it her own carefree projection disappeared. 'We were friends, weren't we?'

'We can never go back to that now, Kate.'

'I know... But we *were* friends, weren't we? I didn't imagine it, did I?'

The yearning to reach his hand across the table to her was so strong he fisted it and held it to his stomach. 'No. You didn't imagine it.'

She closed her eyes and inhaled deeply through her nose, then picked her fork back up to stab at her pancake.

After she'd eaten a little more, she looked back at him. 'What you said earlier... I get why you're confident Leo will pretend to be you until you go back, but how do you know he won't register the marriage certificate?'

Leander pushed his plate aside and considered his answer. 'He has always been straight down the line, if you know what I mean. His conscience will not allow a falsely signed document to be registered. He will leave that for me to do.'

Another tiny sparkle glittered. 'Is that because you don't have a conscience?'

He gave a half-smile. 'Because he believes I don't.'

She ate one more bite of her pancake and pushed her own plate aside. 'What happened between you? Helena told me it goes back years but I honestly don't understand how two people formed from the same egg can be estranged as you two are.'

He poured himself another coffee and topped Kate's up too, remembering her first breakfast on his island when he'd poured her a cup of it. The face she'd pulled at the taste had amused him and made Helena snort with laughter. Greek coffee was, he'd learned in his thirty-two years on this earth, an acquired taste. Four breakfasts later and Kate had drunk it like a native.

'Before I answer that, answer something for me.' It was a question that kept repeating itself in his mind because of the sheer impossibility of it. 'Could you really tell it was Leo waiting at the altar and not me?'

Her eyes widened in disbelief. 'Could *I* tell? Honestly, I couldn't believe no one else noticed. I watched them exchange their vows fully expecting someone to jump up and point out the wrong brother was standing there. It was the most surreal experience of my life but no one else noticed. I'm pretty sure even your parents didn't clock that it was Leo until the vows were done.'

'But you saw it?' Leander pressed.

'I didn't even think about it.' Her slender shoulders rose and she added a simple, 'It wasn't you.'

For a moment it felt like he'd fallen into a version of suspended animation where the only sound was the blood pounding in his ears.

Clearing his throat, he said, 'People have never been able to tell us apart. They think we are the same person.'

The face she pulled at this made him smile properly for the first time in days.

'We are physically identical but our personalities have always been very different,' he confirmed drily. 'Leo was always very serious, very straight down the line, as I said.' Still staring intently at her, he took a sip of his coffee. 'You know why I have never wanted to marry or be tied down with a partner?'

Her pretty dark blonde eyebrows drew together.

'It's because I spent eighteen years married to my brother and our marriage ended with acrimony. I hurt him very badly.' For reasons he couldn't begin to decipher, it felt imperative that he explain himself, something he'd never needed to do before. 'People treated us as if we were one entity with the same thoughts and opinions. It frustrated both of us, especially in our teenage years. Leo frustrated me. He still does. He is so straight, never willing to take risks. He was always the voice of reason.'

'He was your conscience?'

'In a way, yes. He shackled me but his opinion mattered more to me than anyone's.' He shook his head with a grimace. 'It's complicated.'

'It sounds it,' she said softly.

'We were close growing up.' It had only been since hearing Leo's voice that he'd remembered just how close they'd been. All the fun they'd had. How they could hold conversations without even having to speak. 'We knew for a long time that when we turned eighteen and finished school, we could either join the family business and work our way through the ranks until we gained the experience needed to take over, or we could take a cash sum from our parents and make our own way in the world. Leo stayed and I took the cash.'

'And that caused the estrangement?'

'It's what started it.'

'Because you chose to go?'

'Because I'd let him believe I would stay.'

Understanding flared. 'Ah.'

The muscles of his neck tightening as he related for the first time the day he'd put a knife to all their plans, Leander kneaded at them. 'I told him I was taking the cash the day we finished our education. A week later I left home to make my own way in the world.'

'He felt that you'd abandoned him?' she guessed.

He grimaced, gut curdling with more self-loathing. 'Yes. I fed us both all the excuses in the world but that is what it came down to. I love my brother, he's a part of me, but at the time I just wanted to be Leander first rather than one of the Liassidis twins, and recognised in my own right. I wanted to make my own way, to get out there and *see* the world. I should have been honest from the start but I got caught up in all his plans for our future with Liassidis Shipping and only found the courage to tell him after I'd booked my flight to America.' He kneaded harder at his neck. 'Leo was furious.' He gazed into the jade eyes bruised with lack of sleep and admitted for the first time, 'And hurt. It would have been better if I had given him the knife to stab into his own back.' And stab himself too.

Hurting Leonidas had felt like cutting his own artery. Leander would never change the path he'd taken but if he could go back and find the courage to tell Leo sooner so he could prepare himself for the separation, he would do it in a heartbeat.

She winced but didn't say anything.

'But we are identical twins. The bond between us can never be fully broken and for many years we both made the effort to get past my betrayal—and it was a betrayal—and then all the crap happened with the business... Do you know about that? When Liassidis Shipping came close to going under?'

'Helena told me a little about it,' Kate said, thinking hard through the exhaustion creeping through her veins that zero sleep and a full stomach had set off. She knew Helena's parents had been business partners of a sort—the details were currently hazy in her mind—with Leander and Leo's parents, and that after Helena's father died her mother had done something or other with her share that had put the business in jeopardy. 'But it was all resolved, wasn't it?'

'It was resolved and the business is thriving now,' he agreed, 'but Leo has never forgiven me for not going home and helping to resolve it, and until I called him Saturday morning we hadn't seen or spoken to each other in five years.'

Although Kate knew the Liassidis twins were estranged, this was the first time she'd really contemplated what the estrangement meant. Her brothers infuriated her at times—and she no doubt infuriated them—and she'd seen little of them during her university years, but she couldn't imagine cutting them out of her life altogether.

She smothered a yawn and finished her coffee, hoping another shot of caffeine would help fight the encroaching sleepiness. This was all the time she would ever have left with Leander and she didn't want a second of it lost in the fog of exhaustion. 'Don't you miss him?'

His jaw tightened, a pulse throbbing below his ear. 'In the years after I left home we only saw each other sporadically. We were already accustomed to our lives being separate.'

Not a direct answer, she noted, her heart twisting for him being unable to admit what to Kate was obvious. Instead of pressing it, she tried another tack. 'Why didn't you go home when the business was in trouble?'

'Because he didn't want me there.'

'But you just said he hasn't forgiven you for not being there,' she pointed out, confused.

'He told me that he didn't want me there and that he would deal with it. I took him at his word—his brain is laser sharp. He can solve a problem before anyone else has identified that there even is a problem. My field is technology, not shipping. I had nothing practical to offer apart from my cash and he made it very clear that he didn't want that either.'

She smothered another yawn and blinked hard to refresh her gritty eyes. 'Do you think he was hoping you'd ignore his order to stay away and go home anyway?'

'Whatever I did, I was damned in his eyes. I think he was waiting for the excuse to justify to himself severing the final ties between us. Up to then, it had been me who'd made all the effort to keep our relationship going but after that he stopped answering my calls or responding to my messages.'

'Maybe it was support of an emotional kind he wanted from you, the kind that you don't always know you need until you receive it or miss until you don't get it,' she suggested, thinking of all the times she'd been too frazzled with exams to call her parents and let them know she was alive and them turning up at her digs with bags of food that required no greater preparation than sticking in the microwave. They'd understood what she needed in those times better than she had.

Leander gave a guttural laugh. 'Emotional support? I thought you'd met my brother.'

'He's like an ice box but he's still human,' she said quietly. She felt wretched for both brothers. She'd always been prepared to dislike Leo after the way Helena had spoken about him but now she felt a huge pang of sympathy for both men, one too stubborn to tell his brother that he needed him, the other too stubborn to see his brother needed him.

A yawn sneaked up on her which she couldn't suppress and which she only just managed to cover with the back of her hand. She blinked hard again at the gritty tiredness in her eyes. 'Excuse me.'

The dark eyes that had barely left her face the entire conversation softened. 'You're exhausted.'

She tried to inject some lightness back. 'Well, it's almost morning and I didn't get much sleep last night.'

His wince of self-recrimination showed her attempted lightness hadn't landed. 'I'm sorry for what I put you through. A thousand times sorry. It was unforgivable of me.'

'It's already forgiven.'

He held her stare for the longest time before exhaling. 'That's more than I deserve.'

'Stop it. You did what you had to do. If I'd understood my own feelings sooner then—' She cut herself off before she could say words that could never be taken back, and gave a frustrated, helpless shrug. 'Toothpaste.'

He shook his head. 'If it's any consolation, I hardly slept either.' Then he added with a short laugh, 'Toothpaste.'

Her own short laugh was interrupted by a wide yawn she only just managed to raise her hand to cover.

Leander didn't know if it was the exhaustion etched on Kate's face that did it or the valiant way she was trying to fight it, but his heart turned over. 'You should sleep.'

She shook her head vehemently. 'I'll sleep on the plane...' Another enormous yawn overcame her.

Before he could stop to think, he pushed his chair back and got to his feet. 'You need sleep, Kate. It might be hours until it's safe to fly. Get some proper sleep in a proper bed, if not for your sake then for mine—let me absolve some of my guilt.'

CHAPTER SEVEN

LEGS FEELING LIKE dead weights beneath her, knee throbbing, the toe she'd hurt throbbing too, Kate followed Leander up the winding stairs and onto the dimly illuminated mezzanine.

It was still black outside but the night would soon be over. When she woke, the dying storm would be over too and with it her time with Leander. The dejection she felt at this...

He opened the door of the pretty, neutrally decorated guestroom she'd showered in and stepped aside. 'If you need anything in the night, food or drink, just dial—'

'One on the intercom?'

His smile was as bleak as the dejection in her heart.

'Can I ask you something?' she asked before he could make the move that would finally separate them that night. As exhausted as she was, she wasn't ready to say goodnight to him. Not ready for oblivion. Not when to wake from oblivion would likely mean saying goodbye to Leander for ever.

'You can ask me anything.'

'Why were you so cold with me after your party?' This was the one question she needed answered before she left.

'Because I wanted to throw Dimitri out of a window for dancing with you.' Leander swallowed the bile that had risen at the gross overreaction of his thoughts that night. 'Once I went to bed, I tortured myself for the rest of the night that the two of you were in a room alone together. I was...' Realising he was about to say something forbidden, he cut himself off. 'Toothpaste.'

The understanding that flashed in her eyes told him she understood what he'd stopped himself from saying. That he'd been jealous. That it had been the night his desire for Kate had smacked him as hard in the face as he'd wished to smack Dimitri.

'Not my finest hour,' he admitted wryly.

He'd never been jealous before. Like his cruelty towards Kate, it was a side to himself he would never allow to take control of him again.

'Nothing happened between us,' she said softly, and she looked so beautiful and so damned ravishing standing in the doorway with only his shirt wrapped around her naked flesh and the guest bed mere feet behind her that the desire he'd controlled to a simmer while they'd been eating slammed back into him.

'I wouldn't think less of you if it had.' He gave a low laugh. It was time to back away and remove himself from the breathing temptation that was Kate. 'We both know I am in no position to judge.' With a bow of his head, he stepped to his own room and was about to open the door when she called his name.

He turned back to her.

She hadn't moved from the threshold of the guest door. 'I haven't slept with anyone.'

It was like she'd thrown a bucket of ice over him. 'What? Never?'

Beautiful jade eyes locked on his. 'Never.'

Mind completely blown, he walked slowly back to her. 'Why not?'

Her lips curved into a tremulous smile and she rested her cheek on the doorframe. 'Do you remember me telling you about that orangutan documentary I watched with my mum when I was seven?'

He remembered everything she'd ever told him. 'The one that made you announce you wanted to be a vet?'

She nodded. 'Everyone kept telling me that only the really clever kids could be vets. I'm not naturally clever like you, Leander. I was the youngest in my class which put me at a disadvantage when I was little and made me feel stupid. I had to work twice as hard as the other kids just to learn my words and numbers, and that's basically been the story of my life ever since, and always with goals that needed to be reached: working for the scholarship, working for my GCSEs, working for my A-levels and then five years spent working for my degree.'

'I understand all that but Helena has always spoken about all the fun the two of you got up to over the years.'

Her smile was rueful. 'I never said I lived as a nun but I went to an all-girls boarding school. The opportunities to go out and live it up were so limited that they didn't really impact my study schedule. Once I started at university I thought I could cut loose a bit more and I got together with this nice lad studying physics, but seeing Euan made me take my eye off the ball and I stopped studying as hard and came close to failing a module and losing my whole place on the course. It scared the life out of me and I ended things with Euan way before we'd reached the getting our clothes off stage.' Eyes shining, her chin wobbled. 'Back then I assumed it would happen once all my studies were over and the time was right.'

Fighting to control the emotions smashing through him, fighting to breathe, Leander backed himself against the mezzanine.

'What are you thinking?' she whispered in a small voice.

He smothered a groan and rubbed the back of his neck. 'I'm thinking I wish you hadn't told me.'

Her silent hurt at this sliced through him.

'Kate...' This groan refused to remain smothered. 'You do know this means I am now destined to spend my life wondering if it has happened?'

Her attempt at laughter sounded like a sob. 'I can message you when it happens to stop you wondering if you like?'

His own effort at laughter was a failure. 'I don't know if the confirmation would drive me more insane.'

Their gazes stayed locked for the longest time before their chests rose in unison.

'Get some sleep, *agápi mou*.'

Her chest rose again at his endearment, a sad smile curving her pretty little mouth as she backed into her room. 'Goodnight, Leander.'

The door closed softly behind her.

Kate hadn't thought it possible that she'd fall asleep. Her talk with Leander had wiped away her exhaustion. Or so she'd thought. Moments after her head hit the pillow she fell into vivid dreams that all revolved around him, and woke with a sob in her throat, an ache in her heart and a heavy pulse throbbing between her legs. She could still feel the imprint of his mouth on hers.

She cuddled tightly into her pillow.

A tear crept out.

The feelings she had for Leander were all wrong. She was only here to take him back to Helena, and...

And Helena didn't want him.

Not in the way Kate wanted him.

Helena was marrying Leander out of desperation. As soon as the sham honeymoon was over, she'd set the ball rolling to get her inheritance and as soon as she had it, the sham marriage would be over.

Helena loved Leander as a brother, and Kate's heart panged sharply as she recalled a long-forgotten conversation from a few years ago. Leander had been due to visit London and Helena had, as she often did, invited Kate to join them. She'd been studying frantically for her final exams and had needed a break and so had, for once, agreed, only to get herself into a lather at the last minute and beg off, terrified that the time she'd have to spend eating with the two of them would be the difference between pass and failure. Helena, used to Kate's last-minute exam time panics, had laughed. 'One day, I *will* get the two of you in a room together,' she'd said. 'If any man's going to make you want to throw away your chastity belt it's Leander.'

'I thought you said he was a playboy,' Kate had said, confused that Helena was seemingly trying to play cupid.

'He's a playboy but he's a good guy, and seeing as he won't settle down until he's at least fifty and you're planning to marry an orangutan, does him being a play-boy even matter?'

Her heart beating harder than ever, Kate replayed that forgotten conversation again, forgotten because she'd sat her exams soon after and then she'd left university for good and resumed her volunteer role with the vet team at the zoo twenty miles from her family home, a role she'd undertaken every term break since her second year at uni. Her head had been too full praying not to have failed her degree to even think of Helena's cupid game, and then once it was confirmed that everything she'd worked so hard for had paid off and she'd become a per-manent, paid member of the veterinary team, she didn't give Leander Liassidis another thought. She didn't give any man a thought, by now too intent on getting the ex-perience she needed to take the final step of realising her dreams. When Helena had confided about her mar-riage to Leander and the reasons for it, Kate had been in the process of arranging visas and the vaccinations needed for her imminent move to Borneo, too excited that her dream was almost close enough to touch to re-member Helena had once implied Leander was the man Kate should lose her virginity to.

This time next week, she would be in South East Asia, finally realising her lifelong dream. All the sacri-fices Kate and those she loved had made had paid off. Nothing could derail her from achieving it because it was already done. She'd already reached the finish line.

And now Leander had invaded her dreams. He'd taken them over so effectively that it was like he'd always lived in them, and her heart beat even harder at the realisa-tion that what she was feeling now was so strong that it was impossible to imagine that anyone else could ever make her feel a fraction of what Leander did.

Feeling like she was falling into another one of her Leander dreams, she threw the duvet off and, her heart thrumming, padded to the door.

The sun was starting to rise and still Leander's brain would not switch off.

He'd brushed his teeth to within an inch of their lives but still all he could taste was Kate. He could still feel the heat of her body in his arms. Could still feel the smoothness of her flesh beneath his fingers.

He closed his eyes and fought harder than he'd ever fought for control of himself.

What madness had let him believe he could sleep with Kate only two rooms away from him?

The worst part was knowing that two rooms away, Kate was trapped in her own tortured awareness of him lying here.

Theós, he wanted her so badly. So badly. More than he'd ever wanted anyone or anything.

And she wanted him too...

The tap on his door was so light he thought his febrile mind had conjured it. It was only the surge of his pulses that made him climb out of bed a few moments later and open his door.

Kate was standing with her back against the mezzanine, facing him.

He swallowed, hardly able to breathe. 'Is everything okay?'

'I...' Her voice dropped so low he could hardly hear it. 'I don't want it to be with anyone else.'

His grip on the door tightened and he had to clear his throat to hoarsely speak. 'What are you saying?'

Her voice might be barely audible but there was no mistaking the clarity in her eyes. 'I want it to be with you.'

Another of those silences where a falling feather could be heard enveloped them until, with a groan that rose from the pit of his stomach, he took the three paces needed to scoop her into his arms and any remaining fight in him evaporated.

What was he even fighting for? he wondered dimly as he carried her into his bedroom, soaking in the colour heightened cheeks and all the delicate pixie features that made Kate so unutterably beautiful.

He laid her on his bed. The beats of his thundering heart echoed through the entirety of his body.

A trembling hand pressed into his cheek. The warmth of her touch scorched him. Slowly, her fingers tiptoed to cup the back of his head. Her throat moved numerous times before her chest rose. Her lips parted, shallow breaths escaping and she slowly craned her face to him.

God in heaven, he ached to be a part of her.

Dipping his head, the last thing he saw before their mouths locked together was the melting of the jade into liquid.

The first brush of her lips against his melted *him* into liquid.

Kate's heart was racing so hard and so fast she could no longer feel the individual beats. Everything— *everything*—had become Leander, and she scraped her fingers through his soft hair to knead his skull as the tender caress of his mouth deepened, her nerve endings zinged into life and the entirety of her senses were filled by his dark taste and musky scent.

She couldn't stop this even if she wanted to, and she didn't want to. She wanted this, wanted Leander with every fibre of her being. Nothing else mattered. Nothing in the world but this. Him. Her. Them.

Who else could she give the whole of herself to? Who else could make her feel like this?

She wanted it all. Needed it all.

When he lifted his face to stare back into her eyes, the hooded desire she found contained in the dark depths made her heart catch.

'Leander, I...' She only just caught herself from saying words that could never ever be taken back.

His gaze flickered, lips tightening as if he too were having to stop himself from speaking. Seeing the mirrored torture only made her heart crash to a stop all over again.

Bringing her face back up to his, she stroked her soft cheek against his stubbly cheek and whispered, 'Make love to me. Please, Leander, make love to me.'

His breaths were ragged and heavy in her ear. 'You have no idea what you do to me,' he muttered hoarsely before his hungry mouth recaptured hers and sent flames burning through her.

Her core and heart on fire, Kate closed her eyes and sank into the pleasure of Leander's assault of her senses.

Sensuous lips brushed the swan of her neck, stubble scratching her sensitised skin as he slowly kissed his way down to the top button of her—his—shirt.

Loath though he was to tear an inch of his flesh away from her, Leander dragged himself to his knees and gazed down at the woman who'd become the only woman in existence for him. Never had he seen such open passion in the eyes of a lover. Never had the heat of a touch turned his body into liquid.

But it wasn't just the unadulterated desire radiating at him that made his heart feel so weighty. The trust radiating from Kate's beautiful eyes landed with equal weight.

This gift she was bestowing on him...

Hooking his thumbs in the sides of his boxers, he pulled them down past his hips, lifted his knees to skim them down his legs and chucked them aside with no further thought.

She opened her arms for him.

Painfully aware of how close he already was to the edge, Leander swooped to recapture her mouth.

Kate dissolved into the dark taste of Leander's hard hungry kiss and then the whole of her dissolved into a fever of sensation as he stripped the shirt from her.

Working from the top, button by button was undone, his lips trailing kisses over every millimetre of exposed flesh all the way down to her pubic bone where the shirt had ruched around her waist.

He pulled it apart.

Fully naked beneath a male gaze for the first time in her life, Kate's throat caught tightly at the expression on Leander's face. He was gazing at her like he'd unwrapped a personal gift from the heavens.

How could she have mistaken that look for disgust? she wondered in dim amazement, then stopped wondering about anything when he covered her breast and the sensations that careered through her felt like their own gift from the heavens. When he replaced his hand with his mouth, head spinning, blood on fire, Kate became fully lost in Leander's worshipful touch.

Hands and mouth roamed her body, kissing, stroking, licking, biting, kneading, the delicious scratching of his stubble against her skin only intensifying the pleasure.

So lost in the sensations had she become that when he gently spread her thighs and rested his face in between, it felt like the most necessary and natural act in the world.

She wasn't his gift from the heavens, she thought hazily as she writhed into him. He was her gift, and the more he gave the more she wanted. Her hunger for him was limitless. Every inch of her body was aflame, burning for more of his kisses, more of his touches and when their mouths fused back together and he put his hand where his tongue had just been, she kissed him deeply and arched into him, incapable of doing anything but obeying her body's demands. All of its demands were for Leander. Just him.

Leander was hanging on by a thread. The need to take full possession of Kate had become an agonised fever in his blood, his arousal tipping into unendurable, but through it all, words repeating over and over to keep his passion leashed, *she's a virgin.*

He could scarcely believe how much it felt like his first time too, as if her succulent breasts were the first breasts he'd ever caressed... *Theós*, her body could have been created especially for him, her scent, taste and texture aphrodisiacs designed purely for his own chemical makeup to respond to, everything about her so much more than he'd ever imagined possible.

'*Theós*, Kate, you're so beautiful,' he groaned into her mouth. 'I want you so much.'

Her mouth slanted against his with such passion it spoke louder than any words could that everything he was feeling was shared.

It took the last remaining fragment of his sanity to murmur, 'Let me get protection.'

Her hold around him tightened, her eyes begging him not to let go of her. 'I'm protected.'

Swallowing hard, trying to control the beats of his heart, he clasped her hip, fingers sinking into her bottom, then shifted himself so his erection pressed between her legs. Just knowing he was so close to being where he so desperately needed to be made his arousal throb hard enough to pulse blood to his head.

This was it. The point of no return.

Threading his fingers through hers, Leander captured Kate's mouth for another heady taste of paradise and slowly pushed into her tight velvet heat.

The shock of Leander's huge arousal pressing into her was matched only by the thrills fluttering through her entire body.

It felt like she'd waited her whole life for this moment.

With one of his hands holding hers, the other gripping her hip, the security of his touch would have doused any fear. But she had no fear, not with Leander, and she submitted her body, soul and trust in their entirety to him.

Lips brushing like feathers, he inched inside her, setting off nerve endings buried so deeply inside her she'd never known they were there waiting for his touch to awaken them from dormancy until, finally, their groins were fused as one.

For a long moment they stayed locked like that, Kate gazing with wonder into dark eyes filled with equal wonder until he groaned her name and kissed her tenderly, withdrawing to the tip.

With a half-stifled groan, he filled her again, withdrew, filled her, his movements intense but unhurried, giving her all the time she needed to become accustomed to his possession.

Slowly, the tempo increased. Slowly, Kate felt the core of herself unfurl and bloom as the pleasure of his possession intensified. So slowly did they go that when she instinctively raised her thighs and the friction increased where she most needed it, she was unprepared for her climax, one moment luxuriating in the bliss of being made love to by Leander, the next caught in a rollercoaster of pulsations that had her clinging tightly to him and crying out his name as the rollercoaster shot her to the stars.

Never in his life had Leander witnessed anything as beautiful as the widening of Kate's eyes as she thickened around him and pulled him deeper into her tightness. Her cries of his name echoed dimly in ears that were drowning in the roar of blood as he fused himself as tightly to her as it was possible for two humans to be and cried out at the almost violent pleasure of his own desperately needed release.

Kate had never believed that time really could stand still, but in those seconds or minutes or hours of silence, broken only by the pounding of her heart in her ears that followed their lovemaking, she finally understood what it meant. Time had ceased to have any meaning. There was no meaning left in the world. Only Leander.

She had never imagined it could be like that, that it

wouldn't be just her body that she gave to him but the whole of herself. And that he'd given the whole of himself to her too.

It had been so beautiful.

He'd made her feel beautiful.

Whatever happened when time reset itself, this was a night she would keep close to her heart and cherish for the rest of her life.

Leander could have stayed wrapped in Kate's arms, the beats of their hearts smashing together, breathing in the sweet scent of her hair and cheek for eternity. Only the fear of his weight suffocating her gave him the impetus to move. Even then, he could only bring himself to shift slowly, clasping her hand to pull her with him so she rolled into him.

Nuzzling his mouth and chin into the top of her head, he stroked her back, marvelling anew at the soft silkiness of her skin, marvelling too at how damn pleasurable Kate's delicate fingers making tiny circles over his chest was.

There was no need for words. No need to rehash what had just taken place.

He could barely comprehend how incredible it had been.

'When is your flight to Borneo?' he murmured after the longest, most peaceful time he thought he'd ever spent had passed.

She lifted her face to meet his stare. 'Monday evening.'

He kissed her gently. 'Then stay. Stay with me until Sunday.'

Her jade eyes swirled starkly. 'And then you'll go back to Greece?' she whispered.

'I gave my word,' he said heavily, the weight in his stomach at the thought of returning to his homeland pulling at his vocal cords. Pulling at all of him.

Tears filled her eyes. 'Then give *me* your word that if I stay, you'll go back to Greece on Sunday. You and me... It can't go anywhere. I'm starting a new life thousands of miles away and your place is with...'

To Kate's horror, she couldn't say Helena's name, and suddenly it hit her, the depth of her betrayal of her best friend.

Concern flickered in Leander's stare and then he must have read her thoughts for in seconds he'd rolled her onto her back.

'Listen to me, Kate,' he said, staring intently into her eyes. 'You have done nothing wrong. Helena feels nothing for me. You know that.'

'I know, but—'

'There is no but,' he told her firmly. 'You and I are both free, consenting adults. If she knew about us she'd be pleased, you know that.'

She blinked frantically before taking a deep breath. When she'd gathered herself together, she forced firmness to her own voice. 'You have to be her husband.'

His jaw clenched then loosened. 'I know. And I will. When you fly back to England to pack for your new life, I will return to Greece.'

It hurt more than she could have believed to say, 'You promise?'

'I swear.' Leander kissed the tip of her nose. 'We will go back to the real world on Sunday.' Whatever it cost him. 'But until then, let this time be for us. Just us. Let us pretend the real world doesn't exist.'

She inhaled slowly before the tiniest smile played on the corners of her little pixie mouth. 'I thought it was impossible for you to pretend.'

He kissed her again, harder, arousal stirring back to life. 'For you, my little pixie, I will pretend anything.'

CHAPTER EIGHT

'WHERE ARE WE GOING?' Kate asked as she climbed into the leather passenger seat of the small sports car. She had no idea how Leander had been able to fit his body into the driver's side. She supposed it helped that the roof had already been folded back. She didn't know why he bothered opening the door—his legs were so long he could have just stepped over it.

After two days spent barely surfacing from his bed, Leander had announced as their breakfast was being cleared away from the balcony of his bedroom that he was taking her out.

'Shopping,' he now told her.

'That's the big surprise? Shopping?'

'You don't look impressed.'

'Well, you did big up the surprise aspect.'

He grinned and leaned over for a kiss. 'I assumed you were bored with my wardrobe—you seem reluctant to wear any of it.'

Heat flushing through her, she gave a knowing smile and lifted her feet onto the dashboard, deliberately letting the black shirt of his that she was wearing fall to her thighs.

'Behave,' he growled, putting the car in gear.

'You're the one who insisted we go out. I was happy mooching around your house…'

'Mooching?'

'You can work it out.' She opened a button on her shirt—and it was her shirt. Kate had determined to take every one of the shirts she'd borrowed since her arrival in California with her as mementoes—and exposed her naked breasts. 'Is it me or is it hot here?'

Two days of near constant lovemaking had completely opened Kate's eyes to pleasure. If Leander was a willing teacher in the art of sensuality then she was a very enthusiastic, committed student. Who wanted to waste time browsing through shops when they could be in bed? There was little enough time left as it was…

He kept his gaze on the road in front of him. 'If you are trying to distract me, it's not going to work. I am taking you shopping, Kate, whether you like it or not.'

'I thought billionaires brought the shops to them,' she sulked.

'I'm not buying for me, I'm buying for you, and there isn't time to have you fitted and clothes made bespoke for you, not without employing an army to work around the clock on you, which will take up even more of our valuable time than going into Marina Sands and buying off the peg.'

She sighed and closed the shirt back up. 'Leander, that's very generous of you but I don't need any clothes.'

He turned off his private driveway and onto the main road, changed gear and put his hand on her thigh. 'Believe me, I prefer it when you don't wear *any* clothes.'

She pushed his hand away and primly said, 'Behave.'

Laughing, he captured her hand and brought it to his

mouth so he could kiss her fingers. 'I'm taking you out tomorrow night and as sexy as you look in my shirts, you will feel uncomfortable wearing one where we're going.'

Her happy mood dimmed. 'I don't want to go out.'

'Trust me, you'll want to go where I'm taking you.'

'But it's…' She couldn't say it. Couldn't say that it would be their last night together. To vocalise it would make it real. Instead, she said, 'What if you're recognised? You're supposed to be on your honeymoon.'

It was the first time either of them had mentioned the elephant in the room since she'd agreed to stay. There had been no talk about either of their immediate futures at all. Kate's only communication with Helena had been a message she'd sent soon after Leander had made love to her a second time, in which she'd been able to tell her friend truthfully that Leander had promised to return to Greece on Sunday. She'd received some praying emojis in return. Her only other communication had been to her mother, apologising that she wouldn't be home until Sunday. That this would give Kate barely twenty-four hours with her family before her flight to Borneo was something she couldn't bring herself to think about because since then it had been just her and Leander cocooned away from the real world, making love and just…*being*.

They had been the best days of her life and now, leaving the sanctuary of his home only brought home how fleeting the time they had together actually was.

'Kate…' It was his turn to sigh. 'We're safe here, I promise. The only local people I've become friendly with are surfers. No one here follows European tabloids. I'm just another rich guy.'

Accepting defeat, Kate closed her eyes and enjoyed

the sensation of the breeze on her face. If they couldn't be in bed together then just being with him was a perfect second best.

'How did you get so rich?' she asked idly as they rounded a sweeping bend. 'Did you have lessons on it at school?'

He laughed. 'Lots of components. Luck and timing played a big part.'

'My dad always says people create their own luck.'

'Your father makes a valid point. I've always had an aptitude for technology and I knew it was the most likely route for me to earn my fortune. When I launched the instant payment app there were three other similar apps in development that I knew of,' Leander explained of the first app he'd created and developed. Its launch had launched his career and founded his wealth. 'My product was better and the security aspect unsurpassable, but if I had made one wrong move or my rivals a better move I would have had to return home.'

'It was all or nothing for you?'

'I invested the entirety of the lump sum my parents gave me in it.'

'So if it had failed you'd have lost everything?'

'It made it easier to take the risk, knowing I had my family to fall back on.'

'Would they have let you join the business seeing as you'd already walked away from it?'

'I wouldn't have joined the business. Shipping bores me. I'd have moved back into my childhood bedroom and found the money to open my own cocktail bar.'

Expecting her to laugh as most people did when he

revealed his adolescent fantasy, a warmth filled his chest when she musingly said, 'I can imagine you doing that.'

He pulled a face. 'For real?'

'You make excellent cocktails and you're so outgoing and gregarious that people would flock to your bar.' He could feel her eyes on him. 'To be honest, I think it would suit you better than being a tech gazillionaire, and as you now are a gazillionaire, aren't you ever tempted to just sell up and buy yourself that cocktail bar?'

'I have wild moments when I fantasise about it,' he admitted, turning into the main Marina Sands car park.

'What's stopped you? Surely you've proved everything you need to prove?'

He reversed into an empty bay. 'I've never been out to prove anything.'

'If you didn't have something to prove you'd have used your parents' money to open the cocktail bar and become one of those people who doodle their clever ideas on napkins in quiet times with reggae music in the background rather than make their clever ideas a reality.'

He turned the engine off. 'There's no money in cocktail bars. That's why I went into technology.'

She unbuckled her seatbelt and leaned her face into his. 'That's my point, Mr Gazillionaire. You're rich enough to live thousands of lives without running out of money. Retire. Open your cocktail bar. Doodle your clever ideas on napkins…' Her eyes glittered. 'Unless I'm right and you really are still set on proving that your decision to go your own way was the right choice.'

Astounded at her wild observation, Leander responded to the kiss Kate planted on his mouth automatically.

'Let's get this over with,' she declared before fling-ing her door open.

She'd skipped round to his side of the car before he'd closed the door.

Shades on, hands tightly clasped, they made the short walk to the boulevard, their footsteps leaving indentations in the fine layer of sand covering all the roads and path-ways. The breeze would wipe the indentations away by the time they returned to the car, he thought with a stab in his chest. Everything about him and Kate was imperma-nent, and he strongly suspected that it was the imperma-nency that made everything between them feel so intense and allowed him to fully commit the whole of himself to what they were sharing. Saying goodbye to Kate would be hard, he did not doubt it, but life was hard and he'd have the sweetest memories to remember her by. No regrets.

What they were sharing was perfect and their ending would be perfect too.

He could not bring himself to contemplate what came after they'd said goodbye.

They'd reached the wide tree-lined boulevard.

Kate's eyes widened in amazement at the array of shops and cafés and the richly dressed people, many of them car-rying or walking tiny dogs of a host of varieties, wander-ing in and out of them. 'Is everyone who lives here rich?'

'Not everyone. The surfers I'm friendly with share a one storey home on the beachfront that was inherited from Danny's grandmother. They work the local bars and restaurants to pay their bills and spend the rest of their lives in the ocean.'

'Was it the surfing that made you buy a property here?' she asked as Leander stopped to check out the name of a boutique, remembering his complete mastery of the board he'd surfed the enormous waves on.

'The surf and Marina Sands being only a short helicopter ride to San Francisco. I usually surf every day when I'm here.'

She adopted an innocent expression. 'Then why has your wetsuit stayed dry these last few days?'

He caught her off-guard by hooking an arm around her waist and burying his face in her hair to whisper, 'Because the competition between catching the surf or staying in bed with you is no competition at all.'

'Then stop wasting time here and take me back to bed,' she whispered back, gripping his hip and pressing herself into him. For the first time since they'd become lovers she was in the frustrating position of having to wait to act on her desires. And she wanted him all the time. Probably it was the strict time limit on what they had together at play, combined with her body making up for twenty-five—nearly twenty-six—years of chastity, together with the fact that Leander was a walking hunk of testosterone. She just could not believe how she'd spent that week in Greece with him, oblivious to how ruddy sexy he was... or wilfully ignoring it as she now accepted she'd done. The more they made love, the more she wanted to make love, her desire for him an ever-expanding hunger that could only be satisfied for short periods of time.

He growled quietly into her ear then brushed a kiss over her mouth. 'Choose a dress and anything else you want and then we can go home. This is the shop I wanted to bring you to.'

In moments Kate was plunged into the alien world of what looked to her inexperienced eyes to be bohemian haute couture. She was quite sure she would normally be in raptures to be brought into a shop like this and told to choose anything she wanted, but right then she was having trouble keeping herself upright. The worst bit was the gleam in Leander's eyes that told her he knew exactly the state he'd put her in.

The shop manager came to them. Leander gave his instructions—let Kate have anything she wanted—and then excused himself.

'Where are you going?' she asked, startled that he was leaving her.

'Not far. I'll be back before you're finished.'

The plunge her heart made to see him walk out of the door...

In two days that walk out of the door would be permanent, a thought that made her heart plunge even deeper.

Breathing deeply to expel the sudden distress nibbling at her and telling herself firmly not to think beyond Sunday, Kate let the manager guide her through the array of beautiful clothes and lingerie. In the end it came down to three dresses that she couldn't decide between, a handful of bras and three pairs of shoes to choose from, and the manager carried the items past an opulent waiting area and through to a dressing room that was like no dressing room she'd ever been in before. No dressing room she'd been in before was this private and plush and spacious and equipped with its own coffee machine with pods, bottles of water and a velvet sofa.

'Shall I stay and help you dress?' the manager asked.

'I'm good, thanks.' And also stark naked beneath the shirt, which wasn't a problem as it practically reached her knees but still meant there was no way she was getting undressed with a stranger in the room.

Starting with the bras, each of which she guessed must cost what she'd spent her whole lifetime on bras, Kate was dismayed to find they all fit her perfectly and all felt glorious to wear. How on earth was she supposed to decide? She'd choose one of the dresses and then make her mind up. The first dress, a silk navy number with a plunging neckline, showed way too much flesh for her liking and didn't need a bra but wanting to see it fully done up and unable to pull the zip all the way up by herself, she pressed the assistance buzzer.

In moments there was a knock on the door.

Opening it, she found Leander standing there.

His eyes locked onto hers. A sensuous smile playing on his lips, he took in the whole of her in one long sweep that sent her pulses surging. His tone one of the utmost deference and politeness, he said, 'You rang for assistance, madam?'

She had to swallow a mouth filled with moisture to say, with equal politeness, 'I need someone to do the zip up for me.'

'May I help you in this matter? Or shall I call for the manager? I'm afraid it will be a few minutes before she can attend to you.'

She cleared her throat and raised her chin. 'I'm afraid time is money and I don't have the time to wait for her.'

A knowingness gleaming in his eyes, he stepped into the dressing room and locked the door.

Giving her another long, desiring sweep, he took a step towards her and straightened. 'Turn around.'

Trembling with excitement and anticipation, Kate obeyed.

Her skin danced as his fingers plucked the zipper and slowly pulled it up.

A shiver she was helpless to do anything to stop raced up her spine. Somehow she managed to stay on her feet and turn back around to face him. 'What do you think?'

Leander didn't know what was the most beautiful aspect of the sight there before him. The melted jade of desire in Kate's eyes, the heightened colour on her cheeks, or the skimpy dress that revealed more flesh than it covered.

Lightly slipping his fingers beneath the flimsy material barely covering her breasts, he pinched the erect nipple with the exact amount of pressure guaranteed to make her moan with pleasure.

'I think,' he said huskily, kneading the whole of her breast with his palm, 'that if I take you out wearing this I'm going to be arrested for gross indecency.'

Eyes glazed, she made another mewing moan.

Placing a finger to her lips, he gently walked her backwards so her back was to the wall and rubbed his cheek against hers. 'Don't say another word,' he whispered, reaching down to her thigh and skimming his fingers under the silk and up her inner thigh to cup her naked pubis.

Theós, she was already hot and sticky for him.

Without a single word being exchanged or item of clothing removed, he used his hand and fingers to bring her to the orgasm her body was telling him she was in desperate need of. He didn't care that he would have to wait until they returned home for his own pleasure and release. Watching Kate climax was a hedonistic pleasure all in itself. Being the one to bring her to that climax…

Never had he been so fully attuned to another's needs and desires. For the first time in his life, Leander understood the pleasure that came with giving without the expectation of receiving, and as she convulsed against him, mouth pressed into his neck to stifle her moans of ecstasy, he knew he could spend the whole of his life searching and never find another Kate.

After dissolving for Leander in the dressing room, Kate had been in no fit state to try the other dresses on and so Leander had firmly insisted on taking all three of them, along with the shoes, bras and their matching knickers. After arranging for them to be delivered to the house, he then insisted on stopping for a coffee before returning home, telling her that to travel all this way without experiencing anything of life in Marina Sands was criminal.

Now, seated on the terrace of a smart little café, looking out over the ocean that was such an intrinsic part of Marina Sands, feet pressed together, they sipped coffee and spooned slices of chocolate torte.

Kate couldn't believe how happy she was. Ridiculously happy. So happy she was in danger of doing an injury to her cheek muscles.

'It's so peaceful here,' she observed.

'It is,' he agreed. 'Of all my homes, this location is one of my favourites.'

'That's a high accolade, considering the ruddy number of them.'

He grinned.

'So which one *is* your favourite?'

'Hmm… Impossible to decide. Marina Sands has the best surfing, New York has the best nightlife, Milan has the best shops. The Seychelles has the best snorkelling, Switzerland the best skiing—'

'Switzerland wasn't on my list of your properties,' she interrupted.

'I sold my original chalet last winter and only completed the purchase of the new one ten days ago.'

'Klosters?'

'Gstaad.'

'Loads of the girls at my school used to have second homes in Klosters and Gstaad.'

'Did you ever go?'

She shook her head. 'My parents hated me being at boarding school. They wanted me home every weekend and the holidays. Not that I was ever asked to go.' Only Helena had invited Kate places.

Helena's name had barely been mentioned since they'd become lovers.

'I remember you saying the school was in the next town to your home. Why did they let you board if they hated you being away from them?'

'Because it made practical sense. The school days were long. My mum worked shifts so it would have been Dad doing all the running around.'

'She's a nurse?' Leander remembered.

'Yes.'

'And your father's an electrician?'

'Yes. By the time he'd finished work and fought through rush hour traffic, the chances of him collecting me and getting me home before seven were slim. He'd have done it gladly and we'd have made it work if I hadn't been awarded the full scholarship and had my boarding fees included. None of us expected that. The most we hoped for was to have my day fees paid for.'

'Your parents sound like amazing people.'

'They're incredible. They've supported me in everything and in so many ways. "My brothers too, even though George teased me chronically about it when we were growing up.'

'He's the brother closest to you in age?'

'An elephant would be jealous of your memory. George is three years older than me. He was always winding me up and telling me I was too thick to get the grades I needed and that I'd be lucky to get a job feeding animals. I swear, every time I opened any test or exam results, I'd imagine him laughing at me and saying *I told you so* if I'd failed.' She sniggered. 'Luckily, I was always able to wave my results in his face.'

'Luck you created with your own hard work,' he pointed out.

'But with their support, and they all made sacrifices. There is no way on this earth that I would be flying to Borneo next week if not for the sacrifices they made. I mean, I only got a full scholarship because they paid for extra tuition so I could reach the needed standard and when I was there, there were always extras that needed paying for, and then more private tuition when I was struggling with my chemistry A level. All the money to pay for that came from Mum working extra shifts and Dad taking on extra clients, and my brothers accepting without any complaints that I was being given opportunities they hadn't even dared to dream of having. They could easily have resented me but they never did. They just loved and supported me.'

'Did you become so focused on your studies because you were afraid of letting them down?' Leander asked. He just could not wrap his head around the lengths the entire Hawkins family had gone to pull together and help make the dream of a seven-year-old child come true.

She sighed and looked up at the sky. 'I think,' she said slowly, clearly thinking aloud, 'that it was fear of their sacrifices going to waste that stopped me from throwing the towel in when things got really hard. They helped keep me motivated. I suppose my dream became their dream too.'

'Do you ever think you would have chosen a different path if you weren't so scared of letting them down?'

She looked back at him with surprise at the question. 'Gosh, no. Honestly, I've never come across anything else where I've even wondered what it would be like to do. Apart from motor racing.'

He raised an eyebrow.

She grinned. My brothers are motor racing fanatics. Occasionally I'd have a wild daydream of getting behind the wheel of a Ferrari and leaving them all to dust but considering I'm a slower driver than my grandad, that's a fantasy that's never going to happen even if the opportunity arose.'

He grinned back and took her hand. 'I suppose your family is already accustomed to the day you move continents?'

'Oh, yes. They've had nearly twenty years to get used to the idea of me going. It'll still be a wrench, I know that, but we'll video call regularly and I get a return flight home for Christmas each year as part of my contract, so it's not as if I'm completely disappearing from their lives. And they can come and visit me too. We've always managed to work it out.'

'That's good.'

But it only served to remind Leander that he'd left Greece and moved continents having given his twin only a week's notice. He'd left knowing that taking his freedom would compromise their relationship but not the extent that compromise would take.

He hadn't known it would end with him losing Leo. Losing the other half of himself.

Memories suddenly flooded him from nowhere, of all the times they'd switched identities in their childhood, in the days before Leander had grown to resent not having an identity that was entirely his own...

Kate's toes prodded into his foot. 'Earth to Leander.'

He caught her eye and smiled ruefully. 'I was just thinking about your family having all those years to prepare for you leaving. It made me think of my parents when I took the cash and their lack of surprise. Looking back, I think they already knew what I'd do.'

'It was just Leo who hadn't known?'

Frustration had him shaking his head. 'Of course he knew. We come from the same egg. He knew me better than anyone in the world. He just refused to see or acknowledge it.'

'He might have suspected but if you didn't actually tell him...' Her words trailed off with a light but sympathetic shrug.

He drained his coffee. 'He knew but he didn't want to see.' And in truth, he *had* gone to great lengths to hide his real intentions from Leo, doing everything to delay the day when he would have to loosen the bond between them and break his brother's heart.

'And you knew but refused to say, and then when it came to the business being in trouble the roles were reversed, with Leo refusing to accept your support and you refusing to accept that he needed you to force it on him. For twins who have absolutely nothing in common, I'm getting the feeling that you both suffer from a huge dose of too much pride and stubbornness.'

For the first time since they'd become lovers Leander felt a kernel of anger unfurl at Kate. But then he saw the soft understanding in her eyes and the anger evaporated as quickly as it had formed. He'd brought the subject up, not Kate and if her observations felt a little close to the bone...

'I'm not judging you,' she said quietly, reaching over the table for his hand. 'I just think it's sad that you've lost so many years together.' Pulling his hand to her mouth, she pressed a kiss to it before a spark rang out in her stare. 'Ready to take me home, Mr Gazillionaire?'

That was better. Desire was much easier to handle than talk of ancient history, and his desire for Kate was seemingly limitless.

Kate's relief when Leander leaned over the table to kiss her and murmur, 'More than ready, my pixie princess,' was physical in its intensity. She'd seen his flare of anger at her comment over something that was, when all was said and done, none of her business.

All the same, walking back to the car, hands clasped, easy conversation flowing, she couldn't help thinking about how much courage it must have taken for Leander to pick up the phone to his brother to ask for his help last Saturday.

CHAPTER NINE

KATE WOKE TO the most delicious sensation of Leander covering her face in featherlight kisses.

'Time to wake up, sleepyhead,' he murmured, gently biting her earlobe.

Flinging her arms around him and trying to hook her legs around his waist, she was chagrined to find his arousal contained beneath a pair of shorts, and opened one eye to scowl at him.

His smile was knowing and seductive before he kissed her deeply. He tasted of toothpaste. He smelled clean.

'You had a shower without me,' she accused when he pulled his mouth from hers.

'That's because you were snoring so loudly I thought you needed the sleep,' he teased.

'Oh, no, was I doing my warthog impression?'

'You were. It was torture to my ears.' He kissed her again then shifted out of her arms and out of her reach so quickly she was forced to scowl her disappointment at him again.

Grinning, he whistled as he walked to the other end of the bedroom.

Kate lifted her head and her mood perked up to see him pick up a breakfast tray and carry it over to her.

Catching the scent of bacon sent off a hunger pang and she quickly decided to wolf down the food and then get those shorts off him.

He lifted a silver lid to reveal a mound of bacon sandwiches.

She beamed her pleasure and scrambled to sit upright, holding the bedsheets under her arms so she didn't get crumbs over herself. A bacon sandwich was her all-time favourite breakfast food.

He placed the tray on her lap with a flourish and perched on the edge of the bed beside her. Along with the sandwiches were two flutes of what looked like diluted fizzy orange juice and two cups of coffee.

'Before you start...' he said, raising one of the flutes. 'To your health.'

Bemused, Kate tapped the other flute to his and, thirsty, tipped the contents down her throat. The last thing she expected was for it to contain alcohol. 'What *is* that?' she spluttered.

'Bucks Fizz,' he said smugly.

'Bucks Fizz for breakfast?'

He simply grinned, helped himself to a sandwich, and took a huge bite.

Biting into her own, Kate had another of those sensations like she'd had in the café the day before, where she'd felt she might actually burst with happiness.

Between them, they demolished the mound, and when they'd finished their drinks, Leander took the tray back to the table on the other side of the room.

Flicking the stray crumbs away, Kate threw the sheets off her and leaned back to welcome him into her arms.

That knowing, seductive gleam she so adored in his

eyes, he stalked towards her but, before she could grab at him, he stopped and dug into his shorts pocket.

Her mouth fell open when he produced a square gift-wrapped box that fit perfectly in the palm of his huge hand.

Heart suddenly thrashing, she looked from the box to his gorgeous face and scrambled upright.

'Happy birthday, *agápi mou.*'

Utterly gobsmacked, she could only stare at him.

'Go on,' he chided, sitting beside her. 'Open it.'

She shook her head, not in refusal but disbelief. 'How did you know?' She'd been so caught up in the magic that was Leander that she'd barely given her birthday a thought. The times it had crossed her mind, she'd determined not to tell him, thinking it would sound needy to casually drop it into the conversation, like she was angling for a gift.

'When you mentioned being the youngest in your school year it reminded me that Helena turned down a night out with me for your birthday last year. She wouldn't let me gate-crash.' Leander had to force a smile at the memory; force it because now that he was thinking of it, it came to him all the different turns his life could have taken if he'd met Kate a year ago, before Helena had needed to get her hands on her inheritance. There would have been nothing to stop him and Kate—

Blinking the errant thought away, he added, 'I got my PA to go through my schedule for when I visited London last summer.'

She shook her head again and tucked a lock of hair behind an adorable sticky-out ear. 'Is this why you disappeared yesterday?'

'Well detected,' he said with forced lightness; this time forced because it had just dawned on him that he'd never bought a gift for a lover before. Not personally. Usually he got Sheree to do it for him.

It hadn't crossed his mind to get Sheree to organise Kate's present for him. He'd *wanted* to go into the stores and choose the perfect gift for her himself. He'd already had in mind what he would get her. It had been sheer luck that he'd found it so quickly.

'Are you going to open it or were my efforts for nothing?'

If Kate had thought she was happy before, it had nothing on the joy zipping through her veins now. Plucking the box from his hand, she tugged at the ribbon wrapped around it and carefully laid it on the bedside table. She would take it with her as another memento. Then, carefully peeling at the tiny heart-shaped sticker holding the beautiful gift-wrapping in place at its base, she flattened it out to reveal a black jewellery box.

Her heart punched into her ribs and suddenly she found herself as terrified to look at Leander as she was to open the box.

Pulses racing madly, she pinched the tiny clasp on the box with shaking hands and had to snatch a breath before she could bring herself to open the lid.

She had no idea if it was relief or dejection that slammed into her when she caught sight of the sparkling contents.

Nestled snugly in the box was a pair of diamond stud earrings.

Leander could hardly breathe as he waited for Kate to respond. He was used to lovers being profusive in their thanks and adoration of his gifts. Too profusive. As if that was what they thought he expected. And maybe he *had* expected that kind of response. Become so used to the monetary value being praised—he was always generous with what he told Sheree to spend—that the lack of meaning behind any of the gifts hadn't mattered in the slightest.

Kate was different. This gift was different.

This gift mattered.

'I remembered you saying you didn't think it would be safe to wear anything but ear studs in your new job,' he said into the silence.

Her eyes lifted to his.

His chest tightened to see the sheen in them.

'You should be able to wear these all the time. If you want,' he added.

'Oh, I want,' she whispered. Blinking back tears, Kate gazed again at the diamonds shining so brightly under the morning light then leaned into him and palmed his stubbly cheek. 'Thank you. They're just beautiful. Perfect. I'll wear them always.'

Emotion threatening to explode out of her, she pressed her mouth to his, sliding her hand round to cup the back of his head and deepen the kiss, fighting even harder against the encroaching tears.

Kate replied to the message from the head of the plane's cabin crew and then messaged her mother.

Her heart felt so heavy she could feel its weight all the way down to her toes.

Putting her phone on the ledge, she carefully applied the mascara and lipstick she'd dug out from the bottom of her handbag and stepped back to look at herself properly.

It was for the best that they were going out, she thought morosely as she attempted a smile for the bathroom mirror. She would still be with Leander but with a new setting and probably people to help distract her from the dread that had been steadily growing in her that day. Since the messages with the flight crew started, the dread had accelerated.

Go out on a high, she told herself, giving her hair one more brush and tucking one side behind her ear. The diamond studs sparkled in her lobes. Under certain angles and lights the diamonds gave the illusion of being shaped like roses.

The earrings were simple, practical and utterly exquisite. She would cherish them for the rest of her life and try to forget that brief moment when she'd held her breath in a combination of dread and excitement that the box contained a ring.

She stepped from the bathroom to the bedroom at the same moment Leander entered the room, dressed for their night out in a tailored dark blue suit with a pale blue shirt unbuttoned at the throat.

Just the sight of him lifted her weighted heart. Kate had only seen him wear a suit once, her second night in California when she'd still believed he loathed her and had been coming to terms with her mushrooming attraction to him. She'd acknowledged to herself the suaveness of Leander in a suit but, being so intent at the time on not letting her feelings for him show, hadn't fully acknowledged the full sexiness of Leander in a suit.

In truth, Leander was just sexy, whatever he wore and whatever he didn't wear. He was even sexy in his sleep.

She was going to miss him desperately.

His gleaming dark eyes slowly looked her up and down. He gave a low whistle. '*Theós*, Kate. You look wonderful.'

All she needed was a crown to sit on her blonde hair and she'd be his pixie princess come to life, Leander thought, although he was quite sure pixies weren't famed for being irresistibly sexy. He could laugh. Of the three dresses from the boutique, she'd chosen to wear the least revealing of them. Created with large black and red embroidered roses interlinked with red lace, the long-sleeved dress scooped across her collarbone and fell to just above her knees. On her feet were sandals held together with a thin black strap across the toes and another around her ankles. The heels were high enough to elevate her so the top of her head almost reached his chin. Without them, she barely reached his shoulders.

The least revealing dress and already his loins were tightening with anticipation of stripping it off her.

Kate could wear sackcloth and she'd still be irresistible to him.

About to haul her into his arms and show her just how irresistible she was, he caught a bleakness in her stare. 'What's wrong?'

She gave a tight-lipped smile and a small shrug. 'I need to leave earlier than I thought tomorrow.'

'When?'

'I need to be in the air by eleven.'

There was a sinking sensation in the pit of his stomach. 'In the morning?' They'd made loose plans to leave for Europe simultaneously late afternoon.

She nodded forlornly. 'I'd forgotten to factor in the time difference between California and England. I'm being collected at ten. If my flight leaves here by eleven, I'll land around five Monday morning British time. I'll be lucky to make it home before six. I'll only have a few hours left to sort myself out before I head back to the airport and I've got so much I need to do and people to say goodbye to.' Another forlorn smile. 'I knew all the travelling I did coming to find you had screwed my sense of time but hadn't realised how badly.'

Finding his lungs had tightened, Leander stroked her soft cheek and grazed a kiss to her sweet mouth, inhaling the scent of her skin to loosen his airways. They'd known from the outset that their time together was limited so it was futile to waste the hours they had left envisaging the moment they had to say goodbye. 'It is only a few hours earlier. If we forget about sleeping tonight we won't lose any time.'

Her lips relaxed into a smile against his. 'I like your way of thinking.'

He slid a hand around her slender back to clasp a peachy buttock. 'And I like that you like it.' Not wanting to ruin her lipstick, he restrained himself to another light kiss before taking her hand and stepping back. 'Come on, birthday girl. Let's go and celebrate while the night is still young.'

Leander sat in the back of the car with Kate's hand clasped in his, her head resting against his shoulder and her sweet scent filling his senses, trying to tune out that this was their last night together. Trying but not succeeding.

The healing wound on her knee was a reminder of how close he'd come to escaping her. If she hadn't tripped, he would have got in his car. He would never have experienced the hedonistic joy of making love to her.

Someone else would have shared her first time with her.

As some point in her future, someone else would take his place.

He wanted that for her, he told himself firmly. Kate had an earthy, sexual side to her nature and now that it had been unleashed, it was unreasonable to imagine she would leave California and be satisfied with a life of celibacy.

For all that he tried to make himself sound reasonable in his own thoughts, Leander didn't deny that knowing she'd be living and working in such a remote location and so would have limited opportunities to meet potential lovers made it easier to have his reasonable thoughts, but that only set his mind racing to her colleagues, the people she would live and work with. What if one of them swept Kate off her feet? A likeminded colleague she could have not only as a lover but build a life with. Maybe marry. Have children...

'You're hurting my hand.' Kate's murmured voice cut through his thoughts.

Realising he'd been squeezing too tightly, he immediately loosened his hold and kissed her delicate fingers in apology. 'Sorry.'

Concern shone in her eyes. 'Are you okay? You've been very quiet.'

He forced a smile. 'Just exercising my brain cells… and we're almost there. Look.'

Figuring that he'd share what was on his mind in his own time, not daring to think that time might have run out for them before that happened, Kate followed his stare. Excitement pushed much of the melancholy out of her and she opened her window to see more clearly, taking in the enormous fairground on the pier they were passing far to her left, the high rides aglow in neon colours illuminating the dark. She could almost hear the screams of the thrill-seekers, practically taste the scent of doughnuts and candyfloss.

Exactly twenty minutes after they'd set out from Leander's home, the driver took a right turn onto a wide street lined by high buildings with architecture that made her think of Spanish cities and soon they were crawling down what was obviously a theatre district, the pavements packed with people in various guises of dress, from haute couture to wacky, a smorgasbord of visual delight.

The car stopped.

'We're going to watch a show?' Kate asked.

He tapped her nose lightly. 'In a way. You'll see.'

Stepping out of the car and breathing in the energy of the place was enough to zap the last of the melancholy out of her.

This was her last night with Leander. It was her birthday. What kind of masochist would she be if she didn't make the most of every last minute with him?

Grinning, she raised herself onto her toes and planted a kiss to his mouth. 'Thank you.'

'Don't thank me yet—you don't know where we're going.'

'I don't have to know that to know I'll enjoy it.' Leander had taken her to a variety of places during her time on his family's Greek island and she'd loved all of them. Loved them because he'd been with her with his infectious good humour. Leander could take her on a date to an academic library and she'd still adore every moment.

'No pressure for me then,' he observed with a flash of his teeth, taking hold of her hand.

With a giggle, she happily let him lead her to a narrow arched door that, in comparison to the other doors along this street, was nondescript, a simple non-neon flashing sign above it in italics: *Trevis*. Leander had his phone ready and showed whatever was expected to a burly bouncer who nodded them through with wishes for them to have a good evening.

There was nothing nondescript about the interior.

There was a fleeting moment when Kate thought she'd travelled back in time and that Marilyn Monroe or Audrey Hepburn or Bette Davis would sashay down the golden cantilevered stairs, a sense that if she breathed in hard enough she'd be able to smell decades-old cigars and Scotch.

Around them, treading on the thick maroon carpet, were dozens of people dressed so glamorously she could believe they were at a movie awards ceremony. Everything in this reception room screamed glamour, from the golden chandeliers to the art deco artwork to the waiting staff hovering semi discreetly with trays of canapés and champagne.

Catching Leander's stare, she laughed. 'What *is* this place?'

'A private theatre.'

'So we *are* watching a show?'

He grinned, caught the eye of a waitress and plucked two flutes of champagne from her tray. After tapping their glasses together, he led Kate through the milling crowd and down wide marble steps into a vast auditorium. Where rows of seats would normally be at the front of the stage were dozens and dozens of tables already filled with yet more glamorous people.

An official greeted them. After Leander again showed his phone, they were taken to a table for two only feet away from the stage.

What followed was the most surreal yet entertaining show Kate had ever been to, an immersive mystical acrobatic cabaret like nothing she'd ever seen, with black magic and comedy that made her gasp and laugh and hide behind her hands, often all at the same time. Throughout it, course after course of beautifully presented and delicious-tasting food, champagne and cocktails were served to them. Kate was so enthralled with what was happening both on the stage and above them that she could have been eating cardboard for all the attention she paid to it.

By the time the finale came, she was giddy with the joy of it all and so at first didn't realise that the acrobat dressed as a water nymph swinging on a giant gold hoop suspended from the ceiling held a cake in her nimble hands, not until the hoop was lowered and the nymph, to loud screams of delight from the audience, swung upside down and expertly dropped the cake on their table.

She had barely clocked the iced *Happy Birthday Kate* inscription and array of candles before the *pièce de résistance* came. For as long as Kate lived, she would never work out how she did it but the nymph exhaled and lit the candles with her breath of fire.

To see the awed wonder on Kate's face made the hours Leander was forgoing that could have been spent in bed with her worth it. To have those jade eyes lock with his and feel the emotion shining from them…

She kissed him on the mouth. 'Thank you,' she said reverently, squeezing his fingers threaded through hers.

He kissed her back. 'My pleasure. Blow your candles out.'

Smoothing her hair away from her face, she extinguished the candles with one long breath then beamed at him and shook her head. 'How did you do all this?'

He gave a modest shrug that made her laugh. 'However you pulled it off, thank you.'

'I don't sleep as much as you,' he teased by way of explanation.

Her eyes gleamed. 'Then you must be running on no sleep at all.'

'The time we've had together has been worth any lost sleep.'

'I'll drink to that.' She lifted her cocktail to him.

Clinking his champagne to it, they finished their drinks in unison.

Glasses placed back on the table, Leander covered her hand and leaned his face close to hers. 'I wanted to give you a night to remember me by.' As he spoke, the sinking sensation in his stomach of earlier returned and it took all his control not to let his fingers tighten their grip on her delicate hand the way they reflexively wanted to.

Soon, this delicate hand would be working on giant apes and the hardworking, learned brain in Kate's beautiful head fully focused on her orphaned orange patients, and he, Leander, would be nothing but a distant memory to her.

He'd never felt the need to create memories with anyone before.

The lightness of her features dimmed a touch before she laughed. 'Then consider your plan a success because this is easily the best night out I've ever had and hands down the best birthday.'

All around them, the crowd rose, clapping and whistling enthusiastically as the performers took to the stage for the adulation and applause they'd worked so hard for, and Kate rose with them. Putting her fingers in her mouth, she wolf-whistled loudly and grinned widely at Leander's admiration, her grin almost splitting her face when he put his own fingers in his mouth and followed suit.

The giddy joy of the evening had turned into a fizzing sensation in her veins, and when Leander asked if she wanted to check out the private nightclub on the top floor and she glanced at the time and saw they still had a maximum twelve hours left together, she happily clutched his hand and walked with him back into the reception and up the cantilevered stairs.

The top floor was a warren of corridors and doors but the nightclub was easy to find by following the throbbing music.

Kate could feel the throbs deep in her fizzing veins

and when they entered the darkened room with its glamorous maroon and gold sensual vibe, and they both drank a glass of champagne before heading onto the hardwood floor, she wound her arms around Leander's neck and thought that if she hadn't had that minor panic attack before her final exams and begged off that night out with Helena and so met Leander back then, her life might have taken a very different direction.

He wouldn't have been promised to Helena then. Kate would have met him safe in the knowledge that Helena was playing cupid. Her time at university almost over, she would have looked at him with her mind already open to possibilities, and she'd have been sunk. She saw that clearly. If she'd met Leander back when Helena had tried to fix them up, she would have found him irresistible from the off. She saw clearly, too, that if he'd fixed those dark brown eyes on her the way they were fixed on her now, she would have fallen for him. He would have filled her opened mind to the point where he was all she could think about and she would have failed her finals.

And if he'd taken her dancing and held her the way he was holding her now, with the scent of his warm skin and cologne darting through her senses, she would have fallen in love with him and given up her dreams of Borneo to be his for ever.

CHAPTER TEN

THE DANCE FLOOR of the private nightclub was packed. Leander wasn't complaining. It meant he was forced to keep Kate and her hot little body close.

With their bodies grinding together to the deep R&B beats pulsing through the floor and Kate's arms hooked around his neck, arousal thrummed strongly in him.

Arousal always thrummed with Kate.

He could do nothing to stop it firing into his loins.

Tightening the clasp on her bottom, he ground her against him, letting her feel his hardness.

Her lips parted in a throaty exhale, the jade of her eyes melting with the same heat that heightened the colour on her cheeks. Fingers of one hand slipped under the collar of his shirt, the other skipping down his arm and tightening around his back.

Eyes and pelvises locked, their bodies continued the sensual grind to the music, desire flowing in a current that grew stronger with every passing beat.

Theós, he'd never known it was possible to want someone so much, for arousal to infect every atom of your body, for the want to multiply with every coupling. Never known he was susceptible to addiction.

Two weeks ago he'd collected Kate from his family's

airfield. The roof of his car had been down. Helena had sat in the front, Kate in the back. Kate had poked her head between them and asked him to turn the music up because a song was playing that she liked. Before they'd had a proper conversation they'd sung along, badly, to a tune he knew he would spend the rest of his life thinking of Kate whenever he heard it. By the time they'd arrived at his family's home, a strong friendship had established itself.

He'd never had that with a woman before. Helena didn't count because Helena was like family to him.

He'd been addicted to Kate's company before he was even aware of wanting her. He'd not allowed himself to see her as a woman because she was only there to act the role of maid of honour for his fake marriage and then when the blinkers had come off his eyes as Dimitri had leered all over her, the depth of his want had scared the hell out of him.

He could never have imagined those two short and yet so long weeks ago that he would find himself addicted to making love to her. Addicted to the sound of her voice, her laugh, her smile. Kate Hawkins touched something in him that no one had touched before and when her nails dug into his neck and she rose onto her toes to breathily whisper in his ear, 'Is there somewhere private we can go?' the pulse that shot through him almost brought him to his knees.

Spearing her hair, he gazed deep into her eyes. The meaning of her words reflected in their liquid depths.

Hands clasped tightly, desire thrumming like an infection in his blood, he led her through the heaving bodies on the dance floor and out of the nightclub room. The first two doors in the corridor were locked. The third opened into an empty, perfumed, sensuous cloakroom with a maroon leather sofa and mirrored walls.

The burning ache inside Kate meant she didn't hesitate. Locking the door, she pushed Leander against the wall and pulled his head down to her. Devouring his mouth with all the passion she possessed…she felt like *she* was possessed…she yanked his shirt free and set to work on freeing him. The moment his erection was released she dropped to her knees, gripped the base and closed her lips around him.

His groan of pleasure fed the ache in her.

Too big to fit whole in her mouth, she used her hand along with her tongue and lips to pleasure him, thrilling at his moans and the way his big hands held her head, the pads of his fingers clasping her skull without restricting her. His groan when she cupped his balls was guttural. Lifting her stare, she found his hooded eyes on her, his features ablaze.

'*Theós*, Kate, what are you doing to me?' he muttered hoarsely before closing his eyes and throwing his head back.

Loving you, she would have replied if her mouth hadn't been full.

Loving Leander. The most natural, beautiful, intoxicating feeling in the world. What he'd done for her that night, the effort he'd gone to…

This might be the last chance she'd have to show what it all meant to her. What *he* meant to her.

He meant everything. For Kate, Leander had become everything.

How was she supposed to say goodbye to him? She

couldn't. It couldn't end like this. There had to be a way...

Although Kate had pleasured Leander with her mouth before, it had never felt like this, like the pleasure could split him into atoms. Release had never felt so necessary but as heady as it felt to reach climax this way, there was no single pleasure greater than finding release buried inside her.

Sensing the point of no return speeding towards him, he tightened his grip on her head and tilted her face. 'Come here,' he said thickly.

Her arms were wound back around his neck and her hot mouth on his in moments.

Twisting her around so it was Kate's back to the wall, he slid a hand up her thigh and clasped her bare bottom.

Theós, and he'd thought he'd been close to coming before?

'No underwear?'

She grinned into his mouth before her tongue continued its dance with his.

He didn't hesitate. Lifting her up, he thrust straight into the tight confines of her sticky heat.

Her legs wrapped around his waist, Kate closed her eyes and clung tightly to him as he pounded into her, softly moaning as she extracted every ounce of the pleasure Leander was giving them both.

So hot and ready was she for him that her climax came quickly and she clung even tighter, closing her eyes as the waves of ecstasy shot through her, trying to drown out the thought that it was now Sunday and that very soon she would have to say goodbye to all of this.

She would have to say goodbye to the love of her life.

* * *

Kate flopped into Leander's arms in the back of the car and blew a lock of hair off her face.

What a night. The most fun, magical night of her life. The best birthday of her life.

Shifting to make herself comfortable, she nestled her head under his chin and stroked the hand resting under her breasts. She closed her eyes and expelled a contented sigh. His breath was warm in her hair. She could feel the rhythmic thumps of his heart through her back...

'Wake up, sleepyhead, we're home.'

Blinking herself back to life, she jerked upright and was astounded to find they'd reached the top of Leander's private drive.

In another blink, all the joy and contentment drained from her.

She'd just wasted twenty minutes with Leander sleeping. A quick look at her watch showed there were only eight hundred minutes left. Her car was collecting her at ten a.m. It had just turned two.

'Take a shower with me?' he asked knowingly after they'd stepped inside and he'd thrown his phone into his study.

She tried to coax her lips into the beaming smile that had been ever present since she'd made the decision to stay, but this time it was an effort. Making her legs bounce up the stairs to his bedroom was an effort. The only thing that was no effort at all was stripping herself naked, stepping into Leander's walk-in shower and making love to him. This time she tried to draw the pleasure out for as long as she could but her body was so responsive to his touch that her climax came as quickly as it had in the nightclub…and when it did come, the usual separation from her body failed to happen and instead of crying out her bliss she found herself pressing her mouth tightly against his neck to stop herself from crying tears.

After he'd wrapped her in a big fluffy towel and carried her to his bed, they made love again, and even though the pleasure was drawn out this time and her climax as powerful as she'd ever experienced, still she couldn't find the separation she so desperately sought, still she fought back tears.

The worst bit was afterwards, lying in Leander's arms, exhaustion trying to lull her into wasting more of her precious time with him in sleep.

Rubbing at her tired eyes, she sat up. 'Can I have a coffee?'

His smile was half sad, half knowing. 'Extra strong and extra sweet?'

Her heart filling that he knew she needed the caffeine and sugar dose to stave off the sleepiness, she nodded.

The coffee was delivered to Leander's room soon after. The night's weather was for once relatively balmy so they took it out onto his balcony, Leander in a pair of shorts he hadn't bothered doing the button up on and Kate in one of his sweaters that, like all the other items of his clothing she'd borrowed, she had no intention of giving back to him.

She would take every memento she could. She might make a shrine to him with it all, she thought, trying to jolly herself along with absurd thoughts.

The balcony had a small round iron table and two chairs on it. Sitting beside him, she slung her legs over his lap and fingered her earrings. At least she would always have something of Leander as a part of her, she told herself valiantly, then looked out over the black sky and the dotted white crests of the ocean reflecting off the stars, and breathed in the salty but sweet night air. The ocean was calm that night, the usually loud crash of waves hitting the beach muted.

Not even Leander's hand stroking her thigh could soothe the crash of Kate's heart hitting her ribs or stop the hand holding her coffee cup from shaking.

This would be the last time she'd share the same night sky as him. When the sun rose it would be the last day-break she'd share with him.

How could she bear it?

She'd thought she was prepared but now, with time picking up speed and the moment of her departure less than six hours away...

Time was slipping away from her and with every second that passed, the ache in her heart spread.

'You're very quiet,' Leander observed. Kate hadn't spoken a word since they'd sat down and was now on her second cup of coffee. There was a tension in her body that had never been there before.

She finished her drink and leaned over to put the cup on the table. 'Just exercising my brain cells,' she said, mimicking his earlier comment. If the night wasn't so still and Leander so attuned to her, he wouldn't have noticed the tiny choke in her voice.

Gently lifting her chin with his finger, he gazed down into eyes that shone with misery.

For a long moment they just stared at each other and then her pretty heart-shaped chin wobbled and a tear rolled down her cheek. 'I can't do this,' she whispered with a quiet sob.

Leander closed his eyes and pulled in a breath as he wrapped his arms around her. Kissing the top of her silky hair, he kept his mouth there and fought the swell of emotions her tear had let loose in him.

For another long moment they stayed locked as they were, with Kate's wet cheek against his chest and her small hand gripping his bicep, Leander's mouth on her head and his hands stroking her back. Her slender body was trembling.

A long time passed before she disentangled herself to look back at him. It was as if her whole face had crumpled. 'How am I supposed to say goodbye to you? I *can't.*'

The pain in his chest was like nothing he'd felt before. 'You can and you will. It has to be this way.'

More tears filled her eyes and she shook her head. 'It *doesn't.*'

'It does. We always knew it would have to end.' They'd been over before they'd even started.

Her voice was barely audible. 'I didn't know it would hurt so much.'

He hadn't known either.

Lightly, tenderly, he stroked her cheek. 'It hurts now but in a few days you'll be in Borneo. This is it, Kate. Your dream is coming to life, and when you're there you'll be so busy that the pain will fade to nothing.'

'Is that how it was for you when you left your brother?' she whispered.

The pain in his chest sharpened. 'That was different, and I didn't leave Leo.' Ultimately, Leo had left *him.*

Her swimming eyes held his before she blinked sharply and her back straightened. 'I can wait for you.'

Unsure what she was suggesting, he stared into her eyes.

Fevered animation suddenly lit her face. 'The two things stopping us being together are your promise to Helena and me moving to Borneo. I don't have to go to Borneo. Well, I do, but I don't have to stay. You need to go back to Greece and play the role of Helena's husband and help her get her inheritance but that'll take a few months to sort out, which is enough time for the charity to find a replacement for me, and then we can—'

Hardly able to believe what she was saying, he cut her off. 'Kate, stop.'

'But this is the perfect solution, don't you see? Helena will be happy for us, we both know that, and I'll still get a few months in Borneo and then—'

'Are you seriously suggesting that you would give up the job you've spent your whole life working for, for *me*?'

Jade eyes bright, she nodded.

Nausea rolled violently in his guts. God help him, she *was* serious.

Thinking hard and quickly through the nausea and the roar of blood in his head, Leander tried to find the angle needed to make Kate see that what she was suggesting was impossible.

She was prepared to give up everything for him. Give up everything for the man who'd destroyed his own brother in pursuit of his own selfish needs.

He could not let her do that.

'And your family?' he asked, stalling.

'They will understand.'

'Kate…' He filled his lungs with air and hardened himself to speak the words that would set the ball rolling for the first unselfish act he would make in his life. 'You can't do that.'

'I promise you, if I'm happy then they're happy.' That was one thing Kate was quite sure of. 'They made all those sacrifices for me because they love me and want me to be happy.' It had been her own fears of wasting their sacrifices that had driven her forwards when she would otherwise have given up. Thanks to them, she'd reached the finish line of her marathon. The destination she took now didn't have to be fixed in stone. 'And I'm sure they'd secretly be happier if I got a job somewhere a little less remote. I can start my own small practice or work for another zoo or—'

'Have you forgotten my aversion to long-term relationships?' Leander cut in. 'You would be throwing away your dreams for a man who doesn't want to make a commitment to anything permanent.'

Confusion clouded her beautiful features. 'But…' Her voice trailed away for a moment. 'Don't you want to try? There's lots of ways we can make it work. I'd give up Borneo for you but there could be a way for us to be together without me having to do that, and—'

Loathing himself for the hurt he was inflicting on her, a hurt that lanced his own heart, Leander had no choice but to inflict more of it. 'What we have shared these last few days has been great, but I haven't said anything that would make you think I want more than this.'

The last of the brightness and animation vanished. Her voice was stark. Bewildered. 'You're happy to never see me again?'

He couldn't tell her a bare-faced lie of that magnitude. 'I wouldn't say I was *happy* about it.'

The bewilderment of her voice was mirrored in her eyes. 'Then what? Why are you being like this?'

'We became lovers knowing—both of us—that our time here was all we could have.'

'That was then, and you can't expect me to believe after everything we've shared that you're happy for us to be over.'

'I just said I wasn't happy about it, but lust is a powerful emotion.'

She flinched as if he'd physically wounded her. 'Lust?'

'Lust,' he confirmed firmly, confirming it to them both. Leander's feelings for Kate were stronger than anything he'd believed it was possible to feel and he'd known from the moment they became lovers that saying goodbye to her would be a wrench, but that wasn't reason enough to let her throw away her life's work on something that would never last and for a man like him, someone selfish, who put his own needs and wants above those he loved. 'And the lust between us is strong. You're only feeling like this because our time together has been short and we haven't had the chance to work it out of our systems. There is no way to make it work between us that doesn't involve one of us giving up the things most precious to us and the end result would still be the same, whichever one of us made the sacrifices necessary—our desire for each other coming to a natural end. I'm not built for sustaining a relationship.'

He watched the colour drain from her face and thought he had never hated himself so much.

There was truth in being cruel to be kind, he thought grimly. And truth in the truth hurting.

'You don't mean that,' she whispered.

'I do mean it. You know me, Kate. You know the kind of man I am. I am sorry if your feelings have changed, but mine haven't. I think the world of you but we wouldn't have a future together even if Borneo wasn't a factor.'

CHAPTER ELEVEN

KATE HAD TO fight the painful ripples of her thundering heart to focus on what was radiating from Leander's eyes. There was a hardness in them she hadn't seen since the days before they'd become lovers. It was a hardness he'd deliberately adopted to drive her away. If not for her tripping over, he would have succeeded. She would not let him succeed now.

She couldn't. Just to imagine it…

'I do know the kind of man you are,' she said slowly, not dropping her stare, knowing the second she lost her focus then the panic that had been building inside her since they'd arrived back at his home would take control of her. It had already come close to doing just that and with time accelerating at the same rate as the panic, she knew she had to keep her head together and fight, however hard, for both their sakes. 'And that's why I don't believe you.'

His jaw tightened, an edge coming into his voice. 'As you pointed out less than a week ago, I'm known as Leander the Lothario for a reason.'

She covered his hand and meditatively said, 'You ran away from Greece and your wedding to Helena because of your feelings for me.'

His hand tensed beneath her touch. The edge deepened. 'I didn't run away. I needed time and space to get my head together.'

'Because of your feelings for me.'

The bones of his jaw were straining against his stubbly skin. 'No, for my conscience. How could I make vows to someone if it was the maid of honour I wanted to bed?'

If she wasn't feeling so wretchedly sick, she would laugh. 'Your conscience didn't stop you agreeing to marry Helena to begin with though, did it? It didn't bother you that you would be making vows that were lies. You thought it would be *fun* to marry her, and let's be brutally honest here, you've bedded so many women that I'd be a fool if I thought I was the only woman attending the wedding you would have taken up with given the chance.'

Yanking his hand away, he pushed her legs off him and got abruptly to his feet. 'I'm trying to do the right thing here, Kate,' he said, pacing away from her. 'I would give anything to have more time with you, but our time has run out and now we must go our separate ways. You need to accept that.'

'How can I?' she asked starkly. Rising unsteadily to her own feet, she fought with everything she had to keep the panic controlled and her voice calm. 'The thought of leaving you behind and never seeing you again is *killing* me and I know it's hurting you too.'

He lifted his head and breathed in deeply through his nose. 'Nothing lasts for ever, not hurt and not lust. Lust always burns itself out.'

'We feel more for each other than lust and you know it.'

Features unreadable, he opened the patio door. 'I

think it's time to end this conversation before words are said that cannot be taken back.'

'We are way past that point, Leander. The toothpaste has already been squeezed out.'

He moved so swiftly that he caught her off-guard, one moment standing at the threshold of his bedroom, the next his hands on her shoulders, leaning down so his taut face was right against hers. 'I don't want to hurt you, Kate,' he said roughly, nostrils flaring, 'but when you leave here, that is it for us. You have to accept it. Move on and embrace your new life—God knows you deserve it after all those years of hard work.'

Seeing the implacability in his eyes shifted something in Kate. All these hours, time had been slipping away from her and now it was Leander himself. For the first time she understood on a cellular level that she was losing him and when he let go of her shoulders and made to step away, desperation had her snatching hold of his wrist. 'Stop making it sound as if you're doing me a favour and that I'm the one who needs to be all reasonable and accepting when you're the one who won't accept the truth. You *know* we've found something special—'

'Oh, I know it, do I?' Leander interrupted as blood that had been slowly filling with something that felt very much like fury at Kate's refusal to accept things the way they were meant to be suddenly surged to his head. He had done nothing wrong except fail to follow some sad script Kate had written in her head where she expected him to declare his undying love and embrace a future he had never wanted and had never lied about not wanting. 'Did sharing my bed give you magical mind-reading abilities?'

Her hold on his wrist tightened and her despairing

face drew even closer. 'I don't need magical powers to know you've spent so many years hiding from human relationships that you'd rather throw away what we have than deal with your feelings for me.'

He only realised his hands were still clasping her shoulders when he had to fight to stop himself from shaking them. 'You don't know what you're talking about. I've never hidden from anything in my life.'

A visible shot of anger merged with the despair. 'You've been hiding from emotions since you were eighteen and told Leo you weren't going to join the business with him,' she said, disbelief in her voice. 'You waited until the last minute to throw that bombshell at him and because you knew how much it would devastate him, you ran away rather than deal with the wreckage that *you* created, and you've been running ever since. You wouldn't even go home when the business was in trouble and he needed you most...'

'He didn't *want* me to go home,' he reminded her angrily.

'Stop lying to yourself,' she cried. 'He didn't need your help but he needed *you*—just you, and if you would just take your blinkers off for two minutes you'd see that you need him too. But you've been so intent on proving to yourself that you don't need anyone and that you're more than just one of the Liassidis twins and that breaking your own twin's heart was worth it, that you won't admit how much you miss him or admit that you've effectively shut out anyone from getting close to you again. Properly close, I mean. Only people like Helena are safe for you to love because they don't expect more than you're prepared to give.'

The dark, dangerous fury on Leander's face, an expression far beyond anything she'd seen before, was enough to make a sane person quail but in that moment, Kate was far from sane. It felt like only minutes ago that he'd been making love to her in the shower, only seconds since he'd tenderly wrapped a big fluffy towel around her, a mere beat since he'd touched the diamond studs in her ears and then kissed her as if she were the most precious thing in his world.

'If I hadn't come with an end date attached, you would never have made love to me,' she continued, uncaring that she was close to shouting now. 'You'd have carried on running because that's what you were doing when you escaped from Greece and broke your promise to Helena and then treated me so cruelly—running from your feelings for me. Well, I've spent my whole life running too, so damn determined to be a vet and fulfil a dream that came to me when I was a *child* and so frightened of letting my family down after everything they'd done for me that the only friendship I ever properly embraced until you came along was with Helena. Learning was so hard for me and I was so frightened of anything distracting me like it did with Euan that I developed a tunnel vision I didn't even realise I'd become trapped in. *You* smashed that tunnel down, Leander, and for the first time I can see how dreams can voluntarily be broken and discarded because being loved by you is the best feeling in the whole world. But now I ruddy well wish I hadn't tripped on that stupid step because tripping pushed me into falling in love with you and now I've got to face the rest of my life knowing the love of my life is at heart a selfish bastard who—'

Kate's unplanned diatribe came to a sudden halt

when Leander clasped the hand gripping his wrist and brought his face so close to hers that the tips of their noses touched. 'If you'd been paying the slightest bit of attention you would know I'm not a man to break dreams over,' he said quietly but harshly. 'I didn't ask for your love. I didn't ask for any of this. I came here to get my head together without any distractions so I could fulfil my promise to Helena. You forced your way in and refused to leave. If you hadn't lived your life shunning relationships you would know that sharing a man's bed doesn't make him magically fall in love with you, and now I think it's best that you leave.'

Prising her fingers off his wrist, he dropped her hand and stepped into his room.

Moments later she heard him speaking on the intercom. 'Please bring a car to the front. Miss Hawkins is leaving.'

The white noise in her head was so dizzyingly powerful that she had to grab the side of a chair to stop herself from falling.

Somehow, she managed to stagger inside.

Seeing Leander shrugging a shirt on through the open door of his dressing room made her rapidly bruising heart thump painfully. He'd already replaced his shorts with a pair of black jeans.

'Don't do this,' she whispered, clutching the door frame.

Fingers working deftly on the shirt buttons, he fixed his implacable stare on her. 'Get your stuff together. Mason is going to drive you to the airfield. I suggest you call the flight crew so they can prepare.'

'Please, Leander.'

Leander blurred Kate's tear-stained face from his vision. He'd always known their parting would be painful and had prepared himself mentally for it. The only aspect he hadn't foreseen and prepared for was Kate's devastation. *Theós*, it hurt to witness it, hurt enough that he already forgave her ridiculous amateur psychoanalysis of him.

One day she would understand that he'd acted for the best, that he'd been thinking about her best interests as much as his own.

'Assure Helena that I will be back in Greece at some point tonight,' he said stiffly as he tucked the shirt into his jeans.

'Leander, *please.*'

Clenching his jaw at her audible pain, he strode past her, making sure not a cell of his body brushed against her. From his bedside table he picked up his thick Omega watch and secured it to his wrist. 'I have work I need to catch up on before I leave.'

'*Leander.*'

Leander caught Kate's stare one last time. 'I wish you well with your new life. Embrace it, Kate, and forget about me.'

And then he left his room and strode the mezzanine to the stairs. On the ground floor he entered his study for the first time since he'd arrived in Marina Sands and locked the door behind him.

Only when he'd sunk into his office chair did he expel the breath he hadn't even been aware of holding and cradle his head in his hands.

Cheek pressed against the car window, Kate cuddled her handbag tightly to her heaving chest. Tears she had no control over blinded her so greatly she didn't notice they'd left Leander's land until they'd made the turn onto the main road and flashing lights broke the darkness. The driver beeped his horn at a driver trying to squeeze into a gap between vehicles lined on the verge and making a right mess of it, but she didn't have the energy to care about what they were there for or care why some of their owners had flashed their cameras at her car.

She'd never imagined pain like this existed.

Had she really got it all wrong? Had she only imagined that Leander's feelings for her ran as deeply as hers did for him? Had it really been nothing but naive wishful thinking on her part?

The road her driver was taking her on that early morning was the coastal route. On the horizon, the first glimmer of light.

Closing her eyes, she breathed deeply in a vain effort to stifle the agony ripping through her that Leander had snatched their last sunrise together away from her.

He hadn't even left his study to say goodbye. The last words he'd said to her were *'forget about me'*.

How could she do that when he'd brought her more joy than she'd experienced during the rest of her life combined?

She couldn't.

Spotting a sign for Marina Sands Boulevard through the car's headlights only hit her with memories of their one shopping trip. He'd sneaked away to buy her the earrings...

The earrings were still in her ears. She was still wearing his sweater. She'd failed to take any of her other mementoes. Had forgotten all about them. The agony of knowing she would never see him again had taken her over. She'd barely made it through the conversation with the flight crew, and thinking of this came with a vague recollection of seeing a missed call and voicemail notification on her phone.

Snatching at the needed distraction, Kate rubbed furiously at her eyes and pulled her phone out of her bag. The nausea that had been simmering in her belly bubbled higher when she realised the missed call was from Helena and that it had been left six hours ago at midnight.

She put the phone to her ear.

From the first spoken syllable, she knew something terrible had happened.

'Kate, the press know.' Helena's panicked voice rang out. 'Please, *please* be careful. They're everywhere and they'll be looking for you and Leander too...' A sound like a sob being stifled. 'I'm so sorry for dragging you into this. I'm sorry for everything. I should have known...' Another stifled sob. 'Please forgive me.'

The voicemail ended.

Leander knew he shouldn't watch Kate being driven away from him. He knew it and still he did it, standing at the window long after the car's lights had disappeared, still standing there as the first rays of the dawn's light penetrated the darkness. For all he knew, he could have stood there for ever, haunted by Kate's complete desolation, if his phone hadn't rung loudly.

It was the ringtone he used for his PA.

No point in ignoring it. Today he must return to his real life and fulfil the promise he'd made.

There was a lethargy in his limbs that made him fumble to answer it and which carried through to his tired voice. 'Yes, Sheree?'

'Oh, thank God. I've been trying to reach you for hours.'

'Have you?' he asked dully. How many hours had passed since he'd put his phone in the study when he'd returned to the house so there was no chance of his last night with Kate being interrupted? It felt like a lifetime. It felt like no time at all.

Sheree cut straight to the chase. 'There are date and time-stamped pictures of you and a woman who isn't Helena kissing in a theatre. They were taken last night.'

He pinched the bridge of his nose. 'Tell the press it's Leo.'

'They know it's you. A Greek blogger has been touring the Californian homes of famous Greeks for a series he's doing.'

'What?'

'You know the kind of blog I mean.' He dimly imagined the eyeroll she made at this. 'He located your home and it's your bad luck that he found it and was about to try his luck and explore the grounds when you drove past him with a blonde lady. He thought the place would be empty, seeing as you're supposed to be in Greece on your honeymoon.'

Leander swore under his breath.

'He followed you into the city last night and when he saw where you'd gone, found the staff entrance and bribed an usher on a break to get pictures of the two of you. The pictures were enough for the press to run with it. They've been looking at flight manifests and know that you're the Liassidis twin in California and that Leo is still in Greece. They know Leo is masquerading as you. The only way to deny this is to play it that Leo used your passport to enter the US, which is highly likely to be a federal offence.'

'We can't do that,' he said automatically. The weight that had been in his heart since he'd watched Kate drive away had sunk to his toes and filled his every crevice.

In one night he'd destroyed the three people who meant the most to him. If he'd ever held an iota of hope that he and Leo could one day rebuild their relationship then this would be its death knell. He doubted Helena would forgive him either. He wouldn't forgive himself if he was in their shoes.

This was everything Kate had warned him about.

It was almost ironic that he hadn't been recognised as himself but through his home.

'I've got extra security coming to you. They should be with you any minute.'

'Thank you. See that Kate has security when she arrives back in England.'

'That's the blonde?'

His hackles rose at this casual, dismissive observation. 'Yes,' he answered shortly, well aware the dismissive observation came from Sheree having spent a decade dealing with a myriad of Leander's lovers who never stuck around long enough for her to get on first name terms with. 'I'll send you her details. Tell them it might be necessary to travel to Borneo with her.'

He couldn't be with her but he could keep her safe until she reached the safety of the Borneo rainforest.

No sooner had he put the phone down than it rang

again. A different ringtone. One he'd programmed when he'd bought the phone new but had never rung.

It was the ringtone for his brother.

For the first time in five years, Leo was calling him.

Kate couldn't bring herself to leave the car. The jet's steps had been lowered, two members of the cabin crew at the opened door ready to welcome her in, and all she could do was stare at the photos of herself and Leander sharing a kiss and the headlines screaming about the Liassidis twins' deception.

If she'd thought she felt sick before, it had nothing on how she felt now, but now it wasn't herself she felt wretched for. All her tears were for Helena, the loveliest, kindest friend an eleven-year-old girl thrust into a brand-new overwhelming world could have wished for and whose steadfast loyalty and unconditional love had been a mainstay of her life ever since.

Just as she was about to press the button to call her back, the phone rang in her hand. It was Helena.

For a moment she was too choked to speak.

'Kate?'

Hating to hear the hoarseness in her best friend's voice, she swallowed hard. 'I'm so sorry. I've ruined everything.' And with that, she burst into tears.

'Don't cry,' Helena beseeched. 'Please, Kate, don't cry. It's not your fault. This is all on me. I begged you to find him when—'

'You *didn't.*'

'I *did.* I was so wrapped up in my own problems that I ignored the signs that something was happening between you and sent you to him.'

'Nothing was going on before the wedding, I swear. I never meant for anything to happen.'

'I know you didn't,' Helena said softly.

'He's coming back to you today, and—'

'I can't be married to Leander, not now. Tell him to stay in California. It's a feeding frenzy here and it's going to get worse before it gets better because I can't do this any more. I'm calling a press conference. There's been so many secrets and lies and so many people hurt that I can't do it any more. I need to tell the truth and—'

Panic scratched at her throat. 'Helena, *don't*! You'll lose—'

'I *have* to. I have to put things right. I've hurt so many people.'

Kate's heart ached to hear the pain in her best friend's voice. 'You haven't. You tried so hard to do the right thing and it was for the best of reasons. I'm the one who's screwed everything up.'

'What happened was inevitable. You and Leander are meant to be together.'

She had to summon every ounce of courage to whisper the admission, 'It's over.'

There was silence down the phone then, 'Oh, my love, I'm sorry.'

Something in the way Helena said this sparked an understanding in Kate that made the ache in her heart sharpen acutely. 'Oh, Helena. Did it happen for you as well?'

A barely audible, 'Yes. And it's over too. I wasn't enough for him.'

Kate closed her eyes and sighed, wishing with all her aching heart that she could magic herself to Greece and tightly embrace the woman who was as good as a sister to her.

'Helena?' she said into the silence.

'I'm here.'

'Were the Liassidis twins born unfeeling bastards or is it something they cultivated individually as they got older?'

Helena's surprised snort of laughter triggered Kate's own laughter and though the laughter from them both was laced with a huge dollop of pain, Kate felt the better for it.

'You know what, when all this is sorted I'm going to take you up on your offer and fly out to Borneo...' A touch of alarm came into Helena's voice. 'Tell me you're still going.'

Kate sighed heavily. What else could she do? Throw away her life's plans for a selfish man who didn't want her love? 'I'm still going, and it would be the best thing ever to have you come see me there.'

'I'm not going to kiss any orangutans,' Helena warned.

'Good, because that's my job, remember?'

The silence after the next bout of laughter had a poignancy to it. It was time to say goodbye and face their individual demons.

'Are you sure you want to do this?' Kate asked.

'No, but I have to.'

'I wish I could be there to hold your hand through it.'

'I wish you could be too. Have a safe flight to Borneo.'

'I will.' She closed her eyes and said goodbye in their own language. 'Loves ya.'

'Loves ya too.'

The call ended, Kate finally got out of the car and

climbed the steps onto the jet that would fly her away from Leander.

Taking her seat, she breathed in deeply and looked out of the window. The sun had fully risen and she welcomed its soft golden rays on her face. It gave her the strength she needed to make one last communication with Leander.

CHAPTER TWELVE

LEANDER FOUND A channel showing the press conference—a whole host of European channels had decided to cut their planned broadcasts short to televise it live—and tried not to look at the sofa Kate had spent her first two nights under his roof sleeping on.

While the Greek presenter gave an enthusiastic and highly speculative account of the 'Liassidis Twin Swap', Leander looked again at the message that had pinged in a short while ago.

The press know everything. Helena is going to hold a press conference and confirm the truth. Not sure when but very soon. Your husband services are no longer required. She says it's best you don't go back yet.

He thought back to that night in Athens. He'd insisted Kate store his number on her phone when they'd set off to the nightclub, just in case she became separated from the rest of them.

He cradled his head. He was still reeling from everything that had happened since the early hours. Leo's call had sent him spinning.

Theós, he'd never expected that. Leo calling. An unexpected outpouring Leander had been unprepared for.

He still couldn't get his head around it.

Strangely, there had been nothing satisfying in hearing his proud brother admit that he'd been wrong to behave the way he had. Nothing at all. Not when he had Kate's accusations about his part in their ongoing estrangement still ringing in his ears.

'Leo,' he'd said when his usually uncommunicative brother had paused for breath. 'Believe me, I appreciate what you're saying but right now isn't a good time for me. I'm sorry for dragging you into this mess and please, tell Helena that I'm sorry for letting her down.'

The silence that had followed this had been stark, reminding him that Leo had never enjoyed the easy friendship Leander had always shared with Helena. Not since Helena hit adolescence, in any case. Before then, Helena had followed them both around like a little puppy. That had been in the days when the Liassidis twins had been closer than borlotti beans from the same pod.

The only person he'd ever experienced a closeness like that with was Kate, who at that point would have been high in the air, flying away from him.

The blood whooshing in his head had increased to a roar, and he'd had to breathe deeply to cut through the silence and say, 'I need to go. When I come home, we'll talk properly. Okay?'

'Okay,' Leo had agreed slowly. 'I would like that.'

He'd swallowed a sharp pang. 'So would I.'

Now, minutes—or was it hours?—since that conversation and the magnitude of it had finally penetrated.

Leo had called him. Leo had reached out for the first

time in five years. More than that, he'd reached across the divide created fourteen years ago, *truly* reached out. As a brother. As a twin. As the other half of his coin.

What had happened to his brother to make him so reflective and actually reach out and say all he'd said? Something had happened. It must have done.

So lost was he in trying to remember everything his twin had said to him that he almost missed the start of the press conference. One look at Helena's drawn face filling the screen and suddenly it became clear to him what had happened to his brother and explained the stark silence that had followed Leander's first mention of Helena's name.

Helena had happened to him.

Just like Kate had happened to Leander.

Helena's statement was short but heartfelt, taking full responsibility for the Liassidis twins' deception. When she'd finished and the audience was invited to ask questions, Leander could watch no more and turned the television off.

He rubbed the back of his neck and expelled a long breath.

It wasn't fair for Helena to take all the blame. Whatever had subsequently happened between Leo and Helena, Leo had been an unwilling party in the whole affair. Leander was the one who'd enthusiastically agreed to the deception. The blame for the whole sorry situation lay with him too.

Leander carried his surfboard across the sand and was knee-deep in the ocean before setting it down and lying on it. The pull was strong and he paddled out with spray drenching him and his board rising and falling sharply with the motion. The latent violence tugging beneath him in that early morning surf didn't faze him. He welcomed it. He needed to feel something.

He'd been numb since he'd released a written statement shortly after watching Helena's press conference. He'd kept the statement itself short.

Helena is an honourable woman who was doing the wrong thing for the right reasons. I make no excuse for my own part in the deception. Leonidas is my twin and his actions were those of a brother protecting a brother. I request that people respect his and Helena's privacy, and also the privacy of Kate Hawkins who is blameless in all of this.

He knew from his parents, who'd been unable to conceal their bewilderment at the situation, that the media frenzy hadn't abated in Greece, but his security staff had been able to assure him that Kate had arrived in Borneo without any paparazzi following her.

His Californian home was still surrounded by them. He was too numb to care.

Trying to block his thoughts off, he chased a wave that surfed him back onto the beach and then paddled back out again. The wind was picking up. The size of the waves was increasing. Adrenaline was bound to start pumping soon.

How was she getting on? His discreet calls had revealed only that she'd made it to the remote orangutan orphanage safely and without being followed. He had no way of knowing how she was settling in. If she was pleased with her accommodation. How she was finding the food. How she was finding her colleagues. How she was finding her orange orphans. How she was finding the weather.

He shook water off his face and the image of Kate's face from his retinas. He was here to surf, not to think about the woman whose heart he'd broken.

He seemed to have made it a habit to break the hearts of the people who loved him the most. And Kate did love him. Loved him enough to give up her dreams for him.

His parents loved him too. He'd broken their hearts, not by refusing to join the family business but by moving continents. His mother had understood his reasons but that didn't mitigate the hurt he'd caused by leaving so suddenly and then expecting her to psychically know he was safe and well rather than checking in more than once a week to keep her worries for him to a minimum.

A larger wave was swelling, and he chased it. Judging when the time was right, he manoeuvred his feet onto the board and stood up, spreading his body weight to keep himself balanced.

As he rode the wave, he experienced a tiny shot of adrenaline but when the ride was over, his heart was barely pumping harder than it did at rest.

He let the swell carry him back out.

Leo loved him too and, until three days ago, Leo was the one he'd hurt the most. The price of Leander's freedom had been his brother's heart. And his own heart too.

For fourteen years he'd been the Leander he'd wanted to be. Fourteen years of living his life for his own pleasure, on his own terms, not having to consider anyone else's opinions or needs. They'd been good years in which he'd accumulated unimaginable wealth. And all to prove a point, not to Leo but to himself. To prove to himself that he didn't need Leo.

Just as Kate had intuited.

But all to prove to himself too that he didn't need Leo and that he didn't miss him when the truth was he'd missed him every minute of every day. When the truth was that he did need him.

Spotting a wave forming further out but just within his reach and paddling furiously towards it, he realised the numbness had gone. Realised it because he was suddenly acutely aware that the absence, which Leo's olive branch should have healed, had deepened into a pulsating open wound and, with it, Kate's devastated face when he'd told her to forget about him flashed before him.

The adrenaline he'd been seeking pumped hard, but it was the wrong adrenaline and at the moment he realised he'd mistimed his chase of the forming wave and instead of being on its open shoulder was in the impact zone, he saw another picture of Kate, in his Athens apartment, holding a cocktail and waving a joyful arm in the air as she sang along loudly and badly and gloriously to the music playing.

His last thought when the lip of the giant wave tipped over and slammed into him was that it had been the moment he'd fallen in love with her.

Dark eyes opened and locked onto Kate's face. She stroked the dear little head. 'You okay, little one?' she murmured.

Fingers so much like her own reached up for her.

'Just a minute longer,' she told her new charge, who'd

been given the name of Mari. Mari was a two-year-old orphan who'd arrived at the orphanage the day before, three weeks after Kate's arrival. Her history was a blank canvas, the assumption being that she'd been traded as a pet and then abandoned. That was the theory seeing as she'd been found in a box on a busy street in Kota Kinabalu, a coastal city surrounded by rainforest. Mari's guardian angel had reached out to Kate's charity, who'd swung straight into action. Within days she'd arrived at the sanctuary that would nurture her and teach her all the skills needed to be let out in the rainforest proper when she became full grown. At some point the poor mite had been bitten, likely by a stray dog, and infection had set in. Kate and her team had sedated her so she could clean the infection and given her a carefully measured dose of antibiotic. Just like with human children, orangutan infants had marvellous powers of recovery and she was confident that Mari would soon be playing in the nursery with all the other infants.

Once Mari's appointed carer had carried her to the special recovery room where she would be watched continuously to ensure she didn't rip off her bandage, Kate removed her mask, helped clear up, scrubbed her hands, then set off to do her final check of the day on her other inpatients, who currently ranged in age from six months to six years. Once she was satisfied that all was well, she headed outside to where the juniors were being led back from the rainforest canopy and a day of being taught how to climb trees, forage for ants and the like, and herded into their own special clearing filled with climbing and swinging equipment. Smiling broadly at Aishah, one of the carers, who currently had one of her charges clinging to her leg rather than walk himself, Kate waved flies and mosquitoes off her face and walked over to the accommodation block.

It was only once the sights and sounds—and smells, they were unavoidable—of the orphanage had faded that her own smile faded and her mood sank.

Being around the cheeky, irrepressible orangutans always lifted her spirits. Since Kate's quarantine had ended and she'd been allowed to start work properly, she'd worked her long shifts with a smile and gratitude. In her short time there, she'd been embraced as one of the team. If melancholy grabbed her, one look at the infants playing was enough to erase it.

Every step away from the sanctuary was like a slowly deflating puncture until she reached her tiny studio apartment and her mood would be completely flat.

Other than dining in the staff canteen—the staff apartments contained only a fridge and a microwave—she had no plans for the evening. No video calls with her family. No video call with Helena.

It still made her chest go cold to remember getting off the plane in the humid Borneo heat to a call from Helena where her friend had tentatively told her about Leander's near-death experience while surfing. She'd quickly reassured her that he was recovering well with nothing more serious than a bad concussion from where his board had hit his head. It had been his good fortune that local surfers he was friendly with had seen him in the ocean and had been paddling out to join him. They'd seen immediately that he was in trouble and rescued him.

The minute that call had ended, Kate had brought up

all the food she'd eaten on the plane and then physically shook for three hours.

In all their video calls since, Kate had refused outright to discuss Leander. She couldn't even bear to hear his name. Her family were forbidden from mentioning him too, or talking about Greece or California.

That evening, she had nothing to distract her from thinking about him.

She didn't *want* to think about him. She wasn't a masochist.

And she didn't want to look at the photos she'd taken of him during that wonderful week in Greece, before he'd gone cold on her. Despite knowing how unhealthy it was, the first thing she did once she'd trudged up the wooden steps and stepped into her apartment was curl up on the decades-old sofa and bring the pictures up.

It was a pattern she'd followed every working day since her arrival.

It didn't matter how much her head told her to follow Leander's advice and forget about him, her heart refused to let go. That was just a sad fact. As another sad fact of her life had been that to get the grades she'd needed meant working harder than everyone else, she knew the only way for her heart to let go and reach acceptance that she would never see him again was to work hard at it.

After scrolling blindly backwards and forwards through pictures of his gorgeous face for a good twenty minutes, she took a deep breath and straightened herself.

It was time.

She would never forget him if she had these photos as a constant reminder.

She brought the first picture up, a selfie of Kate, Helena and Leander leaning against the car he'd collected her from the airport in. Delete.

The next photo was another selfie. The three of them around the Liassidis family swimming pool. Delete.

The next was just Leander. He was walking towards Kate carrying a pitcher of sangria that she'd cheekily requested. The camera had captured the magnificence of his body and that devastating smile. Delete.

One by one, all the images of the man who'd turned his back on her love were erased. By the time she'd finished, the screen of her phone was soaked with tears and her heart was shredded.

It was a long time before she was able to bring herself to head to the canteen for her first meal of the day. Because that was something else she needed to work at. Eating. Her work clothes were already loose. She didn't have enough body fat on her to lose any more weight. She would force her appetite to come out of hibernation.

And she would let go of Leander.

Leander had travelled all over the world. He'd climbed mountains, skied mountains and trekked the Gobi Desert. Those were just the things he remembered off the top of his head. Even with the things that didn't immediately spring to mind, he had never been in an environment like this. Never felt the humidity actually soak into his skin. When they reached a huge clearing at the edge of the rainforest and he got out of the truck that had collected him from the airport, the noises assaulted his ears.

A tiny, formidable-looking woman with salt-and-pepper hair steamed over to him.

'Mr Liassidis?' she said in perfect English that contained only the trace of an accent and not the slightest trace of warmth.

'Call me Leander,' he said, extending his hand. 'You must be Yuna.' The woman who ran the orphanage.

She ignored his hand. 'That's me. Your documents.'

Prepared, he handed everything over. He would have been here weeks sooner if the concussion from his mistimed surf and then bureaucracy, not from the Malaysian government but the charity itself, hadn't held him up. This orphanage was too precious for them to risk allowing shortcuts of any kind. Only a sizeable donation had got the trustees onside. Yuna had been vocal in her resentment of his special treatment. If Leander wanted to see a member of her staff, then he should make private arrangements to meet at the house in a local town the staff used on their weekends off. As she'd then refused to tell him when Kate's weekend off was, he'd gone through every expected hoop to get this far.

Unhappily satisfied all was in order, she started walking. 'Remember, you must not enter any building our charges are in.'

Even though the sun was falling, there were plenty of workers around, all going about their business, and he followed Yuna past buildings of varying sizes that all buzzed with life and activity. If he wasn't feeling so sick with nerves, he'd find it fascinating.

The orphanage's buildings behind them, they followed a narrow path until they reached what looked like a low, wide temple.

'Wait here,' Yuna commanded. 'I shall see if she wants to see you.'

Leander clamped his lips together and gave a short

nod. That had been one of Yuna's many conditions. If Kate refused to see him, he would be escorted straight back to the truck.

Yuna disappeared around the side of the building and returned tight-faced.

His heart plunged. 'She won't see me?'

She shook her head. 'No, she wasn't in.'

The relief almost knocked him off his feet.

'She must be eating. Come.' And she set off again.

CHAPTER THIRTEEN

KATE SWIRLED NOODLES around her fork and, ignoring the expectant faces of two of her colleagues barely suppressing their laughter, popped it in her mouth. The chilli heat this time was instant.

Mouth on fire, she finished her glass of milk. 'You two are evil,' she seethed, only half joking.

Her photograph deleting spree meant she'd been the last to arrive in the canteen. The only main course left was the noodles with chicken and prawns and peanuts, which was absolutely delicious excepting the abundance of Thai chillies infused in it.

'More milk?' Stefan, the only other European who worked there, asked.

'Bring the cow,' she laughed, and added another forkful into her mouth.

So much for her not being a masochist!

But this was good. A little companionship and conversation and laughter. The days here were long and people rarely lingered after dinner, most grabbing their needed sleep. The nature of their jobs meant a full night's sleep wasn't guaranteed. Kate was looking forward to her first weekend off and the promise of a sightseeing trip with one of the nurses. Anything to fill her days and keep her brain busy. Stop her mind from taking over.

The main door opened and Yuna, Kate's slightly terrifying boss, walked in. She clocked Kate and zoomed over to her.

'You have a visitor.'

Kate stared at her blankly.

'A visitor,' Yuna repeated, this time more slowly. 'Shall I let him in? Or kick his ass back to the airport?'

Him?

Her stare zipped to the door ten feet from where she was sitting.

Standing at the threshold…

She shoved her chair back with such force it would have toppled if the wall hadn't been there to break its fall.

Leander knew he was breaking the cardinal rule. Yuna had been explicit. He must let Yuna ask Kate privately if she was willing to see him.

His legs had disobeyed before his brain realised what they were doing, and the first thing he'd seen looming through the opened door was Kate sitting with two men whose company she was clearly enjoying.

To see her animated face in the flesh after all this time had sucker-punched him.

It was the face he'd seen when he'd come round from his near drowning on the beach and known in that instant that he'd made the biggest mistake of his life.

The animation had fallen the instant she'd spotted Leander.

Yuna followed the direction of Kate's now-ashen face.

Features contorted with fury, she pointed a finger at him. '*You*. Do *not* move.'

To Kate she asked, 'Well?'

The two men Kate had been seated with had also risen and were flanking Kate and the diminutive boss, staring at Leander with the deepest suspicion. As they were barely taller than the women, the sight of them geeing themselves to square up to him would have been comical if he'd been focusing on anything but the face he'd missed more than it was possible to believe.

Forcing his body to remain at the threshold, he asked hoarsely, 'Can we talk?'

Talk, Kate thought dazedly. Leander wanted to talk. That was if it even was him. Wasn't it known that too high a dose of chillies could make a person hallucinate? It wasn't actually possible that the figure standing in the canteen doorway was Leander. People didn't just turn up here. This was a rainforest, for goodness' sake!

He'd told her to forget him.

'Can I kick him out or not?' Yuna asked impatiently.

Even though she knew this wasn't happening, Kate shook her head, at the same time grabbing Yuna's skinny wrist to keep herself anchored and hoarsely whispering, 'Please stay.'

The noodles she'd been eating were churning in her stomach, clashing with the violence of her heartbeats.

'You hear that?' Yuna taunted. 'She wants me to stay. So get on with it.'

There was something strangely reassuring in Yuna's protective stance and in the body language of the two men with them. Leander wouldn't allow himself to hope that he had a future with Kate. If he left Borneo with her deserved rejection ringing in his ears then at least he would have the comfort of knowing she was amongst people who would care and look out for her.

He had to clear his throat and then clear it again.

'Kate, I'm sorry. I'm here to beg you, on bended knee if that's what it takes for you to take me back.'

Even with the distance between them, he heard the whimper that came from her closed mouth. It was a sound that sliced through his heart.

'Since you've been gone…' He shook his head and breathed deeply. He could never explain in mere words the hole that existed in him. And then he sighed and filled his lungs with more of the humid air. 'I say *since you've been gone* but you only went because I pushed you away, and I pushed you away because I'm the biggest fool on this earth. I knew you were the best thing that had ever happened to me. I was too stupid to admit it to myself but deep in here…' He made a fist and pressed it to his heart. 'I knew I loved you.'

Her eyes widened.

'What I didn't know was that living without you would be such torture. It's a torture I deserve. I've hurt you so many times and all because I was too damned stubborn—and frightened—to accept that the life I'd built around my own needs and pleasures was crumbling around me. It started crumbling the moment you first jumped into the back of my car on the island and now it's nothing but ruins.'

Her hand fluttered to her mouth.

'I've always been selfish, Kate,' he admitted starkly, wishing he could peer deep into her brain and see what she was thinking. 'But you already know that. You've already accepted that. You see me exactly as I am and still you love me... Loved me.' He swallowed a lump that had lodged itself in his throat. 'You are the only person in the world I can't be selfish with. Your happiness is all that matters to me. You don't make me want to be a better man; I have no choice in it. To hurt you is to hurt myself. Since you've been gone...since I pushed you away,' he corrected himself, then grabbed the back of his head, trying desperately to find the words he needed to say before the fear gripping his heart and lungs took full control of him. 'Everything you said about my estrangement with Leo was true. I functioned for fourteen years without him and it's only now that he's back in my life that I can acknowledge just how badly I missed him in those years.' He attempted a smile. 'What you said about us being identically stubborn is also true.'

One of the first things Leander had done when he'd come round after his surfing accident was call his brother and apologise properly for the first time for leaving the way he had all those years ago and for being a selfish coward in the way he'd gone about leaving. With Leo insisting the blame lay with him and being adamant the deterioration of their relationship after the family business trouble was his fault, while Leander saw clearly now that it was his fault and that he should have gone home and insisted his brother lean on him for emotional support, the twins had been forced to agree that they had both played their part in the whole sorry mess and that it was the future that mattered now. A future as brothers. Twin brothers.

Who cared if people couldn't tell them apart? The one

person who mattered most knew with one glance that he was Leander. She saw *him*.

Soon, once everything with Kate was resolved for good or for ill, Leander would fly to his brother and they would sit down for the first time in too many years and share a beer together. Whether he would be able to taste the beer and take enjoyment in his brother's company all depended on what came next now.

'I could function without Leo, but I can't function without you. I don't just miss you, Kate.' Something hot was stabbing the back of his eyes. 'The world still turns but it turns without me, because without you in my life, there is nothing for me. My life belongs to you. I love you and I don't know how to live without you. I…' His voice cracked as suddenly it hit him that he really could walk out of this place and never see her again. That Kate, his beautiful, joyful, funny pixie princess might have already moved on emotionally. That he'd hurt her too deeply for her to be able to put her trust in him again.

He would have no one to blame but himself.

Kate had listened to Leander's almost rambling speech with the sensation that she'd stepped out of her body and was watching weightless from above, only her grip on Yuna's wrist stopping her from floating up to the sky. It had been all too incredible, and even as she'd listened to every word he said, a dazed voice had kept repeating in her ear that it couldn't be him.

It was the break in his voice that pulled her back down to the ground. A break that speared straight into her heart, and suddenly she saw him clearly. Leander.

Her Leander, the man who had lit her heart from that very first smile and switched on unimaginable passions and joy and a zest in her veins that had all dimmed into nothing without him.

Her Leander, looking utterly wrecked.

He'd lost weight. That wasn't stubble around his jaw but a thick, unruly black beard. His hair looked like it hadn't ever seen a comb. His eyes were those of a man who'd lost the ability to sleep.

Those eyes shone with tears.

Those eyes shone with agony.

Staring into them...

She saw it. The truth. It was right there, his heart shining through his tortured stare.

Leander had come to her.

There was a gentle push on her back. She didn't need it, or know or care who'd done it and didn't look to see. Her gaze was glued in its entirety to the man her heart had gift-wrapped itself for long before her head had realised it.

She walked to him with that floating sensation drifting through her again.

Leander couldn't breathe. Couldn't speak. Couldn't hear anything above the roar of noise in his head. Couldn't tear his gaze from the figure walking like a dream towards him. Diamond stud earrings glittered in her ears...

She reached him.

Her throat moved. Her chin wobbled. A tear spilled down her cheek.

For the longest time neither of them spoke.

Her throat moved again, and then her chest rose and fell like a sigh, and she put a trembling palm to his bearded cheek and quiveringly whispered, 'If you ever push me away again or run from me then I will rip your heart out with my hands.'

A scintilla of the weight compressing his lungs lifted.

Covering the hand against his cheek tightly, he nuzzled into it. 'Take it now. It's yours.'

Jade eyes fixed on his, she cupped the back of his neck with her other hand. 'For ever?'

He almost closed his eyes at the rush of emotions her touch on his neck evoked, but he kept his stare locked on hers, willing her to read the sincerity in them. 'It's yours, Kate, for as long as you want it.'

The tiniest curve tugged at the side of her mouth. 'I want it for ever.'

'You have it. My heart and my soul.' The soul she'd saved without even trying.

Faces inching closer, her stare bore into his for what seemed an eternity before the curve widened a little bit more and he felt it, felt Kate's heart and soul reaching out to meet his and fuse together, lifting the weight inside him in its entirety.

'I love you,' Kate breathed as their mouths brushed together, and as she was pulled into the deepest, sweetest and yet most passionate kiss of her life, the last shreds of her heart flew back together and knitted seamlessly into place, leaving her whole.

He loved her. Leander loved her.

An unsubtle cough behind them broke their mouths apart.

They'd both forgotten they had an audience.

Not loosening their hold on each other, they locked eyes again. Overwhelmed by all the emotion flowing through her, still only half believing that all this was really happening, that Leander did love her and that he'd come all this way for her, Kate giggled and tightened her grip around his neck. 'I love you,' she repeated.

'And I love you. Always, always.'

The unsubtle cough sounded again. 'I suppose this means I'm going to have to advertise for a new vet,' Yuna grumbled.

'Absolutely not,' Leander said firmly before Kate could even think what to answer. 'Kate will stay here for as long as she wants to be here. I'll be making the changes necessary to make our marriage work.'

Kate's eyebrows lifted like a shot. 'Marriage?'

'If you'll have me.'

If she'd have him? In the space of a few hours Kate had gone from rock bottom to feeling that she'd been lifted to the top of the world.

Smiling so widely her muscles screamed in protest, she kissed him with a passion so deep it left him in no doubt what her answer was.

EPILOGUE

THERE'S A GREEK ISLAND, only a short hop from the Li-assidis family's island, that's a mecca for travellers of all varieties. A long stretch of its golden beach is en-tirely private but at its border with the public beach sits a wooden shack with an open front and outside tables.

Tourists and locals alike have learned that the best months to visit Kate's Cocktail Bar are May and June, when its gregarious owner can be found behind the bar welcoming familiar faces and strangers as old friends. His wife, the eponymous Kate, is a regular presence in those months too, although she leaves the cocktail-mak-ing to her husband. Come the end of June, the couple fly out to Borneo, where they spend six months living in a bespoke treetop house in the sprawling grounds that constitutes the orangutan orphanage his non-cock-tail-making wife works at. Every year, a week before Christmas, they fly back to Europe to visit their respec-tive families, often bringing them all together in their magnificent Greek villa, before they move on to Cali-fornia, where the husband enjoys weeks of surfing and his wife pretends her heart isn't in her throat every time he carries his board to the beach. February, March and April are spent wherever they fancy it.

It's a semi-nomadic life Kate absolutely adores but one that must soon come to an end, and with excitement and a tiny bit of nerves sloshing in her stomach, she wanders out of the villa in search of her husband. It's a short search.

He's sitting on a wooden stool at the bar of Kate's Cocktail Bar scribbling on a napkin. Music's already playing. It's still a little early for even the hardened drinkers, and his concentration is such that at first he doesn't hear her approach. When he does, the wide, beaming smile that's entirely for her lights his face.

He pulls her between his legs, squeezes her bottom and kisses her as if they were still newlyweds. She has no doubt they will always kiss like newlyweds. And then he must see something on her face for his eyebrows draw together in question.

She grins.

A moment later he understands what the grin means and an almost dazed smile comes close to splitting his face.

The front of the shack's shutters are closed so they can celebrate the life they've created together in private.

Their lives will have to change again.

Neither of them has any doubt that they will make it work.

They always make it work.

* * * * *

HER VENETIAN SECRET

CAITLIN CREWS

MILLS & BOON

CHAPTER ONE

NO ONE SAID no to the fearsome and ruthless Cesare Chiavari and lived to tell about it, according to all the rumors that swirled around the very idea of the man, but Headmistress Beatrice Mary Higginbotham certainly *tried.*

"I'm so sorry," she told his man, who had appeared in her soon-to-be-relinquished offices at the Averell Academy in England, a desperately exclusive and extraordinarily private school for misbehaving heiresses. She was not sorry at all, but she was very good at appearing as if she might be for the benefit of the parents, guardians, and benefactors of the students. "I have no interest in private tutoring."

Or any other kind of tutoring. For anyone, but especially not for the fifteen-year-old in question, Mattea Descoteaux, who had made quite a few names for herself at the school over the past year. All of them uncomplimentary.

It had been Mattea's first year at Averell. Maybe it was not a coincidence that it was Beatrice's last.

As tempting as it was to imagine such a thing, however, Beatrice knew that it wasn't true. Though there would be some poetic justice in it if it was. She maintained her polite smile and braced herself for the inevitable argument. Because with these great, wealthy men—and their typical representatives, like the one before her now—there was always an argument.

But Cesare Chiavari's man did not argue. He did not attempt to convince her of anything, not with words. He merely sat opposite Beatrice with a pad and a pencil and upon that pad he wrote a number. A rather large number.

Every time she demurred, he added another zero. Then another. And yet another. Until Beatrice was only continuing to murmur that she *really couldn't* to see how far he would go…but he seemed to have no end point.

The result was that Beatrice felt very nearly cowed by the man's complete indifference to the amount of money he was offering.

"Are we in agreement, then?" he asked smoothly when Beatrice could only stare at the parade of zeros, unable to let herself fully grasp how utterly and completely her life would be changed if she simply…accepted.

It wasn't even a particularly difficult job, she reasoned, staring at that absurdity of a number. At all those zeros. Mattea was a uniquely difficult child, but then, they all were. And it was only temporary. Just for the summer. There were no metrics to measure her performance, like exams or reviews or regular slatings by families, guardians, and benefactors who expected nothing less than the total transformation of the young girls whose behavior they'd usually had a hand in crafting. All she needed to do was keep Cesare's troublesome half sister out of trouble, which his man had told her she could broadly define as out of the papers and out of Cesare's way, so he could marry whoever it was he planned to marry in peace.

Behind her desk, she let her hand rest on her belly—the real reason she had resigned from her position. She was still trying to wrestle with all the implications of this completely unexpected pregnancy, but she'd intended to raise the baby on the little bit of money she'd set aside for her own retirement one day. And with a different sort of teaching job, perhaps, one that did not require her—a soon-to-be single mum with no bloke in the picture—to act as any sort of moral authority the way she did here.

But that was a whole lot of *maybes*. How could Beatrice refuse the opportunity to drastically change her child's circumstances, no *maybes* required?

"When do I start?" she asked the billionaire's man, pressing her hand tight against the belly her pencil skirt still hid, but wouldn't for very much longer. One of the snarkier younger girls had called her *a bit hippy* only the other day.

"Mr. Chiavari will be delighted to welcome you to the family estate in Tuscany in two days," his man told her, betraying no particular satisfaction at her acquiescence. Because, she realized then, it had been a foregone conclusion to him. Which he then made clear. "All the details of your transport have been arranged. You need only present yourself at this address in London." He wrote the address in the same sure hand, right there beneath the page of zeros. "You are expected promptly at nine o'clock in the morning with everything you will need for a summer abroad. If you have any questions, please do feel free to reach out to me at any time."

He jotted off numbers for a mobile phone, presumably his, and then ripped off the paper from the pad to slide it to her across the polished surface of her desk. "Mr. Chiavari looks forward to a fruitful relationship."

"Everyone loves a bit of fruit," Beatrice murmured.

And if it hadn't been for that piece of paper, she might have thought she'd imagined the whole thing.

Because it took far less time than she might have imagined to wrap up her life's work at the school that had been the only real job she'd ever had after her teacher training. First as a member of staff, and for the last six years, as headmistress. And still it didn't take that long to say her goodbyes to the staff members she would miss, because she had agreed not to tell any of them the real reason she was leaving. The Board of Directors had been very clear on that point. After all, how could they continue to sell themselves as standard-bearers for moral behavior in young women when the headmistress of the school had gone ahead and gotten herself knocked up with no husband in sight?

It didn't matter what year it was in the outside world. It was always medieval on the grounds of the Averell Academy.

"Live by the sword, die by the sword," Beatrice told herself stoutly, as she marched herself off said grounds for the last time. She had set herself up as a paragon of correct behavior. She should have known that it would only be a matter of time before behavior tripped her up, too. Wasn't that the way things worked?

She still didn't understand how this had happened, she thought later that same night in a hotel room in London. She'd cleared out the rooms her role at the Academy had provided for her—meaning she'd put what few belongings she had into a few sad cases and had carried them off with her when she'd left. Now she found herself sitting on her hotel bed, staring at the lot of them.

Beatrice thought that surely a woman in her thirties ought to have more worldly possessions than the contents of three medium-sized suitcases, but she didn't. Her parents had both died when she was young. She'd had no benefactors or caring relatives, and had been raised in care. Everything she'd made of her life since she'd done on her own, with a certain ruthless single-mindedness, until four months ago.

She stretched out on her bed in the tidy room a short walk from Covent Garden. Tomorrow she would take herself on a bit of a shop for loose, voluminous clothing that could hide her condition throughout the coming months, which she did not expect to be terribly hard. In her experience, no one ever paid that much attention to the staff. And especially not wealthy people like Cesare Chiavari. She didn't have to know him personally to know that. All she needed to do was stay beneath the radar and earn those zeros.

She owed that to the baby she'd never meant to conceive, and now planned to love ferociously and unconditionally forever, no matter how different her life was going to be once the child arrived.

It had all started innocently enough. Beatrice had been one of the chaperones on a trip to Venice with a set of their graduating girls who had distinguished themselves with their excellent behavior and comportment, turning themselves into examples of everything the Academy could do. The trip was their reward. Teachers and students stayed together in one of the grand houses that lined a quiet canal, generously donated to them for the annual trip by a grateful father of an Averell graduate. The girls went on a tour of all Venice had to offer, from art to music to glass to history. And on their last night, after a happy dinner out beneath the stars on a piazza, the girls had gathered in the grand house's sprawling lounge and decreed that it was time to give the headmistress a makeover.

Beatrice had always kept firm boundaries between herself and the girls. It was the only way to maintain order, and she knew it. But on these trips abroad, with the deserving girls who would soon graduate, she allowed herself—and them—some slight bit of leeway. And this year had been a hard one, with Mattea Descoteaux like a troublemaking plague that infected everything. Beatrice had been in a mood for perhaps even more leeway than usual, and so she had allowed them to take down her hair and apply their curling irons and creams and gels with abandon. She'd let them take off the glasses she always wore to paint her face in a way she never had and never would again. She'd even let them cajole her into trying on a completely inappropriate dress in a shocking shade of red.

When she'd looked in the mirror, she'd seen a scandalous stranger.

"Now, miss, you must take the final step," the boldest of the girls had declared, her cheeks red with her own daring. "You must walk out into public like this and see what happens."

"It will be a grand adventure!" one of the more romantic girls sighed.

"I will do no such thing," Beatrice had replied immediately, though she had been smiling. And thinking that really, she could do with a quiet glass of wine where no one knew who she was or had any expectations about what she should *do*. Just an hour or so of anonymity would sort her out far better than any spa, she was sure of it.

"Think of what you told us when we embarked upon our final projects," the first girl had pressed. "Fortune only ever favors the bold."

Beatrice had laughed at that, at the stranger in the mirror with smoky eyes. "Hoist with my own petard," she'd agreed.

And she'd decided it was a gift, this challenge they'd set her. She would take a short walk in the sultry Venice evening on a warm spring night. She could take in the canals, the mystery of this city that seemed built entirely on imagination, and revel in the sheer joy she always felt when she was traveling.

Besides, she'd thought once she'd left the house as commanded, she didn't know a soul in Venice. There was very little chance that anyone would recognize her. And this was a good thing, she assured herself when she caught another glimpse of herself in the window of a shop already closed for the evening. Because she looked nothing like a headmistress.

She turned in a different direction than the one she usually took to lead the girls toward Piazza San Marco. Then she followed her whims, turning this way and that, until she found herself walking toward a little *vineria* up ahead of her, with people spilling out from the brightly lit interior into the walkway.

It looked like no part of the life she knew, and so it felt perfect for this strange version of herself on this odd night. Inside it was bright and loud and happy, and she was shown to a table tucked away in the corner with a boisterous family on one side, and a lone man on the other.

Beatrice had thought about what had happened that night a thousand times, and she liked to imagine that had she been left to her own devices, she would have drunk her glass of wine and nibbled on the little plates of delicacies they'd delivered with it. Then she would have found her way back to resume her life in precisely the same way she had always lived it.

She would have told the girls a story, and maybe even embellished it, secure in the knowledge that nothing much had happened.

That was what she'd *expected* would happen.

But instead, the man at the table beside her turned his head, caught her gaze with his own—the darkest, deepest blue imaginable—and had changed everything.

Beatrice still couldn't believe that it had happened. She'd been so heedless, so reckless—

But even though she liked to castigate herself in that manner, she knew better. It hadn't been like that at all. There had been an electricity between them, so intense that they had both laughed at the impact of it. It had been the way he looked at her, perhaps. Or it was that she was playing the part of a stranger who'd felt no need to restrain herself. She did not attempt to bite back her laughter. She did not deny herself a second glass of wine, or the bites of cheese and honey he offered her from his own fingers.

The stranger in a red dress who she'd been inhabiting that night denied herself nothing.

And when he asked her if she wanted to find a place where they could dance, Headmistress Higginbotham could think of a hundred reasons or more why she should say no, but the stranger she was that night said *yes* instead.

They'd danced in a hot, wild place with bodies pressed in all around, though she had seen only him. They'd danced on the crest of a *ponte* arched above the dark water, and then over it to a *fondamenta* while a street musician played for the quiet canal, weaving his beauty into the night.

Beatrice had felt nothing but magic. It had to have been magic that made her feel beautiful in his arms. So beautiful that when he'd kissed her, she'd melted against him.

So beautiful that when he'd taken her to the private hotel where he was staying, she went easily. Happily.

And she'd tried ever since to tell herself that she had disgraced herself there, rolling around and around in that bed with him.

But even now, when she knew how it all would end, she still couldn't quite bring herself to use that word. She still felt all the same magic every time she thought about the baby she carried.

The child of a man whose name she didn't even know, making her just as bad as all the young women she attempted to mold into ladies with far better manners than she had displayed that night. Far better morals that she could claim, now, as a truly fallen woman in every sense of the term.

And still when she fell asleep that night, the same as every night, she dreamed of Venice.

The next day, Beatrice gathered herself a brand-new wardrobe that made her look round in every way, so that the rounder she became over the summer, the less likely it was anyone would notice. And the following morning she presented herself dutifully at the address she'd been given, and was swept off into a waiting car. She was swiftly driven to an airfield, where a private jet waited to whisk her away to the Chiavari estate, a location so celebrated and well-known that she was sure she'd seen pictures of it many times without even looking.

She knew the man himself by reputation only. Even though the school had been teeming with too many powerful men to name, all of them deeply concerned with the misbehavior of the young women in their care, Cesare Chiavari seemed to hold a special place in that pantheon. Beatrice saw his luxury goods everywhere. The family name was stamped on everything from chocolates to silks to buildings to sports cars. Beatrice possessed the same awareness of that branding that anyone did, by simple dint of being alive, but then Mattea had arrived at the school last fall. She had been hand-delivered by a curt woman who had spouted off her master's instructions and made it clear that he would hold Beatrice personally responsible if the school did not live up to its many promises.

And since Mattea had gone out of her way to make sure that a tremendously difficult feat, Beatrice had spent a lot of time thinking about Cesare Chiavari ever since.

The approach to his estate was spectacular. Rolling hills undulated out beneath the azure sky. Cypress trees marched in rows up this hill and down the next. It was like a perfect postcard of an Italian masterpiece, and this was where she would be spending her summer…

With the most obnoxious fifteen-year-old alive.

Beatrice closed her eyes as the plane went in for its landing. She envisioned a cozy little cottage, on a stretch of beach with the sea *just there*. She imagined gardens filled with bright blooms in summer and a fire inside, keeping her warm when the weather was gray.

She would take all the zeros she would earn this summer and buy herself exactly such a place. She would raise her child there, far away from the concerns of billionaires, and their fifteen-year-old half sisters. She would learn how to cook. She would bake her own bread, the way she only vaguely recalled her own mother had done. She would make her baby the home she had always wished she had while she'd been in care.

All that she needed to do was survive a few short months in a true Tuscan masterpiece.

When the plane set down, she opened her eyes again, and decided that it would only be hard if she let it.

Beatrice decided then and there that she would not let it be anything of the kind.

After all, she had successfully run the Academy for years. She had ushered a great number of young women into the successful futures their families wanted for them. And she was very, very good at the job or she wouldn't have remained employed at Averell as long as she had.

She would not fail to be just as good for a few months with one single, solitary girl, even if it was the provoking Mattea Descoteaux. How could she be anything else?

Beatrice exited the plane feeling a great deal more like herself. Which was to say, she felt like a ball of optimism in steel-toed boots, which is what she'd always told the girls. They'd always groaned in embarrassment, but eventually they'd all usually admitted that it really was the perfect description of Headmistress Higginbotham.

She found herself humming songs from *The Sound of Music* under her breath as she climbed into the waiting SUV that took her down tiny, winding lanes that carved their way through seas of vineyards, armies of cypress trees standing tall to mark the way, and glimpses of red-tiled roofs tucked here and there.

Though even she fell into an awed sort of silence when she saw the house come into view.

It was immediately apparent to her that it was *the* house. *His* house. Because it could be nothing else, and because she recognized it, vaguely, the way she did grand palaces in all sorts of places she'd never been.

The house spread itself out in all directions, claiming the top of one of the rolling hills. The approach was a leisurely drive along the banks of the sparkling blue lake surrounded by groves of olive trees, and it was so immediately charming and picturesque that it only made the house itself look more dramatic in the hills. It was all so pretty it almost hurt.

It was a house built to intimidate, she understood, but it was also stunning work of art.

And for some reason, she thought of that man in Venice. Her lover, as she sometimes liked to think of him, in the privacy of her bed. Because it was such an odd, old word. And because it should have had nothing at all to do with her fastidious life.

But then, perhaps that was why she liked it. It reminded her of a strange woman in a bright red dress, with her hair in a wild, deliberate snarl down to her hips.

The car pulled up before a great grand entrance where two women in starched black uniforms waited, expressionless. The driver of the car got out and opened Beatrice's door, which left her feeling off-balance.

"Thank you," she said as she crawled out with as much dignity as she could muster, not having spent a great deal of time in her life learning how to exit cars elegantly. "There's no need for any fuss. You could drop me off at the servants' entrance."

"The master's orders were clear," said the older of the two women. She had what Beatrice could charitably call the face of a hatchet, and the blade of it was aimed directly in Beatrice's direction.

Beatrice smiled, because she wasn't afraid of a sharp edge.

"Be that as it may," she said, serenely, "this is not the Victorian age. I'm not a gentlewoman fallen on hard times, suspended somewhere good manners cannot quite reach. I'm an educator and quite proud of what I do. I'll need no special treatment here."

The older woman sniffed. Next to her, the younger woman did not have the same control of her facial expressions and when her elder turned and headed toward an entry concealed beneath the grand stair, she broke completely and smiled wide.

"That's taken the wind out of Herself," she confided, her eyes bright. "She has spent days puffing and huffing about who is above the station, and all the rest."

And in the spirit of friendship and the fact she had only just arrived, Beatrice did not take it upon herself to correct the woman's language. Because she had spoken in English, which was clearly not her native tongue.

All she did was smile. "You know precisely what my station is," she said. "And I would like to remain at that station during my stay."

More than that, she knew a thing or two about grand households like this, having observed them many times during her travels as headmistress, forever meeting donors and future donors where they lived. And often *had lived*, for generations.

Even so, she couldn't manage to wrestle her three sad cases away from the driver, who was now acting like the footman she didn't need. All she could do was follow the older woman who was clearly the housekeeper, trailing after the woman's unflinchingly straight back through into the bowels of the great house.

It was only when they all filed their way up a set of stairs that she began to get glimpses of the house's true splendor. A great hall that rivaled the palazzos they'd toured in Venice. Chandeliers beyond description, with what looked like diamonds hanging in each and every one of them. The space was cavernous, yet elegant, arranged around an open central courtyard that rose up to an intricately frescoed ceiling.

The place was operatic.

The housekeeper continued up the servants' stairs for another flight, but then stepped into one of the house's main halls. There was a library on one side and great terraces on the other, opening up to let in the view that seemed to roll on in pastoral splendor as far as the eye could see. There were sitting rooms, rooms that were filled with art and fine furnishings, and by the time they stopped and the woman threw open the doors of a great suite at the far end, Beatrice was shaking her head.

"This looks very much like the sort of room given to honored guests," she said as she peered inside, taking in the high ceilings and painted shutters flung wide to even more astonishing vistas. Not to mention the eternity pool and a riot of trellises and pagodas.

"You are a guest of the Chiavari family, are you not?" returned the housekeeper in perfectly neutral tones, but her gaze was assessing.

"I'm honored by the suggestion that I rest my head where no doubt kings and queens aplenty rested theirs before me and will again long after I cease to be a memory here," Beatrice said, aware that with each word, the younger woman was grinning all the wider. "Yet for what I am here to do, it would be inappropriate to stay anywhere but in the servants' quarters. Surely we can agree on this."

Once again, the older woman said nothing, but this time Beatrice did not have to look to the younger woman as a barometer to understand that she had passed some sort of test.

She knew she had. It would have been the easiest thing in the world to make noises about knowing her station, only to take the luxurious accommodations offered her.

And it wasn't that Beatrice had anything against luxury. She quite enjoyed it, particularly when it was something she'd earned. She imagined her seaside cottage would be the kind of luxury she loved most.

But today she had far more prosaic concerns. "This is a beautiful suite in a stunning house," she said as she followed the older woman back toward the servants' stairs once more. "I must assume that something so lavishly appointed is closer to the family's rooms. That can only be unsuitable, given my circumstances here this summer."

The older woman stopped, and so Beatrice and

the younger maid stopped with her. Then they all ex-changed a speaking sort of look.

"Indeed it is," the housekeeper said after a moment or two. She inclined her head down the length of the hall. "Miss Mattea is only two doors down."

Again, they shared a look.

Beatrice inclined her head. "I feel so much better knowing that the rooms you set aside for me can be left open for someone more deserving of such comfort."

And she knew that while she might not have made new friends quite so quickly, she had certainly risen in the estimation of the housekeeper by simply making it clear—without being indiscreet—that she did not wish to be quite so close to her charge. Because no one in her position would...unless they thought such proximity could lead to an elevation of station.

Beatrice had just made it clear to the household staff that she, like them, was here to work. And she let out a sigh of relief when she was settled in one of the rooms beneath the eaves, spare and tidy, with precisely what she needed clean and ready for her. No dramatic reading rooms and such. Nothing more and nothing less than was necessary.

"Why don't you settle in," the housekeeper advised her. "Mr. Chiavari anticipates that you will meet with him when the clock strikes noon. He will be in the main hall at precisely that time. Do you intend to wear a servants' uniform while you're here?"

"I think not," Beatrice said, with very real regret. "I have no wish to distinguish myself in any way, but I suspect that I will need to cling to what little authority I have over my charge. It would be better if she did not think that just because I'm here, she can order me around in a way that I would never permit her to do at the Academy."

"Just so," the older woman said, inclined her head. "I am Mrs. Morse. Please feel free to ask me any questions you might have."

Then, with what seemed to be something terribly close to a click of her heels, she quit the room.

"I think you might have impressed her," the younger girl said in tones of awe. "And she is from England and never impressed. I am Amelia. Mrs. Morse said that I am to show you the threads."

Beatrice blinked. "The ropes, I think. She'd like you to show me the ropes, no?"

"*Sì*...yes, the ropes," Amelia agreed happily. Then she straightened. "But you must not keep the master waiting. It is not done. I will guide you down to the great hall, for it is very easy to get lost. I grew up here and I still do."

And while that did not exactly instill a great deal of confidence in Beatrice regarding Amelia's abilities, she nodded, and when the girl stepped out, she set about freshening up with her usual efficiency. She could admit that she was curious about the master of the house, but the way she was always interested in finding out where her girls came from. Who had raised them and how. The truth was that she was well used to dealing with men like Cesare Chiavari. She'd faced down irate parents from almost every possible high-society echelon in every country around. The only real difference was that she was in this one's ancestral home, where she would be staying for the next few months.

She tended to her hair, scraping it back more firmly into its typical severe bun. She had discovered early on that the more she made herself look like a stereotypical headmistress, the more she was treated as one. She'd been wearing thick glasses only she knew weren't prescription ever since. She blew her hair straight and pinned it up ruthlessly. She had made a study of dowdy clothes, which was why the girls in Venice had been so gleeful that she'd let them dress her up as the very antithesis of herself.

If she could have, she really would have worn the house uniform. It would allow her to disappear into the wallpaper in the eyes of all the well-to-do residents, and it did not take a terrific amount of imagination to understand why that would be a boon to a woman in her position. No one noticed if a servant grew fat or thin. Not in places like this. No one noticed the servants at all.

She merely had to inhabit a space that was somehow a little bit of a headmistress and a servant at once. She needed the authority of one and the built-in invisibility cloak of the other.

But the good news was that she only had to find that particular balancing act for the next few months.

In record time, she cleaned herself up and exited the room to find Amelia waiting as promised. She followed the girl down from the attic, only half listening as she chattered on about this and that, lapsing in and out of Italian as she went.

These grand houses really were museums, Beatrice thought as they walked through the gallery, making their way around the square of it so they could walk down the great Y-shaped stair on the far side. It was the true gallery here, because the light that poured down from above, and a great glass ceiling several floors above them, did not shine too brightly to all the works of art that graced the walls. She was sure that if she walked the length of the gallery, and the floors above, she would find formal portraits of the family, because that was the sort of thing people with money like this always seemed to have on hand. But the paintings she saw on this level of the gallery were not family portraits, historical or otherwise. They were extraordinary. Beatrice didn't have to have a degree in art history to recognize that a great many of them were famous, and others looked as if they ought to be familiar, suggesting that she was in the presence of the Great Masters whether she could identify them or not.

Not quite the same as the sketches and photographs of old headmistresses that had been on the walls of her rooms at Averell, along with the maps of the grounds from different eras that served as her decor.

A bit hushed—she would never say *awed*—she started down the great stair, waved on by a suddenly bashful-looking Amelia.

And as she descended the stairs, the clock that took pride of place there on the landing where the arms of the Y met the stem, began to toll.

She marched down the left arm of the Y, turned, and there he was.

And for a moment, like a small death, everything stopped.

It was like that crowded little wine bar in Venice all over again.

Beatrice looked up, and it was as if they were all alone. There was only his gaze, like a dark blue touch, so intensely did it meet hers. There was only his face, harsh and beautiful at once, intimidating and yet its own kind of art.

She knew. She had tasted it. She had seen the kind of art he made.

And despite the parts of her that were already melting, and the riot inside her, she couldn't seem to stop herself from taking one step, then the next. She felt her eyes widen. She felt her whole body shiver, and then the heat she recognized too well by now took its place. It wound its way through her. It filled her. It sat heavy in her breasts, between her legs.

If she knew his name it would have been on her lips, like some kind of song of praise.

She didn't understand, but she couldn't stop moving, and still the clock boomed on and on.

It had struck twelve as her foot finally hit the marble floor of the great hall.

And she opened her mouth to speak, but he was looking at her...quizzically, yes.

But not at all intensely the way he had that night.

That was wrong. That didn't make sense—

"Welcome, Miss Higginbotham," he said in that voice that she still dreamed of, all these months later. She had heard it rough in her ear, a rumble against her throat, and as a dark, deep laugh between her legs. "I'm pleased that we were able to come to an arrangement. As you are already aware, my sister is a handful. All I ask is that you maintain an appropriately tight grip on her antics until I am wed."

It took her spinning head entirely too long to catch up. To catch on. Because this didn't make sense. Or maybe Beatrice didn't want it to make sense.

But all that shivery heat changed inside her as the penny dropped. It twisted all around, turned cold, then seemed to flood straight through her to hit the same hard marble floor.

She understood too many things in that moment.

Almost too much to bear—but one thing above all.

This was Cesare Chiavari. There was no doubt. And he was not only her new employer, he was the man she'd met in Venice. He was the only lover she had ever taken into her body. He was the father of the child she carried.

And she could tell by looking at him, and that vaguely impatient, arrogantly polite expression on his face, that he didn't recognize her at all.

CHAPTER TWO

CESARE HAD NEVER met the legendary headmistress of the Averell Academy, because her reputation—and that of the school—had preceded her. After Mattea had been expelled from four schools in one school year, Averell had been the only remaining choice.

That place might as well be a jail! Mattea had protested.

It is Averell or a real jail, Cesare had told her flatly. *Choose carefully.*

And since Mattea had actually remained at Averell for an entire school year, a new record for her, Cesare had not had any need to confer with the headmistress or anyone else about her sins. He had therefore thought about the school only when paying the astronomical tuition fees. If asked, he could not possibly have pulled the woman's visage to mind.

But she certainly looked the part, he thought now. Precisely as a headmistress should. Her hair looked black, scraped back as it was to lie smoothly against her skull and then fastened into a torturous-looking bun on the back of her head that would make even the most hardened ballerina wilt. She wore huge glasses that obscured the better part of her face, and he thought it must be a trick of the light that he was tempted to imagine her skin looked smooth. Supple, even.

He dismissed the bizarre observation as he took in the rest of her. She was not *quite* as dowdy as he had expected, given her profession and the way Mattea had complained about her as if she was the Wicked Witch of the West in all regards. He had expected warts at the very least.

But this woman was significantly younger than he'd assumed she'd be. A fact that should not have sat upon him the way it did, as if it had weight. It did not. Of course it did not.

The only other immediately notable thing about the headmistress was that she was round. And dressed in dark colors, so she resembled nothing so much as an owl.

She eyed him—yes, *owlishly*—and she stood there, somehow looking as if there was steel down her back despite the *roundness*.

She also looked at him directly, unsmilingly, as if she was inspecting him—and finding him wanting.

It was unusual, but he decided he liked that, too. She was exactly what was needed to keep Mattea in line while Cesare was off tending to the tedious, yet necessary business of securing the family legacy.

"And where is your sister?" the woman asked, and something about her tone…got to him, though he could find nothing objectionable about it. Maybe it was her voice itself. It made something in him react.

Cesare told himself it was his hackles rising, and quite rightly, because it had been a long while indeed

since he had been spoken to with anything but rever-
ence and respect from someone he had never met before. Someone who worked for him, no less.

He told himself that it was likely good for him to
have someone about who did not regard him as something akin to a local god, but it was going to take some
getting used to.

Especially when he had a fifteen-year-old sister who
handled daily irreverence quite well herself.

"I imagine she is still fast asleep," he said, surprised
that it took him a bit of work to keep his tone neutral.
As if this was an important negotiation when it was
not. He usually didn't bother to meet new staff at all.
He left that to the always efficient Mrs. Morse, who
had stepped in when the curt former governess responsible for Mattea had quit after delivering her to Averell.

The headmistress gazed back at him in that same
steady manner. "And do you have a set of instructions
for how her days ought to be ordered?"

"Do I detect judgment?" he could not seem to help
but ask.

"Judgment is often assumed, because of my position," she replied smoothly, which he supposed was a
nicer way of saying he was imagining things. When
Cesare Chiavari was not, as a rule, known for his imaginative flights of fancy. "I reserve my judgment for my
charges. Everyone's happier that way, I find."

Yet he felt judged all the same.

He could not account for the fact that this woman
had him standing in his own ancestral hall, *feeling
things*.

But he thrust that aside. Because it was unaccountable. And because she continued to gaze up at him through those enormous glasses as if she knew exactly what he was trying to pretend he was not feeling.

Cesare could not say he enjoyed the sensation of being *easily read*.

"My sister has a useless father who cares only about himself and a mother who was renowned for her bad decisions," Cesare told her shortly.

"*Your* mother?" she asked. He stared at her, affronted, and she curved her lips, but barely. "You and Mattea shared the same mother, is that correct?"

He suspected she knew perfectly well that it was correct, and more, that she was reading into the fact that he hadn't claimed his mother outright. He could feel a muscle in his jaw flex. "Mattea has been taught to communicate via temper tantrums and questionable behavior. All I can tell you is that she came by these skills...organically."

What he wanted to say was, *She is just like her mother.* But he didn't. And the fact that he had altered something simply to please this woman, or not to *displease* her, appalled him.

"I'm familiar with Mattea's communication style, Mr. Chiavari."

Cesare knew he wasn't imagining the flint in her voice then. It was the way she said his name, as if she'd taken quiet, yet irrevocable, offense to it. He supposed it was possible that she was one of the great many who claimed they were offended at his family's wealth. The simple fact of it. And he supposed he could not blame her. Or anyone else, come to that. Some found it obscene that anyone should have so much, he knew. No matter how tasteful a vast estate was, it was still a vast estate.

Still, he would not have thought that a woman who made her living thanks to the offspring of wealthy people much like himself would have such a reaction.

But how could it be personal? "I do not wish to psychoanalyze my sister unduly," Cesare said in what he hoped were sufficiently quelling tones, "but she did not react well to my announcement that I plan to marry. I expect her to take this as an opportunity to act out all the more."

This time, there was no doubt. The headmistress stiffened, her surprisingly clear hazel gaze going glacial. "Change is always difficult. Whether one is a lonely teenager or not."

He lifted a shoulder. "Left to her own devices she would fill the estate with her friends and throw a party that would raze every bit of it to the ground, dancing all the while in the flames she ignited herself."

The headmistress did not relent. Not one centimeter. "That will not make her less lonely. If it could, it would have done so already. Instead, I imagine such antics have only made her loneliness worse."

Cesare frowned down at the bespectacled creature before him, not sure why he felt almost...jagged inside.

Whatever *that* meant.

"By all means, then," he found himself saying, as if she had challenged him directly. "Let us wake her. If that is what you wish."

He thought that this woman—Headmistress Higginbotham, if ever there was a more unwieldy name—looked at him oddly. Too closely.

As if she could see things in him that no one else could.

Things even he did not know.

If he were a different sort of man, Cesare thought, he might find this woman unnerving.

He did not. What he felt was that *jaggedness* and so he told himself, with great confidence, that it was merely irritation. If it was anything other than that, he did not wish to understand it.

Instead, he inclined his head, and beckoned her to precede him back up the stairs.

But when she did, he thought there was yet more judgment implied in the set of her back as she moved—somehow with obvious umbrage, yet surprisingly lithely, up the steps before him.

None of this made sense and Cesare did not care for things he could not immediately classify. He liked order—it was precisely why his sister, and his mother before her, chose chaos to shriek their endless, torturous *feelings* at him.

But there was nothing chaotic about the little owl with ruffled feathers marching up the stairs before him as if *she* was leading *him* somewhere.

Cesare had no previous experience with a headmistress of any sort, so he doubted very much that he was reacting to the simple *fact* of her and all that authority she was clearly not shy about casting this way and that. Even here, in his own home. He had been sent off to boarding school in England when he was eight and in many ways had been raised by teachers he'd had there, far away in the cold. The rain had seemed to sink into his bones, making him shiver from the inside out.

It had been the making of him, those cold, distant years.

Cesare had much preferred his teachers—good and bad and indifferent—to his elderly father and his flighty mother. He had enjoyed his independence. He had liked the adventure of it, when he was younger. And he had grown to take pride in the fact that he had not been required to depend on anyone, and therefore still did not.

Where other men had weaknesses, Cesare had only strength.

He wished he could teach his sister the same lessons.

Unlike Mattea, Cesare had never fought against the expectations of his birthright—nor had he used it to take advantage. Even if he might have wished to experiment with that life, there had been no time for the sowing of any oats, wild or otherwise.

His mother had waited for him to achieve his majority before she'd remarried. Not out of any sense of delicacy, of course, but because that was what she'd agreed to when she'd signed the marriage documents that had made her Vittorio Chiavari's wife. Once Cesare was eighteen, she had married with great fanfare, and he had always assumed that she'd stayed with Mattea's father out of fear. That people would blame her if the marriage fell apart. That they would imagine that she was to blame when she preferred to project an image of quiet serenity to the world outside the walls of her home.

He had even told himself that she was not his problem, because that made it easier to watch his mother scrabble for the attention of a man that, even at eighteen, Cesare had considered his inferior.

But what mattered was that never would there ever be any but Chiavari hands on the grand and glorious family legacy.

Cesare had assumed the reins of the family holdings when he was eighteen, some years after his father's death. He'd learned that having been sent away so young made the occasional notion that he'd been abandoned by both of his parents in the space of a handful of years...easier. He had been raised to take care of himself, hadn't he? And he'd had dreams of going to university, but that had not been at all realistic. Not when his mother was not there to help him. It was not the first time he'd sacrificed something for the good of the family legacy, and it would not be the last.

He liked to tell himself that, as with everything else, he had come to his resilience both honestly and young.

Sometimes he thought it was a blessing that Mattea had not had to do the same. Sometimes he thought he almost envied her that innocence she did not know enough to treasure. Perhaps he might have liked to throw a temper tantrum along the way himself, but the difference between him and his rather spoiled sister was that the only person he would have hurt with a tantrum was him. If he had behaved the way she did, he would have proved to all the vultures watching his ascension that he could not handle the task set before him.

He would have made himself a laughingstock.

Cesare had been determined that would never happen, and so it had not.

He had been left to his own devices by his father first, then his mother the moment she legally could leave, and he hadn't had a meltdown. He hadn't flailed about. He had kept any stray feelings he might have had about those things to himself and had made sure the devices he'd been left to were nothing short of stellar.

Then he had dominated, as was his wont.

Now all he needed to do was enact the final part of his duty to his legacy, that being the continuation of it. He had not been avoiding it. Not exactly. It was only that he had decided that he had so many other things to do first. Like build his own, separate fortune, so he need not do anything with the family fortune but grow it.

He had accomplished this masterfully, silencing any vultures who'd imagined they could circle him way back when, and so it was time.

Like it or not, it was time.

And he would not allow himself to deviate from the plans that had been laid out for him, as they were for all Chiavari heirs. His wife would be dutiful and biddable in all things. He would guide her as necessary, so that she could imbue her role with a seriousness his own mother had lacked. Together they would prepare for the next generation of Chiavaris.

Familial duty sorted.

If he was less…invested in that duty than he had

been before he'd taken that trip to Venice some months back, well. That was between him and the moon. He would leave it there.

He couldn't comprehend why he was thinking of that night just now.

At the top of the stairs, he moved ahead of the round owl he had hired and led the headmistress and her judgy back around to the entrance to the family wing, where Mattea had been accorded a set of rooms as far away from his as possible.

Once he married, he and his wife would follow long-standing tradition and move into the grand master suite that took over the top floor of this wing. The rooms up there were arranged in the old-fashioned way, with a significant separation between the master and the mistress's bedchambers, so that once the necessary heirs had been produced, the couple could maintain their privacy as they wished.

The mistress's chamber sat directly above the nursery, with its own private stair between them, though Cesare had always seen that as a curiosity more than anything else. He had certainly never seen the slightest evidence of his mother knew it was there. And he had never taken advantage of it himself.

His mother had not been a comfort to him when he was small. And she had been a deliberate thorn in his side when he was older. He did not allow himself to indulge any softer feelings on the subject, much less any *what-ifs*. They changed nothing.

And Cesare tried not to discuss these things in his sister's presence.

"When is the wedding date?" the little owl asked from beside him as they walked down the hall of the lower family rooms, built when families were larger. Or perhaps for parents who had liked each other more than Cesare's ever had, to his memory.

"It will be sometime in August, I assume," he replied.

Though he was struck with the strangest notion that the woman who now walked beside him, quite as if she imagined herself his equal, ought to have been taller.

It was the oddest sensation. Perhaps it was that air of authority of hers. Perhaps he thought she should be at least as tall as she was round.

She made a sympathetic sound. He discovered he did not believe it. "I understand it's hard to pick a date."

"The date is not the issue." He found himself in the exceedingly unusual position of having to explain himself and did not care for it. "I have yet to propose."

"I see."

He glanced beside him and lifted a brow at the expression that was *not quite* on her face, what little of it he could discern behind the gigantic glasses. "Once again I seem to have earned your judgment, Miss Higginbotham."

"Not at all, Mr. Chiavari." Once again, there was something in the way she said his name. Something very nearly...chiding. He disliked it, but he could hardly continue to insist that her judgment existed when she claimed it did not. It made him look delusional. Or emotional, which was worse. "I was under the impression the wedding was already set."

He gazed at her in amazement. "I do not anticipate that my proposal will be declined."

The very notion was absurd.

"Have you chosen a bride? Or will there be a selection process?"

Her expression was smooth and unreadable, as far as he could tell, and yet he still could not get past the notion that she was making a mockery of him.

Then again, he was unfamiliar with such things. It was entirely possible he was mistaken.

"I appreciate your interest in my personal affairs," he told her in the sort of freezingly polite tone that most people took for the scathing put-down it was. She, naturally, appeared wholly unfazed, so he carried on, from between gritted teeth. "I assure you, I will be well and truly wed by the end of summer. You need not concern yourself with the details. Your one and only concern is keeping my sister entertained enough—or busy enough, or incarcerated enough, I am not picky—that she does not set off one of her typical bombs in the middle of the festivities. Or in the papers before any such festivities. Or at all."

Last summer Mattea had been fourteen. She had crashed a stolen Ferrari into a famous fountain in Rome, then attempted to evade capture on foot, dressed only in what Cesare could euphemistically call a *gesture* toward a yoga ensemble.

He had been forced to decline "modeling offers" on her behalf ever since.

"I don't think she would bother to take the time to set off an actual bomb," the irritating woman beside him replied, almost cheerfully. "So there's that, as a positive."

He stopped with some flourish at the door at the end of the hall, and waved his hand. He did not need to point out the obvious. They could both hear the pounding beat of music—if it could be called music—thundering from within.

This was how Mattea greeted each day and celebrated most every night.

"That is very loud indeed," the headmistress said, but with a little *tsking* sound, as if he was to blame for allowing it. The audacity was breathtaking.

He forced himself not to react. "In my experience, my sister does not play her music unless she is at home, the better to make certain it is annoying as many members of the household as possible."

The headmistress considered this. Or him. Or possibly she was looking at the moldings, so impossible was it to tell with her glasses in the way. "And where is she going when she is not home?"

"In the half week she has been back from school this summer she has attempted to make a break for at least five distant European cities," he said mildly. "With or without the company of the lovesick young men who attempt to gain access to my property. On her own she has stolen, in order, a utility truck used primarily for viticulture, a bicycle belonging to the postman, a delivery van, and the groundskeeper's all-terrain vehicle. She never attempts to leave on foot, of course. She says that would feel like work. In every case, she was apprehended before she left the property."

He did not know how to process the fact that the woman did not seem particularly surprised by any of that. *He* was outraged simply recounting it all.

It had only been *a few days*.

"But it's quite a bit of property, isn't it?" Miss Higginbotham was saying. "You could trek for ages in all directions before you found any hint of civilization."

"A fact of which my sister is well aware, but chooses to ignore." Cesare lifted a shoulder. "Possibly because what she really wants is attention."

"Have you considered giving her that attention, then?"

He stared down at this owl of a woman, who he had employed for less than a day. She was not here because she possessed some vested interest in his sister's well-being. She was here because she was being paid handsomely, and perhaps they both needed to remember that.

"You are to give her that attention, Miss Higginbotham," he told her softly, making no attempt to keep the menace from his voice. "And you are to direct her focus away from me, and the woman I will marry. That is your purpose here. Am I understood?"

"Completely understood," she replied.

And there was nothing impolite or edgy at all in the way she said that. It sounded like a simple statement of fact, nothing more.

There was absolutely no reason that he should find himself frowning as he walked away, as if she'd taken a swing at him.

And more, landed it.

He left the family wing behind as quickly as he

could, not sure why he felt as if he was…escaping a haunting of some kind.

Perhaps it was because he did not, as a rule, spend any time with women like the headmistress. He preferred his women soft and obliging, not sharp. And he liked to see their faces, for God's sake, because he appreciated feminine splendor however he found it.

But he was done with all that. In preparation for his future, he had drawn a line under his usual exploits. If such they could be called. He preferred dependably excellent sex from women who knew that they were in no way candidates for a ring, but now that he planned to take a wife, he had stopped calling them.

In his father's day, there would have been no expectation of fidelity in a marriage like the one he planned to have, but he knew that in this day and age, there were different expectations. At least at first. He was prepared to remain celibate for the remainder of the summer and to sleep only with his wife until they completed their family.

After which he expected that they would come to a different arrangement. One that suited them both.

But even when he had the freedom to indulge his appetite as he pleased, he would steer clear of women who stirred up reactions in him like this little owl did.

Though he had to stop walking at that thought, and shake his head, because surely he was being possessed by some demon to even imagine such a thing was possible. He was not *reacting*. He was Cesare Chiavari. He did not lower himself to the likes of starchy headmistresses who were happy enough to hector their own employers.

The very idea was absurd.

He forced himself to think instead of the lovely Marielle, the meek and proper heiress he had determined would be perfect for the role of his wife. It had been no easy selection.

The mother of his heirs had to be pure. Untouched. She should exude virtue, not because of any ancient stipulation in that regard, but because Cesare's own mother had fallen short in that regard. Vittorio had been so charmed by her beauty, and the presence she'd brought to her roles in the cinema that had made her a household name in Italy, that he had thrown all caution to the wind.

But he had never trusted her. Ever.

The actress he had become obsessed with became a wife Vittorio had watched over jealously. Angrily. Convinced that every man she encountered was her lover.

Until, according to all reports, she decided that if she was already to be accused of the crime, she might as well commit it.

And thus she had.

Cesare did not intend to make his father's same mistakes. He would choose a woman who was appropriate, not one who set his blood afire.

He had always avoided the very hints of such elements. He had watched his father suffer, and his mother too, and he wanted no such affliction.

When he and his wife decided, as coolheaded and thoughtful adults, that they might prefer other partners, there would be no jealousy. They would conduct themselves discreetly. They would keep in mind, always, that their children did not need to know the contours of their relationship.

Dynastic marriage was by necessity a business arrangement, and Cesare wanted no talk of love or emotion or unpleasant feelings to pollute his. He would regard his wife well. He hoped for the same in return.

He wanted no part of any *hauntings*. He did not wish to sit around in his own office, in his own house, puzzling over the behavior of a woman he hardly knew and did not wish to know any better.

He spent enough time doing exactly that over his sister's antics. But Mattea was fifteen. He intended to stamp out her behavior and when he did, he would make certain there were no more disruptions in his life.

There would be peace. Continued prosperity. And the perfection he had prided himself on since he was eighteen.

He just needed the surprisingly disconcerting Miss Higginbotham to do her damned job.

CHAPTER THREE

BEATRICE STOOD STILL outside Mattea's room for a long
time. Much longer than necessary. If there had been
anyone there to see her, she never would have allowed
herself to *linger* like this, because it was a clear sign
that she'd been thrown for a significant loop and normally she made certain to present herself as completely
and totally unflappable.

But this situation was…beyond her.

She was frozen into place, grateful that the music
from behind the door was so loud. It drowned out her
own too-fast breathing, so while she could *feel* the way
her pulse pounded and she could *feel* the way the little
air in her lungs sawed in and out, she couldn't *hear* it.

It seemed a blessing and she was in dire need.

She didn't know how she'd managed to…have a conversation with him. To talk to him the way he was talking to her, as if they had never met.

At first she'd wondered if he was playing some kind
of game. Had he hunted her down and lured her here?
Her heart had leaped at the notion—but he hadn't broken. He hadn't called her *cara*, the way he had in Venice.

She still couldn't quite believe that he didn't recognize her. Was she really *that* altered in appearance? It

wasn't as if she was wearing a costume. But she'd given him the benefit of the doubt. If he hadn't engineered her coming to Italy *because* of their night together, it made sense that he wouldn't expect to see the woman from that night in his home today. And she knew full well that no one saw *her* when they looked at her. They saw the headmistress. They saw the school.

That had always been the only thing she wanted them to see.

Still, she'd waited for him to recognize her anyway. Her voice. The color of her eyes. *Her.* But as the conversation went on and he didn't seem to catch on, it became hideously clear to her that he really, truly didn't know who she was.

And though Beatrice was certain that she would have recognized him anywhere and at any time, even if she was blind and deaf, she started to realize that it would be far worse if he *did* recognize her now.

That he would likely think that *she* had somehow contrived to meet him here, to track him down in this house that would never have admitted her otherwise. That he was the sort if man who would assume that anyone with less wealth than him—meaning, most people alive in the world—would by definition wish to seek him out to exploit whatever connection they could claim with him.

The idea that he would look at her and see some kind of *gold digger* made her skin go clammy.

And now here she was. Neck-deep in a mess she didn't know how to get out of—and never would have gotten into if she'd had any idea who he was.

She had realized, too late, that she'd assumed she knew what he looked like because she'd heard his name so often.

Perhaps you should make a note to look these things up, she told herself acidly. *Should you find yourself in this position again.*

The idea of this happening *again* made her think she might actually break out in hysterical laughter, but she held it at bay. She tried to get her breathing back under control. She tried to *think*.

Because she needed to find a solution to this…but none came to mind.

Beatrice had found the father of her child. But instead of celebrating that the way she wanted to—the way she'd imagined she would if she ever came upon him, the way she'd hoped she would one day—she had discovered that he didn't know her when he saw her.

That she was that unmemorable. Or perhaps it was simply that he had such nights all the time, so why would theirs stand out—though *that* thought made her want to do something truly out of character. Like scream to drown out the music.

Or cry.

And that was because of the situation on its own. That wasn't even getting into the fact he had just discussed his upcoming nuptials to a lucky bride he had yet to propose to with her.

The lucky bride that he had yet to *select*.

She hated that she knew anything about this. Or him. She preferred the man he'd been in her head since Venice. That mysterious, miracle of a man who had come from nowhere, given her the best night of her life, and left her changed forever.

The man who had claimed he was not passionate, but had showed her nothing but.

She wasn't prepared to let go of that version of him. But she had no choice, did she? Particularly since *this* version of him seemed about as passionate as a glacier.

Beatrice urged herself to buck up and carry on, but instead she stayed where she was. Reeling around and around inside her head while Mattea's obnoxious music pounded on and on and on.

For the first time in as long as she could remember, Beatrice wanted nothing so much as to turn and run.

Away from this place. Away from a man who could have turned her inside out the way he had…and yet not know who she was when he saw her again. Away from the possibility, now that she hadn't introduced herself, that he would discover that he knew her—and that she was pregnant with his baby—and wreck her life once again.

"A person could argue that it's the smart thing to do," she muttered to herself. "To run away from here before that can happen."

But she didn't make a move. She didn't march for the servants' quarters, grab her cases, and ask Mrs. Morse to provide her with a ride to the nearest village so she could make her own travel arrangements. She wanted to. Oh, how she wanted to. She could perfectly visualize every step she needed to take…

Yet she didn't walk back down the hallway to begin the process of leaving this mess behind her.

Beatrice Mary Higginbotham did not run away from her problems. She solved them.

She stood straighter, there outside Mattea's loud door. She squared her shoulders and forced herself to breathe, slow and deep, the way she advised the girls to do when they felt otherwise moved to shout and carry on.

What she absolutely did not do was give in to the deeply uncharacteristic urge to simply...collapse. And curl herself up on the floor where she could weep and weep and weep.

Because whether she liked it or not, her feelings had nothing to do with this. It was just as well she'd learned that today. Before she'd had time to really settle in here and imagine that things were different.

The truth was that she had nursed some romantic notions about the father of her child. She'd assumed that after the child was born she would return to Venice and seek him out, if it was at all possible. That was the thing she hadn't dared to admit to herself even last night, lying in that tiny hotel room, thinking of the night they'd shared.

It had always been her intention to do her best to find her child's father and see if what had bloomed between them that night was worth pursuing. If it was still there at all.

Now she knew that by the time she found him, if she'd been able to find him, he would have already been married. So this was a gift, it really was, to discover that he was the kind of man who could look at a woman he had tasted as thoroughly as he had tasted her and not recognize her at all.

And though there was still something in her that urged her to run, she tamped it down as ruthlessly as she could.

Because all the practical considerations that had brought her here were precisely the same, recognition or no. She had already expected her months here in Italy to be difficult, because Mattea was difficult and because she needed to hide her pregnancy while she handled the girl. She had expected her personal feelings to involve exhaustion and exasperation, nothing more.

But no matter what she felt, it was still only a summer. A few short months. Not very long at all.

How could she possibly do anything but stay? Surely she owed her child what this summer promised to deliver, if nothing else. If she couldn't give her baby its father, she would give it the next best thing: a life without financial insecurity built on the foundation of her father's money.

It was more than most women in her position had, and she knew it.

Armed with what felt like the first weapon she'd managed to wield since she'd walked down that stair and laid eyes upon the last man she'd expected to see today, Beatrice knocked sharply at the door. She waited, not surprised when there was no answer from within, then knocked again.

When there was only the same pounding music and nothing else, she opened the door and walked inside.

If she'd thought about it, she would have understood that she would not be walking into a dormitory room like the ones the girls lived in at school. Obviously. The Averell dormitories boasted far nicer rooms than any

she'd lived in when she was the same age, despite the
many complaints from the usual pampered inmates.

Even so, it took her moments to process that Mattea's rooms were even more spectacular than the guest
rooms she'd been shown earlier. She had to find her
way through a rabbit warren of interconnected cham-
bers, salons, an indoor hot tub and sauna, what looked
like three separate libraries, and an expansive media
center. All to find her way to the actual bedchamber,
where Beatrice was not in the least surprised to find
the notorious Mattea Descoteaux herself.

The girl was a sullen lump beneath a mound of lin-
ens in the center of the high, canopied bed, though she
was clearly not asleep. She had her knees up and her
mobile in her hand, and she did not appear to notice
that she was no longer alone.

How could she, in the midst of this racket?

Beatrice looked around for the speakers responsible for the clamor and found them quickly. There
were only two of the tiny ones the kids used these
days, tossed haphazardly on the polished surfaces of
ancient antiques with a thoughtlessness that could only
be achieved by someone who had never spent even a
moment of her life considering the actual cost of things.
Much less the whole of her adolescence.

Not that Beatrice could begrudge her for that. She
would not wish the kind of childhood *she'd* had on anyone, and she'd been lucky enough in the care homes
she'd lived in. Far luckier than some.

Nonetheless, the automatic calculations she did
whenever she saw anything dear kicked in whether

she liked it or not. And it was going to make her dizzy if she kept doing it here. It was like sitting across from Cesare Chiavari's man again, watching zeros fill his pad. She gathered up the speakers, found the buttons to power them down, and did so.

And when the room was suddenly, glaringly silent, she waited. She stayed where she was, watching the mound in the bed.

Mattea groaned as if attacked. She sat up in a rush of drama and irritation—

Then caught sight of Beatrice.

For a moment, the two of them did nothing but gaze at each other.

Like so many of her students—former students, Beatrice corrected herself—Mattea had been gifted with a significant amount of genetic privilege to go hand in hand with the fortune she was likely to burn through before she was thirty. Where her half brother was dark and brooding, Mattea had the face of a celestial choir girl. Cheeks like a cherub with a sulky mouth and eyes the limpid blue of the lake just outside the windows.

She used her angelic looks to her advantage, always. She had not liked that Beatrice was unaffected.

"I knew that I was stuck in a never-ending nightmare already," Mattea said, in that cultured, accented English she used that made her seem interesting even to the girls at Averell who shared her background. "Wait, though. Is this a bad trip? Or no, it's worse than that, isn't it? I've actually died and gone to hell."

"It's a delight to see you again too, Miss Descoteaux," Beatrice replied smoothly.

And it felt like another gift, to slide so easily back into this role she knew so well. It was easy to sound arch and frigid at once. It was easy to take on all her headmistress attributes, as if they were simply another part of her instead of a role she'd taught herself how to play.

When she was playing headmistress, a voice inside her pointed out, there was no room for personal feelings. There was no possibility of any crumpling to the ground and weeping like an opera heroine. There was only her authority and the way she wielded it.

She smiled at the girl. "Am I to understand that you were not made aware that I would be joining you for the summer?"

"Who would make me aware of something so horrific?" Mattea replied, her voice shifting over into that sulky sort of drawl she used when she was of a mind to be the most provoking. "No one would dare."

Beatrice made as if to consider that a moment, then smiled a bit more pointedly. "I wonder if that is because you treat your family and the staff here to the same outrageous and unacceptable behavior that we were at great pains to do away with over the school year."

Mattea scowled and even then she looked almost cute instead of sulky and insolent. It was one of her superpowers.

Luckily it had long since ceased to work on Beatrice. In truth it never had.

"I thought you quit," she said, her expression clearing when Beatrice did nothing but gaze back at her. "Everyone said you did. Obviously, that was the best news anyone had received in ages. A great many parties have been planned for next term, let me tell you."

"It is true that I am no longer headmistress of the Averell Academy," Beatrice confirmed. Mildly. "But too many celebrations on your part would, I fear, be premature. Your brother has hired me for the summer. I am to be your constant companion, Miss Descoteaux. Are you not filled with joy at the prospect? I know I am."

She watched the girl closely. The way she flared her nostrils as if trying not to react while color flooded her cheeks. The way her eyes widened as if she felt betrayed.

Beatrice felt a pang for her, because she knew too well what it was like to have her life forever in the hands of others. She wanted to sympathize, but knew Mattea would not accept it. Not from her.

But what she was really looking for came next, when Mattea pulled in a dangerously deep breath.

"If you begin to scream bloody murder, as I know you love to do," Beatrice told her quietly, "you won't like the consequences. Allow me to promise you that straight off."

"We're not in that jail you call a school anymore," Mattea threw right back. "You can't possibly believe that you're going to get away with treating me like anything but what I am. A member of the family. And if you work here, I'm your boss."

"Your brother is my boss, child," Beatrice said, with a laugh. "And do you know what he hired me to do?" She didn't wait for Mattea to offer suggestions, though she was sure they would all be creative. "All he asks me is that I keep you under control. Now ask yourself this. Do you truly think that he cares how I do it?"

Mattea's cheeks grew brighter, and her sense of injury was like a living thing in the room between them. "If I complain..." she began.

"I imagine you complain loud, often, and long." Beatrice raised her brows. "What have those complaints achieved, do you think?"

She already knew the answer. She knew, very well, the profile of the girls whose families sent them to a school like Averell. Sometimes they truly were dangers to themselves and others, but usually that was something that could be addressed with the proper counseling that their relatives preferred to pretend no one in their august bloodlines required.

More often, the girls were simply lost, like Mattea. Desperate for the attention of the very people who had not only stopped giving them any, but had sent them off to a place like Averell so that they could not be bothered with the behaviors they had likely helped encourage.

It was another reason to be glad Cesare had not recognized her. Beatrice liked people who helped others instead of throwing money at problems and expecting everyone else to clean up the mess.

That was what she couldn't help but think while Mattea sat there in her bed, looking much too young and as if, once again, a rug had been torn out from under her. This was what Beatrice had reminded the other teachers at the school. When Mattea tried to sneak off the school grounds, taking entirely too many of her classmates with her in the vehicle she'd stolen. When Mattea had broken the House Rules every single day for a month and laughed when given the usual chores as punishment, doing her best to encourage a rebellion in the other students. When Mattea had dyed the hair of every first-year purple, green, and pink the day before the term ended and all the girls were headed home for Christmas with their disapproving families.

During each of these disasters, Beatrice had reminded everyone that, while maddening, Mattea was still a kid. More than that, she was a kid who had lived through a lot of loss in her life. The death of her mother. The loss of her father, who had surrendered his parental rights. Her only family was her brother, now her guardian, who was clearly too busy to deal with her.

And was now in a rush to marry and no doubt produce perfect little children who would not behave the way Mattea did.

No wonder the girl thought she had no course of action but to misbehave.

"This is not something I would say at the school, were we there," Beatrice told her, because she always thought that the girls who came to her were talked down to quite enough. She leveled with them, like it or not. Mattea was too aware of her place in the world and yet had no power whatsoever. Beatrice could relate to that.

"Is this where you think we're going to become best friends?" the teenager asked, with scathing disdain. "Because thank you, I'm good."

If Beatrice could be deterred by teenage contempt, she would not have made it through her first day as a teacher, long ago. "I know you like to imagine that I take some pleasure in crushing young girls' wills, Miss Descoteaux, but you could not be more mistaken. My goal has only and ever been to teach young women how best to use the tools they have to claim their own power and whatever roles they might find themselves inhabiting."

She lifted a hand when Mattea started to argue. "Negative attention is not power. It leads to this. To my being hired to deal with you for the summer instead of allowing you to do things that you might like to do on your own."

"You could let me do what I like," Mattea offered, but not as if she thought Beatrice might.

"No one can trust you to behave in a manner that would allow you independence," Beatrice said, not unkindly, though she saw the girl hide a wince anyway. "And only you can change that."

"That sounds like a great laugh. Cheers."

Mattea was looking away then, as if bored. Beatrice pushed on. "I won't be surprised at all if you feel you must test me, likely as soon as possible, to see if I really intend to maintain the sort of order here that I did at the school. I can tell you now that I do intend exactly that. And when you decide to push at those boundaries, remember this. You have yet to set me a test I did not pass, Mattea. If I were you, I would learn from that."

Beatrice waited for a moment, watching the color deepen in Mattea's cheeks and wash all over her face. She didn't point out that she could see it or that she knew it meant there was a war going on inside the girl. What she did was incline her head as if they'd come to an agreement. "The first thing we will be instituting are reasonable hours, many of them quiet. Regular meals, regular exercise, no subjecting the whole of Tuscany to your music. This is nonnegotiable."

"I don't get up before noon and I don't *exercise*," Mattea shot back, the temper making her flush then, the way it always did. Beatrice assumed it felt better than the misery. "You can't make me."

Beatrice saw no need to argue about that. Not yet. "You look out of sorts, Mattea," she said instead. "As if you stayed up too late, slept terribly, and are in dire need of sustenance. If you looked happy, strong, and well rested, it wouldn't matter what hours you kept or how you cared for yourself."

"You should do something about your weird obsession with other people's lives," the girl told her, with a sneer.

"Prove to me that you can care for yourself," Beatrice said gently, "and I will not feel the need to impose care upon you."

This time, Mattea looked something like ashamed, and clearly hated that she did. Because she immediately flung herself backward into her bed and pulled the covers up over her. "Go away," came her muffled voice.

"You have an hour," Beatrice told her. "I would like you to rise, shower, and dress yourself in something appropriate for walking. I will need a tour of the house and grounds and would like you to give it to me. That is how you and I will spend our first day together. And no," she said as the mound of covers shook with obvious outrage, "I will not go off and wait for you somewhere else in this rambling mansion so you can pretend you can't find me. I'll be right here."

The covers moved slightly, so Mattea could peer out at her.

And Beatrice said nothing further. She didn't need to.

She didn't need to threaten the girl or list out the consequences Mattea might face if she refused. She knew that Mattea was running through all the times Beatrice had been as good as her word—that being every time. And all the times Mattea had bested her—that being none.

They stayed like that, locked in a silent battle of wills, for a long time.

So long that Beatrice had to remind herself that at the end of the day, what Mattea liked most was attention. And she had proved extremely interested in getting Beatrice's over the course of this last year.

Besides, she was fifteen, very pampered, and thought she was far tougher than she was.

All Beatrice had to do was maintain her cool and refuse to break.

And sure enough, Mattea eventually let out a theatrical groan. She threw the covers back and stormed up and out of the bed. She muttered things that Beatrice did her a favor by pretending not to hear while she stomped into the adjoining bathroom suite and slammed the door.

Beatrice, true to her word, did not quit the bedroom. When she didn't hear the water go on inside the bathroom, she went and knocked on the door. "Do you need help turning on the water?" she called.

And smiled when she heard a clattering sound that she suspected was a mobile tossed with some force onto a counter. Then something that sounded suspiciously like a scream of rage before she finally heard the sound of water.

She went over to look out Mattea's windows and was

struck once again by the sheer, unimaginable beauty of this place. Mattea's rooms looked out over a perfectly maintained garden, with summer flowers in full bloom. The hills in the distance were covered in neat rows of vines. Beatrice thought it must be possible to stand here for an eternity and never get sick of the view.

But thinking such things was dangerous, because it led her back to thinking of Cesare.

Something she was going to have to learn how to do without giving herself away. She had the urge to slide her hands down over that thickening at her belly that had become a kind of touchstone, but she didn't. Because that was giving herself away too and she had to break herself of the habit.

Because nothing mattered more than her child's future. She needed to keep that at front of mind.

Mattea eventually emerged from the bathroom naked, looking for a reaction she didn't get. She dressed languidly, then condescended to take Beatrice all around the house, the gardens, and a little swath of the vineyards. By the time they were done, she was wilting about, claiming that she was starving. Beatrice conferred with Amelia and had a proper tea brought up to one of Mattea's salons.

And she noticed that like most children and all puppies, Mattea was far more biddable when she wasn't hungry. Once she filled her belly, she stopped trying to prove how bad to the bone she was and was actually rather polite, automatically.

"You've gone to such lengths to convince us all you have no manners," Beatrice pointed out after this went on through a second round of perfectly toasted crumpets. "Apparently that, too, is an act."

The teenager sniffed. "Your whole thing is an act. I bet you don't even look fussy like that when you're alone. *I* don't run around in a costume."

One thing Beatrice knew about kids is that they were often frighteningly accurate.

She didn't react. "The difference is that 'my whole thing,' as you put it, is a job."

"Whatever you need to believe." Mattea shrugged, and then set down the last of the crumpet she'd been eating, dripping with jam and butter. "I know what Cesare thinks, but my mother wasn't the waste of space he pretends. She just didn't like being alone." A vulnerable expression moved over her face but she seemed to realize it, so she blinked and looked down at her lap. "She liked pretty things and delicate behavior, so she taught me both, but not because she was all that fragile. But because the more people thought of her as breakable, the better they treated her."

And there were so many questions that Beatrice wanted to ask at that. About her mother. About Cesare. About whether or not Mattea considered herself breakable, or why she went out of her way not to use the pretty, delicate behavior her mother had taught her—

But the girl stood up, pushing away from the table as if she'd suddenly remembered that she ought to have been in a fury this whole time. "He hired you to be my babysitter because you're the only headmistress who didn't kick me out of school within a month. But that just means that I'm better at manipulating you than the others, doesn't it?"

"That's one story," Beatrice said, with a smile. "Is that what you tell yourself?"

"Anyway, it doesn't matter." Mattea huffed out a sound that managed to convey her bone-deep disgust in all things, but especially Beatrice. "The thing about Cesare is that he thinks I'm an embarrassment. So it doesn't really matter what I do, does it? The fact that I exist embarrasses him and there's no getting past that."

"I'm sure that's not true—"

"It is true," Mattea fired back at her, looking flushed with temper again. "Personally, I'm more than happy to live down to every single low expectation he has of me. I'm certainly not going to flail around, desperate for his approval like my mother. And if that means that you get fired too? I'll consider that a happy bonus."

"I will make a note," Beatrice said, watching the girl.

But Mattea was still going. "My brother is no different from my father or any other man. They think that every time they're ready to move on, they can erase the past, except I have a nasty habit of turning up." She let out a harsh laugh. "Like a rash."

Beatrice knew at once that someone had said that to her. Those exact words. And even as she understood that, she knew immediately that it hadn't been Cesare—because if it had been, she wouldn't have said it that way.

"If I'm going to be a rash, I'm going to be the itchiest, most unbearable rash there ever was," Mattea said in a hard sort of voice that sounded a lot as if she was trying to cover over the glint of emotion in her eyes. "This has been a nice try to attempt to win me over, Miss Higginbotham. But it's not going to work. You might as well give up now."

"Mattea," Beatrice replied, setting her tea down with a click, "you could not possibly say anything that would make me less likely to give up. Ever."

Mattea laughed again, in that harsh way. "That's what they all say," she bit out. "And yet they all do. One after the next, like clockwork. You'll be the same."

And despite everything—not least the child she was carrying inside her—Beatrice vowed there and then that she would not.

Because she could not help feeling for the girl, abandoned like this. So vulnerable and trying so hard to hide it.

She could not help but think about what she'd want for her own child if, God forbid, she wasn't here to care for the baby herself.

Thinking of her own child like Mattea, foisted off on someone who did not dote on her as surely as her mother had and would...

But Beatrice could not allow herself to entertain the emotions that swamped her then. She had to focus instead, and so she did.

On the one thing she could do here, and she vowed that she would. That she would help Mattea whether the girl wanted to be helped or not. That one way or another, she would not abandon this girl. No matter what.

Even if she had to fight Mattea's own brother to do it.

CHAPTER FOUR

SINCE HE HAD installed the confounding headmistress in his household, Cesare had not been aware of his sister in a negative sense at all. No tedious scenes over dinner, a danger to herself and the table settings. No attempts to disrupt his business calls at all hours. No reports of her behavior, delivered in sorrowful tones by Mrs. Morse when he returned from his many trips.

This suggested to him that he had done the right thing, as ever.

And so he had the woman brought before him for a status report at the end of the first week since he had assumed guardianship of Mattea, and she was in residence, that had been…quiet. Usually when his sister was in Tuscany, she made sure to paint the whole of the estate with her particular brand of chaos.

The headmistress herself, oddly haunting though she had appeared to him when they'd met, was doing her job. Nothing else mattered.

It was a lovely summer's night, warm and ripe with the scent of flowers on the breeze. Cesare had spent the afternoon locked away in his offices, wrapped up in a particularly tense set of negotiations with a business concern in the Philippines. He quite liked the heightened tension of high-level discussions but he liked this, too. Sitting out on his favorite terrace, the one with the sweeping views all the way down to the lake and beyond, enjoying *la bella vita* with an *aperitivo*, as the good lord surely intended a Chiavari to do.

Beside him on the small, tiled table, the staff had placed a selection of freshly baked *schiacciata*, tart olives and sun-dried tomatoes from his own land, and his favorite *pecorino*, though he was indulging only sparingly tonight. Later, he would fly up to the Côte d'Azur, where he had agreed to attend a weekend-long party in the house of an old friend and business associate. Cesare had never been much for parties, but this one was different. He was going to the party because Marielle was attending, and she expected him to propose.

He had indicated he might. It was high time he did.

And so he took these sweet, calm moments to sit here, looking out at the legacy in question, and let himself think of how nice it would be to take the next step. To settle the enduring question of who he would marry, and when, and apply himself to the next phase.

Cesare knew it was time because it no longer felt like an imposition. It felt like a piece to a long-unsolved puzzle, snapping into place at last. For it would mean that he had followed his late father's instructions to the letter.

The literal letter.

He no longer carried it with him everywhere he went, but the letter his father had written him so that he might have it long after the old man's death stayed in pride of place in Cesare's office. He kept it tucked just beneath the glass of his workspace, so that he could always be reminded of his father's advice and allow it to be his true north, always.

Vittorio had been elderly when Cesare was born, and Cesare had been off at boarding school for most of his youth. Vittorio had died while Cesare was sixteen and still studying abroad, but he had made certain that his son and heir knew his thoughts on how to maintain the Chiavari fortune, how to expand where possible and hold back when wise. He had advocated in the letter that Cesare wait until he was older and settled to bother with a wife.

Because, he wrote, *the risks are too great that a young man will think too little and act too rashly. An older man, having had all the experiences he might wish, will choose a mate that will benefit the family name above all things.*

What he had not written about was why he had chosen Cesare's mother, when he had only lost himself in jealous rages over her. Cesare had come to think of the letter as not only Vittorio's advice to his son, but a mea culpa over some of his less-than-stellar choices.

Cesare heard the sound of a door opening behind him and turned slightly so he could watch the approach of the headmistress closely. Almost with interest—except there was nothing to catch his interest. The woman was dressed, again, as if she was attempting to disappear in plain sight right there on the loveliest terrace in all of Italy.

Once he thought that, he found himself studying the oversize glasses that covered so much real estate on her face, wondering why anyone would need such a monstrous pair. Because it certainly wasn't for fashion, of that he was certain. There was nothing *fashionable* about her. She was a study in a certain brand of put-together drabness that offended him to the depths of his Italian soul.

He might have learned how to control himself and everything around him when he was still technically a teenager, but Cesare had grown up here. Right here, surrounded by what he confidently believed was the most beautiful bit of earth on the planet. He sought out beauty in whatever he did, wherever he went.

What he did not understand was a person who could have improved their appearance, yet did not.

As she came to stand before him, as round and owlish as he had convinced himself he had misremembered, he reminded himself that how she presented herself was no concern of his. The woman he'd hired to wrestle his problematic sister into good behavior whether Mattea liked it or not needed only to accomplish that. She could otherwise be as drab as she liked, with his blessing.

He beckoned for her to take the seat opposite him, there on the other side of the small table. She sank down in the chair with a surprising show of grace, and the strangest reaction rippled through him, making him frown. It wasn't only that a certain heat bloomed in him, confounding him, when she had displayed so little elegance. When she was so round he could not even manage to discern a figure beneath her garments at all.

That was concerning enough, as a man who considered himself something of a connoisseur when it came to stunning women, but there was something else. It was almost as if she reminded him of something, or someone—

But who could she possibly remind him of? He had only seen her on the day she'd arrived, and now. Perhaps he was simply remembering the way she'd come down the grand stairs, as if there was an elegance deep in her bones no matter what her station in life or what she chose to wear.

Of far more concern was that bizarre surge of attraction—but that he could chalk up to the unusual celibacy he had been practicing for months now.

In any case, he dismissed it.

"I have neither seen nor heard from my sister since your arrival," he said, waving a hand at the *aperitivo* that waited beside her to indicate it was hers. "I must congratulate you."

The headmistress frowned faintly at the drink, as if she thought it might lead her straight into a den of iniquity if she so much as touched the glass.

"I believe your sister is humoring me," she told him. And when she raised her gaze to his, she smiled. In that way of hers that was neither soothing nor placating, and as such, made him...something close enough to *uncertain* as to how he should respond.

He was Cesare Chiavari. He was never uncertain, by definition.

It was clear to him that her smile was a weapon.

"Humoring you?"

She sat back in her chair without surrendering the ruthlessly straight line of her spine, a feat he found himself admiring as if it was architectural. "I believe she is attempting to lull me into a false sense of security, so that her next act of defiance will seem all the more dramatic in comparison and, with any luck, also get me fired."

He considered that. And this strange woman who, everything in him stated with no hesitation, he should not be sitting around with like this. For any reason.

She is dangerous, something in him whispered, but it was connected to that inconvenient heat. He had no choice but to do his best to shove it aside. Hard.

"Do you know what this act of defiance will entail?"

"We have to assume that her target is always you, Mr. Chiavari." She folded her hands in her lap, managing to look serene and something like regal, for an owl. If not remotely comfortable. "It's understandable that you are the focal point for these displays." He must have looked confused, or perhaps irritated, because her brows rose. "Surely the care and interest you have given so generously while raising her marks you as her only remaining family member in any real sense."

And it had been a very long time since anyone had dared attempt to chastise him. So long, in fact, that he could not remember it ever occurring. Cesare was astonished to find that he felt the faintest hint of something like *chagrin* trickle through him.

"Are you suggesting that I do not care for my own sister?" He did not say *Do you dare?* His tone said it for him.

She did not appear to notice. "I believe I said the exact opposite."

"But it was the way you said it, Miss Higginbotham."

Again, that sharp smile. "You must have misunderstood me." He had not. "I am well used to girls like your sister. They all come to the school in the same state. What we try to do is redirect their energies toward more appropriate outlets."

"And what might that be?" He laughed. "Do you imagine she will take up watercolors? The piano? Perhaps we ought to encourage her to *journal*, is that it?"

The woman eyed him, again in a way that made him feel slightly discomfited. "Do you think those are the only acceptable outlets for feminine energy? You are aware, I hope, that this is not the Victorian age?"

"Tell me something." And though he never spoke without knowing exactly where the conversation should go, tonight, somehow, he felt less careful. That, too, felt uncomfortably familiar. "Why are you no longer with the school? I found the statement issued in the wake of your departure notably uninformative."

"I wanted a change," she said, after a moment in which he wondered if she planned to answer him at all. "And no, before you ask, I had no desire to take *this* job. I was thinking more along the lines of something charming that could be left behind at the end of the day. I have long wondered what sort of life *that* must be."

"Boring," Cesare said softly. He didn't mean to.

Her gaze flew to his, and for a moment, something snapped into place between them, and it was more than a memory. It was like a switch being pulled—

But she aimed that bland smile at him again. "You made me an offer I felt I could not refuse."

He felt that switch snap back into place and could not have said why he resented it when he didn't even know what it was for. "It is cheering to know that your morals are no better than anyone else's, I suppose. You are as avaricious as the rest."

"Yes," she said, with that smile at the ready and sharper than before, to his mind. "Of the two of us sitting here, I am the one awash in avarice. You can tell, because you are the lord and master of all you survey. And I sleep in your attic in a room I doubt you have ever entered. But truly, you and I are the very same."

That might have been a stinging critique—he felt sure it was meant to be, and there were parts that landed on him hard, but that had more to do with imagining her asleep—but then she laughed. And he was not prepared for the sound.

It almost reminded him of another laugh he had heard once, musical and light, a stunning descant to a busker's cello on a bridge in Venice—

But this was far more pointed. More edgy, and Cesare had no idea why he was allowing that particular memory to pollute his head once more. It had been one night. He was not in the habit of one-night stands, because he was a creature of habit. He preferred regular sex to adventures with uncertain outcomes. He had told himself that it was far better to lock that night away, and he had succeeded.

It had been months now.

Yet another truth was that he'd woken up to find her gone, that mystery woman in Venice, and he had looked for her with a ferocity that he had never displayed for anything else. Or anyone else.

He did not particularly care for that truth.

He had never been a man of passion, not before that night. Not since.

And in any case, it was all for the best that he'd never been able to find the woman he'd met by chance that night. The woman who had melted all over him like fire and silk, and whose innocence had been as miraculous as it was unexpected. A woman who, he had come to think, must have been in a similar situation to his. With a set future before her, like it or not, and only the one, stolen night to pretend otherwise.

He did not like to think about that, either.

But what Cesare knew full well was that he was in no position to marry a woman who could tie him up in so many knots the way his companion had that night. He knew that passion was fleeting and that his true legacy was in the details he managed over the sweep of time. These were the lessons he had learned, not from his father's letter, but from an analysis of his father's life. His mother's life. His sister's father too.

Whole lives were ruined by the uncertainty of desire. His was not a life of uncertainty—that was its blessing and its curse. Some men in his position took up extreme sports. Fast cars, high mountains. Cesare had never developed the taste for such distractions, too cognizant had he always been that if he died, his family legacy died with him.

And he needed to protect that legacy and provide for it. He had no place in his life for a night like that, so filled with longing and need and something like magic that he could have been anyone. Not Cesare Chiavari at all.

Just a man like any other, struck down by a woman with a single, smoky-eyed glance.

It was all for the best that he had not been able to locate her. He knew that. He did.

"Whatever you are doing," he said in repressive tones as her laughter died away, as he tried to get rid of that unsettled feeling within himself, "I can only hope it continues."

"It won't." She lifted a hand and demonstrated, making it bob up and down like a dolphin. "There will be peaks and valleys. You cannot expect perfection."

He did not *glare*. He was not given to *glaring* at his staff. Still, he supposed the way he regarded her was stern. "I think you will find that I can. I do. I always expect perfection, Miss Higginbotham. That is what I am paying you to obtain here."

She did not look as abashed by that as he felt she should. She did not look abashed at all. "I understand that, but we are speaking of a fifteen-year-old girl with *feelings*. I can be as perfect as it is possible to be. She will not do the same. On that you can depend." Her lips curved as if she was holding back that laughter again. "Mr. Chiavari."

He found himself studying the woman as if she was a game of chess, and one he wished to win, when he could not recall ever feeling such a thing about a person in his employ before.

"What do you suggest should be done with her, then?" he asked.

Again, a curve of her lips, but he could still hear that damned laughter, as if it was *inside* him now. He was struck once more by how haunting it was when it should not have been. When she should have been anything but.

The woman looked like an owl, for God's sake.

"I don't know much about family relations, I'm afraid," she told him, with a disarming directness that he wanted to enjoy—but he knew by now that this woman only attempted a disarm when there were other weapons at her disposal. "I'm an orphan. Both of my parents were only children. So you see, I have never experienced the joys and challenges of the familial state."

"And yet you have worked with children all this time."

She tipped her head slightly to one side, as if he was the one who made no sense. "I don't think one is required to have a family to work with young people. In fact, most families who send their children to Averell do so because they cannot find a way to deal with the child in question. So perhaps it is the opposite. Perhaps I am better suited for the job."

"A job you gave up."

She took a moment to look out toward the hills. Then she turned that same assessing look on him. "I don't imagine you will be able to understand. Because of who you are, I imagine you must always be...this. Who you are. I imagine the person you would be was decided from birth."

"It is called duty," he told her. "And an abiding interest in my family's legacy, which stretches back into antiquity."

"I can see how that could be both a burden and a deep joy," she said, and he did not understand why that felt to him like a breath, finally released. "I have a duty only to myself and no legacy to speak of, save what I fashion as I go."

"That sounds very…untethered," he found himself saying.

Something in her gaze seemed to kindle then, suggesting sparks when there could be none, surely. No switches, no sparks. "But a tether is such an interesting thing, is it not? It can either be a binding, holding us against our will. Or it can be its own safety net, I suppose, holding us fast when we fear we might fall."

And Cesare wondered if it was the owlishness about her that made him wonder what the difference was between falling and flying free…and then cursed himself for his foolishness. He was not in a position to imagine anything of the kind. He had spent years settling on the appropriate wife and now that he'd located her, he needed nothing to stand in his way.

Especially not himself and this…nonsense.

"I will never know," he said, his tone harsh.

He didn't understand why it felt so easy, so natural, to talk with her like this. Of such odd and unnecessary things. Cesare did not normally sit about in the evenings, *conversing* with his staff. He gave directives and orders, and he was not available for explanations about failures when it came to carrying out those orders and directives. He took pride in the fact that he was not an unkind master, but he was always the master.

He could not think of a single time he had ever forgotten himself.

And he assured himself he was not forgetting himself now.

"I think it is easier for people like me to decide on a change," she said, as if she knew all the things he was thinking, when of course she couldn't. She couldn't begin to understand what it was like to be steeped in his own history with every breath, and to *like* that. To see it not as a terrible yoke, but as an opportunity. She was tetherless, as she had told him. An insubstantial creature with a life that would never be recorded into stone, as his would be one day, in the gallery of statues and in the family crypt. "I don't know how you would ever manage to be anything but who you are. The Chiavari heir and all that entails."

But unlike every other person who had said something like that to him, the round little owl beside him did not sound remotely admiring.

"I have no interest in change of any kind," he said, but there was something, then, in the way she gazed back at him. That hint of something sparking in her gaze, perhaps.

A kind of knowledge there that should not have existed.

And certainly should not have felt as if it was mirrored in him.

"Yet you are to be married," she said quietly.

And there was nothing off about the way she said it. What was off was his reaction. Something in him almost…prickled into attention.

But he was Cesare Chiavari and he did not *shiver* before a woman. Much less his own staff.

"I do not foresee my marriage being any kind of meaningful change," he told her, gruffly, after a moment. "Why should it be? It is merely a necessary continuation of the existing legacy of this family, this land. The empire that was built here."

A sort of amusement lit her gaze then. "What a lucky bride she will be, then, whoever she is. To disappear so completely into your...legacy."

He did not miss the emphasis she put on that last word, and could only hope he did not sound or look as affronted as he felt. "There are many women who would consider that a great honor."

"I have no doubt that there are." She paused, and for the faintest moment she looked almost uncertain. But then he thought he'd imagined it when she leaned slightly toward him, her expression intense and her huge glasses catching the evening light. "You do know that it does not have to be all one way or the other, don't you? You can create your own legacy without tearing down your family's. They're not in competition."

"Forgive me," he said through his teeth, "but you have no idea what you are talking about. How could you?"

There was something in the air between them then, making the lengthening shadows feel richer all around. Something in him felt electric, but he knew that must be a misinterpretation, because this was not the sort of woman who inspired such reactions in him. This was not the sort of woman to whom he should find himself telling secrets that he would otherwise assume were his to keep to the grave.

A sunset out on the most glorious terrace in Tuscany could not change that.

He would not let it, no matter what she seemed to know about him. She didn't *truly* know anything. He knew that. He knew she was only guessing.

Because that was all that this could be.

In any case, being unexpectedly seen and understood in that way—that had only happened the once.

It was all for the best, Cesare kept reminding himself, that he would never see his lady of Venice again. Because that stood as the only night in his life that he could recall actually imagining a different path forward. A different legacy altogether. He had held her sweet body close to his and he had slept, dreaming about all the ways he would change heaven and earth if he had to, if he could keep her.

He had no desire to relive those hours. They had rendered him unknowable to himself, and he could not abide it.

And it had been the height of foolishness, because the woman had disappeared without so much as telling him her name.

Cesare could not understand why this odd, inappropriate *owl* made him think about that night the way she did. He doubted she knew the first thing about passion and he wished he did not either. It was far too...messy.

He stood, abruptly, and that too was a betrayal of who he was. He had been trained in perfect manners since the time he was small. There was no reason at all he should abandon the habits of a lifetime simply because a headmistress he employed to handle his sister made him uncomfortable.

But he did not sit. Nor excuse himself.

"I have a plane to catch," he said.

And when her smile widened, it was as if he could hear the words inside her head, pointing out that one did not have to catch a plane that already belonged to him. That it was likely to wait as long as he wished it to.

Only once, in Venice, had a woman looked straight through him, but that night, he had enjoyed it. It had made him feel as if something molten flowed in his veins, and he had wanted nothing more than to burn with her.

Again and again.

Tonight he could not abide it. So he merely turned on his heel and stalked off of his own terrace. Cesare told himself that he was simply removing himself from an interaction that had gone on too long.

He was not running. He was not quitting his own house.

And by the time he made it out to the airfield, he had convinced himself that his reaction had been entirely proper. The headmistress was a maddening woman dressed like an owl and he was the master of the house. He did not have to descend to her level. It had been a compliment that he had condescended to do so for even a few moments, but he would not do so again.

Just as you will not think of that woman in red again either, an arch voice inside him whispered, sounding entirely too *headmistressy* for his taste.

It was a short flight to the Côte d'Azur, and another short drive into the hills above Nice for this party he had said he would attend. He was a man of his word, was he not? This was the only reason he could think of as to why he did not stop off at one of the medieval villages along the way.

This was the only reason he chose to ignore the notion that walking into this party was like fashioning his own noose.

But when he arrived, everything was as it should be, and there was no noose in sight. His friend's home was a sparkling château nestled in the more dramatic hills of Provence. It was a study in elegance, no detail too small or insignificant. His friend, who he had known since they were young boys in far-off England, was as amusing as Cesare recalled him. The friends and acquaintances he had gathered were the same. And Marielle, the heiress he had picked out to become his bride, shined like a well-set jewel in the middle of the expected splendor.

Everything was perfect. The food, the wine. The conversation was sophisticated, entertaining, and intelligent, and afterward, when there was dancing, Marielle moved in his arms like a song.

So there was no reason that later, when he found himself alone in the rooms that had been prepared for him, he found himself studying the ring he had brought with him for the occasion—unable to explain to his own satisfaction why he had not proposed.

It had been the perfect night for it. He had planned to ask her in the accepted way, not in the center of a dance floor but on a walk in the gardens, perhaps. And yet here he was, alone in his room and still without the fiancée he already knew would accept him.

Was desperate to accept him, by all accounts.

He threw open the French doors that led to the balcony off his bedchamber, wearing nothing but the boxer briefs he slept in when he was away from home, should he have to leap up and handle a fire, overly familiar fellow guests, or other such middle-of-the-night calamities.

It was cool, this high in the hills, and he liked the breeze on his skin. The moon was high in the sky, like a blessing, when what he felt like doing instead of praying was letting out a howl as if he was a wolf after all.

And maybe that strange image was what stuck with him when he finally took himself to bed, promising himself that he would address this strange issue he had created come morning. He would find Marielle and propose to her in sunlight, as if he had not disappointed her tonight.

That was what he told himself as he drifted off to sleep, but the moon shined in and got tangled up inside him, making him more wolfish than a dutiful man should permit himself to become. Maybe that was the reason why he did not toss and turn, but fell instead into a deep, rich dream.

It started off in Venice, as so many of his dreams did. But this time, when he brought his mystery woman back to his hotel, he knelt between her legs and drank deep of those sweet, hot mysteries at her core.

And he licked his way into her until she cried out, and he shocked himself awake.

Because when he looked up to see the face of his lover in that dream, he saw Headmistress Higginbotham instead.

CHAPTER FIVE

"SOMETHING IS DIFFERENT with my brother," Mattea said one morning, shuffling along beside Beatrice on what the surly teenager liked to call her daily forced march. Sometimes she even called it boot camp.

No matter what she called it, Beatrice only smiled, and walked faster.

"Perhaps he has gone ahead and become engaged," Beatrice suggested today, and if those words tasted sour on her tongue, she would never admit it. She would swallow them down, every bitter drop, before she gave the slightest indication that she cared what Cesare Chiavari did with himself, his life, or his betrothal.

This was why she insisted on morning walks out in nature. It was healing.

She was *healing*.

"Impossible," Mattea was saying with all of that overweening confidence of hers that she could produce at will. "He might like to keep it secret, obviously, because he's always ranting about escaping the glare of public interest, blah blah blah, but there's no way *she* would go along with that."

As if she knew the woman in question, was all Beatrice could think, when she'd been under the impression that Cesare was still in the process of choosing—

But none of this was her business. None of this concerned her at all.

When Beatrice did not reply, the younger girl sighed. "It's a fact that every woman in Europe has chased after my brother at one point or another. Whoever lands him will be celebrated far and wide. It will be called a coup. You must know this."

"I can't think of any topic that concerns me less than your brother's betrothal," Beatrice said icily, as much to remind herself as to get Mattea to drop the subject.

It had been almost a month now, here in this beautiful place that only seemed to root itself more deeply inside her by the day. But she had other things to worry about when it came to things *inside her*, thank you. Everyone loved Tuscany, but Beatrice's waist grew thicker and her belly protruded unapologetically, and at night she rubbed herself with lotions and was deeply grateful that she'd had the foresight to buy such baggy, oversize clothes that made her look twice her size anyway.

She only looked rounder now.

If asked, she would claim it was the endless supply of homemade pasta that accompanied every meal.

Beatrice expected she would dream about the handcrafted pasta here for the rest of her life.

What she would try to forget was that every week, Cesare called her before him and interrogated her about his sister's progress, whatever that was supposed to be. He was never as open as he'd been that first time, and she told herself she was grateful.

But she also didn't know what progress he was looking for from a teenager who was doing surprisingly well with the constant company of her former headmistress.

After all, she had said last time, with perhaps more asperity than necessary—in his office, because he'd never had her back to that glorious terrace at sunset, and thank goodness—*there are no exams to sit, are there? She will either disrupt your wedding or she won't.*

But now all she could think was that he had not corrected her. He had not said that he *wasn't* getting married, so she had to assume he still was. Even if privately she agreed with Mattea. If a man like Cesare had gotten engaged, the world would know.

I would know, something in her insisted, as if knowing the man she'd exulted in for only one night allowed her to know this cold man who'd taken his place, too.

"Maybe he won't get married after all." Mattea was speculating now as they took their usual route, out into the vineyards, out a little farther every day, and then back when Mattea started to get a bit fractious. Or remember that she *should.* "He doesn't really *need* to."

And it made Beatrice's heart hurt to hear the way the girl said things like that. With so much *hope* in her voice that it would have horrified her, if she could hear herself. It made Beatrice want to turn on her heel and charge back into the house so she could upbraid the man in question about the way he treated this little sister of his. This child who only wanted a relationship with him, no matter how she went about it.

But that was not her place.

And besides, there really was a change in Cesare, but Beatrice didn't think it had anything to do with his plans to marry. For all she would know or be told, the wedding could be next week. It had taken her a week or so to figure out what, precisely, it was that she was sensing during her meetings with him. And when he dropped into the little adventures she and Mattea took around the house and the grounds.

It is almost as if you are showing her how to treat this place, he said on one such occasion, coming up behind Beatrice and nearly making her jump. He had been looking past her toward his sister, who had been laughing with Amelia as the maid tried to teach her how to set a table in the formal style. *Did I hear that yesterday my sister learned how to do laundry?*

Beatrice had dared Mattea to try, claiming she would ruin all the garments and likely flood the house, but she didn't tell Cesare this.

Don't let your sister know it's educational, she whispered in mock horror. *That would ruin everything!*

She'd turned to look at him then and had found Cesare gazing at her in that way he'd been doing for weeks now. And she'd finally realized that it felt a lot like suspicion.

As if he was *actively suspicious* of her.

It told her things she was not sure she wanted to know about herself that her reaction to the possibility that he was onto her true identity—or anyway, the identity she'd flirted with in Venice, because she couldn't say that was her at all—filled her with more delight than despair.

You have been shockingly wrong about the content of your character your whole life, she told herself sternly. *It's only this past year that you have actually met your true self.*

And her true self, it turned out, was a bit shocking.

But these were not conversations she could have with Mattea, who she found she liked a great deal now that the girl was not playing to her classmates. But they were not friends. They could not be *friends.*

"Many men in your brother's position feel that they must marry," she told the girl now instead. And it was possible she was explaining that to herself, too. And the baby inside her. "They feel a tremendous duty to carry on the family line. I think you'll find this is the story of the world as we know it."

"It's stupid," Mattea replied, with an epic eye roll.

That Beatrice agreed with her was, of course, also not something she could share. She gave her charge a reproving look. "In the meantime, dare I hope that this spate of good behavior from you will continue? Last time I met with your brother, he asked if you were ill."

Mattea laughed, but there was color in her cheeks to Beatrice's eyes, and not from temper today. It was fresh air, maybe. Or far healthier emotions than usual.

"I'm too bored to bother," Mattea said, but she was biting back a smile at that lie. "Don't you worry, though. There's loads of time for me to meet every low bar Cesare has in place for me."

Beatrice thought about that later, during the evening

quiet hours she'd instituted over the past weeks. Mattea had protested at first, bitterly, claiming she might wish to do things normal teenage girls did on a summer evening and sometimes that included music as well as a reasonable curfew. Beatrice had been unmoved.

You do not have a single friend in a hundred-mile radius, she'd said crisply. It was her feeling that Mattea had precious few friends at all, because she gravitated toward troublemakers like herself, who were always about the drama they could cause above all else. But she knew better than to share that observation. *So the only thing you could possibly do of an evening is get yourself into trouble. We will not be doing that.*

Maybe I want to watch a movie that it would be embarrassing to watch with my jumped-up governess. Maybe I want to hang about in chats or on video calls making up stories to tell my friends. Maybe I just want to be alone, she'd hurled back.

You can be alone all you like, as long as I know where you are, Beatrice told her serenely. *You can listen to whatever music you choose, using headphones. If you want to interact, I will teach you how to play games that, yes, you can weaponize in various ways when you're older. I suggest you worry about your own reaction to any movies, not mine. If you wish to send sulky and insulting texts to your friends, presumably about me, by all means. Feel free to do so, but you will do it while sitting in the same room as me. These are the rules.*

Mattea had won herself extra quiet hours that day for her profane response to that.

But she had settled into the routine Beatrice imposed upon her with surprising ease. Sometimes they did actually play games. Sometimes they watched movies in her media room, though they got less provocative once the girl realized Beatrice refused to give her the reactions she wanted. And many nights featured Mattea performatively typing into her mobile or her laptop for many hours while Beatrice caught up on her reading.

Lately Beatrice had begun to think that there was probably more to this run of good behavior on Mattea's part than the rules Beatrice had set down. It wasn't that Mattea was suddenly filled with the desire to be obedient.

It was that she was the most outrageous when she had an audience, for one thing. And for another, it was that this might very well be the only time she'd ever had somebody else's full attention.

"Did you spend a great deal of time with your mother while she was alive?" Beatrice asked one afternoon while dealing a hand of cards.

Mattea swiped up her cards and fanned them out before her. "When she was around, I guess."

"Did you do mother-daughter things? Did you have traditions?"

"I told you she liked to have her little *afternoon soirees*. She would dress me up and teach me how to be delightful." Mattea made a face, frowning at Beatrice over the top of her cards. "Why are you asking me this?"

Beatrice gazed back at the girl, trying to keep her expression impassive as her heartbeat picked up speed.

Why *was* she asking such things? She told herself it was because she cared about Mattea, but even as she did, she knew there was more to it.

Maybe she simply wanted to hear what it was like to have a mother for longer than she'd had hers. Maybe she wanted to soak in that bond, no matter what it was like, so she could figure out how to love her own baby as well as possible.

She cleared her throat. "My mother died when I was seven. I remember when I was very small, she'd read me stories. When I was a little older, we would go on walks in the evening and we would talk about the days we had. It made me feel very grown-up."

Mattea didn't actually sneer, but it was a close call. "That sounds sweet, really," she said, making it clear she thought it was anything but. "That's not the kind of mother mine was."

"How was she, then?"

"My mother threw parties or she went to parties. So she slept all day, woke up in the afternoon, spent hours getting dressed, and then went out. She made me sit with her while she was getting dressed, so she could teach me how to be a sultry and alluring woman. She would spray me in perfume and make me taste her champagne. She taught me how to dance for a lover when I was eight. Sometimes she liked to take pictures of the two of us, but only when she looked young and fresh. But none of this made me feel like I was a grown-up." Her blue eyes were hard and sad when they found Beatrice's. "More like I was her pet hamster."

It cost her a lot not to react to any of that the way

she wanted to, because showing the girl the deep compassion she felt—and the anger she wished she could share with a dead woman who should have treated her daughter better—would only make Mattea recoil. She knew that appearing nonchalant was the only way to keep her talking. "And what about your father?"

"Oh, he forgot he had a kid." Mattea shrugged when Beatrice only gazed back at her. "He always seemed surprised to see me. Too surprised. You know."

Beatrice had to bite her tongue as she discarded some cards and picked up others.

"It was always the most fun when Cesare visited," the girl said a few moments later, unprompted. "I thought it would be like that all the time when I came to live with him, but it's not."

"And why do you think that is?" Beatrice asked her.

Mattea looked at her, then looked down. "I know what I'm like, Miss Higginbotham. And so do you."

Then she was done with cards in a sudden, swift storm of a mood change. She threw hers onto the table and whirled around, making her way back to her favorite couch and curling up with her mobile, refusing to look up again until late.

You can't make me go to bed just because you tell me to, Mattea had shouted at her on one of the first nights. *I'm* fifteen. *I'm not a* child.

You can sneak out if you want to, Beatrice had replied, unfazed. *But I have instructed the staff to deliver you to me when they catch you out and about. If I can't trust you to stay in your room, Mattea, I will make you sleep on the floor in mine. How does that sound?*

My brother will never allow it, the girl had snapped.

But she also hadn't snuck out since, apparently not wishing to test the theory.

Now that they had discussed emotions and family dynamics and had almost managed to get into Mattea's self-worth, Beatrice supposed everything was back on the table. And so, when she made her typical nightly announcement that it was bedtime and that she would be leaving Mattea to make good choices, she didn't go up to her rooms.

She went downstairs instead, smiling when she encountered Mrs. Morse in the servants' stair.

"Off to bed?" the older woman asked, because she knew everyone's schedule down to the minute.

"I have a feeling that tonight might be a night that Mattea attempts something," Beatrice said. "I thought I'd position myself in the best possible place to apprehend her."

Mrs. Morse sighed. "She has been worryingly quiet of late," she agreed. "Follow me. I'll show you where she normally climbs down."

It was another beautiful summer evening outside. The stars were out, crowding the sky. Beatrice went and found herself a bench to sit on in the gardens, tucked back in the shadows but with a full view of Mattea's bedroom windows one story up.

But while she waited for the teenager's inevitable attempt to *do something,* what she thought about was Cesare.

And that particularly narrow, assessing way he'd been looking at her lately.

She blew out a breath, not surprised to feel it thick and tight in her throat.

He wasn't engaged yet. Not yet.

She knew he wasn't.

It was her secret shame that she looked every morning on her mobile before she got out of bed. Every morning before she rose, washed, and loved on her baby belly in the only place she could. In private. Before she stopped being a mother to the child she carried and became the headmistress. Before she twisted back her hair until her eyes watered, stuck on her glasses, and wore billowy clothes to hide herself.

And it was shameful enough that she looked.

But it was nothing short of sad that every day she woke without news of his betrothal, she felt hopeful.

The same way her fifteen-year-old charge had sounded hopeful that he might decide not to marry at all.

Maybe it was more than simply *shameful*. Maybe it was pathological.

"It is a lovely evening," came Cesare's voice, as if she'd imagined him out of the stars above and the faint breeze that danced over the garden, bringing with it hints of rosemary and night-blooming flowers.

She almost thought she was dreaming, but when she pinched herself, she was still there, sitting still on that bench in the garden. And Cesare was melting his way out from the shadows deeper in the garden, where the hedges were higher, and she heard there had once been a maze.

As if he'd been out on a night constitutional for,

perhaps, the same reason she marched around in the mornings.

Her heart took up a terrible knocking deep in her chest.

But she made herself smile at him primly, the way she always did. "It's beautiful, but then, it's always beautiful here."

She could hardly recall what she was agreeing to.

"I did not realize you enjoyed sitting out and taking the night air," he said, prowling closer.

There was no other word for how he was moving, though Beatrice tried desperately to find one. Because there was no need for her to be reacting to him as if he was some kind of big jungle cat, stalking her where she sat. That could lead nowhere good.

She refused to let herself think about dancing with him in Venice. In that packed little venue. On a bridge by themselves.

Then again, back in his room.

Where he had talked of passion and then taken her through an exploration of it.

Maybe the truth, obvious to her out here in the soft night that blurred everything, was that she hated that this was the same man. She *hated* it.

And she hated that he couldn't see her for who she was.

Yet none of these thoughts were the least bit productive.

Beatrice folded her hands in her lap and sat up straighter, trying to exude so much virtue that some of it sank into her, too. "I'm not sure I've ever met someone who did not enjoy a starry night, Mr. Chiavari."

He seemed to study her for moment too long, then another.

And then he confounded her completely by sitting down beside her.

Too close, she thought in a panic. He was too close, and she could not allow that. Because she knew how much closer they could get—

Seize hold of yourself, Beatrice ordered herself then. *All he sees is a servant.*

"I think it's time you call me Cesare," he suggested, another shock. "After all, Beatrice, you and I are involved in the same great enterprise, are we not?"

And she had not let herself wonder what it would be like to hear her name on his tongue. To yearn for it. She had not thought she ever would. It was like honey. It was like heat, and it was everywhere. It was far, far better and more seductive than she could possibly have anticipated.

It was a disaster.

"I'm perfectly happy to maintain formality between us," she told him, with less control than she would have liked.

"I think not," was all he said.

Beatrice made herself sit perfectly still. She could feel her internal temperature rocket up to something more akin to a forest fire, but there was nothing she could do about that. She gripped her laced fingers tightly, so tightly that it hurt, but she would never forgive herself if he knew these things that were happening to her. If he could *see.*

She did her best to exude a cool she didn't feel, and

for the first time since she'd assumed the headmistress's position years ago, she wasn't sure it worked.

"You are, of course, the final word on all things," she said, agreeing with him in that way she knew was its own arch provocation.

She was not prepared for the rough caress of his laughter, dancing on the breeze. She hadn't heard that since Venice. Not in real life, anyway. Though she knew, the moment she heard it, that it was the song in her head, every morning when she opened her eyes.

It was a trap, she told herself.

But she didn't stand up and walk away, the way a wise woman would have.

"I'm delighted that you accept that I'm the person in charge," he said, after a moment. "As if there was some doubt."

Beatrice didn't understand what was happening, but as her head seemed to spin this way and that, she had to think that this had something to do with the way he'd been studying her lately. She didn't let herself imagine it had something to do with his delayed engagement, because that was madness.

But even though he disconcerted her simply by existing, she had become quite talented at hiding that. Or she hoped she had.

She concentrated on her posture. On the undeniable coolness of her tone. "I anticipate that at any moment, your sister will climb out of one of her bedroom windows," she told him matter-of-factly. "I made the very great mistake of prodding at her emotions and I imagine her reaction to that will be to get herself back into trouble as quickly as possible, because that feels much better. More familiar."

"I would think it would be the opposite. That getting into trouble would be the more emotional path."

"Getting into trouble allows a person to focus on who is to blame for doling out any consequences," Beatrice told him in the tone she reserved for junior staff. She was trying not to use her nose, because the scent of him was *just there*, like the breeze. Pine and rosemary and something warmer. Something she knew tasted deeper and richer when she had her mouth on him. It was entirely him. She felt her breasts grow heavy beneath her drapey clothes. "And to think deeply on how misunderstood one is, etcetera. Discussing emotional things is much harder. It requires a person to be vulnerable and most people avoid that at any cost."

"But not you, Beatrice. You have somehow transcended the reactions of mere mortals."

Her smile felt a bit brittle, but she aimed it at him anyway. "Not at all," she said. "The fact is that I have always recognized my vulnerabilities. Being orphaned will do that to you."

"You do realize that I am also an orphan, do you not?" Again, that laugh of his that cascaded through her like sunlight. "Though I will admit, I do not consider myself one. Still, both of my parents are dead."

She actually turned and frowned at him then, though she knew that wasn't wise. "You are an extraordinarily wealthy orphan, and I think you know that. I, on the other hand, was an extremely poor one. With no options. I made my own way in this world. Added to that,

I'm a woman. And women are always more aware of their vulnerabilities. That is the way of the world."

"You are not the only person alive who misses their parents, Beatrice."

That stung. Deeply. She sucked in a breath, and her hands clenched in her lap were more like a single fist. "I never said anything like that. I never *thought* anything like that."

But he had turned toward her, too, and this should not have been happening. "I will not claim that there are no privileges, but they come with a high price. Is that vulnerable enough for you? Or would you prefer that I tell you, step by step, what it was like to be eighteen years old and suddenly in charge of the vast Chiavari empire while I knew that all the while the world was holding its breath, waiting for me to fail?"

Beatrice would love him to do just that, but that was dangerous ground. And she was already afraid she would never be able to walk away from this garden bench in the moonlight. She was already afraid she'd come face-to-face with the real trouble here.

She didn't want to.

"And if you did fail, what would happen?" she asked him, fighting for her usual calm tones and not quite getting there. "You'd be slightly less rich, that's all. You and I are not the same." She blew out a breath. "But that doesn't make up for losing your parents. I'm sorry."

And she thought she heard his breath, like a sharp inhale.

"It shocks me, Beatrice, that you have spent all these years catering to the whims of these people you so despise." But now he was the one using a deeply sardonic tone. He moved closer and she could suddenly no longer see the stars above, so broad were his shoulders. So intensely did he regard her. And then, impossibly, his fingers were on her chin, tilting her face toward his. Just like that night months ago. "What do you think that precious school of yours would say if I were to tell them that all this time, you have been a wolf in hiding?"

And somehow, she was no longer sure that he was talking about the same thing she was. All she was conscious of was the danger. It seemed insurmountable.

And it, too, felt like that hot, sweet honey inside her.

She pulled back, and then stood. And told herself she could not afford to allow herself to process the touch of his fingers against the skin of her face.

Not now. Maybe not ever.

Not while she carried his baby deep inside her, and he looked at her as if he'd never laid eyes on her before.

Although, though she knew it must be a trick of the darkness, he did not appear to be looking at her like that just now. "I don't work there anymore," she reminded him, as gently as she could. "So you may tell them whatever you wish. And if our arrangement is no longer working for you, I would ask only that you pay me for time served and I'll be on my way."

She didn't mean that. She didn't think she did. It came out of her mouth without warning, but she kept herself from showing any surprise.

"I will decline that offer," he said, with hints of laughter in his voice.

He was going to be her undoing.

Again.

Everything in her pulled tight, because she was sure he was going to leap to his own feet and advance upon her once more, and Beatrice thought she would die if he did. She knew she would die if he didn't.

But instead, he laughed again, and that was worse.

Or better, something in her whispered.

But with a jut of his chin, he directed her attention to the house. To Mattea's windows.

That easily, he reminded her where they were. And what she ought to have been paying attention to. Because Mattea was climbing over the side of her balcony, dressed like some kind of fashion-conscious burglar. Complete with a beanie set *just so* on her blond head, though it was not cold by any measure.

Beatrice didn't mean to—surely she didn't *mean* to—but she drifted back toward the bench, back into the shadows, closer to Cesare.

"Where do you think she imagines she's going?" Cesare asked, his voice low.

"She's well aware that there's nowhere to go," Beatrice said quietly. She folded her arms in front of her, aware that her breasts were tender, and felt swollen, and she could pretend all she liked but she knew it wasn't her pregnancy. Not when she could feel that bright, blooming heat between her legs. "So I have to assume that she has some mischief in mind."

"And what do you, in your infinite wisdom as headmistress extraordinaire, imagine we should do about this?"

Beatrice had never felt less wise in her life. If anything, she felt a strange kinship with Mattea because, deep down, there was no getting away from the fact that she wanted this man's attention too. If she'd been *wise* she would've walked away from this place the moment she'd seen that he didn't know who she was.

But it was too late for all that, so instead she tried to think tactically, knowing what she did about Mattea specifically and teenage girls in general. "She wants your undivided attention and I'm guessing she only gets it when you're furious with her."

"Are you suggesting—again—that I neglect my own sister?"

She shot him a look, but didn't answer that question. "I think part of her good behavior of late has been because she had *my* undivided attention," she said instead. "If I think critically about the year she spent in Averell, I have to conclude that what she's looking for is the full, irrevocable, and undeniable attention of the authority figure in every situation she's in. I assume none of that was available with her parents."

He was silent beside her, and Beatrice cautioned herself. She didn't know him. She might have spent a night with him, but that didn't mean she knew anything about what might be happening in his head *now*.

Though she did.

Because he proved it the next breath. "However neglectful you might imagine I am," he said in a low voice that left a few marks in every place it touched her, "let me assure you, it bears no resemblance to the total lack of regard in which she was raised."

It was only then she realized that there was a trembling, deep inside her, and the fact she was keeping it locked deep inside her didn't make it any better.

"What I suggest is a little bit of a mind game." Beatrice didn't look at him. She didn't dare. She wasn't sure she could count on her own restraint tonight. "If I've read your sister right, she will start attempting acts of defiance and destruction. I suggest we quietly put out whatever fires she sets—hopefully only metaphorically—and never mention them at all."

"That is the very opposite of doing one's duty and learning the consequences of one's actions," he growled at her.

"It is not a tactic I would take with *you*," she retorted without thinking. "But I think it has a very real chance of getting inside your sister's head in a way a lecture never will. She's already heard every lecture there is."

His eyes were too blue, hinting at all that passion she knew was there. She'd felt it. She'd lost herself in it. And she was not strong enough for this. For this coldness where so much heat should have been. She had never been strong enough for this. For him.

But she made herself pretend she was anyway, the way she always did.

Beatrice smiled as if nothing Cesare did concerned her in the least. "Of course, the choice is yours."

CHAPTER SIX

BEATRICE READ HER charge's intentions absolutely right, Cesare was forced to admit. He told himself he was delighted that he had chosen the right headmistress for the job. He told himself he had believed in her all along—or he would not have authorized his man to pay her as much as he was paying her.

That night they'd met in the garden, Mattea had snuck out by climbing down the side of the house using the trellis and an evidently too-hardy vine. When she hit the ground, she wandered into one of the outbuildings and trashed it.

Cesare had the place quietly set to rights before morning and had instructed the staff to say nothing about it. And later that same day Beatrice informed him, with that smile of hers, that Mattea seemed almost spooked by that response. That *lack* of response that was far louder than any threats or lectures.

Which was precisely what they wanted, she claimed.

Not that it kept Mattea from trying again. And again.

But every time his sister acted out, no matter how big or bad the behavior, Cesare did the same thing and had it handled before morning. He set guards on her windows to track her nighttime trail of destruction, though he warned them to never let her see them. And slowly, Mattea's attempts to wreak a little bit of havoc...ebbed.

Before his eyes, without a single thundering lecture or threat of such things as incarceration, he watched his sister's entire demeanor shift.

What he could not understand was why he was so annoyed.

Or rather, he understood that it was Beatrice herself who was getting to him, personally, for all the same reasons he could not explain. Not the success she was having with his impossible sister. He was thrilled about that. But the way she mystified *him* without even seeming to try.

Then again, not understanding Headmistress Beatrice Higginbotham, or her effect on him, was becoming a significant issue all around. As was that dream, which kept coming back to him no matter how he tried to exhaust himself to keep it at bay.

That night in the garden he'd thought he *was* dreaming when he'd seen her sitting there in the dark, like the very fantasy he'd been trying to walk out of his head.

The walking wasn't working.

But since then, he'd avoided more shadows with her, too.

"If I may raise a personal matter," the woman herself said in that prim, arch way of hers at one of their weekly meetings. It was coming on to the end of July by then. And he could not help but notice that she had taken on an internal sort of shine. He found it deeply disturbing, which was to say, he could not look away.

Cesare was fairly certain that if he set her next to the moon, she would have out-glowed it.

And then he was forced to question where such terrible poetry was coming from, deep in his historically unpoetic soul.

"That is highly irregular," he said in quelling tones. "But I will allow it."

Her hazel eyes met his across the width of his desk. And held. "This job was presented to me as a temporary one. Predicated entirely on your betrothal, and then your wedding. I was given to understand that this would all happen in the course of the summer. This summer."

Cesare could not have said why he disliked, so intensely, that a round little owl—who seemed to get ever rounder by the day, to his eye—should mention the betrothal that hadn't happened yet. Or the wedding he should have started planning already.

Just as he could not comprehend how he, who had never dragged his feet where his duty was concerned, had now been doing so for months.

He gazed at her with as much arrogant amazement as he could manage. "I'm struggling to understand how or why this is a topic of conversation you feel is appropriate to raise with me."

"It will be August tomorrow," she said, in that gently intense way she used on Mattea all the time. Cesare did not appreciate the comparison. "Time is running out."

He sat back in his chair, pleased—and that was the right word, he assured himself—that he had moved their meetings to his office. Better to keep things on the right foot with no more meetings on a lovely terrace at sunset. Better to make sure his father's letter was at hand. Even if they were having an inappropriate conversation about his personal life anyway. "Do you imagine that I will have any trouble marrying in whatever timeline, accelerated or otherwise, that I wish?"

Her eyes seemed to glitter. "I only want to make sure that you're aware that *my* timeline cannot go past August." When he raised a brow, he thought she nearly flushed, then wondered why he wanted her to. What that would *mean*. "That was the agreement that was made."

There was no reason that should scrape at him. What did he care what life this woman had waiting for her out there, wherever she was from?

"As it happens, I have decided to throw a great party," he found himself saying. "My intended will be here, of course. I thought perhaps I might use this party as an opportunity to propose." He stared at her. "If, that is, my plans for my personal life meet with *your* approval, Miss Higginbotham."

And he didn't think he was the only one who felt the tension in the room, then.

"I'm sorry if I overstepped," Beatrice replied, and she sounded appropriately apologetic. But there was that way she was looking at him. There was that challenging glint in her gaze. He doubted very much that she was apologetic at all. "My interest in the matter is only in how it relates to my calendar. You understand."

He did not understand.

Just as Mrs. Morse did not understand when he informed her, perhaps a bit shortly, that he intended to throw a gala.

"You mean next year, surely?" the woman sputtered.

When she never sputtered.

"I mean next week," Cesare growled.

He had hired the indomitable housekeeper when he was leaving England, and his schooling, so he could come back to Italy and somehow take charge of the Chiavari empire. She had been overseeing the domestic workings of an entire public school's worth of posh boys, all of them neck-deep in too many pedigrees to count. At eighteen, he had thought she was a marvel.

He still did.

She proved herself to be exactly that when all she did was force a smile. "Everyone adores a summer party, Mr. Chiavari."

And she set about making it happen.

Most people could not throw a grand party on a moment's notice and expect anyone of worth to attend. Certainly not in the depths of summer, when so many people were committed elsewhere and had been for months.

But he was Cesare Chiavari. People would always do his bidding. Besides, most of Europe would kill for the opportunity to have a nose about the famous Chiavari estate, known for generations as the jewel of Tuscany. To prove his magnanimity, and perhaps to predispose her to consider behaving, he even told Mattea that she could invite some friends.

And yet as the party drew closer, he was…not right.

If he was a different sort of man, he might have

called it agitation. But Cesare did not get agitated. He did not allow himself that lack of self-control.

Still, he found himself awake late into the night, holding that ring in his hand and turning it this way and that as if a new view of it might change things.

But no matter how hard he tried, he could not imagine it on Marielle's slender fingers.

When he thought of the ring that had once belonged to the grandmother who had died before he was born, he thought instead of the hands he'd seen clenching down hard into the bedcovers in his Venetian hotel. The fingers that had scraped their way down his back, leaving marks that had taken a long time to heal.

Marks he had missed once they were gone.

And worse by far, every time he closed his eyes, every time he drifted off to sleep, he dreamed of Beatrice.

Something about the woman drove him absolutely mad.

None of it made sense.

But Cesare was certain he had mastered it the night of the party.

Because he needed it mastered. Tonight was the night he would propose to Marielle, making her the next Chiavari wife, and ushering in the next era of the family legacy.

He should have been filled with the deep contentment that came from taking one more step toward the future he'd always known awaited him, the way he had at the start of the year. Back when he'd decided that it was time to stride with confidence into the next phase. The phase that had always been planned for him.

Cesare told himself that was exactly what he felt. *Contentment.* Though tonight it seemed like nothing so much as a deep pressure in his chest.

The guests had been trickling in all day, taking up residence in the guest quarters here in the house and in cottages spread out all over the property. The staff had prepared the estate, making it sparkle even more than it usually did, and Mattea—perhaps in anticipation—had kept her nighttime activities to the barest minimum. The last night she'd snuck out she'd only gone and sat by the lake for a time. There had been no cleanup crew required.

Perhaps you should view it as a gift for your betrothal, that infernal headmistress had suggested.

Now Cesare stood at the bottom of the grand stairs, waiting for the night—and his future—to begin. *Content* straight through. And as he watched, Marielle started down one side of the Y-shaped stair, making her way down from the guest wing side of the gallery. She was dressed to shine, and she took her time with each step, no doubt expecting that he would take the opportunity to appreciate her.

He did, Cesare assured himself. Of course he did.

From the other side of the gallery, Mattea ran down the opposing arm of the Y, entirely too fast for anything approaching the propriety she ought to show, given her position. He frowned at her as she shot past him, but he didn't bother to react to the insolent face she made.

His gaze was caught by the woman who followed

after her, dressed in what he assumed must be a formal version of her usual shroud, hair scraped back and what looked like the faintest hint of lip color somewhere beneath her monstrous glasses.

And suddenly, irrevocably, he was faced with an unpleasant truth he had been avoiding for a very long time.

To the left, there was Marielle. She was all that was elegant. The sort of woman men wished to possess simply because she looked like what she was: expensive and exclusive and out of most men's reach. Blonde and slim and tall, she glided instead of walking. She had the sort of long neck that was made to showcase dramatic jewels. She had a pleasing face that would always look good in a photograph. She knew precisely how to style herself to look her best at every occasion. She made a good impression without even trying.

And to the right was a woman who looked like nothing so much as an owl, feathers ruffled in perpetual outrage—or, perhaps, condemnation. She was decidedly round. She dressed in dark-colored shrouds and would look like a dark orb in any picture. Her glasses had ridiculously heavy frames that hid most of her face. She was not precisely a servant, but she wasn't a guest, either, and even the usually unimpressed Mrs. Morse had indicated that she liked the headmistress. Like everyone else in the house who was not a surly teen.

Yet it was a truth he could no longer deny that he spent uncountable hours imagining what it would be like to get his hands into that strict bun of hers and let her hair fall free. He had spent many, many nights wondering what her hair even looked like. Was it long? Thick? Did it curl when left to its own devices?

And that was but one, small fraction of his obsession with the woman.

He didn't understand it, but it had been happening for a while. And only now, faced with both Marielle and Beatrice practically side by side, could he accept this thing that baffled him as much as it made him uncomfortably hard.

He did not want the woman he intended to marry. Not like this. Not with a deep hunger that seemed to have no bottom.

Cesare wanted that little owl.

In a manner he would call *desperate*, if he were someone else.

And sometimes, in moments like this one, when her steady gaze was on his and something in the hazel depths glittered, he suspected she knew it.

But it was not as if that knowledge was any help to him. Not now. *Not ever,* a voice in him growled.

For any number of very good reasons, but particularly the blonde, lovely, and blue-blooded reason who glided down the rest of the stairs to stand before him. Presenting herself for an inspection that she likely expected would end in adoration.

What was the matter with him that he could not give even that to her?

"I have very few requirements," Marielle said quietly after a moment. "But one of them is that you at least *try* to pay attention to me when we are alone."

And she said that with her winning smile, the one

that he could tell was lovely but left him cold. Because it turned out that what he wanted in a smile was a bit of weaponry. A dangerous edge, a hint of chastisement or judgment. Not centuries of breeding, apparently, with the perfect manners to match.

As he thought these things, his little owl passed behind them, and Cesare realized that she existed completely beneath his intended's notice.

The way she should have existed beneath his.

"My apologies, Marielle," he murmured, drawing her arm through his. "I will attempt to focus my attention where it ought to go."

But he didn't. Because Cesare was aware of the typically determined sound of Beatrice's footsteps as she disappeared, ducking out of the great hall into one of the open, airy salons that flowed one into the next, clearly in search of Mattea and the friends who'd joined her for the weekend.

If he was not so afflicted by his own round, drab owl, Cesare would pay no more attention to the doings of his sister. He would assume that the person he'd hired to handle her was doing the job.

And yet as he led Marielle into the salon where the most important guests were already gathering ahead of the banquet, none of them fifteen-year-olds, he found he could barely track the conversation. Instead, he wondered if this was what he had to look forward to for the rest of his life. All of this gentility and talking around things, or past them. It had never occurred to him that cocktail conversation was nothing more than a means of passing the time. And that the fact that there were those who felt that it should be elevated to an art—and judged those who could not manage the task—suggested that the people indulging in such pastimes were idle enough that they required a certain kind of wit to animate the time allotted to conversations like this, because they had little else to do with it.

He stood slightly back from the group, watching Marielle play games he knew she'd been coached in since the cradle. She was good at all of it, of course. It was one of the criteria he had judged her on.

She had gotten high marks across the board. She was innocent, but had not spent her formative years locked away in a tower, like some. She was bright, educated. She was a keen runner and enjoyed testing her times in the races she ran. She'd had multidisciplinary interests at university yet had gone into charity work upon graduation, though not the way so many other heiresses did. She was not merely marking time. The charity she worked with was more hands-on and she'd spent a significant amount of time getting her hands dirty. And while Cesare did not require a wife with dirty hands, he admired her dedication.

But most importantly, Marielle had been raised to prize a strong legacy above all things. She had her own. As many questions as he had asked her about her future prospects, she'd had the same number of queries for him. She'd wanted to know what it would mean to be a Chiavari, how her children would be received by the world, and how best they could craft a life for them that could honor both of their august bloodlines.

She was a woman who knew her worth and expected her treatment to match.

And yet as he watched her shine in her own inimitable way, all Cesare could think was that she was…a lovely chandelier, made to give off good light, but always dependent on her surroundings to reach full strength.

He broke away from the group and told himself it was only because he, as host, needed to greet the rest of the guests. But he made short shrift of that and soon found himself moving through the parade of salons until he found the little huddle of teenagers in the one farthest away from the one he'd been standing in.

And Beatrice was there in the middle, somehow managing to have all the magic and mystery of moonlight. As if she was the moon itself.

She saw him coming and walked away from the group, but not before muttering a few words that Cesare did not have to hear to know were sharp.

"Surely you have better things to do, Mr. Chiavari, than monitor the children," she said crisply. Likely to make sure the teenagers heard her refer to them as children.

Because *this* woman did not appear to concern herself with him or his wishes at all, and he should have hated that.

Cesare knew that under any other circumstances, with any other woman, he would.

"I'm making certain that everything is under control," he said, because…he needed to say something, didn't he.

He needed to explain why he'd sought Beatrice out like this, when all the guests who mattered waited for him at the other end of the house. And a glance at his sister showed that she had a bit of hectic color in her cheeks, and a look in her eyes that usually led to bad decisions, but he supposed that was only to be expected with her friends in the room.

"They look as if they're plotting something," he said.

Beatrice did not have to follow his gaze. "Because they are. They're teenagers. That's their job. I can guarantee you that unfortunate decisions will be made, but the hope is that I can minimize any collateral damage."

"I would think your role is to prevent it."

"My goal for the evening is not to prevent scandalous behavior, Mr. Chiavari," Beatrice said with that serenely patient smile. "But to keep it off the internet. To that end, I've confiscated every single one of their mobiles. I have the staff on high alert. All *you* need to do is concentrate on your party."

Cesare realized in that moment that he'd forgotten all about the party.

Something in him turned over at that. As if it was yet another message he couldn't afford to ignore.

Though he tried anyway.

Later, at the banquet table, he watched Beatrice sit with her usual smile in the midst of a pack of teenagers, managing to keep them at a dull roar, with only hints of high-pitched mirth running through the lot of them like an electric current now and again.

But he must have been staring that way for too long. To his right, Marielle stirred, gazing down the length of the table, and then beaming when she looked back at him. "I'm so looking forward to getting to know your sister, Cesare." She paused. Delicately. "She seems like such a colorful girl."

And Cesare found that he did not care for anyone's critiques of Mattea, save his own. He did not frown at Marielle. Not quite. "My sister has not had an easy time of it."

"What I hope, Cesare," Marielle said, reaching over and putting her hand over his on the tabletop where everyone could see, "is that I might offer myself as some kind of role model for your sister as she moves through these formative years. As we both know, a reputation is a legacy waiting to happen. Sometimes it happens against one's will."

Cesare discovered in that moment that he was not particularly interested in discussing either reputations or legacies when it came to Mattea. And he realized he hadn't thought enough about the fact that any wife he brought home might feel, as Marielle clearly did, that it was her job to instruct Mattea on how to behave.

Everything in him balked.

Because there was only one woman he trusted to keep his sister's best interests at heart. Only one he would allow to chastise her. Only one who he would ever permit to speak to Mattea as if she was simply a girl, instead of *his* sister.

And he was not at all certain that Mattea needed a self-professed role model who he had earlier this evening compared to a light fixture.

"Marielle," Cesare began, pulling his hand out from under hers.

He watched panic flash over her features. Or perhaps it something else, something more like determination.

Either way, Marielle leaned in. And without waiting for any sign from him, she pressed a swift kiss to his mouth.

Then she turned, beaming down the length of the table, and let out a laugh that was nothing short of *peals of joy*, wholly unsuited to the moment.

It made the rest of the guests fall quiet, as he understood then that she'd known it would.

"Cesare and I are getting married!" she cried, clasping her hands to her chest.

And the analytical part of Cesare's brain could not blame her. He had told her he meant to propose, then he hadn't. This was supposed to be a business arrangement. It shouldn't matter in the least that she was the one who had called his bluff here.

Especially when she did it so masterfully, leaking a tear or two and throwing herself into congratulatory hugs and praise on all sides as everyone surged to their feet and clustered around the happy couple.

Making it impossible for him to correct her.

Cesare was aware of friends and acquaintances slapping him on the shoulders, offering him the expected felicitations, but his focus was on the far end of the table. The teenagers looked confused. Mattea looked worryingly stone-faced.

And then, though he knew it would hurt—and did not wish to ask himself why—he found Beatrice.

She appeared to be studying her empty plate with tremendous focus, but as if she could feel the weight of his gaze upon her, she looked up.

And for moment, there was only that.

There was only *them*.

There was an honesty between them, at last. Too late. An acknowledgment. An unspoken certainty that made the pressure in his chest all the worse.

When she finally pulled her gaze away, Cesare found himself bereft.

And more than that, engaged.

CHAPTER SEVEN

BEATRICE WOKE UP early on the morning after the party, because she had a job to do.

It was possible, she thought as she marched through the hushed, quiet house, that the simple fact of that job was how she had managed to make it through the night unscathed.

Well. Not entirely unscathed. Not really.

But at least she knew that the places where she'd taken hits, where the way Cesare had looked at her as if she was the only woman alive while literally in the middle of his own engagement to someone else— were invisible.

If the appearance of invulnerability was all she had, she would take it. And hope it became true. In time.

Because the alternative was that she would have to live like this forever, with her foolish heart crushed flat.

Mattea had looked stunned by Marielle's announcement. Then as crushed as Beatrice felt. Then she had looked Beatrice right in the eye and announced to her friends that she intended to make this party one for the history books.

You do not want that, child, Beatrice had told her.

Unsurprisingly, the girls got silly, fast. When the

dancing started, the teenagers started stealing bottles of wine and hiding in unused rooms to chug them down, squealing with laughter when caught. When Beatrice finally herded them up to Mattea's rooms, there was too much music—so loud it was a shock they couldn't hear it in the civilized party below.

The *engagement party*, a voice inside Beatrice had kept on repeating, like a death knell.

The girls had pleaded for internet access and when repeatedly denied, had started playing the kind of shrieking, out-of-control games that led to breaking things—or would have, had Beatrice not been there to quietly remove the most delicate objects from their haphazard range.

And then, later, she had been on hand to quietly dispense cold washcloths for clammy brows and buckets for the girls who had chugged the most contraband wine.

Now it was a clear, bright morning, and she could have them sleep, but Beatrice believed in the power of consequences.

So she rousted the lot of them from their slumber, ignoring all the whining with the ease of her years of practice. She dispensed tablets for headaches, insisted each of the girls drink at least twenty ounces of water, and then made the most sullen group of teenagers in Europe keep her company as she stretched her own legs on an extra-long loop through the vineyards.

Twice.

When they came back to the house, drooping and moaning, she had the kitchens deliver up a proper meal to sop up the excesses of their behavior the night before. She shepherded the girls into showers, and supervised their unnecessary makeup and hair routines, all of which went on for ages. It was past midday when she handed off Mattea's friends, who had only been permitted access for one night, to the waiting SUV that would whisk them off to the airfield.

Beatrice allowed herself not one single moment to concern herself with the night Cesare might have had as an engaged man.

Not one.

When she returned to Mattea's rooms, she found the girl curled up in a ball on her favorite couch in the media room, looking as if she didn't know if she wanted to go to sleep...or maybe cry her eyes out. She was everything that was limp and wan, and Beatrice ignored her entirely.

She bustled around the room instead, tidying everything she could. She threw open curtains throughout the suite, opening the windows and the balcony doors to encourage airflow and light, knowing that sooner or later both would revive Mattea.

And she found herself grateful that she was working today. That she had things to keep her busy. She didn't have time to sit around and think too much about the fact that Cesare had finally, actually, gotten himself engaged.

Engaged. To be *married.*

It was no longer a theoretical possibility. It was no longer something she needed to look up on her mobile every morning. She hadn't bothered today, because she already knew the answer. She'd been there to see it with her own eyes.

She couldn't decide how, exactly, she felt about the fact that it was clear—to her, anyway—that he hadn't wanted it to happen like that. It had been Marielle who'd seized that moment and made her announcement.

Beatrice had waited for the powerful and mighty Cesare Chiavari to correct her...but he hadn't.

Instead, he'd looked at Beatrice. And she'd had the most ridiculous urge to claw her way up that long banquet table—anything to get to him—but she didn't know if her end goal was to save him or to slap him.

What she did know was that she didn't have the standing or the right to do either of those things.

She'd been grateful when the girls had started acting up, because she would rather handle overexcited teenagers forever than dig into how she actually felt, having witnessed the father of her child allow the whole party to congratulate him on his engagement to another woman.

And the night had been so busy containing her charges, then handling their splitting heads and tender stomachs, that she'd happily had no time to herself to curl up in a ball, hold her baby belly the way she wanted to, and daydream about a night in Venice that seemed farther away now than it had ever been.

"I don't understand why you can't just *be still*," Mattea moaned then, reminding Beatrice that she was still here. Doing her job. Not in a position to lapse off into daydreams.

Something else she knew she should be grateful for.

"It does no one any good to get stuck in despair," Beatrice told her, or perhaps she was talking to herself. She kept the bustling going, tidying up every surface that she could find, still as amazed as she always was that packs of girls could make such a mess. "These are called the wages of sin, Mattea. I hope you're enjoying the rich, ripe fruits of the choices you made last night."

"Oh, my *God*," Mattea moaned with all the drama of an entire theater run. "Why can't you just say *I told you so* like a normal person?"

Beatrice almost cackled out a laugh at that, more proof that the emotions she wasn't letting herself feel were all over the place. She bit it back at the last moment. Then she glanced over at her charge, who had gone from curling in a ball into lounging about like a full opera heroine. Complete with one arm over her eyes, awaiting her inevitable tragic end.

"Did you enjoy having your friends here for the night?" Beatrice asked mildly, because there was no point adding oxygen to opera.

Mattea made a noncommittal noise. "I guess."

"They all seem particularly high-spirited. I don't know why they've never darkened the doors of Averell."

That inspired Mattea to sigh and shift to a sitting position. "None of their parents care if they get kicked out of school. It's not like they need to be educated. They'll all get their money at eighteen."

Beatrice sniffed. "Imagine having nothing at all to live for."

"It's the opposite of that. It's just that you get what you're looking for at eighteen, without having to get old and weird and having to go on yoga retreats to find yourself."

"Mattea," Beatrice said, quietly. "I don't how to tell you this in a way that you will understand, because I'm afraid it's the sort of thing you have to grow into. But there's so much life beyond eighteen. So very much. Eighteen is scarcely a memory to hold on to, at my age. It was so long ago. And in the fullness of time, it means so little."

And she knew as she said it that it was breaking her own boundaries, but that was the trouble with today. She felt broken.

Besides, it was possible she needed to hear those words herself.

"Right." Mattea only rolled her eyes. "But I'm guessing nobody handed you a memorable trust fund. So."

"What I got was much better than that," Beatrice replied, straightening from the bureau she'd been attempting to clean, though she feared the scratches she'd found there might be permanent. "I had no trust fund, you're quite right. What I was given instead was complete and total independence, and I took it."

"Sounds great," Mattea said insincerely, looking and sounding sulky. But Beatrice saw the glint of something else in her eyes. A tiny hint of curiosity she didn't want to show, but couldn't hide. "Can I have my mobile back now?"

Beatrice reached into one of the deep pockets in the smock she was wearing and pulled out the girl's mobile phone, tossing it to her. Mattea missed it and let it clatter to the floor, but then only stared at it where it lay. She didn't even reach for it when the screen lit up, alerting her to a new notification.

"The thing about my friends is that they're not really friends," Mattea said after the screen went dark again. "It's more like whenever one of us got into trouble in the various schools we all went to, the other ones were there to make it worse. And then, later, talk about how funny it all was. But I think... Sometimes I think that a real friend would do the opposite."

Beatrice understood this as the heartfelt confession it was, and so she didn't rush over to Mattea's side. She sat instead on a chair on the opposite side of the room and kept her expression interested—but not *too* interested—so as not to overwhelm this moment of teenage vulnerability.

"It seems to me that there's a difference between friends and fans," she said when it was clear that Mattea could stare at her mobile on the floor forever. "The fact is, Mattea, you're excellent at giving a good performance. I don't mean that as an insult. I watched you do it all year long at Averell. If I had really wanted to punish you, I would have done it with solitary confinement. Because you truly bloom when you have an audience."

"I've had to sit through a lot of therapy," the girl replied with a shrug. "I know it's bad. Seeking approval. People pleasing. Childhood trauma, blah blah blah."

"That's one take on it," Beatrice agreed. "On the other hand, you could also channel that particular urge, because it's something you're good at, into something more positive."

"Like what? Multilevel marketing?"

Beatrice couldn't hold back a laugh then. "I somehow doubt that your future is in tawdry, tiered sales, Mattea. I was thinking something more like acting."

She watched as the girl's face went blank for a moment. Then something soft and deeply emotional took root there, making her look young and sweet and almost wistful.

But in the next moment, all of that was gone, replaced by scorn.

"Because of my mother?" She sat up straighter so she could wrap her arms around her chest, and then hold on tight. "What would make you think I would want to be anything like her?"

"Acting is a noble profession," Beatrice said matter-of-factly. "More than that, it's an art. I might even call it a privilege. To inhabit the skin of others, to truly have the opportunity to walk in their shoes? That doesn't sound like work to me. It sounds like a gift."

Mattea was up and on her feet, then. Beatrice watched in as much amusement as compassion as she began to pace back and forth in the room, protesting this idea that had clearly hit a button for her.

"You don't understand, because you didn't know my mother, but that's the whole problem. No one knew my mother. She couldn't be known. There was nothing there." She shook her head. "She was just…a collection of scenes and bits she'd found along the way so she could make herself into her very own personal Frankenstein."

"By all accounts, your mother was a very accomplished—"

"My mother made a handful of artsy films," Mattea bit off, sounding cold, though her blue eyes were wild. "And then she married into this family. And after that, the only acting she ever did was pretending she was happy."

Beatrice didn't know why that winded her, when she'd never known the woman. She'd only ever seen the same still photographs that everyone else had. She had been shockingly pretty with her sky blue eyes and flaxen blond hair. It was not the least bit surprising to Beatrice that people still wanted to project their imaginations onto a face like that.

"All I'm suggesting is that you might enjoy a bit of theater," she told Mattea now, as the girl continued to pace. "As a way to channel some of the desire for new experiences into more worthy avenues."

"So I can be just like her, is that it?" Mattea asked, her voice rising. "Everybody's favorite when the spotlight is on, but what happens in the dark? What becomes of something so shiny then?"

Once again, Beatrice found herself almost speechless, when she knew she couldn't let that happen. She knew she had an obligation to show up for the girl. No matter how difficult it was for her. This wasn't about her.

It didn't matter that it resonated.

"Mattea," she began again.

"Our mother," came a voice from the door, "should have shined like the beacon she was, for all of her days. It is a tragedy among tragedies that she could not."

And when they both turned toward the sound, Beatrice's jaw wasn't the only one that dropped slightly at the sight of Cesare there in the doorway.

Though for different reasons.

He had been in formal attire last night. He was usually in formal attire, Beatrice thought with some surprise, though she had never really put that together before. Here, in his own home, he preferred bespoke suits—as if he liked to remind himself that he was meant to be an institution, not merely a man.

This afternoon he wore nothing but a pair of visibly soft sweatpants and a gray T-shirt whose sole purpose seemed to be clinging to every single plane of muscle in his chest. Not to mention his ridged abdomen.

Beatrice had the great pleasure and deep agony of knowing exactly what was underneath that stretch of gray, as well as the sweatpants that emphasized his strong thighs and seemed to love the most rampantly male part of him too well.

It took her too long to come to the obvious conclusion that he'd clearly just returned from some kind of workout. But then the silly little fool inside of her was far too quick to wonder if that was because he'd woken up this morning and tried to chase his demons away.

Hopefully, the one he'd agreed to marry last night.

You are delusional, she chided herself. *And for all you know, his fiancée is lovely. Her only sin is not being you.*

Mattea was staring at her brother, with that same mix of too many emotions on her face. But the one that stabbed Beatrice through the heart was hope.

A wild flash of *hope*.

"It is not her fault that she could not stay as bright as she started," Cesare told his sister, his voice and his gaze intent. "There are some men who find beautiful things in this world and wish to possess them. They take them in their hands, they hold them too tight, and then they blame the things themselves when they are crushed."

"Is that what you think?" Mattea's voice was small. "I used to hear my father yelling at her. That her glory days were long past. That she should have been more grateful he was willing to tolerate her in her decline."

Cesare made a low noise. "I'm sorry you heard that. You should not have."

Mattea blew out a breath. "She always said that the best way to make people remember you is to be unforgettable, by any means available. And she could throw parties. She could cause scandals. All I had was school. And my father didn't remember me when I was home. So I thought I might as well...use what I had to remind him."

Cesare was still in the doorway, and the darkly intent look he shot Beatrice made everything in her stand on its head. Then cartwheel all around.

As if he knew her. Or at least, as if she had something to do with him showing up here like this.

She wanted so badly to imagine she had gotten through to him somehow. That whether he remembered her or not, something deep inside him *knew* her all the same.

The way she knew that man he'd shown her in Venice.

The one she persisted in believing was still in him, somewhere.

Right now she didn't have to look very hard.

Soon enough, it wouldn't matter what he remembered or recognized, because nothing that occurred in this house or this family would be her concern any longer. Beatrice needed to find a way to hold on to that.

"I have never forgotten you, Mattea," Cesare told his sister, shifting all of his force and intensity back to her. "I never could. And there's something I should have told you a long time ago. I am not your guardian because your father wanted to get rid of you. I am your guardian because I demanded that he relinquish you to my care. Because I did not think he was doing a very good job."

Beatrice knew she wasn't the only one holding her breath, then. But she was sure that she was the only one who had suggested that he'd been something less than the perfect guardian to his sister. The only one who had wondered if, maybe, he might try being there for her with more than just his money.

She had never felt anything like this. The sheer joy that he had *listened*. And that he was here now, saying these things to a shaken, lost girl who needed desperately to hear these words, straight from him.

"You seemed to like me more when you saw me less, Cesare," Mattea said, with that shattering teenage honesty.

Cesare, to his credit, had the grace to take that hit. To look chagrined, and to let his sister see it.

"I realized last night that I have not explained these things to you," he said, and he did not sound as if he thought that was an excuse. "When I was your age, I was being prepped to run an empire. And the way I made myself memorable was with perfection. Because I could not afford to do anything less. It is possible that I expected you to simply do the same, when you have no empire to run or enemies waiting to see you fall. All you need to do, Mattea, is try not to let anyone take your shine." He inclined his head. "Even me."

His sister looked down, and seemed to remember the night before, and the shenanigans she and her cohort had engaged in. Or perhaps it dawned on her that it was not normal for her brother to make appearances here. "You never come to my rooms. Are you going to send me away again? Because I didn't behave like a proper little princess at your party?"

"Did you not?" And again, Cesare's dark gaze slid to Beatrice and made her throat go tight. While it seemed everything else in her lit on fire. "I will confess, I did not notice."

"I contained it," Beatrice said, shooting for a crisp tone and not quite getting there. "As promised."

She told herself it was a relief when he turned that dark blue gaze back to his sister.

"I realize that I have not discussed with you what will happen when I marry," Cesare said. "I only mentioned that I wished to do so."

"Well," Mattea said, forthrightly, with a resigned sort

of shrug. "You were always going to marry someone like that Marielle."

Beatrice would have left the room immediately if she could, because this was none of her business. But Cesare was blocking the door that led toward the exit with that unfairly beautiful body of his. And only she knew she'd gotten to taste every bit of that body, thoroughly. And if she closed her eyes, she could taste him again right now.

And it didn't matter what he knew or didn't know.

What she knew beyond any shadow of a doubt was that she did not want to stand here and listen to a discussion of his fiancée. It was too much. In a summer of entirely too much, this was...*beyond*.

She wasn't sure she could take it.

"What do you mean?" Cesare was asking and not in that quiet, dangerous tone he sometimes used, when he was warning off any follow-up questions. He seemed genuinely interested. "What, precisely, is 'a woman like her'?"

"Like she's made of reflective glass," Mattea said, and she was getting her equilibrium back. It was there in the color that was slowly coming back into her cheeks. Even her tone had returned to its usual dismissiveness. "So she can mirror all that Chiavari legacy stuff you like to go on about. I thought that was why you were getting married in the first place."

Cesare let out a small sound, as if he had taken a hit to the gut, and Beatrice kept her eyes firmly on the floor. She expected him to launch into a defense of his betrothed.

But he didn't.

He didn't, something in her whispered, as if that meant something.

As if it was personal. To Beatrice.

How shameful that she wished it was.

Cesare crossed over to the couch Mattea had vacated. He swiped up the remote control and pointed it at the screen on the far wall. "I have an idea," he said. "Why don't we watch one of the films?"

Mattea reacted as if someone had slapped her. "One of... Our mother's?"

Cesare sat, clicked through a few menus, then patted the cushion beside him. "I am not an actor in any regard, but I have always been very good at negotiations. And what is a negotiation except a kind of performance all its own? If I were you, I would ask myself what gifts our mother left you. Not what stories people tell about her. Even if those people are me."

"People sometimes say I look like her," Mattea said, in a small voice. "They don't say it nicely."

"Because beauty like hers is not a gift," Cesare said, very seriously, holding her gaze in a way that made it clear that he agreed that Mattea resembled her. "It was her curse. People remembered her face, never her. So she thought she had nothing more to offer. But you and I know better, do we not?"

And this time, when he pointed to the cushion beside him, his sister went and sat there next to him. Through one film, then the next.

Beatrice sat through the first one with them, only because when they had both protested when she'd tried

to leave. Almost as if they weren't sure how to be together, she thought. But while they'd watched their
mother, she had watched them.

And had wondered if she would have to *actually* bite
her tongue to keep herself from asking all the questions
she wanted to ask. Like where was Marielle? What
had brought Cesare here to make things better with
his sister?

Did this mean he no longer needed her to play her
headmistress role?

She was dismayed at how sad the prospect of leaving this place made her, when she should have rejoiced
that she could go, her secret still safe with her.

During the second movie they screened, she made
her way down to the kitchens and sorted out a late afternoon meal for them. The house was quiet, as most
of the guests had left in the first part of the day. The
servants' quarters were sparsely populated as well, as
the bulk of the cleanup had already taken place and
many were off having well-deserved personal time.
Beatrice carried in a tray of food and slid it onto the
table nearest the couch, but then stopped short.

Mattea had fallen asleep, her head on her brother's
shoulder. And Cesare was not looking at the screen in
front of him, where his mother was riding on a train,
looking sadly out of windows streaked with raindrops.

He was looking straight at Beatrice.

"We should find her acting lessons," Beatrice said,
though her voice sounded far more fluttery than it
should have. She cleared her throat. "If she's even a little bit her mother's daughter, she will be extraordinary."

Cesare only looked at her, his gaze dark, brooding.

"And I really do think that if she has a place to channel that energy, she might find that making trouble holds far less appeal," Beatrice continued, though she was aware that something inside of her had caught fire. It was connected to the way he was looking at her, like a livewire that went deep, and everything inside her seemed to...*spark*.

"Little owl," he said, which made no sense, "I do not wish to speak any further about Mattea."

Beatrice wanted to say something, to do something, because she felt she needed to *do something*—

Especially when he turned, carefully cradling his sister's head as he shifted her body until she could curl up against the back of the couch and sleep on.

And as Beatrice watched—somehow frozen still— he stood.

Then walked toward her, portent in every step.

Or maybe it was simply in her, the pounding of her blood in her veins. The honey in her limbs, the heat sweet and slick between her legs.

He advanced, she fell back, and she didn't realize until too late that it was a tactical misfire. Because she let him back her fully out of the room.

Now Mattea was in the room beside them with the film still playing, Beatrice was in some small salon with no witnesses, and then Cesare was there too, taking up all the air. All the space.

All she could see or hear or breathe.

I remember this, something in her said with great satisfaction—

But she couldn't melt into that. She *couldn't*.

"Mr. Chiavari," she began desperately. "I really think—"

"That is the trouble," Cesare said.

His eyes were so dark, she thought, and he was so close now, and she was not immune. She had tried for so long now, but she was still not immune.

"The trouble?" she asked.

But she was whispering.

"Too much thinking," he said, closing the distance between them until her breath felt like his. Until *she* felt like his, when she knew better.

Cesare studied her face for so long that she thought he might fog up her glasses, but instead he leaned forward, slid his palm over her cheek to hold her face steady, and kissed her.

Finally, he kissed her.

And it made her realize in a searing burst of *thank God* that every dream she'd had about him since Venice was a lie. It was all smoke and mirrors, fuzzy and filtered.

Because the real thing was so much better.

The taste of him was so much wilder, and far more devastating.

Their mouths fit together the way they always had. As if they'd been carved from the same bit of sensation and their lives had been an exercise in finding their way here. Finding their way home.

And she was too aware that her body was different now, and even more his than it had been that night, little though he knew it.

He kissed her again, then again, then he took the kiss deeper, and sensation was so sharp it felt like she was being lacerated by the pleasure—

But he was engaged to another woman. There was no mistake. She had been there.

And Beatrice could not be the kind of person who did this, could she?

I won't, she sobbed within. *I can't.*

She pushed herself away from him, horrified. Deeply horrified.

Though what she was really horrified about, she could admit only deep inside herself, was that she wasn't as horrified as she should have been, and certainly not for the right reasons.

Because he felt like hers. He always had.

Yet he was Cesare Chiavari. And she was a former headmistress teetering on the brink of total disgrace.

And she told herself it wasn't surrender but strategy when she whirled around, wishing she was as nimble as she'd been before she was pregnant, and ran.

CHAPTER EIGHT

THERE WERE TOO many things slamming their way through Cesare, then, none of them gentle. All of them catastrophic.

There was a kind of knowing he didn't want to accept. A recognition—

Yet still, something in him refused it. All of it.

Because what mattered was that he had just proved that he was not the man he'd always believed himself to be. The man he had prided himself on being. The man he had assumed he would always be, so pure and perfect were his intentions and his goals.

It hadn't even been that hard to walk the path he'd chosen. He'd assumed that was a testament to the strength of his character, or perhaps a simple acknowledgment that he was right to place the family legacy above all else.

But now he understood that he had never been tested.

He had never been tempted.

The man he'd imagined he was, honorable and brave, would never have allowed himself to be claimed by one woman the night before, then kiss a different one come the morning. The man he'd been certain he was all these years would never have found himself in such a situation.

He would have proposed to Marielle ages ago. He would have married her by now.

He never would have paid the slightest bit of attention to a round little owl.

Cesare realized that for the first time in the whole of his life, he had no idea who he was.

The headmistress turned and fled. He could hear her feet down the length of the hall, then the door to Mattea's suite slam behind her as she burst through it.

Maybe he should take that as a sign. A call to his better self, to be the better man he'd always imagined he was, before today.

But his blood was so hot inside his body that he thought he might scald himself. His sex was so hard it ached. For some reason, he kept mixing up Beatrice and his lady of Venice—

Something hovered, just there, but he didn't want to accept it.

And before he knew it, he was going after her.

He didn't see her when he made it to the hallway. Remembering one of the little jibes she'd thrown at him, he made his way to the servants' stairs and climbed up them, all the way up to the rooms beneath the eaves.

The afternoon light streamed in from the end of the hall. He expected to encounter other members of his staff, only to belatedly remember that he'd given most of them the rest of the weekend off. He thought he should have been able to hear Beatrice in whatever room was hers, and he stood there, trying to control his own breathing so he could hear hers.

And this might have been his house, but he did not

feel right about peering into the private spaces of the people who made this house run. Cesare stood there in the hallway, aware that he was having far too much trouble controlling himself.

It was more evidence that he was lost. That he was not himself. That he had no access to the man racked with need who had taken over his body, his mind, all of him—

Because inside him, still, there was a kind of storm. And he had the sense it hadn't yet hit ground.

A voice inside that sounded a great deal like his memory of his late father whispered, *You do not want that, my son. You know where it leads.*

Maybe it was a good thing that he couldn't find his little owl.

To break the tension—or to find his way back to himself, somehow—Cesare walked down to the window at the end of the long, narrow hallway. It was round and high, and when he looked out at first he saw the same view he always did. Rolling hills, cultivated vineyards, olive groves.

His legacy, arrayed before him like a painting, just as he liked it.

He had gone for a very long run this morning, after a long and sleepless night, much of which had been spent at a party he wished he hadn't thrown, fielding congratulations that sat heavy on him.

Are you pleased with yourself? he had asked Marielle at the end of the night when he walked her to her chamber, because it had seemed expected. And he was a man who always did what was expected, didn't he?

I will be happy when I am the next Chiavari wife, she had replied, with that same smile. *As we have discussed for a long time now.*

I did not realize that happiness was in the cards, he had replied, without thinking.

When he should have known better. He and Marielle could live a long life together, fully content with each other, but it was predicated on not allowing such unnecessary glimpses behind the curtain.

Had he really believed, for so many years, that a life like that was what he wanted?

And for the first time, he thought he'd seen the real Marielle there, lurking in the bones of her objectively lovely face.

We will create a perfect legacy, she had said, almost sternly. *We will nurture it into something robust that will stand the test of time. What is* happiness *next to that?*

He had turned that question over and over in his head ever since.

It was what had prodded him to run faster and faster on his run, but not because he had come round to Marielle's way of thinking. Or back to what his own thinking had been when he'd started this search for an unobjectionable wife, who would fit into his life like the mirror his sister had accused her of being, with a lack of heat that had seemed like an indictment.

He had thought about his lady of Venice, as ever. He had thought about Beatrice.

But it was his sister who had weighed heaviest in his thoughts.

His sister, who Marielle believed needed a role model. And more, that she was the perfect person for the position. She, a woman who would pretend that he had proposed because she was tired of waiting—and not because she was so taken with him that she couldn't bear another moment apart.

He had run faster and farther, knowing that wherever he ran, it would be on land that was his. That the earth beneath him was his legacy. That it would remain long after he was gone, and that was a contentment that nothing could take away.

And more, that he might not count happiness as a virtue worth pursuing—or he never had—but he wanted something better for Mattea.

She deserved, at the very least, to choose.

Beatrice had been trying to tell him these things all along, hadn't she?

That was what had brought him to her rooms, with dirt from the Chiavari vineyards still on his shoes.

Now he was only regretful that he hadn't gone to her sooner, to speak to her of the mother they'd shared.

Still at the window, he let his gaze drop straight down to the pool area that only family and staff knew about. It was separated from the rest of the house by high walls festooned with flowering vines, and over time it had become almost exclusively the purview of the staff, because Mattea had a marked preference for the eternity pool on the opposite side of the house, set against a stunning view in the distance, some glorious landscaping, and shade. For his part, Cesare always meant to swim, yet usually found himself running instead.

But today, he stood there, transfixed.

Not because of the pool itself, though it was a sweet turquoise invitation in the golden afternoon light. But because he could see his little owl, marching across the flagstones toward the pool as if on one of her missions. She was still fully clothed in her usual drab, unflattering shrouds of clothing, with what looked like an extra smock today. Her enormous glasses were still on her face, and he remembered that he had felt them pressed against his own cheekbones before.

Why should that wash over him like heat?

And there was something about her mouth that was sitting on him strangely, urging him to *think*—

But instead, he watched Beatrice, several stories below, as she took herself to the water's edge. She stood there for a moment, and even from this far away he could sense the tension in her.

Until, fully clothed, she threw herself in.

A different sort of drumming began, deep inside of him.

Because he was perfectly clear what was happening here.

She was washing herself clean. She was washing *him* off.

Cesare did not like it at all.

And he stopped worrying about what kind of man he was.

Everything seemed to go narrow inside his chest, a taut spiral that was made of stone and fire. Without intending to move, he found himself charging down the servants' stair. When he got to the bottom, down in the kitchens, he had no memory at all of whether or not he'd passed anyone on his way down. It was all blank space in that fire within him.

He made his way outside, then into the secret pool area through an ancient door set in the thick walls covered in vines that were older than some American cities. The door opened and closed noiselessly, though he would not have cared if it had scared off half the birds in Tuscany. Cesare strode to the side of the pool, scowling down into the water, at first not able to make sense of what he saw.

It looked like there were shadows, everywhere, floating beneath the water—

But he realized in the next moment that what he was seeing were those shroud-like clothes of hers, because she was tearing them off under the surface of the pool.

And the very moment he took that in, his gaze was drawn to the stair across the water, where she was rising up like some kind of mermaid from the very depths of his deepest, darkest fantasies.

Beatrice was completely nude.

And her hair… Her hair was no longer caught up in that achingly tight bun on the back of her head. It flowed down, impossibly long, and the water made it seem as dark and as smooth as ink as it poured down her back.

She turned, as if she heard him. As if she could hear that thundering inside his chest, like it really was a drum.

As if she could feel the ache in his sex.

She froze, there on the stair without a stitch of clothing on a body that was nothing short of a celebration of the female form, looking back over one perfect shoulder toward him.

The first thing he thought was, *She's taken off those hideous glasses.*

And then, at last, he recognized her.

He recognized her.

"You…" Cesare breathed.

And that magical miracle of a night in Venice slammed into him, a cascade of heat and longing and need.

Because she was the very same woman. She was his lady of Venice. She was the woman who had exalted him and ruined him, and he had never been the same.

Now that he knew it, he couldn't understand how he had missed it all this time.

She had lived here, under his roof, and had interacted with him for more than a month and he hadn't known—

Then again, maybe he had.

Maybe his body had always known the thing his mind had not wanted to accept.

Because there was no other explanation for his obsession with a drab little owl who was here to keep Mattea in line, save this.

In his dreams, he had known. His subconscious had recognized what his eyes did not. There were parts of him that had known all along.

She had been haunting him…because she was here. Not a ghost at all, but the woman he dreamed of each and every night.

And he thought that somehow, this must have been

fated all along. Destiny, when he had long believed that Chiavaris made their own destiny, by their will and their legacy alone.

It was no wonder he'd been dragging his feet where Marielle was concerned. It made perfect sense that he had been unable, somehow, to give the family ring to the wrong woman.

Because the woman he truly wanted, the one woman he craved, was right here.

"Sei il mio tesoro," he said, almost roughly. *"Sonno pazzo de ti."*

Because she was a treasure to him, and she'd been right here beneath his nose. And he was more than half-mad for her, in whatever form she took.

But as he watched, feeling as if he had been turned into stone, something changed in her gaze. She took a deep breath. He could see the way she straightened her shoulders.

Then she turned all the way around. And his gaze dropped to take in the unmistakable jut of her belly.

The baby she carried.

Mine, something in him roared at once.

And it was as if everything in him shattered into pieces.

He heard a sound, low and animal, and understood that it was that same roar, from a place he hadn't known he carried inside.

Because it was as if he had spent the whole of his life trying to figure out who he was, and now he knew.

Now there was no doubt.

Now he was *himself,* at last.

He made that noise again, and it was like a song. And then he was moving, rounding the edge of the water, and bearing down upon her with intent.

With unmistakable intent.

"Cesare..." she whispered, as if in some kind of apology.

But he did not want words. He had no need for apologies.

He wanted...everything.

It was as simple and as impossible as that, so he kissed her.

Again, and again and again, a slick, hot claiming.

A reminder.

A deep, hot, long-overdue recognition.

He set her away from him, tugged off his own T-shirt, and dressed her in it. It was almost like a dress on her, though her belly made it shorter, and despite that glorious red thing she had worn on the night they'd met, he somehow knew that his lady of Venice who was also Beatrice Higginbotham did not spend a lot of time wearing scandalous, body-baring attire.

It was all for him.

She was all for him.

And Cesare hauled her close, then into his arms, and carried her into the house.

To his bed, at last.

CHAPTER NINE

BEATRICE HAD LOST herself in this dream a thousand times. A soft bed at her back. The glory of Cesare braced over her. That shatteringly intense look on his face that she could feel all over her, within her, as if they were the same.

As if where it counted, they were one.

She'd had this dream again and again and again, but this was different.

This was better, when that should have been impossible.

The sun was gold and red and molten outside the windows, making them both glow. And Beatrice lay there in that very same T-shirt she'd been admiring earlier, wrapped up in the scent of him. Her body was hungry in ways she'd tried so hard to forget, heavy and needy, and this time she wasn't going to wake up bereft and alone.

Best of all, his hands were on her belly. He was frowning in total concentration as he learned the new shape of her, sliding his palms beneath the shirt and over the mound of the baby they'd made.

And every dream she had involved different reenactments of the night they'd shared in Venice. She had been mining a memory and on some level, she'd imagined she would keep doing it the rest of her life. But this was something else.

This was all new, and better still, they knew each other now.

He knew her name. She knew him.

They had spent weeks together, not a few wondrous hours.

Venice had been like a dream even when it was happening.

This felt like poetry.

Like the passion she'd known was in him all along.

He laid kisses on either side of her navel. His warm palms, hotter by the second, smoothed down the slopes of her bump as he whispered words of praise and adoration in Italian.

Sweet little sonnets all for her, and their baby.

Our baby, she thought, and that was a revelation all its own—and it could not matter, not in this precious moment she had not believed would ever happen, that there were complications hovering there, just outside the bedroom—

Beatrice pushed them aside. Because this belonged to them, and the memory of the night that had changed everything. This was theirs alone, and the future that kicked inside of her, as if the baby recognized its own father.

And somehow, the sweetness of this introduction— not only of herself to this man who had changed her life, but of this father to the baby he should have been expecting from the start the way she had been—made everything...

More.

The sweeter the things he murmured to the baby, the hotter it was. The more carefully and reverently he touched her, the more restless she became, desperate to wrap her legs around him the way she had in Venice— though she supposed that would not be as easy now.

It might not even be possible in her current shape, but the longing only intensified. The *wanting* only deepened.

She had known he was her baby's father, of course, but Beatrice had never understood until now how all the different things he was to her could twine together.

Brother to his sister. Father to their child. Lover of her dreams, finally in the flesh once more.

He was Cesare, and in some way, she had always considered him hers—even knowing that she couldn't have him.

And maybe this was a dream after all, but maybe this was the one she would never wake up from. Because time seemed to flatten out and turn to honey like the rest of her, like the sky outside, as Cesare crooned to her belly, whispered promises, and pledged himself to their unborn child as if he had wanted nothing more than an unexpected pregnancy all this time.

There was so much emotion inside of her that Beatrice hardly knew how to keep it all inside. She tried. She told herself there were things that needed to stay hers—

She did her best, but it all spilled out anyway.

"I thought you would cast me out," she found herself saying. She pushed herself up on her elbows to look down at him as he crouched there, his hands tracing lazy patterns over her belly and a look of wonder on his face. "That you would call me a gold digger, or something in that vein."

"You would have had to know who I was." He lifted his gaze, a deeper, darker blue than any she had ever seen. "There are many things to discuss, Beatrice, this is clear, but I know full well you had no idea who I was. Any more than I knew you. It is a fact I have regretted ever since."

"Cesare…" she whispered, but not because she had anything particular to say to him. More because she felt a wild, deep joy that she could call him that. Here, now. His name was known to her, *he* was known to her. She could lie back, naked and gloriously pregnant, and still sing it at the top of her voice if she wished.

Yet try as she might, she couldn't keep the complications at bay. There was last night. There was still the very same reason she'd run to that pool and tried to scrub her need for him off her skin. It wasn't that the joy in sharing the baby with him ebbed. She wasn't sure it ever would.

But it was layered with other considerations, whether she liked it or not.

"You asked another woman to marry you," Beatrice made herself say. She made to sit up, to pull away from him, and shook her head when he stopped her. "This is wrong."

"Two things," he said, in that dark and stirring way of his. "First, I did not ask her to marry me. I intended to, months ago, but something held me back." His gaze searched hers. "You, Beatrice. Shuffling around in your headmistress costume, right under my nose. I could not understand why you drew my notice, why I could not look away, why I dreamed of Venice but saw glasses and a tight bun instead." He watched as she took that in, flushing with a pleasure she couldn't make herself contain. She wasn't sure she tried. "And second, you can consider things ended with Marielle from this moment forward."

It was shocking, really, how much she wanted to do just that. "I doubt she will consider it ended, however much *I* might."

"Marielle wants a spotless legacy over which she can reign."

"So do you," Beatrice whispered. "You speak of little else."

"I thought I did." He shook his head, his gaze dropping to her belly. "But you and I, this child we made, this is not spotless and still, it is beautiful."

And Beatrice felt her whole body relax at that, in a way she had not let herself relax since she first knew she was pregnant. And certainly not since she'd come to Italy.

Some part of her had not believed, until now, that it was possible she would be okay.

But he thought it was *beautiful*, this mess they'd made. This miracle.

Cesare looked almost rueful. "I have no doubt that Marielle will be delighted to be released from any connection with me."

Beatrice thought she should argue. That she should insist that they sort out the matter of his engagement now, and it didn't matter to her that it was clear Marielle would not have done the same if their positions were reversed. It wasn't about Marielle. It was about the kind of person Beatrice had always thought *she* was—

But Cesare was moving up the length of her body to settle himself beside her, and his face was so close to hers that he was all she could see.

She forgot anything and everything but this. But him.

At first, after Venice, she'd believed that she would never see him again. And then she had, and that had been worse. Then it had all been a kind of torture, but she had soldiered on because she'd truly believed it would be good for her child.

And because she'd discovered that she cared quite a lot for Mattea, whose behavior she understood so much better now. And, of course, because she liked being near Cesare. She craved it.

Even when he didn't recognize her.

But Beatrice was only flesh and blood, in the end. She was only human. Headmistress Higginbotham was the armor she wore, and she had spent years perfecting it, but the reality was this. A woman lying naked and big with child, in bed with the only man she had ever touched. The only man who had ever touched her. The man she had longed for ever since she'd met him, before she'd known who he was and after.

And it turned out she had precious little strength left to resist him.

She reached over, because she could, and she traced the dark arch of one brow, then the other. She tested the line of his proud nose, his sensual lips. She shivered, imagining the way he could use them on every last inch of her, the way he had in Venice.

The way she knew, somehow, he would again now.

"But I have heard you talk about the kind of life you want," she heard herself say, because there were still sharp little poking things, there in the back of her mind, "and it isn't this, Cesare. It isn't the man who showed up in his sister's room today and healed something in her. I... I can't reconcile the two."

"I will tell you."

He pressed his mouth to her cheek, her jaw. To one corner of her mouth, then the other. He found her temple, then the soft spot between that and the shell of her ear.

"Last night I stood at the bottom of the grand stair while the woman I had carefully selected to be my wife walked toward me. But all I was interested in was you, a woman my would-be bride did not even notice was there." A strand of her hair lay between them, sodden and dark, and he paused to curl it around his index finger with great deliberation. "I excused myself from world leaders and men with great power when I would normally speak with them for hours, so I could watch you hold court over a handful of teenagers. And I resented it when I was forced to take my spot at the head of the table, because I was not interested in the tedious conversations and social mores that awaited me. Because, my little owl, though you may not realize this, very little has interested me since your arrival but you."

"Impossible," Beatrice whispered, though she could feel the way her lips curved. "Surely a man of your stature cannot see over the cliff of his own consequence all the way down to a woman of such humble origins as mine."

"I might not have recognized you, Beatrice," he said in a low, thrilling voice that washed through her and over her and made everything inside her *hum*, "but I see you. Hidden behind glasses you do not need, your hair tamed into submission, and swathes of clothes to hide your shape. Still, I saw you. Still I dreamed of you." He made a kind of growling sound. "It was always you."

She thought there was more there, because hadn't he told her something like that, months ago?

I have never been a man of passion, he had told her when he was deep inside of her, keeping her on the edge of that sweet shattering for what had seemed like a lifetime, *but for you, I would learn it. For you,* mi tesoro, *I would become a creature made only of desire.*

Beatrice hadn't let herself imagine that this could happen. That they could finally be together again. He rolled away to kick off his shoes and pants, then came back. He sat her up, stripping his T-shirt from her body and tossing it aside.

And when he lay back down beside her, there was nothing between them but skin, and she wasn't sure she had any arguments left inside her.

"Beatrice," he said, in that dark, thrilling way of his. "Kiss me, I beg of you."

So she did.

Cesare had kissed her in Mattea's rooms earlier, and again by that pool, but this was different. Because this felt like a sacrament.

And Beatrice was greedy enough to think it ought to be. That this kiss should function like a vow, fusing them together. Especially when he moved over her, making pleased, greedy noises as he filled his hands with her bigger, rounder breasts.

"You are so lush," he told her as if the words were too small to contain what he meant, "so beautiful."

And then he laid her back down in the center of his bed, and worshipped her.

Every inch of her, as if this was their new religion, theirs alone to share.

And he wasn't quiet about it. Cesare was inventive and imaginative and he wanted to let her know about each and every discovery he made as he went, so that by the time he made it over her bump and down into that furrow between her legs, she was trembling, her eyes slick with emotion and need.

For he had stretched her out on the edge of that cliff for a long, long while, and he clearly meant to keep her there.

"You are even more beautiful than I dreamed, then I remembered, my little owl," he told her. "But you will be even more beautiful when you come in my mouth."

And then he kissed her there, too.

He licked into her, devouring her, making her arch up to get more of him. As much as she could. There could never be enough. Every touch made her want more.

One lick, another, a twist of his jaw—and she was in pieces.

The lover she remembered took charge then, sliding his fingers into her soft heat and finding his way inside her. And all the while he licked her, again and again, letting her catch her breath only slightly before throwing her out into bliss once more.

Only when she was sobbing, not sure if it was from pleasure—or if she was pleading, or what she was pleading for—did he crawl up the length of her body, moving her hands away when she would have reached for him.

"I wish to worship you," he told her, very sternly. "And I need for you to let me, Beatrice."

And what could she do but obey.

Cesare lay down beside her and rolled her over him, helping her kneel over him. Then he guided her, lowering her down on top of him while they both watched the thick head of the hungriest part of him sink into her soft heat.

He made a rough, low noise and then he gripped her hips. He looked like every dream she'd ever had, true at last. He gazed up at her with those dark blue eyes gone electric.

And then he used his hands at her hips to lower her onto him, inch by inch.

It was a slow, wild stretching. He was so big, so hot and so hard, and her body ached as it accommodated him—because it felt so good. Because it was scalding hot and so beautiful.

Because it was everything she had told herself she would never have again.

Beatrice already knew how beautifully they fit together, but she remembered, too, how he had murmured praise and wonder in her ear as he'd worked himself inside her that first time. How he'd taken such care with her untried body. How he had eased his way inside, a fraction of an inch at a time, until she had been shuddering all around him—not sure if she was sobbing or singing.

Until he'd reached between them, taken that proud little bit of flesh there between his fingers, and introduced her to herself.

Beatrice could see that Cesare was remembering the same thing now. That miraculous first joining in Venice. It had been a culmination of the magic of their meeting, their dancing, their astonishment of having found each other—

And it had only been the beginning.

Tonight, he eased his grip just slightly, though his jaw was tight and his gaze narrow. She could see the faint tremor in him as he held himself in check, his control its own wonder. And she didn't waste the opportunity. She rocked a bit as she straddled him, experimenting with moving one way and another, expecting to feel strange and unwieldy in this new body of hers that kept changing by the day.

But she only felt more beautiful.

And she felt him *more*.

"I would have said that there was no way that you could be more beautiful to me, *mi tesoro*," he told her, his voice hoarse with awe and wonder and that driving need that had its teeth sunk in her, too. "But you have proved me wrong."

"I couldn't believe you didn't know who I was," she told him, looking down so their gazes could be as locked together as the rest of them.

And, however disapproving she might have attempted to sound, it all trailed off into a sigh as he smoothed his hands up higher. Then began to tease her breasts, finding them significantly more sensitive than they'd been before.

Just like the rest of her.

"You will forgive me," he said.

"Will I?"

Cesare's eyes were on hers, and he moved his hands again, back down to her hips until he was moving her, too. Raising her, lowering her, and it was like sunburst, like fire.

It was the whole world, and she'd spent a lot of time and effort convincing herself that nothing could be this good. That she'd made that up. That she'd been making excuses for how she'd behaved in Venice, so unlike herself. And how she hadn't even bothered with protection. And all the other things she'd failed to do that night, like guard her feelings, her dreams, her heart—

But this was a revelation all over again.

Her head tipped back of its own accord. Her toes curled.

She had to brace herself on his chiseled chest with her palms as he lifted her up, then slid her all the way back down the hard length of him.

So slow.

So deliberate.

And so good it should have been illegal. It shouldn't have been *allowed*.

Beatrice started to shake all over again, simply because this was happening again. When she'd been so sure that anything that fierce and that glorious could only occur once in a lifetime, on one magical night, to be dreamed of ever after—

But then she was shaking all over again, falling apart, hurtling off of that cliff.

She heard him laugh, and knew that he wasn't going to stop. That this wasn't a dream.

That this was real, and even better than before, and she would be lucky if she survived the intensity of it this time.

In that moment, she wasn't sure she cared.

He gave her no quarter. There was no time to rest, no time to catch her breath.

She fell off of that cliff, but he kept bringing her back and bringing her back until she didn't think she was holding herself up anymore. Cesare was the one who was holding them both there, maintaining that perfect rhythm.

That thrust and parry that made them new every time.

Beatrice couldn't count the number of times she'd broken apart. She lost track of anything and everything but this, this wild communion, this twining of far more than simply their bodies.

Because it really was sacred, this thing between them. This riot of light and color, fire and need.

When she felt him lose track of that rhythm, when his pace broke down and his thrusts became jerky and mad, she held on tight. As best she could.

And when he roared out his pleasure, she felt it from the inside out, and hurtled off into all the light and heat beside him.

It was dark outside the windows when she came back to herself.

She discovered that she was lying on her side, and he was at her back, his arm slung over her with his hand resting on the baby.

It brought home the fact that this wasn't a dream, because all of her dreams had been renditions of that night in Venice. A beautiful night, but only the one night.

She hadn't been pregnant then.

If she was honest, it had never occurred to her that he would accept her pregnancy so easily now. She'd assumed she'd never have the opportunity to tell him about it and if she did, he'd reject the possibility the baby was his without proof. Wasn't that what men like him did in situations like these?

"Don't you want a barrage of tests?" she asked into the dark room. "Don't men in your exalted position insist on establishing paternity, as a matter of course?"

She felt a new sort of shaking and realized he was laughing. That she could *feel* him laughing, just there behind her.

And this was the man she remembered. Not the Cesare Chiavari she'd met here, brooding and tightly wound and in danger of flying apart at any moment. This was the man she'd remembered all these months, with that voice like a simmering fire and a certain languid confidence that moved through her bones like molten gold.

"The lawyers will demand it," he said, sounding lazy in her ear.

"But you're not concerned."

"Should I be?"

Beatrice felt the faintest brush of irritation, then, though she couldn't have said why. She wasn't sure it made sense. She looked back over her shoulder, shoving her still-damp hair out of the way.

"You could have had a thousand lovers since that night in Venice," she said, though that was the last topic she wanted to discuss. Still, it was realistic, and surely she should cling to such things now, no matter how far removed from *reality* she might feel at the moment. It would help with any whiplash on the other side of this. She hadn't liked that much when she'd experienced it—first when she'd discovered she was pregnant. And again when she'd recognized him instantly, and he had not known who she was. Maybe she could mitigate it. "I assume you have."

"I have not." Cesare moved then, rolling her over so she was more on her back and he could prop himself above her. Once again, he found a thick strand of her hair and played with it, as if looking for hints of red in the dark mass of it. They glinted, as if it at his command, in the soft light from fixtures he must have switched on without her noticing. "I told myself it was because I should not expect an innocent wife if I was not willing to curtail my own activities. But the truth of it, Beatrice, is that I wanted only you."

And she wanted nothing more than to melt into that. Into him.

But this time around she had a child to think of. This time around she needed to protect the both of them.

"How convenient for you that I walked into your palatial home, then," she said, and she could hear that touch of asperity in her voice. She could feel it crashing around inside her.

But he didn't seem to notice. "I have already had my staff reach out to Marielle," he told her. "She was already told that she was not to make any broader announcements, and now she has been made aware that there will be no announcements made at all. I am told she took the news with only a sigh."

Beatrice flinched a bit at that, but could not keep herself from touching him. She traced her finger along the edge of one of his pectoral muscles, then let it go where it would, finding its way along those spectacular abdominal ridges that had haunted her for months now.

"Maybe all she really needs is someone to love her for her," she said but he did not reply.

And that felt like a warning. Beatrice knew she should heed it.

Then again, he'd seen who she was. He'd been inside her, again. He had even accepted the baby. Why should she imagine that this was all happening a little too easily? A little too quickly?

Maybe, she told herself, *you're simply unfamiliar with getting what you really want. It's never happened before.*

Here in his bed, with her hands on his beautiful body, wrapped up with him as if they'd never let go, she could finally admit that he was what she'd wanted all along.

That night in Venice had changed her, profoundly.

She had only been pretending otherwise because she had to. Because she could not say, *I fell in love with a stranger during a one-night stand and I will never be whole again without him,* not even to herself.

"The girls gave me a makeover," she told him now, almost shyly. "They were being funny, obviously. It was a bit of a lark to dress up the headmistress and dare her to go out like that, looking like a total stranger. It never occurred to me that I would do more than have a glass of wine somewhere and let myself be anonymous for an hour or so, then return."

If there were warning signs here, she didn't see them as he shifted, pulling his fingers through the length of her hair, as if testing its weight, its luster.

"I was in Venice for business," he replied after a moment or two. "I had decided at the dawn of the new year that it was time I took the next steps, and I was certain that I had found an acceptable woman who fit my criteria. Everything was as it was meant to be. And then, there you were. You set all of my good intentions on fire."

She searched his face and what she saw was that same intensity. She remembered it. She'd seen it here, too.

It was part of this thing that always burned inside her, and in him too.

"At first I was glad I did not know your name," she whispered, a new confession. "That made it seem not quite real. Like a dream. I thought that night was a secret I would keep forever. But I missed a period. Then another. And by the time I took a test, it could only tell me what I already knew."

"I looked for you," he told her gruffly, in that same hushed manner, as if this bed of his was a confessional they shared. "I woke up, you were gone, and I could not accept it. I looked for you everywhere that following morning. But no one had seen a ravishing woman, dressed in red, a siren to make men run ashore at the slightest glance. It did not occur to me that she was a costume you had worn."

"I didn't look at a picture of you before I came here," she said, with sudden urgency. "It didn't occur to me that Mattea Descoteaux could have any connection to that man or that night. If I'd known it was you I would never have come like this. I had imagined I would go to Venice once the baby was born, and look for you then."

"But you are here now, little owl."

Cesare kissed her then, long and deep and slow.

And she forgot the other things she might have said, because the kiss caught fire.

This time, he had her brace herself on her hands and knees as he took her from behind, holding her hair in one hand like a rope, so he could find her mouth when she looked back. When he encouraged her to look back and find him.

It was possible that she might have lost a bit of consciousness, there, when he reached beneath her legs and found the center of her need, then pinched it.

Or maybe it was simply that there was a kind of starry sky within her that only he could find.

Over and over again.

And Beatrice fought to find her breath again, Cesare stretched out like a god beside her, and thought, *This is all much more than I ever believed I would have. It's enough. It's more than enough.*

Because it should have been.

But the truth was that she felt like crying.

He rolled out of bed and then hoisted her up in his arms again, carrying her off into his shower to wash them both clean, making them both smell like him.

And maybe she did cry as he used his hands between her legs to make her fall apart once more.

Maybe she sobbed, riding his hand and kissing him like she would never see him again, while heat and steam billowed all around them.

Afterward, he pulled his T-shirt and sweats back on again. Then he took more time than was strictly necessary to help her into a robe, until she was flushed and perilously close to *giggly*.

So close that she almost pulled him close and whispered those words that were heavier on her tongue by the moment—

But she didn't.

Cesare had been so quick to accept all of this, but he'd never mentioned love.

And Beatrice could not raise her baby without love. She wouldn't. It was the one gift her parents had left her, the greatest inheritance imaginable. And for her, it was a simple thing, there beneath the role she'd played here while she'd waited for him to recognize her.

There had never been another man in her life. There never would be.

She had accepted that a long time ago, never imagining she would see him again. He was it for her.

But though she was brave in so many ways, because she'd had to be, Beatrice could not bring herself to tell him. To say the words that would make her feelings clear.

He walked her back to her attic room, as if this was some kind of date. He stood outside the door to her little room. He looked down at her, and ran the back of his fingers down the side of her face.

Beatrice thought, *This can be enough. I can make this enough.*

And when he bent to take her mouth with his, sending all those stars and all that molten light spinning through her, she believed she could do it.

She truly believed she could.

But then there was a soft, strangled noise from farther down the hall, and he lifted his head.

And when they turned, Mattea was standing there at the top of the stairs, looking pale and shocked, and worse still, terribly betrayed.

"This was about him," she whispered, her wounded gaze on Beatrice. "This was all about him, wasn't it? It was never about me at all."

"I came here for you," Beatrice managed to say, because that was true.

"Mattea," Cesare began.

But his sister turned that same deeply betrayed expression on him. "You don't care about me at all. You're just as bad as the rest of them. Worse, because they never pretended." She pulled in a ragged breath. "I hate you both."

And then Mattea turned toward the stairs again, and ran for them, her feet like a drum as she raced down toward the bottom of the house.

CHAPTER TEN

LATER, CESARE WOULD castigate himself for a great many things but chief among them that his first response was astonishment.

He froze.

He and Beatrice stared at each other.

"You must go after her," Beatrice said huskily. Shakily.

And he didn't know why he needed her to tell him that. It was as if he didn't know how to behave in the face of that much anguish, but then it didn't matter.

He tore down the stairs, trying to anticipate where his sister would go.

His second bad decision was assuming that she would go to her rooms and barricade herself inside, as she had done on other occasions. He got down the stairs and across the house in record time, but she wasn't there.

And by the time he made it outside and around the front of the house, it was too late.

His sister, who'd long had an affinity for vehicles she was too young to drive, had helped herself to one of the groundskeeper's carts, leaving nothing behind but a cloud of dust.

She was headed for the vineyards. And likely the hills and winding roads that would lead to tiny, medieval villages, and, eventually, Firenze.

He called for the keys to one of the SUVs and followed.

Up one hill, down another, and Mattea knew he was following her. She kept trying to go faster, and when that failed, she began to drive more and more recklessly, as if she thought she could shake him off her tail that way.

Cesare was beginning to wonder if he should fall back, so she would stop the wild stunts with a cart that was not built for such maneuvers—

But then it happened.

Mattea tried to take a sudden turn, too quickly. And Cesare watched in horror as the cart hit stone in the makeshift roadway, launched into the air, and threw his sister free, face-first, into the dirt.

And when he ran to her, she did not wake.

Everything after that seemed like a greasy, slick wheel of adrenaline and self-loathing. Cesare gathered her up as best he could, fully aware that choosing to do that was a risk itself, as he was no doctor and he could not be sure she had not damaged her neck.

But he did it anyway, laying her in his vehicle and calling in for help as he drove back to the house.

Like a maniac.

Then there was the rush to get Mattea up to her rooms again, to lay her out carefully on her bed, as they waited for the doctor he'd sent for to arrive. He had sent his helicopter.

"You must step back and let me look at her," Beatrice said, sounding unnaturally calm to his ears. His blood was so loud in his ears he could hardly bear it, but he let her push through, remembering that she had cared for a great number of students in her time.

That she was not the problem here. He was, just as Mattea had accused him.

"She is breathing. Her pulse is weak, but there." Beatrice frowned up at him. "There is no blood. No broken bones, as far as I can tell."

He could not bring himself to hope. Or even respond.

Cesare knew he would never forget standing by his sister's bed, wondering how exactly he had let this happen. He, who had always had a plan. He, who had been merciless in the execution of that plan across the years.

He, who had prided himself on his perfection.

More than that, he had looked down on those—including his sister—who could not live up to his expectations of a perfect, blameless existence and it was all for nothing. It was all a lie. Some foolishness he'd told himself to prop up his own ego.

Because the truth was that he was a man without control who'd had a one-night stand in Venice. Without protection. And now had a broken engagement, whether he had done the proposing or not. He was about to have a baby out of wedlock with a woman he might find fascinating, but he knew full well his own father would consider her beneath him. Because deep down, wasn't that where Vittorio's fury at Cesare's mother come from? He had believed that an actress was beneath him, and was therefore furious that he could not control her as he felt was his due.

And none of that mattered, because he'd only had one true responsibility in all of that, and it was to keep his sister safe.

He'd thought that taking her away from her useless father had achieved that, but it hadn't.

Cesare had failed in the only way that could ever matter. She was hurt. It was his fault.

He could not bear to imagine all the ways he would fail Beatrice and his own child too.

When the medical team arrived, they were thorough. When they were done examining Mattea, making certain that her minor cuts and bruises were attended to and that any potential for serious injury was explored, they delivered the verdict.

Their expectation was that she would be fine.

Though they were going to have to wait for her to wake up to be certain.

"Leave us," Cesare muttered, because he could not allow himself to feel relief. Not until she woke up and they knew for certain. "Thank you."

And though he'd meant that all the staff should step out, he was somehow unsurprised that Beatrice did not obey.

"I wish to be alone with my sister," he said gruffly.

She didn't even look at him. "No."

He glared at her, and that felt better. It was someone to blame, and he liked that.

But Beatrice only swallowed, hard, her eyes on Mattea, and he couldn't blame her for anything. "She was very clear, Cesare. She felt both of us betrayed her. I'm not leaving her side again. Not until she wakes up."

Cesare found himself pacing, and he ran his hands through his hair as he moved. "This is my fault. I have always known what is required of me and I should not have lost sight of it. I should never have allowed myself to lose sight of it. Of her."

And he could admit, when Beatrice did not react the way he expected her to, that he was spoiling for a fight. That he really did want to put this at her door, when he knew better. Pretending that she was the problem when he knew it was him was just weakness.

His weakness.

He was the one who had leaned in, back in that *vineria*. He was the one who'd asked her to dance. He had extended the invitation to her to join him in his hotel.

If there was any fault here, it was his.

It was always and ever his.

"When she wakes," he said then, in a voice that did not quite feel like his. It was too precarious. Too uncertain and rough. "I will make absolutely certain that she wants for nothing. That her every need will be met, always. That there is never any—"

"I have an idea," Beatrice interrupted him. He stopped, because he was so seldomly interrupted that he was not certain how one was meant to behave. And she aimed that steady gaze of hers straight into him. "Why don't you try loving your sister? Why don't you start a new legacy with that? How about, when she wakes up, you hug her and say it? *I love you.* See? It's that simple."

But if it was simple, it would not feel like a tectonic crisis, deep within him.

"You forget yourself," he managed to say. "I will not deny there's a passion between us, Beatrice, but you know nothing of this world. It is the world that Mattea and I live in, and always have, and believe me when I tell you I know it well. I do not need childish advice—"

"Childish?" Beatrice threw that word right back at him, her voice rising. Quite as if she was shouting at him. *Shouting.* At *him.* "I'm not the one who had a night like we did in Venice and then decided that a great idea would be to go out and get engaged to another woman. I'm not the one who failed to recognize the other thanks to a different hairstyle and a pair of glasses. How is it possible, Cesare, that a person can be as obviously intelligent and powerful as you are, and yet so very dumb?"

He thought that something in him...exploded. He felt it, shattered pieces everywhere, and it wasn't as simple as temper. He knew how to deal with that. He'd learned, long ago, to shove it down, to keep it out of sight, to make sure he did not lapse off into jealous rages like his father.

But he was in pieces all the same.

"I was raised by two people who talked all the time about the love they shared when they were in public," he found himself thundering back at Beatrice, across his sister's still form. "And yet at home they were toxic. It was poison."

"People aren't perfect, Cesare," Beatrice threw back at him. "Not a single one ever has been nor ever will be. People are messy. They make mistakes. They hurt each other, and they can't always fix it. They seek forgiveness, and they don't always get it. The most you can hope for is to love the people that you love, as hard as you can and as best as you can, because that's the only thing in this world that you can be sure of."

"Beatrice." And her name came out of his mouth like a plea. "I can give you anything you desire. We will make more children, as many as you like. If what you truly want is a family, I will give you one. But do not speak to me of love. Ever."

And she looked crushed, then. As if she was the one who'd been tossed out of a cart like that, breakable and so fragile, then thrown face-first into the dirt.

That image broke something in him.

But if there was a way to repair it, he didn't know it. He had the terrible notion that all of his wealth and all of his power could do absolutely nothing at all to fix this.

Why don't you try loving? she had asked him.

Beatrice, his unflappable, indomitable headmistress, was shaking now. There on the other side of his sister's bed, she shook, and he had done this. He had delivered that wound.

Cesare had never wanted to go to her more. The pull to her was so intense he thought it was possible it would cut him in half—

But then, the real tragedy was that he lived. He took a breath, and nothing was better. Another, and still she only stared back at him. One more, and his sister stayed still, while Beatrice waited for him to be the man he wasn't.

Cesare could not seem to make himself move. And Beatrice's gaze grew more and more haunted as she looked back at him.

This was how a vibrant creature like his mother, capable of lighting up a screen with her smile—not to mention every room she'd ever walked into—became so small. It happened over time. One disappointment after the next, each and every one of them delivered by the men she wanted to trust.

He opened his mouth to tell her this, but he couldn't make his throat work. He slashed a hand through the air instead, but it did not convey the message he wanted. It did not warn Beatrice off.

All it did was change that look in her eyes to something worse. It looked like compassion.

"I can't keep you from hurting your sister," she said quietly. "All she wants from you is what you gave her today. Just love her, Cesare. Spend time with her, like she matters. That's all she needs. That's all anyone needs. Love, time, and hope that there will be more of both."

"I can give you anything in the world," he managed to get out, his voice the faintest scrape of sound. "But I can't promise you that."

"You don't want to," she corrected him. Cesare watched as she stood a little straighter. He could see her throat move. "But you need to understand that I won't let you do this to my baby."

That hit him like a blow. "Both of you will be cared for. Always. How can you doubt this?"

Beatrice's eyes took on a light Cesare did not like at all. "I don't want care. I had *care*, Cesare. I even had decent care, which is more than many people in my position could say. But I want love. And for this baby? I demand it."

Her own words seemed to shock her. She drew in a breath as if she hadn't quite intended to say that.

Cesare could only look back at her, stricken.

But she wasn't done. "I want love," she said again. "And if you can't give it, I want you to leave us alone. I want a real family, Cesare. I refuse to give my child anything less. This baby will know only love at home, all its life. I don't think that's too much to ask."

And he wanted to tell her whatever it took to make her stay, but he couldn't. He couldn't make his throat work. His sister still lay so still in that bed, and he was responsible for that, too. On the very day he had tried to tell her that he loved her as much as he was able. And now the mother of his child was standing before him, asking him for things he could not give.

It was all a mess. It was *his* mess. But he could see no way out of it.

Across from him, Beatrice lowered her gaze. She'd pulled on clothes, but left off the glasses. Her hair was swept back into a bun, but this one was far looser. It was soft, with tendrils that fell out and framed her face. It suited her far more.

In the midst of all of this, it felt like a gift.

Maybe that was why, when she turned and headed

for the door with something close to her usual determined stride, he let his eyes fall shut. He let his head go back.

And somehow, though his throat was tight, he got out one single word.

"Don't."

And when he didn't hear her open the door, he forced himself, with everything he had inside, to get out one more. The one that mattered most, and one he rarely uttered.

Not when it could only be what it was. Cesare Chiavari, begging.

He almost thought he wouldn't manage it, but he did.

For her, he managed to eke it out. *"Please."*

CHAPTER ELEVEN

BEATRICE WAS NO stranger to heartache.

But this was different.

Her parents had not wanted to leave her. If they could have lived, they would have. They had not *chosen* the accident that had taken them away from her.

Cesare was choosing this. He was *doing* this.

She had barely accepted that she was in love with him, and already, he was tearing her heart out. The worst part was, she knew him well enough by now to know that it was not something he would do lightly.

He truly, honestly believed what he said. That love was toxic. A poison.

That she could stay, but that he would never love her. He wouldn't even try.

There was nothing she wanted less than to walk away from him, not now that they'd found their way back to each other, but how could she do anything else?

She turned back to look at him. "Try to understand. My parents died when I was young. And the rest of my childhood wasn't easy, but I always, always knew that they'd loved me. It made a difference." Beatrice pulled in a shaky breath. "There were other children in care who didn't have that, but I did. It was like…a candle in a dark night. You might think that doesn't matter, but if you do, it's because you've never had to look around for that kind of hope."

"Don't think that when I say love is not on the table that that means it will be…" But he couldn't finish that, whatever gritty thing he'd tried to say. He tried again. "Beatrice… You know you wrecked me that night in Venice. You must know this."

That jolted straight through her. It was the way he was looking at her now, with that wreckage right there in his dark blue gaze. She felt it wash over her, making her breath come too hard, too fast.

And she knew it would be too easy to give in, to back down. Because she wanted whatever she could get of him—the fact she'd stayed here all summer proved that. But her hair was down now. The truth was out.

Beatrice didn't think she could pretend again.

There was a very real chance that if she tried, it would kill her.

"I looked for you and I looked for you, but you were nowhere to be found," Cesare was saying. And I am not a man who does not get what I want. That is not who I am. But I could not find you."

He was still by the side of the bed, but he had turned toward the door. And he looked different than she'd ever seen him. It was that starkness on his face. As if he'd been stripped down to his elements and what was left was what she saw now, a man haunted.

As if grief lived in him now, too.

Because it had come so close today. She thought she understood. It wasn't his father, who had been so old.

It wasn't his mother, whose choices he openly questioned. It was his sister, a fifteen-year-old who should have a whole life in front of her, but had nearly seen that snatched away.

And he had watched it happen, knowing that he was the reason she had jumped in that cart in the first place.

"I knew I had to let you go," Cesare was saying, stark and serious. "But I couldn't. I dreamed of you every night, though I knew that was not realistic. I knew there was no moving forward with a dream. And you might not think much of the Chiavari legacy, but I was raised to believe it was the only thing that mattered." He shook his head. "I have made sure that it's the only thing that can ever matter."

"You matter, Cesare," Beatrice whispered. She pointed at the bed. "She matters." Then she put her hand back on her belly. "And this child matters. That's your legacy. Don't you see that?"

He lifted up a hand, as if he intended to order her to stop. But he didn't.

"I went through the motions, Beatrice. This is what I'm trying to tell you. I did all the right things. I followed the plan my father laid out for me before he died. I—"

"Why?" Beatrice asked baldly. "He sounds like he should have sorted himself out before he dispensed advice to others."

And for a moment, she thought she'd gone too far. Cesare looked as if he didn't know if he would collapse beneath the indignity of her remark—or if it might have left a mortal wound.

But he pushed on. "If I could not have the woman who made me think that passion was possible. If I could not find the woman who had torn apart the carefully sewn-up world that I'd been living in for so long, then why not a woman who might as well have been a settee? A dresser? That is all the thought and emotion I put into the question of my marriage. I want you to know that."

Beatrice realized then that she was holding her breath. And even when she told herself to breathe, she wasn't sure she was capable of actually *doing* it.

"And then you arrived." He shook his head, and she thought he looked one part disbelief, another part wonder, but no little bit of temper in between. "This...absurd woman, marching around my family's ancestral seat, issuing orders and dressed like an angry little owl."

"An owl," she repeated. "You keep saying that."

"It's the glasses," he muttered. "I hate them. I want to bronze them. And I, who have never been seen in the company of a woman not held to be among the most beautiful in the world, found myself in pieces over a little round owl profoundly lacking in every possible way. The headmistress who was here to discipline my sister, but appeared to have censure aplenty for me, too." He ran an agitated hand through his hair. "I don't think you can possibly understand how egregious this was. This obsession. This preoccupation with the woman who I should never have even noticed was here."

"How marvelously tender," she snapped at him. "I am all aflutter, Cesare. Truly."

"Why does that not offend me? No one speaks to me as you do, Beatrice. No one except my surly, impossible sister, who everyone assures me will grow out of it once she is old enough to know better, and yet you certainly have not done so."

"The thing about children, Cesare, is that they do not suffer fools until we teach them that they must." Beatrice was still frowning at him. "Maybe that is something you should sit with for a while."

"I don't need to sit with it," he threw back at her, his voice rising in a deeply imperfect, un-Cesare manner. Almost as if he couldn't control himself. "I am Cesare Chiavari. Great men tremble when I enter a room. Women beg for a scrap of my attention. And *you*— You live in my home. You never seek out my company, I must demand it. You dress to hide your beauty and you want nothing to do with me and my obsession with you grows by the moment."

"Cesare," she began, but he ignored her.

"I thought that never being able to find my lady of Venice was the worst thing that could happen. But living without you, thinking that I would never find you, was tolerable only because I came to believe that nothing could possibly be as good as I remembered it being that night." He shook his head. "But once again, Beatrice, you defy me."

"Because it's better," she whispered. "It's so much better now."

They still stood in their respective places, Beatrice frozen by the door and Cesare next to the bed, as if he could not bring himself to step away from Mattea's prone form. As if something held them in place like two strong hands, holding them apart but not allowing Beatrice to end this by walking out the door.

"I can't bear it if you leave me again," he told her then, gruff and low. "And I want all of you. I want my child. I want you, as my wife. My lover. And everything between. And I don't know how to reconcile this with who I have been, who I have wanted to be for the whole of my life. But Beatrice, I look at you and I do not see the point of my duty. Not if it means losing the only woman who I have ever dreamed about—"

"Oh, my *God*," came a sulky, scratchy, deeply disgusted teenage voice from the depths of the bed, and Beatrice felt the tears hovering at the back of her eyes spill over, because she had never heard anything more beautiful. Better yet Mattea's eyes were open. She was already scowling, clearly cranky and out of sorts, and she was glaring at her brother. It was glorious. "You're obviously in love with her, Cesare. And you are *rude*. Why are you *shouting* like this when I'm obviously *dying*?"

"You're not dying," Beatrice whispered, and she didn't care if Mattea could see the tears as she moved toward the bed. She didn't care if Cesare could, too. "You're not dying, child. Thank goodness, you're not dying, because I couldn't bear to lose you. You have to know that I was always here for you first. Always. But I do think you're going to have a terrible headache."

"That's so unfair," Mattea moaned.

And when Beatrice came over to the bed, Cesare met her at the foot. He drew her close, so that the pair of them were looking at his sister. He gazed down at Beatrice. Then he reached over and ran his thumb below one eye, then the other, collecting moisture as he went.

"I think I'm in love with you, little owl," he said quietly, and Beatrice felt her heart seem to quiver behind her ribs. He looked over at his sister. "And I have always adored you, since you were red and squalling and tiny. I'm sorry I made you doubt this for even a moment."

Mattea didn't look remotely shivery. She made a face at her brother, every bit of her alive with disdain.

"Don't *think* you love her," she told him, filled with the contempt that only a teenage girl could manage. "Or me. Just…*love*."

And so, not always easily or gracefully, but always deliberately, Cesare did.

CHAPTER TWELVE

WHEN MATTEA WAS fully recovered, they started to take their morning walks as a trio, and Beatrice forced— she liked to claim she *encouraged*—brother and sister alike to discuss their history, and their feelings, in a way they never had before.

"I hate this," Mattea complained.

"As do I," Cesare agreed.

Beatrice, in headmistress mode, only smiled. "Excellent. We'll make it a family tradition."

They found a prestigious acting camp in the States and Mattea, grumbling all the way, allowed them to pretend to bully her into going. She assured them that the whole thing was dumb and she would hate it, but when it came time to come home after the agreed-upon week, she stayed. For the rest of the summer.

A summer during which there was much speculation in the press about the engagement that wasn't, until Marielle ended it by marrying a minor royal, and even the gossips moved on. A summer, hot and sweet and long, that allowed Beatrice to make amends with the staff who thought she'd infiltrated their ranks to get to the master. Something she insisted was necessary, despite Mrs. Morse's support, though Cesare disagreed.

But he had nothing to argue about. For the first time in his life, he was simply *alive*. He took Beatrice to his bed at night, he loved her with all the passion he had inside him, and he woke up with her every morning.

"If this is an obsession," Beatrice liked to whisper when he was deep inside her, making them both grown, "at least we share it."

They saw the doctors together, took all the tests his attorneys required, and discovered they were having a little boy.

"I do not want to raise a son the way I was raised," Cesare confessed one night, out on the terrace where the setting sun bathed him in gold. "I could not bear it."

"Then we will find another way," Beatrice agreed at once.

One night as the summer came to a close, they sat with his father's letter and Cesare read it to her, point by point. And they agreed that a man could be imperfect and still deliver good advice—but also that it was not necessary to take that advice as gospel.

And so Cesare carefully folded up the letter, tucked it back in its old envelope, and secured it behind the portrait of his father that hung in the gallery. Where he could find it again if he needed it.

But he didn't think he would.

Mattea returned from her acting camp bright and happy. And when it was time for her to go back to school, she took Beatrice aside, and confessed that she didn't know how to go back to a place like Averell and *not* be the troublemaker she'd been before.

"It will be your best role yet," Beatrice told her.

And somehow, Cesare knew that his sister was going to find her feet. And very likely the stage lights, too.

In September, when Mattea was back in school and already involved with her first theater production, he took Beatrice back to Venice.

This time, they both stayed in the private hotel that he had bought in the meantime, so that it could always be theirs when they wanted it. They walked along the canals, held each other close in the piazzas, and she took great pleasure in tossing coins into this fountain and that.

"So we will always return to the people and the places we love," she told him.

And one night, as he danced with her to the sound of a street musician's instrument on a bridge in this city of sighs and wonder, he stepped back. He got down on one knee, held her gaze, and placed his grandmother's ring on the only hand where it could ever belong.

"Please," he said, a word he was getting better at all the time. "My little owl, *mi tesoro*, I love you with all that I am. Will you marry me?"

She did, with none of the fuss or pomp that he had previously imagined his wedding would require. They did it quietly with the village priest and a trip to the estate's ancient chapel, a beaming Mrs. Morse and Amelia and Mattea as witnesses.

Then they celebrated by walking back through the fields in the vineyards, toward the grand old house that was, he finally realized, just a house without these people he loved. Just a place.

They were the heart, and they made his beat.

Because Beatrice did not simply teach him how to love, she insisted upon it. She loved him back and she told him so all the time.

And for every step he took her closer and closer to the kind of love he thought his wife deserved, he dedicated himself that much more fully to expanding her imagination when it came to the things they could do between them. He did love to watch her eyes go wide.

He also gave her the great big family she'd always wanted.

There was Mattea, who was not their daughter but who they loved as if she could be nothing else. Their son was born that first fall, dark-haired and golden-eyed, like a cannon blast straight through the center of everything Cesare had imagined he was.

"I had no idea love could be like this," he whispered, holding his precious child in his arms for the first time. He gazed down at his miracle of a wife. "But you did. You always did."

"It will only get better," she promised him.

And as with most things, Headmistress Higginbotham was right.

Over the years, they made seven more little creatures, each and every one of them messy and sticky and wild and feral—and absolutely perfect.

And at the end of those years of baby bellies, sleepless nights, and love so great it left them hollow with all that laughter, they sat out on his favorite terrace. They listened to Mattea lead the children in the musical revue that, by that point, people would pay to see her perform on stage, and smiled at each other.

They sat the way they had so long ago, Tuscany a gleaming bit of glory all around them. But all Cesare really needed was Beatrice. Even when he wasn't touching her, he could feel the things that held them together.

Like steel girders. Unbreakable and true.

The real legacy was this. Them. This passion that only deepened with time.

The family they'd made and the laughter they shared.

And the love he'd almost turned away, far brighter than any single candle in the darkness.

Because their love was molten gold, day after day and year after year, as bottomless as the sky and as dependable as the dawn.

And forever was a foregone conclusion. That was the only plan that mattered.

* * * * *

MILLS & BOON MODERN IS
HAVING A MAKEOVER!

The same great stories you love,
a stylish new look!

Look out for our brand new look
COMING JUNE 2024

MILLS & BOON

COMING SOON!

We really hope you enjoyed reading this book.
If you're looking for more romance
be sure to head to the shops when
new books are available on

Thursday 20th
June

To see which titles are coming soon, please visit
millsandboon.co.uk/nextmonth

MILLS & BOON

MILLS & BOON®

Coming next month

MY ONE-NIGHT HEIR
Natalie Anderson

'You stunned me into silence.' His expression softens. 'I was trying to stay in control. I couldn't do this there.'

'This?'

The brush of his lips is balmy, teasing. His tenderness takes me by surprise as does the moment he takes to lean back and search my eyes. I realize he's seeking my consent.

I can hardly think. 'This is…'

'What I've wanted to do all night.' His gleaming gaze bores into me—intense and unwavering. 'You're why my pulse is racing.'

I just topple right into his arms. He scoops me close and then his mouth is there again—on mine. And I melt.

It turns out that kissing is the best ever way to neutralise panic. The best way to stay in the moment, to not give a damn about anything else in life—not even imminent death. Kissing is the best ever thing full stop.

Continue reading
MY ONE-NIGHT HEIR
Natalie Anderson

Available next month
millsandboon.co.uk

afterglow BOOKS

Afterglow Books are trend-led, trope-filled books with diverse, authentic and relatable characters and a wide array of voices and representations.

Experience real world trials and tribulations, all the tropes you could possibly want (think small-town settings, fake relationships, grumpy vs sunshine, enemies to lovers).

All with a generous dose of spice in every story!

OUT NOW

Two stories published every month.
To discover more visit:
Afterglowbooks.co.uk

LET'S TALK
Romance

For exclusive extracts, competitions and special offers, find us online:

f MillsandBoon

X @MillsandBoon

⊙ @MillsandBoonUK

♪ @MillsandBoonUK

Get in touch on 01413 063 232

MILLS & BOON

THE HEART OF ROMANCE

A ROMANCE FOR EVERY READER

MODERN

Prepare to be swept off your feet by sophisticated, sexy and seductive heroes, in some of the world's most glamourous and romantic locations, where power and passion collide.

HISTORICAL

Escape with historical heroes from time gone by. Whether your passion is for wicked Regency Rakes, muscled Vikings or rugged Highlanders, awaken the romance of the past.

MEDICAL

Set your pulse racing with dedicated, delectable doctors in the high-pressure world of medicine, where emotions run high and passion, comfort and love are the best medicine.

True Love

Celebrate true love with tender stories of heartfelt romance, from the rush of falling in love to the joy a new baby can bring, and a focus on the emotional heart of a relationship.

HEROES

The excitement of a gripping thriller, with intense romance at its heart. Resourceful, true-to-life women and strong, fearless men face danger and desire - a killer combination!

From showing up to glowing up, these characters are on the path to leading their best lives and finding romance along the way – with plenty of sizzling spice!

To see which titles are coming soon, please visit

millsandboon.co.uk/nextmonth

GET YOUR ROMANCE FIX!

Get the latest romance news,
exclusive author interviews, story
extracts and much more!

blog.millsandboon.co.uk